TIME ANOMALY

ECHO TRILOGY, BOOK TWO

LINDSEY FAIRLEIGH

RUBUS PRESS

Editing by Sarah Kolb-Williams
www.kolbwilliams.com

Cover by We Got You Covered Book Design
www.wegotyoucoveredbookdesign.com

ISBN: 978-1539540090

ALSO BY LINDSEY FAIRLEIGH

ECHO TRILOGY

Echo in Time

Resonance

Time Anomaly

Dissonance

Ricochet Through Time

KAT DUBOIS CHRONICLES

Ink Witch

Outcast

Underground

Soul Eater

Judgement

Afterlife

ATLANTIS LEGACY

Sacrifice of the Sinners

Legacy of the Lost

Fate of the Fallen

Dreams of the Damned

Song of the Soulless

THE ENDING SERIES

Beginnings: The Ending Series Origin Stories

After The Ending

Into The Fire

Out Of The Ashes

Before The Dawn

World Before

World After

For more information on Lindsey and her books:

www.lindseyfairleigh.com

Join Lindsey's mailing list to stay up to date on releases

AND to get a FREE copy of *Resonance*.

CLICK HERE TO JOIN

For my mom. Because.

PROLOGUE

The Delta, Egypt
c. 3500 BCE

"Quiet, *girl*," Apep said. Sick of the young Nejerette's whimpers, he lashed out with his arm, backhanding her across the face. She fell on the cavern floor in a heap of shapely limbs and bruised flesh. He grinned.

The young Nejerette was pretty enough now, in her pre-manifestation state, but he saw the potential for true beauty hidden beneath her thinning mask of humanity. There was just enough time left before she manifested completely . . . just enough time for her to conceive and bear his child and pass on her beauty to the first-ever offspring of a union between two Nejerets. Just enough time . . .

Apep sneered. She would make a decent enough mother to his new host body, but he cared less about how attractive that body might be and more about the power it was certain to contain. Finally, he would take one giant step closer to defeating Re, to being in control . . . to unmaking *everything*.

"Please," the young Nejerette whispered. "No more." She pulled her legs up in front of her, hugging them to her chest in a pathetic attempt to hide herself from him.

It was useless; he'd already seen all of her. He'd already done what needed to be done. If she wasn't with child by now, it would be too late. He would have to dispose of her, as he'd done with his other failed attempts, and start over.

"Your depths of depravity never cease to amaze me," a woman said from behind Apep, her voice oddly accented and laced with scorn.

He spun around, pulling an obsidian dagger from his woven leather belt.

The intruder, a striking Nejerette, stood in the mouth of the cavern. Behind her, the sky shone with silvery starlight, but not even the heavens could compete with her eyes. They were aglow with fire. With power. He could feel it writhing beneath her skin, seeking a way to expand out into the physical plane. He *needed* that power.

Apep licked his lips, overtaken by an uncontrollable hunger, and took a step toward the stranger. "Who are you?" he hissed. He would rip her apart. He would consume her . . . possess her. He would *have* her power.

The Nejerette sneered. "You are pathetic, Apep."

Apep stumbled. *He* wasn't pathetic. He glanced at his pre-manifestation Nejerette, sniveling against the cavern wall. *She* was pathetic, not him. Who was this woman—this imposter—to call *him*, a Netjer, one of the original universal powers, *pathetic*? He would eviscerate her.

With a bark of laughter, the Nejerette raised her hand, and a tangle of vines made of nothing of this world burst up from the cavern floor and snaked around Apep's legs, restraining him. "You disgust me. If I could erase you from existence..."

His lips retracted, and a vicious snarl clawed its way up his throat.

"But you are needed in the future"—she crossed her arms over her chest—"so all I can do is take young Aset away from you and erase all of your memories of her and what you have done to her . . . and all memory of me, of course." The Nejerette scanned him from head to toe. "And your host body's memories as well, since he invited you to possess him in the first place." She smiled, but there was only vengeance in her eyes. "And I think I shall leave you trapped in that body for a little while longer."

The otherworldly vines climbed higher, capturing Apep's arms and trapping them against his body. He struggled against them, but they only constricted, securing their hold on him.

The Nejerette took several steps, closing the distance between them. She raised her hand and touched her fingertips to Apep's forehead. Her eyes narrowed. "It is a fitting punishment that your freedom will mean his death, but it is not enough. I think I shall add some memories of intense pain as well." She sighed. "Though I fear that, too, will not be enough. Nothing will change what must come."

Apep felt the barely contained power within the Nejerette swell, and a searing pain slithered into his head. For a while—minutes, hours, days, or possibly years—all he knew was pain.

PART I

Cairo, Egypt
Present Day

". . . know this, Heru:
however much time stands between us,
however much distance separates us,
I will find my way back to you.
I will return to you . . ."

—taken from the Hall of Lex, Nejeret Oasis, Old Kingdom, c. 2180 BCE

1

SEX & DEATH

"I swear to some god who *isn't* you, Marcus," I said, closing my eyes and relaxing into our suite's massive Jacuzzi tub. "If you don't get that cute butt of yours in here right now . . ."

"You'll do what, Little Ivanov?" Marcus said from the doorway, his low, silken voice and enticing accent heightening my anticipation.

Keeping my eyes closed, I let the corners of my lips curve upward. *The things that man can do to me with only his voice . . .*

I shook my head ever so slowly and slouched a little lower in the oval tub, the almost-too-hot water scented with the tiniest drop of vanilla essential oil. Over the past week, this tub had become one of my favorite things about our rooms in the Council's Cairo palace; the Florence Palazzo had been stunning, but its accommodations were definitely cramped by modern standards. Thankfully, the Cairo palace, though nearly as old as the Palazzo, didn't suffer from the same historical handicap.

I'd only just left Marcus's side to sink into the water, but even a minute away from the man I was quite literally addicted to, whose bonding pheromones were as vital to my survival as oxygen, was a minute too long. Our bond was both emotional and physiological, and it was both the most wondrous and the most terrifying thing I'd ever experienced.

Marcus's shoes squeaked faintly on the polished marble floor as he entered the palatial bathroom, which meant he was still *wearing* shoes . . . which meant he was still fully dressed. *Damn.*

I sighed and opened my eyes just as he stopped at the foot of the tub. He was staring down at me, his golden irises burning with desire. But he wasn't showing any intention of shedding his gray slacks or pristine white, button-down shirt, of revealing the sculpted masculine body the clothing tried, and failed miserably, to conceal.

"You're not actually going to join me, are you?" I stuck out my lower lip, just a bit.

One side of Marcus's mouth quirked, and he narrowed his eyes. "That depends."

"On . . . ?"

He inhaled deeply and glanced up at the ceiling. "On what you'll do to me if I *don't* join you." His eyes settled on me.

I shifted my legs, teasing him with a different view. "I honestly think you should be more concerned about what I *won't* do to you . . ."

Something dark glinted in Marcus's eyes, far different from the playful, predatory intensity that had shone in them only a moment ago, and an unexpected burst of anxiety twisted in my gut. I shifted in the tub, closing my legs and sitting up a little higher.

And again, Marcus's eyes glinted with darkness. "You really are a little whore, aren't you?"

I stiffened, and my blood ran cold. Despite all the reserved, almost stony characteristics several millennia had chiseled into Marcus's personality, he was never cruel to me—a little frightening, perhaps, and sometimes frustratingly tight-lipped and other times shockingly blunt, but *never* cruel. My anxiety expanded, snaking out to my limbs and electrifying my muscles.

As Marcus stalked around the edge of the oversized tub, an inexplicable instinct screamed inside my head: *DANGER! GET AWAY! FLEE!*

Marcus knelt beside the tub, a cool smile doing little to soften his hardened, achingly handsome features.

I caught another glimpse of darkness in his eyes; it slid around, lurking just beneath the surface of his black-rimmed golden irises in a hauntingly familiar way, like a ghostly parasite. I'd seen something similar far too often during the months I'd spent trapped in the At, the otherworldly plane where time and space mingled fluidly, as Set's—my father's—prisoner. That same darkness had filled *his* eyes, too. At the time, I'd thought it was Set's sanity, sliding in and out of place.

My stomach twisted, making me instantly nauseated. Marcus and Set now shared half of Nuin's power; was it possible that sharing that power had somehow allowed the darkness—Set's madness—to *infect* Marcus? Because this was most certainly *not* normal Marcus behavior.

The chill in my blood seeped into my bones despite the hot water lapping against my skin. "Marcus? Are you feeling o—okay? Wha—"

Tutting me, Marcus reached out and caressed the side of my face with the backs of his curled fingers. There was no comfort in the touch, no sensuality, and there was none of the electric pleasure that resulted from our bonding. It was almost like the man kneeling beside the tub wasn't Marcus, not really. It didn't make any sense, and at the same time, it made me want to scream and cry and run away.

Bile rising, I fought the urge to panic. Whatever warnings my subconscious was shrieking in the back of my mind, this *was* Marcus, after all. He wouldn't hurt me. He *loved* me. It took a colossal effort not to flinch away from his touch, not to hide behind closed eyes, not to shiver, not to scream. I stared at him, my neck stiff and my eyes wide.

"The power is beginning to show in your eyes," he said, and I started to tremble. His accent had changed; he now sounded very aristocratic and very British. He didn't sound like Marcus at all. "Poor Alexandra . . . you cannot hold it forever. In time, it will erode your body until your bones are little more than dust."

My breaths came faster, and I gripped my thighs so hard that my nails cut into my flesh. "How—what are you talking about? Marcus, are you—"

"Oh . . ." Marcus pulled his hand back and raised his dark eyebrows. "The love of your puny little life is in here, of course, and he's not too happy." His lips spread into a razor-sharp grin. "But he's not in control right now."

I shook my head. He sounded like Set . . . *exactly* like Set. It was impossible. Then again, a lot of impossible things had been happening lately.

Clearing my throat, I whispered, "Who are you? Set?"

The man who both was and wasn't Marcus flashed me a brilliant smile. "Not quite, Alexandra, though as far as you're concerned, yes."

My heart hammered against my breastbone. "What—how are you—"

He waved his hand dismissively. "Insignificant."

I had to swallow several times before I could find my voice and ask the only thing that *really* mattered at this moment. "What do you want?"

"Isn't it obvious?" This time, only one eyebrow rose. "I'm here to reclaim the power you've stolen from me."

"I didn't steal it—Nuin gave it to me," I said, somehow managing to keep my voice even. I had absolutely no idea what was going on, but I really didn't think antagonizing this "not quite Set" being who was somehow possessing Marcus would go over well.

"It matters not." One second, his hand was on the edge of the tub, the next it was encircling my neck. He moved faster than I'd ever seen Marcus move, and I'd seen him move inhumanly fast on multiple occasions. This was something else.

My heart rate quadrupled, but shock held me frozen in place. I felt as fragile as a porcelain doll.

His eyes scanned my body through the water. "Such a pretty, delicate little toy . . . I'd hate to break you before I've even had a chance to play." He paused, letting his words sink in, and met my eyes. The tainted darkness had completely overtaken the gold in Marcus's irises. "If the bond still functioned while I was present, there'd be a way . . . I could let you live, and the method of extracting the power from you would be immensely pleasurable for us both." He frowned, then raised one shoulder in a halfhearted shrug. "But it is clear to me now that such a thing is impossible. Pity . . ."

I shook my head. "Please . . . don't—"

Clenching his jaw, he took a deep breath through his nose and tightened his grip on my throat. Before I could react, he shoved my head under the surface of the water.

I fought his hold, kicking and scratching at anything I could reach. The top of my foot made contact with the faucet and I cried out underwater, inhaling sharply. As bathwater filled my lungs, I coughed and sputtered, but it did no good.

Set-Marcus was drowning me.

And because of our bond, if I drowned, whatever was possessing Marcus would effectively kill us both. I'd watched Marcus die in an alternate timeline nobody but me remembered. I refused to let him die again.

Instinctively, I stilled, and Nuin's power exploded from my every cell, surrounding me, *transforming* me.

The world fell away, leaving only a sense of warmth and comfort and eternal well-being. Gone was my warm bathwater. Gone was Marcus's death grip on my neck. Gone was the impending threat of death.

2

PRESENT & PAST

With a flash of smoky colors, the world reappeared, dark and drafty. I fell to my hands and knees on a floor that was both cold and hard, coughing up water on polished black and white marble tiles. I hacked, gagged, and retched until my throat felt raw, inside and out, like I'd been drowning in flames rather than bathwater. Flames seemed appropriate; I'd been drowning in my own personal hell.

Marcus . . . almost killed me . . .

Closing my eyes, I rested my forehead on a dry patch of floor and worked on catching my breath, uncaring that I was naked and had no clue where I'd landed in my panicked flight. Wherever I was, it couldn't be far from Marcus's and my suite; in all of my accidental spatial shifts, I'd never moved more than several hundred feet from my starting point.

Which meant I had to catch my breath—and fast—because I needed to get as far away from the man I loved as possible. Before he tried to kill me again.

Dread wrapped around my heart and lungs as a terrifying thought eroded my resolve to flee. If I was out of his reach, what would he do to the people I'd left behind in the palace—to

Jenny, my human sister, who just a week ago had learned she was pregnant with Set's baby, or to Kat, my half-sister, who'd only just started to manifest as a result of being *forced* in a last-ditch effort to rescue me from Set's At prison, or to Dominic, my half-brother and closest friend . . . or to Marcus? What would that *thing* inside of Marcus do to *him*?

My efforts to catch my breath turned into frantic gasping, and glittering spots floated in front of my vision. I *couldn't* catch my breath. There wasn't enough oxygen in the air. I could barely breathe.

"Lex!" a woman shouted. Her heels clicked hard and fast on the marble tiles. "Lex! Are you okay?" There was something familiar about her voice, about the hint of an accent, but I couldn't quite place her.

I should have looked up, stood, tried to cover myself—done *something*—but with the tremors coursing through my body and my lungs' desperate attempt to suck all the oxygen from the room, I couldn't manage to do anything besides stare at the floor and take gulping breaths.

"Pick her up! We have to get her out of here before that guard regains consciousness and before Apep realizes she's with you, and—"

"I know." The second voice was male and also sounded familiar, but like the woman's, I couldn't place it. "Give me your coat."

Seconds later, I felt rough fabric being draped over my shoulders and my limbs being manhandled as a trench coat was situated on my body. Before I knew what was happening, I was rolled onto my back and lifted off the ground, strong arms supporting me under my knees and behind my shoulders. I probably should have struggled, but I was half-delirious and on the verge of passing out, and the strong, warm arms wrapped around me hardly seemed threatening.

The stranger's hold on me shifted, and he held me closer

against his chest. "It's going to be alright, Alexandra. I swear, I won't let—"

"Don't make promises you can't keep," the woman said. "Lex deserves better than lies, especially from you."

The man grunted, and I could feel the vibration against my cheek. "Apep *possessed* me," he said. "I did not *choose* this." For the first time, I noticed the man's accent. It was similar to Marcus's, with its ancient Middle Eastern notes, but quite a bit thicker. "I have been present during every disturbing moment that Apep is in control of my body, always aware, never able to act. Thinking of how I may one day make amends for all he has done is all that keeps me from ending up as insane as Apep."

The woman cleared her throat. "I—I apologize. That was unfair of me. It is just hard to forget some of the things you—*he*—has done . . ."

"I understand."

I pulled my head away from the man's shoulder and squinted up at his face. And stiffened.

Even in the dim light of what I now realized was the palace's grand staircase, his pale, severe Nejeret features were easily recognizable. I could never mistake that face.

Set.

My muscles tensed, and I twisted in his arms, intending to do whatever possible to break free from his hold. But Set had apparently been expecting a struggle, and he tightened his grip on my body.

"Lex! Stop it!" the woman said in a screeching whisper. "You must stop! We're trying to help you!"

A very unexpected face appeared inches from mine, and I froze, my back arched and one foot pushing on the cool marble banister. "Doc—Doctor Isa?" I had met her only once, in a hospital back in Seattle, after I'd awoken from a coma resulting from a near date-rape. She'd said things—*known* things—about what I really was, and then she'd disappeared.

"Yes, yes, it's me," she said, patting my shoulder. "Long story *very* short, this Set—who is, essentially, a completely different man from the one who's been tormenting you most of your life—is your *true* father." She frowned, then bit her lip. "But he's, well, he's been possessed by a very evil being, who just happens to be the same being who slipped into Heru this evening, and if you remain here much longer he *will* kill you, and then he will destroy everyone you love." She scanned me and, once again, frowned. "You didn't tell me you would be naked." She tsked. "You should remember to do that."

"I—*what?*" Nothing she'd said made any sense to my stunned brain. If not for her knowing about Marcus's so-called possession, I would have been screaming my head off. Instead, I was working on not hyperventilating . . . again.

Sighing, Dr. Isa shook her head and continued down the pale, elaborately carved marble staircase. "Never mind. We don't have time now. I'll explain what I can on the road . . . and you should slow down your breathing, or you'll pass out." She glanced down at her wrist, then shifted her attention higher, focusing on Set. "Pick up the pace. According to what Nik saw in the At, we've got less than three minutes before Apep returns."

Set started moving at a quick jog, and I wriggled in the cradle of his arms. "I can . . . walk. Put me . . . down," I said between heaving breaths. Whatever Dr. Isa claimed, I definitely *wasn't* comfortable with Set carrying me.

"No." Set managed to lace the single syllable with so much heavy emotion that I stilled. "You can barely breathe as it is, and beyond that, this may be the last chance I ever have to hold my little girl."

I didn't bother pointing out that I was a full-grown woman. Likely because I really *was* having a hard time breathing. I stared up at Set's face, and with each consecutive glance he flicked down at me, some of my more tightly wound bundles of hatred and disgust loosened. There was just so much concern, so much warmth in the depths of his rich brown eyes—*brown,* not black, like the eyes of the Set *I* knew.

"W—where are we going?" I finally managed to ask as we reached the bottom of the stairwell.

Set glanced down at me again, his eyes lingering on my neck, where I assumed some pretty nasty bruises were taking shape. It didn't really matter; thanks to my Nejerette regenerative abilities, they'd be gone soon enough.

"To safety," he said.

"Come, come," Dr. Isa whispered. "Hurry." She held open a gracefully carved door and ushered us into a dim hallway. It was one of the many parts of the palace I'd yet to explore.

We quickly made our way down a set of stairs, along another hallway, and through an exterior door, me in Set's arms and Dr. Isa hustling along beside us. When we reached a squat black car parked crookedly on the side of the street nearest the almost-hidden door we'd exited through, Set hugged me closer to him. I tensed immediately.

"I am so sorry for everything, Alexandra." He set me in the front passenger seat. "And I am so proud of you—of everything you have already done and of everything you are about to do."

"Wha—"

He leaned in closer and pressed his lips against my cheek, stunning me speechless, then straightened and shut the door.

I was absolutely and completely baffled, not to mention totally freaked out. Set . . . kissed my cheek. He *helped* me . . . and Marcus-who-wasn't-Marcus had tried to *kill* me. It was like I'd slipped into a mirrored version of the world, where everything was reversed: up was down, good was evil, sane was *not* . . .

Seconds later, Dr. Isa slid into the driver's seat and stuck the key into the ignition. She guided the little car out onto the street, glanced at me sidelong, catching my eye, and returned her focus to the way ahead.

I took a shaky breath, appreciative that my urge to hyperventilate had passed now that Set was no longer close by. "What's going on? Is Marcus okay? Is this . . . oh God, is whatever's wrong with him—this possession thing—is it *permanent*?"

"No, no, Lex, it is not," Dr. Isa said. "If all goes as planned, he will be fine."

"As planned? *What* plan? And what kind of *being* can possess people?" I'd experienced a lot over the past seven months, and my eyes had been opened to an entirely new, unbelievable world of mythical, practically magical beings who could step out of time to observe the past, present, and possible futures, but I'd never heard anything about *possession*.

"I can't tell you much—to do so would invalidate the timeline, but . . ." She paused, shifting in her seat to pull something out of the pocket of her pale linen pants. "This will hopefully help to convince you to believe what I *can* tell you." She handed me an antiquated, almost disintegrating folded-up piece of paper and reached overhead to turn on the dome light. "Careful with that. It is ancient."

I did my best to contain the overwhelming need my body still felt to shiver and unfolded the piece of paper. I sucked in a surprised breath. The paper was, in fact, *not* paper; it was pressed papyrus and, from what I could see of both the craftsmanship and level of deterioration, thousands of years old. The age, however, wasn't the most surprising thing about it; the language and handwriting were. The former was English, and the latter was, well, *mine*.

Swallowing in an attempt to wet my suddenly parched throat, I shook my head. "That's my handwriting."

"It is."

"This isn't possible."

"Read it," Dr. Isa said.

So I did.

Lex,

First off, Marcus will be fine. Well, not fine, exactly—he'll be really upset about what Apep almost made him do—but he'll be okay, really. Jenny, Kat, Dom, Alexander . . . they all will.

I know you're confused, but it will all make sense soon. Or, at least, most of it will. Okay . . . some of it will.

So here's the deal—when Marcus tried to drown you/me/us, he wasn't actually Marcus. Which is the reason you can't stay in our native timeline . . . you know, YOUR time. You have to ~~come back to~~ go back to Nuin's time to learn how to use your borrowed power—it's the only way you and Marcus and everyone else will ever be safe. If you don't do this, everything and everyone we love will be destroyed. But if you do, we'll have a real, fighting chance. I promise you, it's the only way.

Okay, I've thought long and hard about how to convince you, my former self, that what I'm telling you is actually coming from me, your future self . . . in the past. It's confusing, I know. Anyway, this is what I've come up with, the thing that only we know:

Marcus died. We changed the timeline, we fixed it, but for a few horrible seconds, he was really, truly dead.

"Oh my God . . ." Nobody else knew about that road-untaken timeline, because I'd reversed time and set our paths on a different course, one where Marcus was still alive. This ancient note really was from me.

It was the second piece of evidence I'd come across in the past two weeks that suggested that I would eventually tap into the time travel aspect of Nuin's power, the other being a

Renaissance sculpture that Marcus had commissioned Michelangelo to create *in my likeness* some five hundred years ago. I'd been skeptical when there'd been only one piece of evidence, but now, with this note added to the mix, I could no longer deny the truth. I *would* access more of the alien power flowing through my veins, entwining with my ba—my soul—and I *would* travel back in time. It was impossible . . . and apparently inevitable.

Pressing my lips together, I continued reading.

Now listen—you have to trust Dr. Isa. Do everything she says, and I mean every single thing. Go ahead and ask questions, but don't expect too many answers. She holds back things from me, too . . . things that must be from my future, but her past . . . so don't get too frustrated with her. It won't do you any good anyway. Trust me, I know. Just do what she says and try to keep calm and break a leg and use the force and all that . . . and try to enjoy at least some of it.

I'd wish you luck, but I don't think you'll need it.

Lex

I cleared my throat and gently set the ancient piece of papyrus on my lap. "How—" With a dry laugh, I shook my head. "*Where* did you get this?"

"From you."

"I know, but—"

"A little over four thousand years ago."

Mouth hanging open, I stared at her, waiting for some sort of an explanation. "But—but . . ." I shook my head. My brain seemed to have transformed into something akin to gelatin, incapable of processing complex thoughts. *Four thousand years ago . . .*

"Marcus will be fine, Lex." When I didn't respond, Dr. Isa

added, "When you return—and you *will* return—you will find him healthy and whole. This I swear."

I blinked several times, then inhaled deeply and turned to look out the window. I didn't understand. This—Marcus, Set, the ancient letter from myself—all seemed so impossible, and no matter how hard I tried, I couldn't fit the puzzle pieces together. I couldn't make sense of *any* of it. I wouldn't fight it, not when my own words claimed that this path was the only one that would keep the people I loved safe, but accepting that didn't make the whole situation any less convoluted or any more fathomable.

As Dr. Isa drove south along the Nile's east bank, I stared out at the river and attempted to reorganize my chaotic thoughts into something that resembled coherency, or at least logic. The lights of Cairo glowed on the water's surface, creating an ethereal reflection of the city. It was normal . . . logical . . . expected . . . unlike the tornado that had ripped through my orderly, if slightly fantastical, life.

After a few minutes, I asked a question that seemed relatively easy, one that couldn't possibly be answered with another impossibility. "Where are we going?"

"Memphis."

Memphis was the ancient capital of the northern half of Egypt—what had come to be known as Lower Egypt, due to the north-flowing Nile. Considering that the ancient city of Memphis didn't exist anymore, Dr. Isa had given me a region, not a specific location.

"Care to elaborate?" I said.

"You'll see soon enough."

"Okay . . ." I shifted my attention from the midnight view of the Nile to the woman who seemed to be part rescuer, part abductor. "Can you at least explain what's going on with Marcus and Set and this whole 'possession' thing?" I shook my head, my heart clenching. "I mean, last I checked, Set was the one hell-bent on ruining my life, and Marcus was the one equally determined to protect me."

As the reality of what had happened sank in—that Marcus's hands had almost ended my life—hysteria bubbled out of my throat in the form of a shrill laugh. It quickly turned into something that sounded and felt a lot more like muffled sobs. Marcus being "healthy and whole" was one thing, but he would hate himself for what he'd almost done to me. He would obsess about it . . . punish himself for it. I wrapped my arms around my middle, attempting to hold my disintegrating composure together. I ached to comfort him.

Dr. Isa reached over and gave my arm a gentle squeeze. "It wasn't Heru who tried to kill you, Lex . . . not technically."

"That's what he said." As my sluggish, oxygen-deprived mind finally registered the name she'd been using to refer to the man *I* knew as Marcus, I narrowed my eyes, scrutinizing her delicate, feminine features. "You're Nejerette." The last time I'd seen her, more than half of a year ago, I hadn't even known *I* was Nejerette; I'd had no way of recognizing her as such.

"I am," she said.

"You could have told me back in the hospital. It would have saved me a lot of trouble." *And saved me from thinking I was losing my mind . . .*

"You know I couldn't have done that. I was already teetering on breaking Nuin's rules by telling you what little I did." She shrugged. "But it had to be done."

"Why?"

"To preserve the timeline, to get us here . . . to set you on your current path."

"Which is leading me to *where* exactly?"

She smiled, and the warmth contained within the expression muffled *some* of my unease. "I already told you—Memphis." Before I could respond, she added, "But you really should be more concerned with *when*."

I took a deep breath, exhaling a heavy sigh. "Fine, I'll bite. My current path is leading me to *when*?"

"Approximately 2180 BCE."

My mouth dropped open, and for a few minutes, all I could do was gape at her. Remotely, I registered that we'd driven onto a bridge and were crossing to the west bank of the Nile. But really, the direction our car was traveling was small potatoes compared to the doctor's proclamation that I would be heading back a good *four thousand years*. Which, I realized somewhere in the very back of my mind, had to be when I'd given her the note.

"You will learn much," she added, like that explained everything. Or anything.

"Okay . . ." I frowned, my mind racing. "So I'm supposed to somehow find my way back to the end of the Sixth Dynasty?" I paused. "Even *if* I could somehow manage that, I'd be popping in at a really volatile time. That was the end of the Old Kingdom. I'm pretty sure an ancient civil war isn't really the safest place for me right now."

Dr. Isa chuckled. "You have no idea."

"But—"

"You were attacked tonight by what is essentially a 'spirit.'" She shrugged. "Nuin will explain it better, I'm sure . . . but anyway, this spirit just happens to be the *same* thing that's been possessing Set for over four thousand years, turning him into, well . . . an evil bastard."

"Wait—*what*?"

"Its name is Apep, and it is the original owner of the power now split between Marcus and Set. For some reason that I don't fully understand, sharing part of that power opens Marcus up to being overtaken by Apep for short periods of time."

I mulled her words over. Apep was one of the ancient names for Apophis, the ancient Egyptian god of chaos and darkness, commonly associated with a serpent. Was his possession of Set the reason that, over time, the mythological Set had become associated with chaos as well?

I breathed in through my nose, then exhaled slowly. "So . . . while this Apep *thing* was possessing Marcus, I take it that Set was free to, well, *be* Set—the *old* Set?"

Dr. Isa nodded, a tiny, sad smile curving her lips. "He was, though Apep has undoubtedly returned to him by now. That vile creature has had more than four millennia to gain an unrelenting foothold in Set's body. It would seem that even with the inroad he now has into your Marcus, Set is the more comfortable fit, like a favorite pair of boots." She wrinkled her nose. I was getting the impression that she hated Apep just as much as I did.

My eyebrows drew together. "So Set, my father, isn't actually evil?"

Dr. Isa glanced at me. "That is correct, Lex. He is not evil."

Unexpectedly, a tension I'd been carrying ever since learning that the Nejerets' most-loathed and most-hunted villain was my father lessened. It felt like a corrosive iron wire had been wound too tightly around my heart, but had suddenly disintegrated. Set was my biological father, but it was Apep who'd been tormenting me all these years. It was Apep who'd deceived, kidnapped, and impregnated my sister, abducted and tortured me, killed Marcus, and intended to take over the world with Nuin's power. *Apep* was the evil one, not Set.

I laughed, and this time, there wasn't a single trace of hysteria in the sound. "That's just . . . wow." I shook my head. "That's fantastic."

"For you, maybe. Less so for Set, I think."

My laughter died as I considered Dr. Isa's meaning. "Oh . . . oh God . . ." I couldn't imagine the sheer avalanche of horror and despair Set must have felt over the long stretch of time he'd spent as a prisoner in his own body. What he must have watched his own hands do. The orders he must have heard given in his own voice. The lives he must have felt himself extinguish. He'd had a front-row seat to all that destruction, all that terror, and he'd been incapable of doing anything to stop it. "How is he still sane?"

I glanced at Dr. Isa in time to see a single tear roll down her cheek. She wiped it away with a quick swipe of her hand and swallowed loudly. "I'm not so sure that he is."

"I'm sorry. Did you know him . . . before—"

"No more," Dr. Isa said. She shot me the briefest of glances. "I've already told you all I can. Revealing too much could alter the timeline irreparably, and *that* is something none of us can afford."

3

ARRIVE & DEPART

Fifteen minutes later, Dr. Isa pulled the car onto a dirt driveway that led to a small, walled-off complex on the western outskirts of Mit Rahinah, one of the modern Egyptian towns that lay within Memphis's ancient borders. She stopped the car in front of an imposing iron gate and removed a sleek smartphone from a handbag stashed on the floorboard against her door, tapping the face before holding it up to her ear.

After a single ring, someone picked up. Thanks to my heightened Nejerette senses, I could hear the woman on the other end, not that it did me any good. From what I could discern, they were speaking in Middle Egyptian, the same dialect that had long been the accepted standard language among Nejeretkind.

In the two weeks that had passed since our explosive confrontation with Set at Hatshepsut's mortuary temple, Marcus, Neffe, and Dominic had been doing what they could to help me learn to understand the spoken language rather than just the written version, but I'd yet to make much, if any, progress in learning to speak Middle Egyptian. It was too different from Nuin's ancient language—like modern Italian compared to Latin—to make learning it much easier than if I hadn't known Nuin's language at all. I certainly hadn't progressed enough to translate Dr. Isa's rushed words.

When she ended the call, the gate started swinging outward. Dr. Isa eased the car into the compound and parked in front of a modern, boxy building. It was relatively small, tan, and appeared to have no windows and only one entrance or exit so far as I could tell—a heavy metal door with no handle, but with a keypad on the wall beside it, about halfway up. It seemed high-tech, high-security, and more than a little out of place.

"Where are we?" I asked.

"You'll see."

The lone door opened, and a handsome, middle-aged woman stepped outside. She wore a simple, white linen shift, her only adornment the single strand of turquoise beads hanging around her neck. She looked like she would've fit in far better in the ancient world than in modern times. Keeping her eyes lowered and her head bowed, she held the door open.

Dr. Isa gave my forearm a gentle squeeze. "Come on, Lex. We don't have a lot of time."

I glanced down at her hand, zeroing in on the rather exceptional bracelet peeking out from the cuff of her delicate sleeve. I couldn't see the whole thing, but I caught enough of a glimpse to tell that it was at least an inch wide, made of an opalescent quartz or some similar stone, and covered in engravings. It looked—no, *felt*—familiar. I had the insuppressible urge to reach out and touch it.

Which is exactly what I did. As the fingertips of my right hand made contact with the edge of the bracelet, a jolt of recognition flitted through my mind, and I suddenly understood the feeling of familiarity. It wasn't made of quartz, but of the very fabric of the At, just like the chest from the hidden, underground temple "containing" the ankh-At—and the ankh-At itself.

I took a steadying deep breath and met Dr. Isa's eyes. They

were filled with a thousand mysteries. "Where did you get this?" I asked, fearful I already knew the answer.

She smiled a faint, secretive smile. "From you."

A shiver crawled up my spine. "I was afraid you were going to say that."

Pulling her hand back, she unbuckled her seatbelt, opened her door, grabbed her handbag, and started toward the woman standing in the open doorway.

I followed suit, stopping beside her at the building's entrance.

"Greetings, Anai." Dr. Isa reached out to tilt the other woman's face upward. She was shorter than me by several inches, though still taller than Dr. Isa, and based on the fine lines marking her gracefully aged face, she was definitely human. "Much as I appreciate the courtesy, we really don't have time for such formality. I trust you've instructed the others to remain silent while they prepare her?"

Anai nodded and turned away, motioning for us to follow her into the building. Once we did, the door shut behind us with a dull thud. Ahead stretched a long, well-lit hallway, wide enough for Dr. Isa and me to walk side by side as we trailed behind Anai toward another metal door.

I leaned in closer to Dr. Isa. "What's going on? What is this place?"

"Anai and this ancient order of priestesses have been waiting for you for a very long time. They will make sure you're properly attired, and then you will"—she raised her hand, wriggling her fingers to signify something flying away—"slip into the past."

Waiting for me? I shook my head. "But I don't know *how*," I told Dr. Isa, panic resurfacing. *What if I can't do it? What if I'm stuck here and Apep finds me?*

He would kill me to steal my power; after our brief encounter in the bathroom earlier, I had no doubt of that. And then Marcus would die as well. And poor Set—he would be stuck as a prisoner trapped inside his own body for who knew how many more thousands of years. Possibly for all of eternity. And then there was the rest of the world . . . there was no telling what Apep would do with the power, once he had it, but I doubted he would turn into the next great humanitarian. No, domination and destruction were more his style. And according to the ancient papyrus note in my pocket, my future-past self agreed.

None of those were acceptable outcomes. Which meant I *had* to figure out how to travel back to Nuin's time.

Anai pressed her palm against some sort of a scanner on the wall beside the door, and a few seconds later, there was an electronic beep followed by a mechanical click. With the sound of a seal being broken and air pressure equalizing, the door swung inward.

When I saw the ancient structure in the absolute center of the room, my breath hitched. "Wow . . ."

"It is quite remarkable, is it not?" Dr. Isa laughed softly. "It was not easy to preserve all these years, but the Order of Hathur managed."

"What is it?" I asked, my voice barely audible.

"You're looking at the inner sanctuary of the oldest remaining temple to Hat-hur, the goddess you know of as Hathor," Dr. Isa said.

I didn't question the validity of her claim; based on the decaying limestone columns and faded wall decorations carved into the small, square chamber, she was telling the truth. The time-worn structure looked odd and ancient and out of place surrounded by the barren, almost clinical white walls, floor tiles, and ceiling panels.

Anai turned to face us, meeting my eyes for the briefest moment and allowing a tentative smile before lowering her gaze to the floor. "Come," she said in heavily accented English, taking my hand and leading me around the ancient chamber.

"The others await you."

I glanced back at Dr. Isa. She had her phone up to her ear again and was speaking even more rapidly in Middle Egyptian. She met my gaze momentarily and nodded before turning away.

Anai led me through a doorway in the far side of the room and into a smaller, softly lit space. There was a compact, minimalistic vanity set against the left wall, and an intricately beaded garment hanging from a polished silver hook embedded in the wall ahead. Several pieces of extravagant gold, quartz, and turquoise jewelry, fit for an Old Kingdom princess, were set out on a corner table that matched the vanity.

Through another doorway, I could see a spacious bathroom with a toilet, a pedestal sink, and a classic claw-foot bathtub filled with water so hot it was steaming. Everything was white, from the towels and towel racks to the tub, faucets, and ceramic tiles that covered the floor.

And there were women, three of them, each dressed like Anai, and each looking young enough to be her daughter. After a second, longer look at each of their faces, I thought they might actually *be* her daughters. They stood placidly in the center of the room, keeping their eyes downcast.

Anai clapped once, and the three young women jumped to life. They hustled me into the bathroom, stripped me of my borrowed trench coat, and coaxed me into the tub.

"Hey, hey . . . I can wash myself," I told them, knocking away their hands as they started running washcloths steeped in faintly floral, soapy water over my shoulders, arms, and back.

They giggled, and one of them even met my eyes for a fraction of a second before blushing profusely, but they didn't show any signs of giving up on their task.

"You must let them do their duty," Anai said from the doorway. "Like me, and my mother before me, and her mother before her, for over a hundred generations, they have trained their whole lives for the honor of preparing you for your journey. You cannot imagine the joy they felt—we *all* felt—when we learned that *we* would be the ones to fulfill our Order's purpose. Please do not take this from them."

"I—you—" I closed my eyes and forced my muscles to relax, one by one. "But I'm just *me*," I murmured.

Upon hearing Anai enter the bathroom, I opened my eyes, hoping that focusing on her would distract me from the three strange, if gentle, women washing my body.

"My mother told me, as her mother told her, that when you finally found your way back to us, you would be confused. You would not remember us until your journey was complete." She smiled, but despite the joy brightening her expression, her eyes filled with tears. "You—this . . . you are our purpose for existing. I cannot explain to you what it is like to be in the presence of the one who—"

"Anai!"

I glanced at the doorway, where Dr. Isa was standing, her arms crossed over her chest and her eyebrows raised. When my attention returned to Anai, I found that her eyes had once again drifted down to the floor. She wiped tears from her cheeks and took a deep breath. "I shall say no more."

Dr. Isa exhaled heavily. "Wonderful."

Minutes later, I was out of the tub, wrapped in a thick linen robe, and all but my hair was dry. The three young women situated me on a squat, padded stool in front of the vanity and immediately set to work cutting and drying my hair and applying makeup. By the time they were done, I had a very proper Old Kingdom hairstyle—dark, shoulder-length, and very straight—and my eyes were lined in kohl. The black galena liner only served to emphasize the reddish hue my eyes had gained when my Nejerette traits started manifesting.

Anai arranged an intricately worked band of turquoise and quartz beads affixed with gold thread around my head. When she was finished, she smiled at my reflection in the mirror, looking utterly pleased with herself. "It is time for you to dress."

"Alright." It wasn't like I could refuse—not with my future-past self breathing down my neck and Dr. Isa tapping her foot in the doorway.

With the help of the young women, Anai dressed me first in a calf-length, white linen shift of a weave so fine it almost felt like silk. After walking around me with narrowed, scrutinizing eyes, she gave a single nod and guided her helpers through the delicate process of attiring me with the beaded faience dress that had been hanging on the wall. The turquoise-colored ceramic beads made a net pattern that covered the shift from my chest almost all the way down to my ankles. Additional beads of quartz, gold, silver, and actual turquoise dangled from the garment's hem and adorned its empire waist and thin shoulder straps. It was an absolutely stunning piece of craftsmanship, far more intricate than any of the Old Kingdom beaded dresses I'd seen in museums, not that many had survived the passage of time.

Anai completed my look with a menat collar—a necklace often associated with Hathor and thought to be something of a good luck charm—composed of dozens of strands of tiny beads that matched my dress perfectly and finished with hammered gold fastenings and a flat, heavy gold counterweight that dangled down my back. She also slipped a two-inch-wide gold cuff bracelet onto my wrist, the face inlayed with a turquoise Eye of Horus.

Thinking of Marcus and how appropriate it was for me to be wearing *his* symbol, I squeezed my eyes shut. *He must be freaking out.*

But this is the only way to protect him . . . to protect everyone.

My heart started racing, and a lump swelled in my throat. Opening my eyes, I turned to face Dr. Isa and held out my hand, palm up. "I need your phone."

It started buzzing in her handbag, and she pulled it out with a quick "Yes, yes, in a moment." For the third time, she fell into a rapid conversation in Middle Egyptian, but this time her tone was more severe, her words sharper.

One of the young women slipped delicate sandals of leather worked with silver and gold onto my feet, then retreated to the room containing the ancient temple sanctuary with the other two young women.

"She is ready," Anai said when Dr. Isa ended the call. The priestess offered a slight bow of her head to the doctor and a far more substantial one to me before joining the other women of her Order in the temple room.

"Your phone," I repeated.

"I'm sorry, Lex, but there's no time." Dr. Isa took my elbow and guided me toward the last remnants of the oldest remaining Hathor temple in existence. "He's on his way."

"Apep?"

"In Set's body, yes."

"But—how—"

"I've had an exceptionally powerful Nejeret cloaking you since we left the palace, but it would seem Set has one just as strong." Her eyes narrowed to slits. "Not that it should be possible . . ."

"But—"

"He knows where you are, and as long as you're here, in this time, he won't stop until he tears this place apart"—her voice turned grim—"and then he'll tear *you* apart. That cannot happen."

Any response I may have been formulating died on my tongue. I nodded.

We passed between two crumbling columns and into the inner chamber, Anai and the three young women following behind us. The latter positioned themselves around the chamber, one at each unbroken wall, while Anai remained in the doorway, and Dr. Isa led me into the center of the chamber. It was cramped and dark enough that without my heightened Nejerette vision, I wouldn't have been able to see a thing. I doubted whether any of the human women could.

"Will you tell Marcus what happened—where I've gone?" I asked Dr. Isa as she left my side to retrieve a small, cloth-wrapped bundle from a niche in the wall opposite the doorway. "Please?"

She unwrapped it carefully and handed the cloth to the young woman nearest her, then met my gaze. "Of course I will, Lex. I swear it on my life."

As she returned to me, I recognized the object in her hand—a small statuette of the goddess Hathor. I recognized it because it was *mine* and was supposed to be in my apartment back in Seattle.

"How'd you—"

I shrieked as she smashed the priceless antique on the age-worn limestone floor. The alabaster cracked and fell away, leaving behind a smaller version of the statuette. But this version was fashioned from At.

And it was glowing.

Dr. Isa bent down and retrieved the statuette with the quick gracefulness afforded a Nejerette and thrust it at me before I could even think of evading it.

As soon as the statuette made contact with my palm, the world fell away.

PART II

Memphis, Lower Egypt
6th Dynasty, Old Kingdom

4

HELLO & AGAIN

Warmth surrounded me. Endless comfort and well-being. Shock and fear no longer existed. Impossible and possible were irrelevant, the events of the past few hours insignificant. *I* was insignificant. Just a part of a greater existence.

One piece.

Small.

Meaningless apart from the whole . . .

I'd felt something similar before, several weeks ago, when my presence had activated a trigger in the At chest in Senenmut's hidden temple and I'd been transported to a time and place Nuin had created outside of the "real" . . . of the "known." Since I'd never experienced the sensation when I shifted spatially, I figured it had to be a part of the time-traveling process . . . which meant the Hathor statuette—the *At* statuette—had worked much like the At chest, transporting me through time upon contact with my skin.

Without apparent cause or warning, the physical world re-formed around me, bringing with it everything I hadn't missed while I'd been floating in that blissful state of unbeing. Fear. Panic. Loss.

It seemed to take eons for my body to re-form, and when I was finally, wholly within the physical world, exhaustion flooded me. My limbs trembled under the sheer force of such overwhelming fatigue. I lurched forward, barely managing to open my eyes before my hands pressed against a grooved wall.

In the dim light, I could see that the wall was white and was covered in brightly colored images. Those images spun and lurched like the wall was no more solid than water. I squeezed my eyes shut, focusing on steadying my breathing as well as blocking out the psychedelic vertigo.

Deep breaths. The air was warm and still and tasted a little stale, though not unpleasantly so. I heard movement behind me a moment before fingertips touched my shoulder.

My eyelids snapped open, and I spun, which only exacerbated the dizziness. But still, I was able to make out the equally awed and concerned face of the woman who'd touched me. It was strikingly familiar.

"Dr. Isa?"

Her eyes widened as my knees gave out and, once again, the world fell away.

I regained consciousness slowly. When enough awareness returned that I could feel the various parts of my body, I registered that I was lying on my back on something like gravel.

Opening my eyes, I found the same view I'd had when I passed out—the worried face of Dr. Isa. *It didn't work . . . I* didn't *travel back in time . . .*

But the closer I looked at the woman's face, the more I

doubted my initial presumption. She *was* Dr. Isa—there was no doubt in my mind—but she wasn't the *same* Dr. Isa I'd been with only moments ago. Her hair was different . . . and her makeup . . . and her dress; it was bead-net, like mine.

I squinted up at the woman leaning over me and, rather moronically, said, "Dr. Isa?"

She cocked her head to the side and studied me. "I do not know those words—*dot tur issa,*" she said in Nuin's language. "But we have met before, you and I, though you told me then that you would not remember our time together when next we met." She smiled, and it lit up her caramel eyes, even in the shadows. "You may call me Aset."

Aset. The ancient name of the goddess more commonly known as Isis, who I knew was really Marcus's Nejerette sister. Who'd *died* in an attempt to rescue her brother from Set in the conflict that had inspired one of the most well-known ancient Egyptian myths, *The Contendings of Horus and Seth*. But apparently not yet.

Or does that mean she never really died? If Aset is Dr. Isa . . .

"You—you are Aset?" I hadn't spoken in Nuin's language in a long time, and I was definitely rusty. I had no doubt that my accent was thick to the point of being nearly incomprehensible.

She nodded.

"Sister of Heru?" I clarified.

Again, she nodded and smiled. "We shared the womb, in fact."

I blinked several times. "You shared . . . the womb . . ." Which would mean they weren't just brother and sister, they were twins. It made my heart bleed that much more for the loss Marcus must have felt after her death . . . or rather, her "death."

"But, you—how—" I snapped my mouth shut, barely stopping myself from asking her about a future she'd yet to experience. "We have met before?"

"Yes, dear Lex, we have."

She knew my name. How the hell could a woman who lived—and was supposed to have died—thousands of years before me have *known my name*?

Realization struck, and I narrowed my eyes. "Nuin told you about me, and this is one of his strange jokes, is it not?" To say his sense of humor—or any other human emotional response—was *different* was a gross understatement. I loved the guy, but he was definitely one of a kind.

A delighted, tinkling sound erupted from Aset, echoing all around us like we were in a small, enclosed space.

I scanned my surroundings for the first time, focusing on the ceiling, then glancing around at the walls. Though the only source of light seemed to be the doorway on the opposite side of the cramped chamber, I could see well enough to tell that the walls—likely plaster spread over mud-brick—were covered in a glorious array of hieroglyphs and sacred images, mostly of Hathor, the ancient goddess of love, sex, singing, dancing, drunkenness—what most people would agree were the best parts of life. I was in the Hathor inner sanctuary, thousands of years before I'd been in it only moments ago.

"You told me you would say that," Aset said. "No, my grandfather does not know of your arrival; only I do."

I propped myself up on my elbows and shook my head slowly. "And you knew I would be arriving because . . . ?"

She pressed her lips together in a thin line. "Now you are simply being obstinate, I think."

My eyes widened. "Uh . . . no, I really do not understand."

Aset sighed. "You visited me a long time ago, and what you did then—" Shaking her head, she looked away. "I must not speak of it, for I cannot not risk changing what happened. It would be far too dangerous." She took my nearest hand in both of hers. "Just know this—there is nothing I would not do for you. I owe you *everything*."

My brow furrowed. Seeing her extreme gratitude for something I'd yet to do was odd, to say the least.

"Come," she said, taking hold of my elbow with a surprisingly strong grip for such a tiny woman. "Let us get you on your feet. I know how uncomfortable it can be to lie on a bead-net dress." She turned her attention to the doorway, where another woman now stood wearing a simple, white linen shift and silhouetted by bright sunlight. "Denai. Aid me in helping her rise."

The newcomer—Denai, it seemed—said something in what had to be Old Egyptian, assuming I'd made it to the target time period of 2180 BCE. Of course, since I didn't actually *speak* Old Egyptian and could only *read* it, much like with Middle Egyptian, this meant I couldn't understand her. At all.

Shaking my head, I told her as much in Nuin's tongue, adding, "Do you speak this language?"

"She does," Aset said. "Since the Hat-hur cult first came into existence many generations ago, I have made sure that every priestess who serves in this particular temple speaks the original tongue. You claimed you would not arrive until the death of our latest pharaoh, but I wanted to make sure we were prepared." She let out a soft, chiming laugh. "Perhaps we were *over*prepared."

Once again, she'd stunned me speechless.

"Apologies," Denai said, kneeling to take hold of my other arm.

Together, they helped me to my feet, though my legs were still a little unsteady. Once I was standing, Denai continued to lend me a supporting hand while Aset examined the backside of my dress.

"You are lucky that none of your dress's beads were crushed, considering how hard you hit the floor," Aset said. "Perhaps they are constructed of a more durable substance than faience? Certainly they are not all turquoise . . ."

"I—" I swallowed, then cleared my throat. "Honestly, I do not know." I'd thought they were faience, the fired, ceramic material so many Egyptian artifacts were made of, but it was entirely possibly that they were just a lighter-colored turquoise than the other, more brightly colored stones.

"Such a garment must have cost a fortune," Aset said as she reached for my arm. She led me out of the dim sanctuary and down a tan mud-brick ramp to a more spacious room.

It was rectangular, and the white plaster walls were covered with depictions of the goddess Hathor in her various forms—as a cow, as a woman with the head of a cow, as a woman with a beautiful face and the ears of a cow, and as a gorgeous woman with cow horns crowning her head, cradling a crimson sun disk, one of the symbols of the main solar deity, Re. A vast array of small items was placed around the perimeter, where the walls met the mud-brick floor; some were tiny figurines of women, while others appeared quite phallic.

They're offerings to Hathor, I realized. Which made sense, considering that I'd appeared in the inner sanctuary of a Temple of Hathor. Time travel seemed to dim my wits a bit.

I was standing in an Old Kingdom temple the likes of which hadn't survived the millennia—mud-brick wasn't the most durable of building materials. I was *really* there, not just viewing it in the At. It was pure insanity, and the archaeologist in me couldn't help but get excited, despite the traumatic and shocking events of the past few hours.

A woman dressed identically to Denai was standing at the bottom of the ramp. When I met her eyes and offered her a small smile, she shrieked and fell to her knees, bowing forward until her forehead was pressed to the mud-brick floor. And I was pretty sure she was shaking.

I stopped mid-step and looked at Aset, utterly clueless as to what I'd done to elicit such a reaction.

She gave my arm a gentle squeeze. "You are not simply

Netjer-At; you are like the Great Father. We can all see it in your eyes."

"You can see *what* in my eyes?"

"The At," she whispered.

My mouth went instantly dry. Nuin's eyes had always been filled with a swirling chaos of every color, reminiscent of the At. But nothing like that had ever shone in *my* eyes.

Aset leaned in closer to me. "They believe you to be their goddess, Hat-hur."

Hat-hur. It was one of the possible ancient pronunciations of the goddess modern people knew of as "Hathor" . . . in whose temple I was currently standing. With the way I'd simply appeared in the temple's sanctuary, not to mention the power they could see in my eyes, how could they *not* have believed me to be Hathor—*Hat-hur*?

I groaned. "And you did not think it important to let them know that I am *not* their goddess . . . ?"

Aset smiled mysteriously. "What makes you think you are not?"

I simply couldn't respond. So I just stared at her. And when I considered that Hat-hur was the mythical consort of the god Heru, and that *I* was bonded to the Nejeret behind the myth of Heru, I started to think she might be onto something. Of course, the goddess was also recorded as being the consort of Re—essentially the sun god—in various myths, so, maybe not . . .

Aset shrugged. "They truly could not be more pleased."

I felt like I was about to pass out again. "I see."

"Besides, it is how Nuin will be introducing you to the others." Laughing, she shook her head. "He could hardly tell them your name is 'Alexandra' or 'Lex'—nobody is named those things in this time."

I opened my mouth to protest, but realizing that she kind of had a point, I changed tactics. Besides, I was thousands of years in the past and in about as foreign a place as there was—being considered a goddess might come in handy at the moment.

Swallowing, I forced a smile. "You are going to bring me to Nuin?" Because I *really* needed to speak with him. And beyond that, I'd always felt comfort in his presence, and I was craving some comfort right about now.

Aset nodded and shifted her hand, linking her arm with mine. "He should still be at the pyramid complex. We can go right now."

Denai strode toward me, bowing her head as she stopped. "We would accompany you, if it would please you," she said to the floor.

"I, uh . . ." I glanced at Aset, who was watching me curiously. She gave another, tinier nod, so I told Denai, "Yes, that would please me very much."

Denai raised her eyes to meet mine, a joyous smile spreading across her face before she bowed her head again. "Thank you, great Hat-hur. You honor us."

I flashed her an uncertain smile. "The more the merrier, right?"

Denai met my eyes again, this time a quizzical light filling hers. Apparently the saying didn't translate quite right. I sighed. I would have to be careful about that.

5

FAREWELL & WELCOME

I fell in step beside Aset as she headed for an open doorway that appeared to be the temple's only exit. It was wider than the one from the sanctuary, but neither wide nor tall compared to modern grand entrances. The doors themselves, little more than simple wooden slabs, were propped open against the outside of the building. Aside from the vibrant reds, yellows, and blues used in the hieroglyphs and mythological depictions covering the interior walls, the temple was rather modest.

I paused in the doorway to take in my unfamiliar surroundings. I may have been an archaeologist *and* possessed the ability to view the past and future—though that was a skill I'd only had for a little over half a year—but actually being *in* Egypt during the tail end of the 6th Dynasty, just as the glory of the Old Kingdom was dying away . . . *that* was mind-blowing.

I didn't know what I'd been expecting, especially considering the lack of Old Kingdom evidence—ruins, artifacts, human remains—that still existed in my time, but it wasn't what I found spread out before me. It was so cheery and filled with vibrant colors and life, a walled-in oasis in the middle of a barren desert.

The temple was surrounded by a courtyard filled with date palms, fig trees, and some other fruit tree I didn't recognize. They lined the inside of the mud-brick walls surrounding the temple and courtyard, as well as the rectangular pool extending from the temple entrance to a set of more substantial wooden doors blocking the gateway out of the courtyard. The broad steps leading down from the temple were also constructed from mud-brick, as were the paths crisscrossing the compact courtyard.

I followed one of the paths, heading around the right side of the pool, Aset still arm in arm with me and the priestesses trailing close behind us. Stopping at the edge, I dipped the tip of my sandaled foot into the water, watching as the surface sparkled, reflecting the afternoon light. The water was lukewarm and exceedingly clear, unlike everything else in my chaotic life. It all seemed to finally be sinking in—where I was, *when* I was, what had driven me here . . .

I missed Marcus terribly, and I'd only been gone for a few hours. I couldn't help but wonder what he was doing at that exact moment, thousands of years in the future. I couldn't help but worry about him. A black hole, a sucking void, seemed to be taking shape in my chest. I ached to be near him again, body, mind, and soul.

"I wasn't expecting this," I said in English. In truth, I hadn't been expecting anything that had happened over the past seven months, and Marcus attacking me was one of the most shocking and painful surprises of all.

"I do not understand," Aset said. In my peripheral vision, I could see her tilting her head to the side. "What saddens you so, Lex?"

I wiped my cheeks with one hand, swiping away tears I hadn't realized had escaped, and offered her a weak smile. "I would try to explain, but it would sound impossible, and you would think me insane."

Aset turned me away from the pool, leading me further down the pathway. "You will be surprised by what I am able to believe, I think. I have seen and experienced much that is not quite . . . normal, even for our kind." After a pause, she added, "And do not forget that *I* already know you, even if *you* do not yet know me."

I met her eyes. "So you know about me—that I do not truly belong here?"

She gave my arm a little squeeze and nodded. "I know that you are not of this time. As I said, you are not a normal Netjer-At; you are like my grandfather, truly divine. Which, many would argue, means you belong wherever and *when*ever you wish to be."

I bit my lip. "But I am not—*that* . . . not divine. Not really." I felt my eyes tense with a plea. "You know that, yes?" I needed her to understand. I needed *someone* to understand. I needed a friend.

She smiled, and it lit up her beautiful, golden face with warmth and affection. "Yes, Lex, I know."

Squinting up at the bright afternoon sun, I sighed. "I thank you for that, Aset. It means more than you could possibly know."

"Ah . . . but you are wrong," she said. "I understand quite well. We all need someone who sees us for who we really are; otherwise, we risk losing ourselves completely."

Again, I met her sincere gaze and smiled, knowing I would need to change the subject if I wanted to avoid a quick descent into tear-dom. I cleared my throat and flipped through my mental rolodex of Old Kingdom rulers. "Alright, so . . . the pyramid complex you mentioned—it is the pyramid complex of Pepi the Second, correct?" I asked as we stopped at the heavy, wooden gate doors. These were coated in a thin layer of plaster, possibly to make them appear stone, while those at the temple entrance had been left their natural, sun-bleached color.

"If you mean Pepi Neferkare, then yes."

Two of the priestesses stepped ahead of us to open the doors, and Denai slipped through the opening as soon as it was wide enough. I watched her scan the wide, smoothly paved limestone avenue on the other side. She shouted something in Old Egyptian and snapped her fingers.

A young boy trotted across the street, wearing a simple white tunic and with all but a long, braided sidelock shaved off his head. He listened closely as Denai spoke, held out his hand to accept something small and cylindrical from her—possibly a seal of some sort—then spun away and broke into a sprint.

I looked at Aset, my eyebrows raised in question.

"He goes to the canal landing to secure a boat for us." She smiled wryly. "Shemu has been long and exceedingly hot this year . . . again. I do not think you would enjoy walking all the way to the pyramid complex." She glanced at the sun, seeming to measure its height in the sky. "No, we shall sit and relax under the cover of a canopy while some nice, strong young men guide us up the canal to the valley temple."

"I cannot claim that does not sound preferable," I said with a smile.

I let Aset lead me out onto the avenue, relying on her guidance to keep me from running into or tripping over anything as I studied *everything*. I'd expected narrow, crowded packed-dirt streets that wound their way through a warren-like town, but what I found was a several-meters-wide avenue paved in worn limestone blocks and lined with tall mud-brick walls like those surrounding the Hat-hur temple complex.

There were few people standing or strolling along the avenue, and those who were appeared to be either youthful errand boys awaiting a task or priests and priestesses going about their priestly duties. Regardless, all were dressed in unadorned white linen—shifts for the women, baggy, belted tunics for the boys, and for the men, wrapped kilts that almost reached their knees.

Every single person who spotted us, whether man, woman, or child, averted their eyes and bowed their heads as we passed. Part of me hoped that meant they didn't notice my eyes.

"Why are they doing that?" I asked Aset.

"To show their respect," she told me quietly. "Whatever else you may be, you are also Netjer-At, and they recognize this and honor this." Her eyebrows drew down slightly. "Do not the people in your time behave the same?"

"No, not exactly. In my time, well . . . we try to blend in. The *people* are not so accepting of differences as they are here, and they outnumber us by so much that if they realized who we were and what we could do, we would be in danger . . . as would they."

"Surely you would not hurt them simply because they discovered the Netjer-At live among them?"

"No, but some of them would try to use us—our gifts—and most likely end up hurting themselves or others of their kind." At her increasingly confused stare, I said, "It is difficult to explain; I come from a *very* different time."

As we walked, I caught tantalizing glimpses of the upper halves of several different pyramids through the gaps between mud-brick walls. Sunlight gleamed off their polished limestone overlays and positively sparkled off the golden *benbenets*—the capstones topping the pyramids. I'd seen the pyramids of Giza in my own time, and though they were definitely impressive enough to have rightfully earned their place as one of the world's greatest wonders, these smaller pyramids, located in Saqqara, Memphis's city of the dead, looked so much more magnificent than their larger, shabbier, *ancient* brethren. These pyramids were in their prime, not yet stripped of their shiny, valuable exterior.

"They are awe-inspiring, are they not?" Aset commented as we walked.

I nodded without looking away. "They are . . . impressive."

"Well, you will get to see the newest up close; it was long enough in the making. Dear Pepi"—Aset said the late Pharaoh's given name like she'd known him well, which I figured was entirely possible—"has been building his complex for nearly nine decades!"

Pepi II, the ruler modern history books marked as the last king of Egypt's Old Kingdom, was proposed to have lived into his mid-nineties, a truly epic lifespan for his time. As far as we knew, he'd inherited the throne when he was six from Merenre, who was either his father, his step-father, or his brother—in my time, much from the Old Kingdom was a bit of an unknown. We were, at least, *fairly* certain that his mother was Ankhesenpepi, the wife of the previous two rulers. Probably.

The sudden decline of the Old Kingdom, one of the first-ever civilized golden ages, was an even greater historical mystery. Even Marcus was a bit foggy about the cause of it, and he'd witnessed the decline of many civilizations. He'd told me that several years of dwindling floods from the Nile, combined with the excessively long rule of Pepi II and his lack of any direct heirs, had led to a sort of civil war and perhaps the fall of the Old Kingdom. But the one thing he'd been able to tell me with absolute certainty was that Nuin had died shortly after Pepi II.

Which was pretty damn terrifying, from my perspective.

Somehow, a statuette had been fashioned from the At and imbued with the power to draw me into the distant past—a feat I could only attribute to Nuin. He *had* to have been the one who made the statuette, the one responsible for me being here, and if he died soon . . . before he could send me back to my own time . . .

I wouldn't be able to return at all, not to my own time and not to Marcus. And without a steady dose of Marcus's bonding pheromones, I would soon start going through painful withdrawals, and the same would happen to him. And after that, we would die. Physiological codependency was the single greatest downside of being half of a bonded Nejeret pair.

"You look troubled," Aset told me as she guided me around a corner. The street widened, and ahead a short ways, a waterway broader than I'd expected for a canal came into view.

I glanced at Aset; concern lined her face. How much could I really share with her? How much did she know about who I *really* was, whatever she claimed? There was no way to know. "I—I am travel weary, I suppose. Tell me, was Pepi a good ruler?"

A wistful smile broke through Aset's concern. "He was a sweet child, and a kind man. He adored Ankhesenpepi, and remained loyal to her until—"

Confused, I stopped walking. "Ankhesenpepi was his mother, correct?"

Aset shook her head, a crease forming between her eyebrows. "No. She is mother to none."

I frowned. "But . . ." According to our meager historical and archaeological evidence, she was . . .

"Ankhesenpepi is Netjer-At. She has been queen and consort to many Pharaohs, including the previous three, and as Nuin's oldest living daughter, she is the highest-ranking female Netjer-At."

I drew back, shocked. "Oh my . . ." I covered my mouth with my hand. "That explains why Pepi didn't have any heirs." If he'd been so devoted to Ankhesenpepi that he remained loyal to her, refusing to take any wives who could bear him children, then an heir had been an impossibility.

Aset nodded and nudged me to continue toward the canal. "Nuin has long indulged her, but I think he is finally fed up with her endless desire for power." She lifted her shoulders and dropped them elegantly. "He has come to the conclusion that we should let them"—she pointed to one of the two-story, mud-brick buildings on our right, where a human woman was shaking a rug out from a second floor window—"rule themselves, and stay out of their business, more or less."

I pulled her closer and let out a small laugh. "You see . . . that is the way it is done in my time. We coexist with them and interfere when needed, but we do not *rule* them. We let them make their own destinies . . . just so long as those destinies are not *too* harmful."

The priestesses surrounded us, babbling non-stop, and Denai tentatively took my free hand and led me closer to the edge of the canal. "Come," the priestess said, "this is our vessel. Watch your step, please, Hat-hur."

I released Aset's arm and let Denai guide me over the limestone precipice of the canal edge and down some grooved steps to a long riverboat constructed of bundled reeds and rope. *God, it's like walking through a documentary . . .* Except everything was *more*—more detailed, more gritty, more vibrant, more *real*—than any documentary ever filmed.

As the priestesses, Aset, and I settled onto lightly padded benches under a thick, reed-topped linen canopy, reality finally, truly caught up with me.

Marcus tried to kill me . . .

. . . and now I'm in Old Kingdom Egypt.

Marcus tried to kill *me.*

Dr. Isa is Aset, Marcus's believed-to-be-dead sister.

Marcus *tried to* kill *me.*

I can't go back until the spirit—Apep—is no longer a threat.

Somehow, I managed to hold in a whimper as I thought, *I have no idea how to take care of myself here . . . and if I stay too long . . . if I'm away from Marcus for too long . . .*

"He must be very excited to see you, Golden One," Denai said. She was sitting to my right, hands folded demurely on her lap. It took me a few seconds to realize that she was talking to me, using one of the titles commonly attributed to the goddess they all believed me to be. With all of the gold emblazoning my jewelry and my bead-net dress, I couldn't blame her. And, unfortunately, the beads were nearly as uncomfortable between my backside and the barely padded bench as they'd been when I'd been lying on the inner sanctuary's limestone floor.

I closed my eyes, focusing on my scattered thoughts rather than my discomfort. "What do you mean?" I asked Denai.

"Great Nuin—he visited the temple with Aset several times before the Son of Re, Pepi Neferkare, passed on to the land of the dead. His presence made the other priestesses very anxious," she said, as though she herself had been completely calm and collected in front of Nuin. Hell, I considered him my first boyfriend, and even *I* wasn't completely calm and collected when I was around him.

When I opened my eyes and looked at her, she blushed but, for once, managed to maintain eye contact. "And I am excited to see him," I told her.

Aset touched her fingertips to my forearm and pointed to the left. Boats, some smaller and some larger than ours, were approaching, threatening to crowd the waterway. There was no way we could continue moving upstream.

I frowned. A traffic jam delaying me reaching Nuin was the last thing I needed.

To my surprise, the priestesses stood, Denai in the lead. She worked her way gracefully between oarsmen, and when she reached the bow, she produced a glinting, palm-sized golden object from her satchel. The four other priestesses took up positions along the front half of the boat and procured similar items. As they raised them high, angling them slightly to the right—toward the sun—I realized what they were: golden signal mirrors.

The watercrafts ahead began angling toward the left side of the canal, like they were making room for our vessel.

I caught Aset's eye. "I don't understand . . ."

The corner of her mouth turned up. "Consider it a perk of being one of us. The mirrors signal that the divine, usually a royal, is en route. Lucky for us, we are *both* . . . at least, to these people."

I watched, absolutely awed, as dozens, possibly hundreds, of other boats made room for us, and we were able to continue on our way.

By the time the canal widened to a small lake and our boat sidled up to the right-side lakeshore, I was so lost in observing this ancient, foreign world around me that Aset had to physically shake me to get my attention. Some muffled part of my mind was screaming about how insane everything about my current situation was, crying out that I needed to return to Marcus as soon as possible, to assure him that he hadn't truly injured me, but I could barely hear it. I felt detached from reality, though that could probably have been blamed on the *un*reality of the past few hours.

Boats were still crowding the canal, either waiting their turn to pick up their passengers at the landing ramps or dutifully steering their way downstream. On land, people milled in the long gateways leading to the two landing ramps, some watching our boat and elbowing those nearest them to look or move out of the way, or maybe to do both.

It was so strange to witness how aware the ancient Egyptians had been of the Nejerets living among them. I'd been told about it, had understood that my kind were the basis for many ancient religious beliefs and mythological figures, chief among them the man I was bonded to.

An unsettling thought surfaced, something I should have considered much earlier. *What if I see Heru?* How was I supposed to react? I wasn't sure it would be possible to pretend that I didn't know him, that I didn't love him with every fiber of my being . . . that we didn't share a physiological bond that both of us relied on to stay alive. But the Heru of *this* time wouldn't share that bond with me. He wouldn't even know me . . . unless, like Aset, he *did* know me . . .

I wasn't sure if that would make things easier, or harder. Because soon, I would have to leave, to return to my time, to my Heru. It would be best if I never saw him in this ancient time at all.

But it was no use worrying about what might be. I took a deep, steadying breath, shook my head, and followed Denai and two of the priestesses off the boat and up the landing ramp. The smooth limestone blocks were coated in a thick layer of dirt and sand that created a slick paste when mixed with water from the canal. Denai and the priestesses, who were all barefoot, didn't seem to have any trouble ascending the ramp, but the goop was hell underneath the leather soles of my sandals, and Aset was having similar issues.

She caught my eye and raised her eyebrows, flicking her gaze down to our feet. "Shoes always make this part more difficult."

"Then why not go barefoot?" I made a quick assessment of the people who'd stepped to the side to let us pass, and none wore any form of shoes.

"Ah . . . you will be glad of your sandals soon." She pointed to some of the people with her chin. "They have all built up thick calluses that protect their feet from the sunbaked stone, but being what we are, we are incapable of building up such a natural defense. So . . . we wear shoes to avoid the pain." She shrugged. Reclaiming my elbow, she hastened my movement forward. "Come. Once we get into the valley temple, the crowd will thin."

I glanced around at all the people we were passing. Though some of the men wore pristine white linen kilts identical to those we'd seen in the temple district, marking them as priests or wealthier mourners, most of the clothing appeared slightly worn and more off-white.

"I have to admit," I murmured, "I did not expect to see so

many people leaving the temple complex." We passed through a tunnel-like passageway and entered a barren, almost empty courtyard.

Aset glanced over her shoulder at the landing ramp. "I believe this is the tail end of the procession-watchers . . . at least, of those returning to Men-nefer"—she used the ancient name for Memphis—"by boat." She gave my arm a gentle tug. "Let us hurry. The Great Father will be so happy to see you."

I was just fine with that. I needed to talk to Nuin, to ask him how to shield Marcus so Apep's spirit couldn't take possession of him again and how to get back to my own time. Marcus had claimed we could go a few days apart without any ill effects, but based on the withdrawal pain he'd been in when Set had trapped my ba—essentially, my Nejerette soul—in the At, I didn't want to test his theory.

Despite my obsession with all things Egyptian, I zoned out as we passed through the valley temple and walked up the several-hundred-meter causeway to the rest of the pyramid complex. I had too many other, more pressing concerns on my mind. At least the way was partially covered, providing some relief from the unrelenting desert sun. But when we reached the end of the causeway, I couldn't help but shake out of my pensive state and pay attention to my incredible surroundings.

The priestesses headed straight into a cavernous limestone corridor covered in elaborately carved hieroglyphs, passed through with quick nods at the two men filling in a far section of engravings with an inky black paint, and strode into an open-roofed courtyard surrounded by an engraved colonnade. Instead of burrowing further into the mortuary temple, they took a hard right at the end of the courtyard and passed through a doorway leading outside.

Aset and I followed. As we neared the opening, distant moaning and wailing disrupted the peaceful silence of the temple. I shot Aset a confused glance. "I thought you said the funeral procession was over."

She snorted delicately. "It *is* over. The mourners are simply continuing their display of *intense sorrow* as they leave."

The corner of my mouth quirked as I wondered if there was a prize of some sort for the Most Enthusiastic Mourner."

After the dimness inside the temples and causeway, the sunlight was glaringly bright, especially as it reflected off the pale, glossy limestone surface of Pepi's pyramid. I raised my hand to shield my eyes, wishing I had some damn sunglasses.

The priestesses stopped near the corner of the pyramid, falling into a line with Denai in the center. As one, they tilted their faces up to the sun, lifted their arms straight above their heads, palms upward, and began singing. Their voices harmonized perfectly, creating a melody that was filled with both immense sorrow and great joy.

I halted mid-step, drawing Aset to a stop beside me, and watched the priestesses, awed. "What are they doing?" I'd never heard of such a display, either at a funeral or otherwise, but that was what happened when so little survived the millennia. *I really need to spend more time studying the past in the At . . .*

"They are greeting Re, thanking him for another day and mourning his inevitable death, and"—she paused, watching as the five women slowly curved their uplifted arms as though they were holding a large round object above their heads—"welcoming their goddess, Hat-hur, who finally walks among them."

Their slight shift in position suddenly made sense. They *were* holding something large and round, or at least miming doing so; they were using their arms as the cow horns so frequently depicted on Hat-hur's head, holding the sun disk, the symbol of Re. As their hauntingly beautiful song drew to a close, they lowered their arms to their sides and folded their bodies as gracefully as any ballet dancer until they were prostrate on their knees, their arms extended on the ground in front of them, still palm-up.

"And now?" I asked.

"Now they are bowing in supplication to the Great Father, the creator of all that is, was, or ever shall be."

"Nuin," I whispered, realizing that meant he was nearby, possibly watching as the final mourners departed. Without thinking, I slipped my arm free from Aset's and broke into a run. I skirted around the priestesses, around the corner of the pyramid, and skidded to a halt.

There was still a small crowd of people standing in the pyramid's courtyard, clumped in groups ranging from three to over a dozen. I scanned them quickly; it didn't take me long to find him.

Tall, golden-skinned, and regal beyond comparison, Nuin still emanated the last few remnants of his power. He was stunning. He was a man who would stand out in any crowd, in any time period. He'd been staring at the priestesses, but his attention had shifted to me as I'd hurtled around the corner of the pyramid.

Meeting his eyes, I exhaled in relief. "Nuin . . ."

His sculpted lips curved into a slight smile, and he nodded his close-shaven head in acknowledgment.

A handful of people stood around him, both male and female, but I didn't give any of them a second glance. Hell, I barely gave any of them a *first* glance. My legs started moving, a slow, stunned stride. It seemed to take forever for me to cross the distance separating me from this one familiar person, this one thing I could depend on in such a foreign time period, but I couldn't manage to move any faster.

I stopped a few steps in front of him, my arms dangling limply at my sides. I had dozens—hundreds—of things to say to him, but I couldn't think of a single one. Instead, I simply stared into eyes filled with brilliant, swirling hues of every color. Eyes that apparently reflected my own.

Tell me what to do, I thought.

Make this make sense.

Help me, please!

My mind felt numb, and I couldn't voice any of my desperate pleas. I could just stare into those mesmerizing eyes.

A woman said something to him from directly behind me, but I couldn't understand her words.

Mischief filled Nuin's ancient eyes, transformed features that were so similar to Marcus's that it was heartbreaking, and a broad smile spread across his achingly handsome face. "Why, daughter, this is Hat-hur, my wife."

6

GIVE & TAKE

"I—I—your *wife?*" I said.

Nuin's eyes wrinkled at the corners as his grin widened. "Yes, dear Alexandra, my wife. It's to my benefit, and to yours, I think, that nobody questions my marital acquisitions," he said, answering in English. Only then did I realize I'd spoken in my native tongue as well. "I hoped," he said, "though I wasn't sure, that Aset was correct about your imminent arrival, and her early warning has given me the time to weigh your possible identities while you're here."

I shook my head. "But you—"

He held up a hand, cutting me off. "Being one of my wives not only gives you a legitimate reason to be here and me a legitimate reason to spend time with you alone and provide you with ample resources and protection, but it also raises you to the highest-ranking position among the Nejerettes of this time. It's the most logical, practical move to make." He raised one shoulder in a halfhearted shrug, and something in his eyes made me think he wasn't quite telling me everything. Not that *that* was a surprise . . .

My shoulders rose, then slumped. "But . . . your *wife?*"

Nuin's grin faded to the faintest of smiles, and he reached up to brush the backs of his curled fingers against my cheek. "Much is troubling you, my Alexandra. How long has it been since we last spoke?"

I frowned and thought back to the disastrous confrontation with Set in the underground temple, just after Nuin had given me the ankh-At, transferring half of his power to me. "A little over two weeks—my weeks, not yours," I added. The ancient Egyptian week contained ten days. "So fifteen or sixteen days, I think. How long has it been for you?"

"Three long, exhausting years."

"Three *years*?" I blurted, surprised. For some illogical reason, I'd assumed as much time had passed for him as it had for me.

Nuin nodded sedately. "And now that you are here, I'll have plenty of time to teach you—"

"Plenty of time?" I shook my head and leaned in. "What about Marcus? I *can't* stay here, Nuin. We *don't* have plenty of time. You know that." Panic somersaulted in my chest. "I have to get back, but I need to know how to keep Apep from possessing him, and—"

"Calm yourself, my Alexandra," Nuin said, taking hold of my upper arms. "Until you have enough control over your new power and are strong enough to deal with Apep and restore ma'at, you must stay here." Not that I had any idea what he meant by *restore ma'at*. "Your bond-mate will be fine in your time, I assure you. And here, you'll be able to—"

A man spoke directly behind me. The voice was deep and silken, and it resonated with the very core of my being, making my heart beat faster and my lips attempt to curve into a smile. Though I didn't quite understand his words, there was no mistaking his identity: Marcus.

I squeezed my eyes shut. *Not Marcus—Heru.*

He doesn't know me . . . he doesn't know me . . . he doesn't *know me . . .*

Nuin squeezed my shoulder supportively and pressed two fingers to my temple. I felt a wash of power sink into me, reminding me of how it used to feel when he would block and unblock my memories every time he visited me growing up.

My eyes flashed open. "What . . . ?"

Nuin smiled. "I have sealed your new power within you." He spoke in English, which I suspected would fast become our go-to method for keeping the more unusual aspects of our relationship secret.

"Why—"

"To hide your rather stunning new eye color . . . among other reasons. I shall explain what I can later, I promise." Switching to what Aset had called the "original tongue," he said, "Yes, Heru, I have a new wife." He laughed, his gaze shifting to look past me. "I found myself in need of just one more, and this lovely creature practically sprang into existence out of the At itself to meet my needs."

I pressed my lips together, far from amused. And holy hell, was I nervous to turn around. The man who would, in just over four thousand years, become the love of my life was standing behind me. And he had no idea who I was.

Forcing a smile and gritting my teeth, I murmured in English, "Maybe it would be best if you just *told* me how to protect Marcus from this Apep guy so I can return to my own time without having to do *this*." I widened my eyes for emphasis.

Nuin's eyebrows lowered, and sadness clouded his multi-hued irises. "That isn't possible."

"What's not possible, protecting Marcus or me going home?"

Nuin sighed. "At the moment—both."

I leaned in closer to him. "Why not?"

He spent a tense moment searching my face, a moment made even more uncomfortable by the building anticipation forming around us. "Because, if you return now, you'll both die. And . . . *before* you leave this time, *I* must die."

I opened my mouth, but shock stoppered my voice. I'd known, I really had. This was when Nuin died. I'd *known*. But . . . I loved this man. Not in the same way that I loved Marcus, but few people meant as much to me as Nuin, and the thought of his imminent death . . . I swallowed roughly. It was like learning that my sister or one of my parents had terminal cancer. I hadn't been ready for this. I would never be ready for this.

Tears welled in my eyes. "Nuin, I—I—"

He tilted his beautiful head to the side. "Calm yourself, dear Alexandra. All will be well. All is what must be."

But his words didn't stop my heart from filling with sorrow or my mind from whirring with possible ways to save him. It didn't seem to matter to my mind that I had no clue *how* he was supposed to die.

Off to my right, a woman strode toward us, rattling off what could only be admonishments and complaints, however incomprehensible her words were to me.

I turned my head to watch her approach. She was middle-aged, slender, and remarkably pretty. She was also human, which was surprising, considering that the sharp edge to her tongue was most definitely aimed at Nuin . . . and possibly at me. It was hard to believe that *anyone* had that gall to speak to him in such a tone.

"You speak the original tongue?" Heru said. I hadn't noticed him draw closer, but based on the sound of his voice, he was standing a few inches behind me and had to be leaning down to keep his words between only us in a crowd that included more than a few Nejerets.

My entire body tensed, and my spine straightened with the effort *not* to lean back against him. *Not mine,* I reminded myself. *He might as well be a different man entirely.*

He'd certainly never mentioned meeting me in ancient times,

so I didn't think prolonging our interaction to a memorable encounter was wise. Nuin might be able to teach me how to block Heru's memories of me, but the more complicated they were, the harder I feared the task would be.

I considered ignoring him, but that just seemed rude. I gave a minute nod.

The woman reached Nuin, near hysterics in her tirade, and another—an absolutely gorgeous Nejerette—was close by her side.

"But not the common language?" Heru asked.

I shook my head.

"Then I shall translate." There was mischief in Heru's tone, and I started to understand one of the many ways the passing of thousands of years had shaped *my* Heru; he'd lost this playfulness his younger counterpart offered up readily. My Heru was serious and somber, and far too conceited. He emitted confidence and power just by breathing, and when he entered a room, his presence demanded that all eyes focus on him. This Heru was different. Less guarded, it seemed . . . less troubled.

I still hadn't looked at him. I wasn't ready. I needed more time; four thousand years sounded about right.

"The woman scolding the Great Father is his primary wife, Ipwet." Heru laughed, and his breath brushed against my neck, making me shiver. "She is demanding to know when and where he found you. She calls him a rabid monkey. She says he's no better than a"—he cleared his throat—"apologies . . . a horny stray dog who is incapable of controlling his libido and cannot turn down any female who crosses his path. Ah . . . now she is talking about you, and I do not think you would like me to translate."

"Enough!" Nuin said, and the woman fell silent. "It is done." Raising his voice, he added, "Let it be known that any person in my new wife's presence shall speak the original tongue unless they do not know it. Ale—Hat-hur does not speak the common language, and it will be considered a great insult by me if any speak it simply to keep her from understanding. She is from far away, and despite having a legendary divine reputation among our people, she is not familiar with our ways. The adjustment will be difficult enough for her; the least we can do is make sure she can understand us." He stared at his primary wife. "Am I clear, Ipwet?"

She nodded, and when her gaze shifted to me, sniffed.

"Ankhesenpepi?" Nuin said, and when the other woman nodded, my mind was blown. Here was Ankhesenpepi, Nuin's Nejerette daughter who, according to Aset, had been the queen or consort to numerous rulers, including the recently laid-to-rest Pepi Neferkare, and was the highest ranking Nejerette alive. Except for me.

I frowned, thinking she was taking being "dethroned" fairly well.

"Perhaps she should spend some time learning the common tongue so we do not risk upsetting her, dear Father," Ankhesenpepi said sweetly, batting her eyelashes at Nuin.

To my surprise, it was Heru who responded. "Perhaps I will volunteer to spend some time teaching her."

Ankhesenpepi's almond-shaped eyes, as dark and richly colored as the finest chocolate, narrowed to slits. She scanned me from the sandals up, her striking eyes going wide when she reached my face. "She is Netjer-At!" Her irate stare shifted to Nuin. "Why would you take her as a wife? This is not the way! You said you would never—that I would always be—"

"Jealous, Khessie?" Heru said, and she turned her glare on him.

"She—she cannot give him children," she sputtered. "It is not done!"

"It is not done!" Ipwet echoed.

"And yet, I did it." There was a note of finality in Nuin's

voice. "We are done with this conversation. Do not bring it up again."

Both Ipwet and Ankhesenpepi shut their mouths, but I could still feel the outrage pouring off them in waves. Clearly I'd been wrong about the dethronement thing . . .

"I have to admit that *I* am a little jealous, Great Father," Heru said. He stepped up to stand on my left, and when a slender arm linked with my right, I glanced over to find Aset standing on my other side. Brother and sister were flanking me like faithful guardians. "After all, the stories do say that Hat-hur is supposed to be *my* wife, and all can see that she is even more lovely than the stories say . . ."

Pulse racing, I turned my head to look at him before I could stop myself. And as expected, he was exquisite—chiseled features that were both masculine and beautiful at the same time and were unquestionably similar to Nuin's, light golden-brown skin, and a lean physique toned enough to make any woman's heartbeat speed up. And just like the rest of the men in the courtyard, his upper half was completely bare, which just made it that much harder not to stare. Everything about him was so familiar that seeing him was like a balm on burned skin.

Until I looked into his eyes, and my soul shattered. These weren't the eyes I knew and loved. They were the eyes of a stranger. Yes, they were as golden as the sun and rimmed in black, but they were too trusting . . . too open. *Not* my *Heru* . . .

He leaned in closer, his brow furrowed. "Are you unwell, Hat-hur?"

I took several hasty steps backward and smacked into another body, hard. A strong hand gripped my arm, steadying me. I spun around and nearly screamed when I recognized who it belonged to—Set.

"I'm sorry," he said, his voice kind. "I did not mean to startle you." He cocked his head to the side, scrutinizing my face. "Have we met before?"

"I—you—" I shook my head vehemently. "No. No, we haven't."

"Set," Nuin said. "I would like you to meet my newest wife, Hat-hur. I think you two will get along quite well and find that you have much in common."

Like our genetics . . .

Set bowed his head slightly and released me. "I am pleased to meet you, Hat-hur."

This was *too* weird. This man, this version of Set who *wasn't* possessed by an evil spirit, was completely different from the Set who'd taken immense pleasure torturing me over and over again.

"I, uh . . . it is nice to meet you," I said, more or less at a loss for words.

Nuin clapped his hands, making me jump. "Splendid. Now that all the introductions are concluded, we shall return to the city. Hat-hur has come a long way, and we all have another long journey ahead of us. It would do us some good to get some rest." After a brief pause, he added, "Tonight, we will feast in celebration of Hat-hur's arrival. Tomorrow, we will finish our preparations, and as soon as we are ready, we shall leave Mennefer."

MUCH TO MY FRUSTRATION, NUIN AND I SPENT THE short trip back to the temple district on different riverboats. I was joined by my original companions—the priestesses and Aset—along with Set, which only frustrated me further. It was so difficult to convince myself that he wasn't the same Set who'd beaten me until more of my flesh was bruised than not. That he wasn't the same Set who'd killed Marcus. That he wasn't the same Set *I'd* killed in an alternate timeline.

I spent the entire trip focusing on taking deep, even breaths to keep myself from fully embracing the urge to panic. Our boats pulled off to a landing a few ramps down from the one the priestesses, Aset, and I had used when heading up to Pepi's pyramid, but we still appeared to be in the same general area based on the wide, paved avenue and the tall mud-brick walls.

The boat carrying Nuin, along with Ipwet, Ankhesenpepi, and Heru, unloaded before ours, and it was impossible to separate Nuin from the two fairly irate women clinging to him. Call it a hunch, but I was getting the feeling that Khessie, Ipwet, and I weren't destined to be best buds.

"Do not mind them," Aset told me as we walked down the avenue, once again arm in arm. "They are petty. They love power and loathe any who threaten to take theirs."

"But I have no desire to take their power," I said as softly as possible, knowing that with her Nejerette hearing, Ankhesenpepi could overhear our conversation if we weren't careful.

"Perhaps, but you have already taken some of their power simply by becoming Nuin's wife. Add that to the power you already have—"

"But they don't know about *that*." I said.

Aset laughed. "Perhaps, but to me, you practically glow with it, like a hundred stars are contained within your skin. But regardless, I would imagine they must feel like a house cat facing an attack from a desert cat."

"But I'm not attacking them . . . and I have no reason to do so."

With a shrug, Aset said, "I never said they were the most intelligent house cats."

Were I not wound so tightly, I might have giggled. But I was afraid of what lie ahead. And I missed Marcus . . . and my sister, whose pregnancy I feared I might miss completely . . . and my mom and dad, who I hadn't seen for months . . . and Alexander, my Nejeret grandfather, and his human wife, Grandma Suse. I missed them all, and none of them but Marcus had even been born yet.

As I studied my surroundings—limestone paving bricks and mud-brick walls that seemed to glow in the light of the sinking sun, and nothing less than a small parade of Nejerets and humans ahead and behind me—I'd never felt more alone.

7

ENEMIES & NEMESES

Our group of several dozen Nejerets and humans passed through a set of wooden double doors in one of the high, mud-brick walls, entering a large courtyard. It was surrounded by covered walkways on three sides, each lined with fluted columns painted a rich sienna at the base and bright yellows, oranges, and greens around the leaf-like capital.

Nuin pulled me aside almost as soon as I was within the walls and led me toward a doorway on the right side of the courtyard. It opened to a long, brightly painted hallway, at the end of which was another doorway, blocked by a rectangle of heavy linen dyed a cerulean as vibrant as the Mediterranean Sea. Much to my irritation, Ipwet followed. She was so close behind me, she was practically treading on my heels with each step.

"We must speak alone, husband," she said.

Nuin paused with his hand outstretched to push the curtain aside but didn't bother glancing back at her. "We will speak later."

"Husband—"

He looked over his shoulder, shooting a warning glare past me. It was filled with such venom that even I shrank back a bit.

"When I first took you as my wife," he said to Ipwet, "Kari and the others not only made you feel welcome among them, but gave us plenty of time alone. Are you so spiteful that you would deny the same courtesy to Hat-hur?"

I was guessing that "Kari and the others" was a reference to Nuin's other wives, or *previous* wives. Nuin, it seemed, was the proud keeper of his very own harem. Which now included me . . .

"But she cannot give you children," Ipwet persisted. In my opinion, it was a pretty dumb thing to do; angry Nuin was definitely one of the last people I would poke with a verbal stick. "Why do you need to—"

Nuin's gaze, still swirling with vibrant colors, darkened ominously. "If you continue with this argument, Ipwet, I may no longer have need of our union. After all, you have not borne me a child for over a decade. What further use do I have of *you*?"

Ipwet gasped.

"That was harsh, Nuin," I said. Ipwet and I might not have been fast friends, but that was just plain mean, especially when he knew full well that there wouldn't be any sexual relations between us.

He turned his cruel glare on me.

I straightened my shoulders, stuck out my chin, and held my head a little higher.

The angry glint faded from his eyes, and the corner of his mouth rose in a small, lopsided smile. He stepped to the side and turned to face Ipwet fully. With a slight bow of his head, he said, "Apologies, wife. I spoke without thinking."

Much to my surprise, Ipwet turned a furious glare of her own on me. "Do not ever presume to defend me again. I do not care what you are; *I* am his primary wife. *I* am the mother of five of his living children. *You* will never be able to say the same." With a huff, she spun away and strode back up the hallway toward the courtyard.

I watched her storm away, absolutely dumbfounded.

Nuin took my hand. "Ignore her, dear Alexandra. I fear I have spoiled her by favoring her above others. Once, she was not so . . . affected." He sighed. "But come, there is much for us to discuss."

I let him lead me through the curtain and into a small room lit only by the evening light streaming through a line of windows set high in the far wall. Most of the wall to the right was another cerulean curtain, and based on the few carved wooden chairs in the room, I was guessing we were in the sitting room of a suite. Beyond the curtain, I would likely find a larger room containing a bed.

Nuin sat in one of two chairs arranged near the far wall, separated by a small, rectangular table covered in tiny, sectioned off squares. It wasn't a table, I realized, but a game board—senet, I was fairly certain.

I sat in the chair opposite Nuin. "You promised to teach me . . . to explain," I said, switching to English. "So please, Nuin, tell me what I need to know. How am I here? How can I protect Marcus? How can I get home?"

"How you came to be here was not my doing, dear Alexandra. I only knew what Aset told me and hoped that she was right, because however unlikely, it was the only way."

"They only way for what?"

"The only way for there to be a chance that everything will work out in the end . . . for ma'at to be restored to the universe," he said, using the ancient term for balance and order for the second time since I'd met up with him.

I leaned back in my chair and tilted my head to the side and smiled, just a little. "You know, sometimes I think you enjoy being cryptic."

Throwing his head back, Nuin laughed.

I crossed my arms and stared at him. "If *you* didn't bring me here, then who did?"

Nuin's laughter quieted, but his smile remained. He truly was exceptionally beautiful, but it was the kind of beauty that could make eyes bleed after staring for too long. I couldn't imagine *truly* being one of his wives. "You contain the power to make such a leap through time," he said matter-of-factly and lifted one perfect shoulder.

"But don't you *know*? Can't you *see* it . . . how it happened?"

Nuin shook his head. "Your ba is not of this time; therefore, it does not appear in the At. It is, as the people of your time say, 'against the laws of physics.'"

My eyebrows lifted.

"You must have done it yourself," he added. "Tell me what happened, how you came to be here, and perhaps together we can make sense of it."

I frowned, biting the inside of my cheek as I considered what he was saying. "There was a statuette . . . originally from around this time. I thought it was made of alabaster, but Dr. Isa—Aset—broke it open and revealed a smaller figurine made of At." I squinted as I recalled those final few seconds in my own time. It had all happened so fast, it was hard to piece together. "It started glowing, and as soon as I touched it, I was thrust back here—er—now." I pressed my lips together, studying Nuin closely. "*You* didn't make the statuette? Or . . . you *could* not in the future? You're certain?"

He shook his head, his bafflement genuine. "At this point, in this time, there is only one person who could make such a thing and set it with such a trigger."

I held my breath, waiting.

"You," he said.

My mouth fell open. "You're kidding, right?"

"I'm not."

"But—but . . . maybe you just haven't made it yet, or . . ."

"No, my Alexandra." Nuin was shaking his head slowly, a sadness to the movement. "I'm no longer able to make such an object. I've only retained as much of my power as was required to keep this body alive so I could train you, should you successfully make it back to this time . . . and, of course, to maintain appearances." He pointed to his kaleidoscope eyes.

I rubbed one of my temples with my fingertips.

"Does your head ache?" Nuin asked, concern evident in his tone.

"No, I'm just exhausted. Jumping back in time really takes it out of a girl . . ."

"Tapping into your new power will become easier, and the aftereffects will lessen as you strengthen your control over it . . . which is one of the reasons you coming here was necessary."

"*One* of the reasons?"

Nuin nodded. "Eventually, it will consume you, tearing your ba apart . . . sooner rather than later, if you don't learn to control it."

"You—you stuck me with a power that's going to *tear me apart*?" My eyes started to sting, and I gritted my teeth together to hold back tears of outrage.

Nuin held up his hand. "I did, and I also know how to rid you of it safely, but if you don't learn to control it . . ." He raised his eyebrows. "Of course, there is also the reality of what would have happened should you have remained in your own time."

I swallowed, blinking too rapidly. "Which would be . . . ?"

"As I already told you—you would die."

"Why? How? How do you know?" I asked in a rush. "With the Nothingness clouding the At in my time, it's practically impossible to see anything. Can you please just tell me what's going on? What is this *Apep* spirit? What does it want? Why does it want to hurt me? And what's it doing to Set? To Marcus? I need to know, Nuin . . . to understand. *Please*."

Nuin leaned back in his chair and sighed. "The power you contain is fractured, making it unstable, and it will remain so until I pass the final strands on to you. That instability alone is enough to kill you. And if it doesn't, Apep will, through either Set or Heru."

"Okay . . ." I was nodding as I processed his words. This could work. We could do this. "So why don't we just complete the transfer, and—"

Nuin shook his head. "As soon as we complete the transfer, this body will perish."

My heart sank into my stomach. "Nuin, no . . ." Until this moment, part of me had still been in denial. But this was confirmation. The final nail in the coffin. *I* was the harbinger of Nuin's death.

"It is always what had to be, I think." Nuin offered me a consoling smile. "Apep is . . . well, he *was* once as powerful as me, very long ago, but we were both very different then. His behavior forced me to separate his sheut from the rest of his being, and—"

"His *sheut*?" I recognized the word as one of the ancient parts of the soul, like the "ba," except whereas the ba more closely resembled the modern idea of a "soul," this term was historically identified with a person's shadow.

"Yes, his sheut. You may think of it as his 'power,' or the thing that gives him access to his power. Unlike you or Aset or Heru, Apep and I are not Netjer-At, gods of time, but Netjer—beings who belong on all planes of existence—and our sheut, our power, is an essential part of our beings. There are others of our kind, who hold dominion over other universes, though we alone exist in this one."

Holding up a hand, I furrowed my brow. "Hold on. *What?*"

Nuin laughed. "It is beyond what you knew of existence, I know. None of this time truly know what I am. *God,* they call me. *Nuin.*" His laugh turned slightly bitter. "If they only knew my true name, the identity of my ren, that part of me that is eternal, just as Apep is eternal . . ."

"Your *ren,*" I said, my voice rising in pitch. It was another part of the ancient Egyptian concept of the soul, most closely identified with a person's name. It was the reason pharaohs and other wealthy ancients of this culture took such pains to ensure that their name would be remembered centuries—millennia—after their death: as long as their name was remembered, part of their soul lived on.

I leaned forward. "That's the part of your soul that makes you *you*, isn't it? Like my ba is *me*, regardless of whether or not it's in my physical body?"

Nuin's eyes widened, and a moment later, he smiled and nodded. "Yes, my Alexandra, that is precisely it."

"Okay, so why did you have to separate Apep's power—"

"His sheut," Nuin corrected.

I waved my hand between us. "His *sheut*. Why'd you have to separate it from Apep's *ren*?"

"That is an excellent question." Nuin leaned forward, resting his elbows on the edge of the small table. "You see, ma'at—universal balance—is deteriorating, and if it goes unchecked for too long, then this universe and everything in it will unravel into raw, unbridled chaos."

I took a deep breath. Then another. I wanted to interrupt with further questions, but even more so, I wanted to hear what Nuin would tell me, so I forced myself to remain quiet and attentive.

"In the beginning, when our universe first came into existence, there was balance. Two beings known as Netjer in their complete state, Re and Apep, maintained ma'at simply by existing in perfect equilibrium. Each Netjer was made up of a ren—an eternal soul—and a sheut, which functioned as a powerful link between the Netjer and the very threads that make up the universe.

"Together, Re and Apep guided the formation of nebulae, galaxies, solar systems, and individual planets, conscious that every minute change would cause a reaction somewhere else, which was good—right—because this was ma'at. But when Re made a change to a moon near one edge of the ever-expanding universe, resulting in the destruction of Apep's favorite galaxy near the other, Apep grew resentful of Re and dissatisfied with the unpredictability of how ma'at would play out. He became mad with the desire for control.

"He decided that if order could not be maintained through ma'at, then chaos—*im*balance—would be better. He sought this end, this *beginning*, the only way he knew how . . . by unleashing his own sheut on the universe, wild and unrestrained, and by attempting to tear Re's sheut away from the rest of his being. Except Apep underestimated ma'at; he underestimated the power that could come of a Netjer being truly in balance with oneself, as Re was—and Apep *no longer* was—and it was *Re* who tore away Apep's sheut.

"Re maintained a semblance of ma'at by carrying Apep's sheut to a little blue planet that had only recently given rise to a species of sentient beings, and he implanted both his own ren and sheut, as well as Apep's sheut, inside a woman who was days away from giving birth."

"It was your mother, wasn't it?" I said softly.

Nuin nodded.

Awed, I shook my head ever so slowly. "Everything you just told me blows most of what scientists *and* theologists of my time believe about the universe out of the water . . ."

Nuin chuckled. "They are still not ready to know, I think, though I will leave that decision to you."

I blew out a disbelieving laugh. "Great." A moment later, I said, "So you're Re? *The* Re?"

"I am, and I am more," Nuin said.

"I don't quite follow . . ."

He pointed to his own chest. "This body contains not only Re's ren and pieces of Re's and Apep's sheuts, but also a human ba. Together, these pieces combine to make *me*, a being you know as Nuin. Re is very similar to Nuin in many ways, and will retain all of my memories when this body dies, but he is not exactly the same as Nuin, for a human ba is not eternal . . . in death, it will fade as its energy is reincorporated elsewhere."

My mind, stubborn as it was, refused to consider the deeper meaning of his final words. Instead, I licked my lips, thinking it was both strange and sort of appropriate that Nuin was sitting across from me, talking about himself in the third person.

He exhaled, suddenly looking so incredibly weary. "And I only have pieces of Re's and Apep's sheuts *now*, because three years ago, I transferred most of them into the ankh-At and gave it to you."

I leaned forward, my skin crawling. "Are you saying Apep's sheut is the power that's now inside me?"

"No, dear Alexandra. You hold only the majority of *my* sheut." His eyebrows drew together. "It is Heru and Set who absorbed most of Apep's sheut."

"Okay . . . so why'd Apep come after me? I mean, if Marcus and Set are the ones with his 'power' . . . ?"

"In your time, Apep is after both his and my sheuts. And if he wrenches them out of you, Heru, and Set, he will unleash their power fully. Then, he will unmake the universe, much as he'd originally intended ages ago."

I felt like the air in the room had thinned, like I'd suddenly teleported to Mt. Everest, except *my* Mt. Everest was hot and dry, and I really could have used a splash of frigid mountain air at the moment. I took long, deep breaths, trying to slow the erratic beating of my heart. Inhale, exhale. Inhale, exhale. Inhale, exhale.

I leaned forward and looked deep into his eyes. "*Marcus* almost drowned me." I studied Nuin's expression. "You don't look surprised."

He exhaled heavily. "It would seem that, split as it is, Apep's sheut gives him an inroad to possess the Heru of your time.

Apep is still tethered to Set, but because Set and Heru share his sheut, he is able to possess Heru for short periods."

I ran my hands through my hair, yanking off the jeweled headband and scratching my scalp as though I could dig out my frustration and overwhelming sense of helplessness. "I kind of hate this, you know? If you weren't here . . ." I let out a despondent laugh. "I think I'd lose it. I just want to go home."

"In time, my Alexandra. In time."

I had an endless supply of questions, but before I could ask any of them, Aset pushed through the curtain into the sitting room, closely followed by Set, who obviously wasn't currently possessed by a psychotic Apep. *But if Apep isn't possessing Set . . .*

A jolt of panic shot through me, and I half-stood. "Nuin, where's Apep right now?" Breathing hard, I stood the rest of the way, the chair screeching on the limestone floor as I pushed it backward. "What if he comes after me? He could be in any of those people out there." I was breathing too hard, too fast. "I can't stay here!"

Standing, Nuin rounded the table and wrapped his arms around me, hugging me tightly. His skin was warm and dry, his body solid, something I could hold onto. And at that moment, I *really* needed something to hold onto. He was such a good man —god—*Netjer*—and I hated the idea of him being gone.

"Be calm, my Alexandra." He stroked my hair, over and over again, and simply held me as I clutched his shoulders. "Be calm."

"I don't want to be torn apart," I whispered.

"Shhh . . ."

"And I don't want to *lose* you."

"Shhh, my Alexandra. Do not fret. And Apep will not harm you while you're near me. He's certainly around, stirring up trouble, but he knows that coming after me directly would be suicide. There is no reason for him to suspect that you now hold most of my sheut, and the only ways for him to find out would be for him to witness you using your new powers—which he will not—or for someone to tell him."

I pulled away enough to look up into his eyes. I'd always loved his eyes, found comfort in their swirling colors. "Does anyone know besides you, Aset, and me?"

"I know, too," Set said . . . in heavily accented English. I turned wide eyes on him.

"How—what—" I pushed away from Nuin and stared at him. "You taught him English? *Why*?"

A small smile curved his lips. "It seemed appropriate."

8

LEMONS & LEMONADE

Nuin had been teaching Set English for almost two years in anticipation of my arrival. His justification was vague and more than a little dodgy, but I didn't push the subject; Nuin could be the king of non-explanations when he wanted to be, and I was too tired—emotionally and otherwise—to even try.

Nuin *did* explain a little of my situation to Set—in English. It didn't matter that Aset didn't understand, since she already seemed to know everything about me. Set was obviously one of the Nejerets that Nuin trusted most, and it only went to show me just how different this pre-possession Set was from the deranged man Apep would make him into. Set took Nuin's explanation of where and *when* I came from rather well, my connection to the future Heru seeming to be the revelation that shocked him the most.

Nuin picked carefully which parts of my backstory he wished to share with Set. He left out such important pieces as "You are Lex's father," and "You will be possessed by an evil spirit for the next four thousand years."

I watched Aset as Nuin spoke, wondering if she was aware of those things . . . if she knew that Nuin's death was imminent. I made a mental note to ask him later, when we were alone and my fragmented thoughts had settled, along with about a million other questions.

How long must I remain here?

How will I get back?

Why isn't Nuin telling Heru all of this?

What if I bond with Heru, here and now?

What about bonding withdrawals for me . . . and for Marcus?

Does Nuin have *to die? Can't we stop it, since we know about it?*

How do I get rid of this power—Nuin's sheut?

How do I restore ma'at?

Nuin excused himself as soon as he finished his spotty explanation, claiming he had to check on some "arrangements," and Set left shortly after. I'd fallen into such a withdrawn, depressed stupor that Aset didn't last much longer. Wishing to avoid pretty much everyone, I retreated into the curtained-off bedchamber.

My bead-net dress felt too restrictive, only emphasizing the helplessness of my situation. In an act of reckless frustration, I pulled it up over my head and threw it across the room, not caring if threads snapped or beads shattered. Shaking, I crouched in a corner of the room, curled my knees up, and hugged them against my chest. My shoulders shuddered as I cried. I felt so lost . . . so alone.

There was a swish a fabric, then, "I—I am sorry." It was Heru.

My heart sang at hearing his voice, then clenched as I realized this wasn't *my* Heru.

"I checked the At . . . Nuin was supposed to be back here, and . . ."

I turned my tear-streaked face to him. He wouldn't have been able to see me in the At, not with my out-of-time ba. Just further proof that I didn't belong here.

"I should go," he said.

"No." The word came out without thought as I rose on trembling legs, steadying myself against the wall. "Please, do not leave."

Heru scanned me from head to toe, then returned his gaze to my face. The kohl that had been so carefully drawn about my eyes was no doubt smeared down my cheeks. For the briefest moment, his eyes again flicked downward, and I became aware that the only thing I had on—the silken linen shift—wasn't exactly substantial. It was more a slip than a dress.

Covering as much of my torso with my arms as possible, I glanced at the opposite corner of the room, where the discarded remnants of my bead-net dress were scattered in disarray. I wished I hadn't acted so compulsively. Such rash behavior was uncommon for me, or at least, it had been before I'd met Marcus. Sometimes I wondered if I'd been sleepwalking before, if I hadn't been truly awake until I met him. Of course, the fault could just as easily lie with manifesting . . .

Heru followed my line of sight, and as he, too, stared at the ruined dress, there was a long moment of silence. "Not having a good day?"

I started laughing, shocking both of us. It wasn't long before Heru joined me, and all I could do was laugh more and drink in the sight of him. I yearned to sink into his embrace, to feel his powerful arms wrapped around me, to press my ear against his chest and listen to the steady rhythm of his heartbeat.

He took several steps closer. "What troubles you, Hat-hur?"

Comforted by his presence and discomfited by his use of the wrong name, I dropped my arms. "Many things." A sudden curiosity filled me. "How old are you?"

Heru's sure grin slipped, but he caught it before it disappeared completely. "I will tell you my age if you tell me what has upset you."

I bit my lip, weighing my options. I picked my words carefully. "I am homesick."

Heru's golden irises sparkled with mischief. "I am very old."

Unable to hold back a small smile, I stepped away from the wall, toward him. "You do not seem very old." Especially not compared to the Heru I knew so well.

"I am older than I look."

I tilted my head to the side. "As is the way of our kind."

"What do you miss the most?"

The question surprised me. "What?"

"From your home—what do you miss the most?"

You. "I guess . . . a friend." I stopped a few feet away from him and studied his familiar features. "A good friend."

"Good friends are hard to find, but I think I may know where you can find one here." His smile, the warmth in his eyes, did much more to melt me than the evening heat.

"Hat-hur?" Denai stepped into the bedchamber. "Golden One, are you—" Her eyes fixed on the tangle of gold thread and turquoise and quartz beads that had once been my dress, and she rounded on Heru. "You! You scoundrel! Hat-hur is not some loose woman, not like Ankhesenpepi, and I will not let you make her into an adulteress!" She lurched toward him. "You—"

"Denai!" I grabbed her arms, holding her away from Heru before she could strike him. I couldn't believe this was the same meek woman I'd spent so much time with earlier. *Not meek,* I realized, *respectful.* "I did it; I ruined the dress," I told her in a rush. "I was upset. Heru was not here when it happened, I swear."

Despite my words, the priestess continued to glare at him, her hands curled into tight fists. "Ankhesenpepi has been looking for you," she told him. "Perhaps you should focus your attentions where they are wanted."

Wide-eyed, I stared at Heru. The thought of him *being* with Ankhesenpepi both nauseated me and made my blood boil. *But he's not* my *Heru,* I reminded myself. *Not yet . . .*

He's not my Heru . . .

He's not my Heru . . .

He's. Not. My. Heru.

Rubbing his temple, Heru bowed his head to each of us in turn, then retreated through the curtain.

Denai turned to me, her livid eyes scanning my face. "You cannot go out to the feast like this, Golden One. Your makeup . . . and your dress."

A wan laugh escaped from me. "Maybe I can just stay in here?" After all, my appetite was now nonexistent.

"No. This feast is in your honor. Such a thing would be unforgivable."

"Alright . . ." I sighed and held out my arms. "So what do I do?"

Denai pressed her full lips together and studied my face and body with such scrutiny that I felt naked. "Just leave it to me," she said. "I can fix this."

As it turned out, Denai was right; she *could* fix it, or rather, she could fix *me*. She swapped her linen dress for my shift and quickly refashioned a turquoise, quartz, and gold belt from parts of my ruined bead-net dress. I used a washbowl that had been set on a tiny table against one wall to rinse off my smeared eyeliner, then sat patiently on the floor in the middle of the room while Denai reapplied it with kohl from a jar she found in a small, wooden chest under the table. Kneeling in front of me, Denai wore a look of contented concentration.

"There," she said, sitting back on her heels. "That is much better." She rose and held out her hands to pull me up to my feet. "Promise me you won't destroy this dress as well, Hat-hur . . . at least, not until you acquire a few more garments?"

I laughed softly. "I promise." After a moment of hesitation, I said, "Denai . . . you know that I am not really the goddess Hat-hur, correct?"

She squeezed my hands. "You are a very powerful Netjer-At. Besides"—she shrugged—"Nuin would only take a Netjer-At who was very special as his wife. This I know."

"But you do not have to take care of me . . . to *serve* me," I persisted.

"You appeared out of thin air in the temple to the goddess Hat-hur, of whom I am currently the head priestess. Perhaps *you* are the one who is mistaken, and you truly are her. Often we do not know ourselves fully, and must rely on others' eyes to see who we really are."

I frowned. "Maybe," I said, knowing that, despite the wisdom in her words, I was no goddess.

"Come." She released my hands and headed toward the curtain leading out to the sitting room. "The feast has begun, and you are expected."

"Wonderful . . ."

Denai glanced back at me as she walked away, her eyebrows raised. She'd definitely heard the sarcasm in my tone, and though she said nothing, I could practically hear her scolding me.

I held up my hands defensively and followed her into the hallway. "I will behave."

And I did. I acted the part of the joyous and excited new wife perfectly, standing by Nuin's side when he wasn't disappearing into other areas of the villa with this human or that Nejeret. I tried to eat, but I still didn't have much of an appetite, though that didn't stop Denai and the other priestesses from bringing me food and trying to coax me.

The food, arranged on several rectangular tables that had been set up in the courtyard, was definitely *interesting*—a vast array of spiced meat, vegetable, and lentil stews, fresh fruits, and breads—as was the drink. There was an extremely yeasty beer that would definitely take some getting used to, and some light, jammy red wine that I rather enjoyed. I had just refilled my carved alabaster cup and settled on a bench built into one of the many recesses in the covered walkways surrounding the courtyard for a moment of peaceful solitude when *she* found me.

Ankhesenpepi sat beside me, far closer than I was comfortable with. I scooted away a few inches, but she followed. Her talon-like fingers latched onto my forearm, and she invaded my space even further. Leaning away, I tugged against her hold, but her grip was surprisingly strong. She squeezed my arm, digging her nails into my skin.

"Ow . . ." I said. "What—"

"You are *nothing,*" she hissed. "The female Netjer-Ats have been mine for thousands of years, and they will be mine for thousands more. They will not follow you. They will not even listen to you, I will make sure of it. You will be powerless."

"I do not desire power," I said through gritted teeth.

Her eyes narrowed. "You cannot have *him,* either."

"Nuin?" I eyed her. "I am his wife. It is done." Which was true. Throughout most of Egypt's ancient history, there was no such thing as a marriage ceremony. A man and woman simply moved in together and declared themselves husband and wife, and that was that.

"I do not speak of my father," she said. "I know that you and Heru were alone in the bedchamber. I see the way he looks at you. You cannot have him. He belongs to me!"

Anger surged, and my eyes narrowed.

He's not my Heru, I reminded myself. *He's not my Heru . . . he's not my Heru . . . he's not my Heru . . .*

Fighting back the primal Nejerette need to initiate a second claiming on him was difficult, verging on impossible. I gritted my teeth. "Heru is a grown-up. He can make his own decisions."

"Stay away from him—and I will know if you do not, even if

you *are* cloaking yourself in the At—or I will tell my father that I walked in on you and Heru lying together as man and wife." She dug her nails even deeper into my skin, and I felt the warm trickle of blood trail down to my wrist. "Have I made myself clear?"

"Yes." I jerked my arm out of her grasp, not caring that her nails gouged my skin. It would heal—but if I stayed near her for even a moment longer, it was highly possible I would do something that would cause irreparable damage to the timeline. Like strangle her.

Holding my head high, I stood and walked around the courtyard, sticking to the shadows behind the columns, and retreated into Nuin's rooms. The space was dark, lit only by the slivers of moonlight shining through the high windows, but I was able to see that a small box had been set on the bed. As I moved closer, I realized it was a cage fashioned from dried reeds tied together with some sort of twine. And inside, there was a tiny, fluffy sleeping kitten.

"Oh . . ." I knelt beside the bed and searched the little cage for some way to open it. A knot had been tied on the top edge, latching the reed door shut.

As I untied the knot, the kitten awoke, affixing its luminous silver-blue eyes on me. It yawned, emitted a high-pitched squeak, and immediately started purring.

"Well hello there, little guy." There was a tremor in my voice. "How'd you get in here?"

The tiny creature squeaked again when I picked it up and hugged it to my chest. As it snuggled against me, a warm and content little ball of fluff, a bit of the loneliness encasing my heart chipped away.

9

HOLD & WITHHOLD

"Ouch!" I yelped, fairly certain that a porcupine was rolling around on my chest. I opened my eyes to find it still dark in the room and the fur ball that had formerly been a sweet little sleepy kitten now enthusiastically tenderizing the flesh just under my collarbone. I smiled and scratched the kitten's neck. "Not squishy enough for you, hmmm?"

He gazed at me with slitted eyes and purr-squeaked.

A thin leather cord was tied around his neck, and something about the size of a quarter was hanging from the front like a modern pet tag. I raised my head to get a closer look. There wasn't enough light to discern a color, but I could make out the shape of the object; it was an eye, a Wedjat, specifically, the most common symbol of the mythological version of Heru. "What are you doing with an Eye of Horus amulet, little guy?"

"I believe it was meant to identify the giver of the gift, dear Alexandra."

I started at the sound of Nuin's voice. He was standing in the curtained wall, the blue linen pushed to the side as he watched me.

"Sorry, Nuin . . . I didn't mean to fall asleep on your bed."

And honestly, I didn't know *how* I'd fallen asleep. The thin pads set on whatever made up the bedframe didn't exactly create a cushy mattress by modern standards . . . or by any standards, for that matter. My joints felt stiff and creaky, and a dull ache was throbbing in the base of my skull.

I sat up, shifting the kitten down to my lap. It curled into a ball roughly the size of a softball, let out a heavy sigh, and promptly dozed off. "I just—I didn't know where else to go."

Nuin held out his hands, palms up. "My bed is your bed, wife."

"Right . . . you know this is never going to be *that* kind of marriage, right?"

Nuin chuckled and entered the room. He sat beside me on the bed and raised his arm, wrapping it around my shoulders and pulling me close. "I have plenty of other wives for that."

"Is it going to raise any eyebrows if I have my own room?"

After pressing a gentle kiss against my hair, Nuin shook his head. "Such a thing is normal among Nejerets, especially when there are more than two people involved in a union. Otherwise the arrangement can become a bit awkward."

A weak laugh bubbled in my chest. "I bet."

He gave my shoulders a squeeze. "We will be leaving in a day or two, and I'll arrange for you and your priestesses—should they choose to accompany you—to have your own tent, but until then, I would like you to stay with me in these rooms." When I glanced up at him, he smiled. "For appearances. The closer onlookers believe our union to be, the safer you'll be."

Smiling weakly, I nodded. "Whatever you say, oh great and powerful husband."

"Sarcasm is very unladylike, wife."

I snorted.

"As is snorting."

"Look at you, making jokes." I nudged his side with my elbow. "And here I thought your ability to do *that* faded ten or twenty thousand years ago . . ." I yawned, making my final few words unintelligible.

Nuin laughed softly.

"Nuin?"

"Hmmm?"

"Why did Heru give me a kitten?"

Nuin took a deep breath and shifted to lie back on the bed. He pulled me down with him, keeping me close against his side. I rested my head on his shoulder and cradled the kitten against my tummy. I may never have had a truly sexual relationship with Nuin, but I'd always found comfort in his arms. After all, he had been my hidden guardian and best friend for most of my life—my ancient, secret, godlike best friend.

"He came to me this evening, asking what sorts of things bring you happiness," Nuin said. "When I asked him why he wondered such a thing, he told me of the conversation you two had about missing your home. So, I told him of your love of cats. I believe that's what motivated him to give you the creature."

"I don't know how to be around him," I said sleepily.

"I know, child."

"Will it get easier?"

"*That* I do not know."

"I think I'll call him Rus," I said with another yawn. "Short for Horus."

"My grandson? He would be very confused if you did."

"No." My eyes drooped shut. "The kitten."

I was standing in the bedroom of Marcus's and my suite in the Council's Cairo palace. The room had been all but torn apart—the king-sized mattress lay askew against one wall, all the way across the room from the now-crooked bed frame and bronze headboard. Chunks of gold-veined black granite that had once been part of a coffee table littered the polished marble floor, mixed with shards of glass and ceramic in a bevy of colors. And in the center of it all was Marcus.

He was sitting on the floor, leaning back against an overturned armchair, one knee drawn up. His arm rested on his knee, his hand hanging limply. Blood dripped from his fingertips onto the once-pristine ivory marble floor. His white button-down shirt hung open, carmine stains streaking and spotting it here and there, and he was missing one of his loafers.

*There was no doubt in my mind that I was in the At, witnessing the result of Marcus's reaction to what he'd done to me when he'd been under Apep's control. For someone who was so practiced at being in control, the experience must have been maddening. He would have been aware the whole time, watching—*feeling*—himself drown me. He likely blamed himself, and I didn't think self-forgiveness would come easily for him, not for this.*

I knelt on the floor in front of him and reached out, brushing my fingertips against the At barrier that separated me from the echo of him. "I love you," I whispered. "I'll come back to you, I promise."

"Lex? Is it really you?" The man who spoke wasn't Marcus, but he was the next-best thing: Dominic. His faint French accent had never sounded so good.

I spun on my knees and stared at my half-brother. Tall, slender, and pale, he had black hair that was slicked back elegantly and sharp, handsome features. He was the one who'd remained by my side while Marcus had abandoned me in his last-ditch effort to avoid the prophecy that would bind us together permanently. He'd been the one to comfort me when the waves of depression had been so powerful they threatened to wash me away completely. Where Nuin had been my closest friend for most of my life, Dominic filled that role now.

"We can't find you. You've disappeared from the At completely." He closed the distance between us, crouched down to grip my shoulders, and

picked me up, crushing me against him in a hug that was equal parts pain and comfort. Though he had a slimmer build than Marcus, his lean muscles held nearly as much strength.

"Crushing me . . . can't really breathe," I managed to grunt.

"Sorry." He let up a bit. "Tell me where you are so we can come get you. Marcus is already showing signs of bonding withdrawals, and he thinks they'll hit you more quickly because you are so much younger. We need to get you back to him as soon as possible."

"I'm—" I started to say, but despite his unrelenting hold, the rainbow colors of the At swept in, separating us, and both the echo and Dominic disappeared.

"Nooooooo!" I howled. Somehow, I'd managed to actually travel to my own time in the At, not just view the future echo, but that time had slipped away like water between my fingers.

My head throbbed as the colors continued to swirl around me, a furious chaos, and I clutched my nonexistent scalp, trying to keep my skull from exploding.

I screamed with nonexistent lungs.

I tore at my nonexistent hair.

I lashed out at the increasingly frenzied movement of the At.

Nothing helped. Nothing relieved the pain.

As I came fully awake, I groaned and curled into a ball, hugging my knees. The pain that had overwhelmed my ba in the At abated, and I slowly unclenched my muscles and relaxed. My mouth tasted sour, like bile. *Did I throw up in my sleep?*

I opened my eyes to the golden light of morning streaming in through the high windows, flopped onto my back, and sighed. It looked like bonding withdrawals had started. I wondered if that was the reason my ba had searched out the future version of Heru in the At. I would have asked Nuin, except he was no longer in the room.

Patting the thin pads that were pretending to be a mattress, I searched for Rus. When I didn't find his furry little body, I sat up and looked around. As far as I could tell, he wasn't anywhere in the room, either.

I took care of my most urgent personal business first, hurrying into the walled-off alcove containing the Old Kingdom equivalent of a toilet—a sort of u-shaped stool with an opening cut out of the seat and a large ceramic vase set underneath. Feeling much relieved, I left the bedchamber in search of Rus . . . and hopefully someone who could explain the current method for cleaning teeth. I was pretty sure it included a stick and a paste of minerals of some kind, but I wasn't sure where to find such implements, let alone how to use them.

Rus, as it turned out, was chasing insects in the courtyard. It was my first chance to get a good look at him in any sort of substantial light. He had the coloring of an Abyssinian, with tan, ticked fur that darkened to a brownish-black on his back, except his fur was longer and fluffier than any Abyssinian I'd ever seen. I didn't think he would grow into a long-haired cat, but I hoped he would at least always be a little fluffy.

I leaned against a column and watched him for a few minutes, hoping the dull ache in my head and joints was just a remnant of the withdrawal symptoms I'd felt in the At. Why the symptoms seemed to affect my ba far more intensely and quickly than they affected my physical body was just one more thing I needed to ask Nuin.

"Ah, you are up," Aset said cheerily from behind me. "Did you sleep well?"

"Not exactly," I told her as I turned to face her. "This is sort of embarrassing, but can you show me how to clean my teeth?" I raised my shoulders and scrunched my brow. "You guys do things a bit differently here . . ."

Aset's face broke into a kind, almost motherly smile. "Of course. Come with me." She turned and headed toward the doorway to the hall leading back to Nuin's rooms.

I jogged a few steps to catch up to her. "Also, and this is *defi-*

nitely embarrassing, what am I supposed to do about cleaning out the, um, *chamber pot* . . . if it is no longer, um, empty?"

Aset laughed. It was a musical sound that instantly put me at ease. "I have seen much of the future—though not so far as the time from whence *you* come—and I know that many things change, our hygiene practices chief among them." She wrinkled her nose and glanced at me sideways. "And not all of those changes are always for the better."

I laughed, thinking of the Middle Ages in Europe. "I know exactly what you mean. I honestly thought it would be stinkier back, well, *now*, but it is actually a relief to not be overwhelmed by so many artificial scents." There had definitely been a little ripeness when we'd been surrounded by the crowd at the pyramid complex, and there'd been an abundance of floral and herbal-scented oils, but none had been as pungent as some of the colognes and perfumes worn—sometimes practically bathed in—by humans of my own time.

"Well, you are surrounded by people who are aware of the sensitive senses of our kind, so they make an effort to wash often and to not overly perfume their bodies."

"It is an effort I definitely appreciate."

Aset smiled and raised her eyebrows. "As do I."

She led the way back into Nuin's private area, through the sitting room, and into the bedchamber. She crouched before a wooden chest that was about the size of a shoebox and was inlaid with intricate patterns of ivory and some dark wood. Much like a jewelry box, it had a top that could be raised, and the bottom half was divided evenly into three drawers that could be opened by pulling on a polished ivory knob.

Aset opened the left-most drawer, revealing a squat alabaster jar with a wooden stopper and a small pile of sticks with frayed tips. She plucked a stick out of the mass and handed it to me, then selected another for herself. After unstoppering the jar, she dipped her index finger into the chalky paste within and started spreading it on her teeth. I mirrored her movements.

The paste was bitter and a little salty, making me wonder if it contained the ancient predecessor of baking soda, natron.

When she started scrubbing her teeth with the frayed end of the stick, I did the same, being careful not to scrape so hard that I made my gums bleed. I watched as Aset rose and scooped a palmful of water from the washbasin and slurped it into her mouth. She swished it around for a few seconds, retreated into the toilet alcove, and, based on the sound, spit the water and paste into the waste vessel.

"All clean," she said with a bright grin as she reemerged. I did as she'd done, and when I returned to the main part of the bedchamber, she showed me where I could store my tooth stick in the right-most drawer of the chest.

Aset leaned in unexpectedly and gave me a sniff. "You do not smell ripe, so we will wait until this evening to wash, yes?"

"Um . . . okay," I said, feeling a little uncomfortable that she'd just sniffed me and more than a little ridiculous that I had to be shown how to handle basic hygiene. But it had to be done, and if she was offering, I wasn't about to turn her down.

"Are you hungry?" she asked. "The cooks like to make a delicious honey bread in the mornings." She linked her arm with mine and guided me back out of Nuin's private rooms. "I am sure you will like it."

I glanced over my shoulder. "And the chamber pot?"

"They are checked regularly. It will be emptied, have no worries."

"Okay . . ." As we walked, I rubbed my temple, fairly certain that the aches and pains were getting worse. Nuin hadn't been worried about either my or Marcus's withdrawals, so I figured he had to know some trick . . . some way to slow or lessen the symptoms . . . some way for it to *not* be fatal.

I cleared my throat. "Do you know where Nuin is, by any chance?"

"He is out making the final arrangements for the journey, but he should be back later this morning," she said with a nod.

I sighed. It looked like my questions would just have to wait. "Everyone keeps mentioning a journey—where are we going?" I stopped halfway down the central walkway to scoop up Rus. He nestled in the crook of my arm, purring lazily.

"Nobody has told you yet?" She glanced at me, a tiny frown turning down the corners of her mouth. "We are returning to the Netjer-At Oasis, deep in the heart of the desert."

"Oh." It was my turn to frown. "That sounds . . . sandy."

Aset laughed. "The trip there, yes. The Oasis, not so much. It is . . . it is hard to describe, but it is very beautiful . . . very lush." She shrugged. "It is home."

The ache in my head gave a rather enthusiastic throb, and I squeezed my eyes shut for a moment. If Nuin wasn't around to help me, there was only one way to alleviate the withdrawal pains . . . at least, only one way that I knew of.

"Do you know if Heru is around?" I raised my arm slightly, earning a muffled squeak from Rus. "I wanted to thank him for his gift."

"Oh, I am sure he is around here somewhere." For some reason, her response gave me the impression that she knew where Heru was, but she didn't particularly want to tell me.

10

REQUEST & DENY

The honey breads were actually more like muffins, and they were pretty tasty, if a little bland. I couldn't say the same on either account of the tangy fruit juice that accompanied them; it was so tart that my eyes started to water and my mouth stung with the need to salivate profusely after the first sip. Regardless, I ate and drank everything Aset offered to me, knowing I would need the nourishment to make up for my lack of appetite the previous evening. If there was one thing I didn't want to be, it was a malnourished Nejerette—that way lie all sorts of undesirable temporary side effects, like advanced age progression or sudden weight loss, not to mention weakening my body's ability to withstand the bonding withdrawals.

Aset and I sat on one of the built-in benches sheltered within the porticoes surrounding the courtyard as we shared our basket of honey breads and pitcher of juice. Rus spent the time stalking the tiny birds that were hopping around the garden, wiggling his backside awkwardly as he prepared for each pounce.

"It must be very strange for you, seeing him like this," Aset commented.

I looked at her, brow furrowed.

"My brother." She finished the final honey bread and dry-washed the crumbs from her fingers.

"*Strange* is an understatement," I muttered. Taking a deep breath, I asked the question that had been perched on the tip of my tongue the entire time we'd been eating. "I know you were hiding something earlier—when I asked you if you knew where Heru was."

Aset studied me, her gaze unwavering, but she didn't say anything.

"Is it that you disapprove of me—of *us*?" I inhaled deeply and held my breath.

She shook her head. "No, Lex, it is just that . . . well, you must remember that time changes a person, and Heru is not the man you are bonded to, not yet. I do not wish for you to be disappointed, or hurt . . . or worse."

"I understand." With a sigh, I patted her hand. "I think I need some alone time . . . to think. You do not mind, do you?"

Smiling faintly, she shook her head again. "No, dear Lex, I do not. You have been through quite a shock, I think. 'Alone time,' as you put it, would be wise."

I returned her smile, then rose and gathered up the empty reed basket, placing both the ceramic pitcher and the alabaster cups within it. "I will return this to the kitchen."

Aset nodded, making no move to rise.

"Thank you for everything this morning, Aset. You have been an enormous help," I told her, my gratitude sincere, and turned to walk away, scooping up Rus as I went.

After returning the items to the "kitchen," I retreated to Nuin's sitting room. But several minutes of pacing was all I could stand, and my headache seemed to worsen with each step.

I couldn't stay in there, doing nothing. So, alone and barefoot, I headed out to the hallway to explore. And by "explore," I meant "find Heru."

There were four curtained doorways lining the hallway, and

each led to sets of private chambers, much like Nuin's but smaller. They were all empty. When I reached the courtyard, I checked to make sure Aset wasn't anywhere in sight, then snuck along the covered walkway to the next off-shooting hall. It was nearly identical to the one ending in Nuin's rooms.

As quietly as possible, I made my way into the hall. Just as I was approaching the second set of curtained doorways, I caught the hushed sound of whispering voices. It was coming from the doorway on the right. I froze, straining to hear enough to identify the speakers. If Heru wasn't one of them, I would move on.

I focused all of my attention on listening and scowled when I realized they weren't speaking the original tongue, but Old Egyptian. I frowned as an idea struck me. Heru *had* claimed he was interested in teaching me the contemporary language; I wondered if taking him up on that offer, regardless of whether it had been a *serious* offer, might be the best way to spend some time around him to ease at least a bit of the withdrawal pains.

An bark of laughter came from the room, unmistakably Heru's, and it was closely followed by a solitary clapping sound —possibly a slap—and a feminine yelp. Heru *was* in that room, and he was with a woman. And if the sound had indeed been a slap, had he hit the woman, or had the woman hit him?

I inched closer.

Heru was speaking, no longer a whisper, and though I couldn't understand his words, I could distinguish the sharp-edged tone. He was clearly displeased.

At the sound of a moan and a throaty feminine laugh, I second-guessed my assessment. There was one other situation I'd heard his voice take on such an edge, but . . . *no, it couldn't be* that . . .

If I was hearing some sort of sexual interlude between Heru and another woman, I would lose it. I would most likely burst into the room and tear the other woman away from him, and then I would be Nuin's psychotic, voyeuristic wife with a violent streak and an unhealthy obsession with her husband's grandson. I shook my head, working up the courage to just walk away.

Heru said something else, and I heard footsteps nearing the doorway.

I glanced around wildly, then lunged across the hall to the curtain blocking off the doorway opposite the one where I'd been eavesdropping. Thankfully, one quick look around the sitting room told me it was empty. I pressed my back against the plaster wall beside the doorway and held my breath, taking in a full dose of the spicy scent that filled the room. I held in a groan. There was no mistaking Heru's enticing, exotic scent. I had no doubt that I'd hidden in *his* private quarters. *Of course I did . . .*

Much to my horror, Heru pushed through the curtain and entered the room, pausing mid-step when he saw me. An eyebrow quirked up curiously, but he didn't say anything as he continued into the room. He raised his index finger to his lips in the apparently timeless gesture signaling the need for silence and glanced at the curtain.

It seemed that he didn't want the woman, whoever she was, to know I was in there.

There were more footsteps, and they stopped on the other side of the curtain. "Heru," a woman called into the room, then said something else I didn't understand.

My blood boiled as I recognized her voice—Ankhesenpepi. *She* was the woman he'd been with in the other room, the one who'd moaned and laughed far too suggestively. A violent, burning rage flared to life within me.

Heru snapped an answer to Ankhesenpepi, his tone notably dismissive, and not long after, there was the sound of quick footsteps moving up the hallway toward the courtyard. Heru and I watched each other while we listened until the footsteps were no longer audible, and even then, we stared for several more seconds. My back was still pressed against the wall, and my chest was rising and falling too quickly with each shallow breath.

"What are you doing in here?" he asked me in the original tongue, his eyes narrowed. Only when he turned away, breaking our eye contact, was I able to take a full breath.

"I am sorry. I truly did not mean to—" I sidestepped to the doorway, looking anywhere but at him. "I shall go."

"Wait."

I paused and, after a long, painful moment, managed to look at him.

He eased down into a wooden chair beside a narrow senet table on the far side of the room and rubbed a hand over his closely shaved scalp. "Apologies, Hat-hur. You caught me off guard. Please, come . . . sit with me." He indicated the chair on the opposite side of the table.

Slowly, I crossed the room and did as he bid, sitting primly and clasping my hands in my lap. But I couldn't make myself meet his eyes.

"Based on your evident retreat into my rooms, I can only assume you overheard my conversation with Ankhesenpepi?"

I bit my lip. "Sort of, but not exactly. I *heard* some of it, but you should not be worried . . . I could not understand it." I flicked my gaze up to his face, but his expression gave nothing away. "I am *so* sorry. I should not have eavesdropped, but I was looking for you, and—"

Intrigue flashed in his golden eyes. "You were looking for me? Why?"

"To thank you . . . for Rus—" I shook my head. "For the kitten, and to ask if you were serious about your offer to teach me the common language."

Some hidden tension within Heru seemed to ease, and he relaxed in his chair. "I am no longer certain that is such a good idea."

At his hesitancy, my heart started to sink. "Why not?"

"Because you are the wife of Nuin."

"I was his wife when you first made the offer," I reminded him.

"*And* because I would prefer not to make settling in here any harder than it has already been for you."

I leaned forward and licked my lips. "But do you not see, learning the common language will make settling in here easier, and—"

His jaw clenched. "You should ask my sister; you and Aset seem to be getting along quite well."

Sparked by his avoidance, my temper smoldered. "If you have no desire to help me, please, just say so. I merely thought that since you offered . . ." I shrugged and stood. "Clearly I was mistaken. Thank you for the kitten." Turning, I strode toward the doorway.

"Hat-hur. Stop," Heru commanded, and I heard hints of my Heru in this younger version's voice.

I halted in front of the curtain, my spine rigid. Something about him calling me by my false name made my smoldering temper flare. I closed my eyes and took a deep, calming breath. Then another.

"Ankhesenpepi is a dangerous woman to have as an enemy," he said. "How did you manage to make one of her so quickly?"

I glanced down at my forearm. The skin was unblemished now, but it had been marred by angry red scratches only the night before. "You," I said softly, not caring that it was only the partial truth, then passed through the curtain.

11

REVEAL & REVILE

I returned to Nuin's rooms after another quick stop by the kitchen, carrying two bowls, both for Rus. One contained an odd concoction of some sort of grain gruel—likely barley—a raw egg yolk, and chopped up chunks of some light meat that had been stewing in a copper pot over the fire a few feet away from the outdoor oven. The cook, Heni, had mixed it all together in a dish the size of a modern cereal bowl, then handed the bowl to me along with another empty one for water.

Rus was asleep on one of the chairs in the sitting room when I passed through the curtain. He was sprawled on his back, his forelegs stretched above his head and his hind legs extended so his rear paws hung over the edge of the chair, and his round little belly bulged comically. It was ridiculously adorable.

I crossed the room and held the bowl of kitten glop near his nose. His whiskers twitched, closely followed by his nose, and within seconds, his eyes were open and he was stretching his neck out to get closer to the food.

I set the bowl on the floor near one of the chair legs. "You've got to get up, lazy boy."

Rus part-jumped, part-fell off the chair in his eagerness to gorge himself.

"Have at it," I told him, laughing softly.

I retreated into the bedchamber to fill the other dish with water from the washing bowl, then returned to sit on the floor and watch my kitten eat and purr simultaneously. When I tried to pet him, he added a faint growl to the mix.

"Okay, okay . . . your food, not mine. Got it. And here I was *so* looking forward to having a snack . . ."

At the sound of footsteps, I glanced over my shoulder. Nuin had entered the sitting room, wearing the same white linen kilt wrapped around his lower half that every other man of this time seemed to favor. He crossed the room, crouched on one knee beside me, and took hold of my chin, turning my face from side to side and peering into my eyes.

Frowning, he released me and sighed. "Your withdrawal symptoms are advancing more rapidly than I anticipated," he said in English. "This will greatly affect the deterioration my sheut causes to your ba. You won't have time to learn everything you need to learn, complete your task, and rid yourself of the power safely."

"This day just keeps getting better and better," I grumbled, rubbing the back of my neck in a vain attempt to relieve the ache. "So what am I supposed to do about the withdrawals? Because having my soul torn apart isn't really that appealing . . ."

"My dear Alexandra, at this rate, you'll be dead long before the power within you has a chance to do any such thing."

Blanching, I stared at him. "What—what are you talking about?"

"At the rate your symptoms are progressing, the bonding withdrawals will kill you within a week unless we can find a way for you to start feeding the bond."

"But—but I *can't* feed the bond . . ."

"You can."

"No, I really can't. I tried to feed it—" I blushed at what my words implied. "I mean, not like *that,* exactly, but I went to talk to Heru . . . asked him to teach me the common tongue so I'd have an excuse to be around him and soak up whatever residual bonding pheromones he might give off, but he said no." Suddenly overwhelmed, I started blinking rapidly in an effort to hold back tears. "Maybe if we told him, he'd be more understanding . . ."

Nuin shook his head. "I am not convinced that that is the wisest path. Heru has, well, I guess you could call them 'strong opinions' about bonding."

"What do you mean?"

"He views such relationships as weaknesses, and I think you'll agree that weakness is something both this and your Heru detest." He paused. "The possibility that it would drive him away . . . it is too great. All would fall apart."

I stared into his rainbow eyes, so full of intelligence and concern, and swallowed roughly.

Nuin squeezed my shoulder. "You *will* spend time with Heru. I'll see to that, but for now, I'd advise against telling him *anything* about your future relationship. Perhaps when he has come to know you better . . . but not yet."

Feeling the oddest sense of rejection, I nodded. "How will you get him to spend time with me?" I hated the idea of Heru being forced to be around me, especially when he seemed so opposed to the idea. But then, dying would be a whole lot worse . . .

The hint of a smile teased Nuin's mouth. "I'm sure I'll come up with something."

A wave of cold fear washed over me as I recalled what Dominic had told me in the At—that Marcus was already showing signs of withdrawals as well. "Nuin . . . what about Marcus—Heru in my time? He might be a little tougher than I am, but won't he eventually be in as much danger?" I frowned, thinking of the only other instance I'd left my own time. "Am I still anchored to my timeline?" If I was, then however many days passed for me in this ancient time, the same number passed for Marcus in my native time. "Can we, I don't know, *un*anchor me?"

Nuin shook his head. "There are some limitations to your body that even my sheut can't overcome. You will forever be anchored to your original timeline, *whenever* you are."

"So we only have so much time . . . until Marcus"—I blinked, breaking the seal holding my welling tears at bay—"*dies*."

"As matters currently stand, yes." Nuin reached out, wiping the tears away with his thumb before brushing a strand of hair out of my face and hooking it behind my ear. "Which means we must *change* how matters currently stand."

I sniffled. "But . . . how?"

Nuin smiled. "You are about to have your first lesson in how to use your new powers." The vibrant colors swirling around in his irises dulled for a moment, and I realized he'd entered the At. A few seconds later, he returned, blinking as he rose to his feet. "Come, dear Alexandra, there are two more people you will need for this task."

"Okay . . ." I cleared my throat and gave what I thought was a pretty valiant effort to pull myself together. I stood, brushing off my backside and stretching in another vain attempt to alleviate the ache sinking ever deeper into my muscles, bones, and joints . . . into my ba, my very soul. "Who else do we need? And *what* task?"

"Aset and one other, and the task is saving *your* Heru."

We found Aset in the Hat-hur temple, standing on the ramp just outside the inner sanctuary and speaking with Denai and a fairly pale man with light brown, shoulder-length hair and a trim physique. Aset smiled when she noticed us approaching.

Denai bowed her head to Aset and the man as we neared, then turned and bowed to Nuin and me in turn. Her bow to me was deepest, despite what I had confessed to her the previous evening. She slipped away on hurried, bare feet, herding a few stray priestesses as she went. Within seconds of our arrival, Nuin and I were alone with Aset and her companion inside the temple. The man turned to face Nuin and me as we joined him and Aset on the ramp.

For a moment, I forgot all about my and Heru's apparently impending deaths. Because I recognized this man. I'd met him once, on a bus, before I'd learned what I really was . . . so I'd been unable to recognize *him* for what *he* really was—Nejeret. His hair had been dyed blue and styled in short spikes, and his kind, handsome face had been pierced in a number of places, giving him an edgy, menacing look, but his eyes—those pale, almost silvery blue irises—those were the same. He'd claimed they were contacts at the time, but now I knew better.

He was staring at me almost as hard as I was staring at him, a faint, friendly smirk curving his thin lips.

"Nekure," Nuin said. "I do not believe you have met Alexandra . . . ?"

The man—Nekure—grinned, glancing only briefly at Nuin before returning his focus to me and bowing. "A pleasure, my queen."

I, too, glanced at Nuin. "I am not your queen."

Nekure flashed another broad grin and gave a slight sideways nod. "As you wish, my goddess."

I pressed my lips together and breathed out through my nose. "I am not a—"

"He knows, Lex," Aset said. She stepped closer to me and,

linking our arms, pulled me toward the sanctuary. "He is teasing you." She glanced over her shoulder as we passed through the doorway. Side by side, it was a tight squeeze, but we managed.

It was cooler inside the sanctuary than it was out in the main temple and just as dim as it had been when I first arrived, but I was still entranced by the colorful hieroglyphs and symbolic depictions of the goddess Hat-hur.

"He is the only other person who knows the truth about who you are and from whence you come," Aset added, and it took me a moment to realize she was talking about Nekure.

My eyes bulged. "You *told* him? Aset—you cannot go around telling people about me."

Aset rolled her eyes as she sat on the floor, pulling me down with her.

I grumbled internally that the limestone floor would probably leave a dirty smudge on my one and only dress, the same one I'd swapped my original shift with Denai for the previous evening. It was a silly concern, but then, I really didn't love the idea of walking around with a dark smudge on my butt for the next who-knew-how-long.

"Oh, please, Lex," Aset said. "You are the one who told me I could confide in him. That I *had* to confide in him."

Frowning, I shook my head. I felt like I'd been doing a lot of both lately. "You are speaking of when we met in *your* past?"

Aset nodded. "And *your* future."

"Uh-huh . . ."

Nuin and Nekure sat as well, Nekure beside Aset and Nuin beside me, so we made a neat little square inside the sanctuary.

I continued to stare at Aset. "And did I tell you *why* it was necessary to confide in him?"

"Because he is essential to helping you complete the process that will restore ma'at to the universe."

I looked at Nuin, then Nekure, then back at Aset. "Which is . . . ?"

Smiling, Aset shook her head. "Not something that you can know yet. You told me *that*, too."

I took a deep breath, held it for several seconds as I scanned the faces of these three people who suddenly seemed to know more about my past and future than I did. Again, my gaze settled on Aset. "Is there anything else you should tell me that I told you not to tell me about?" I asked, just a touch petulant.

Aset grinned, a mysterious glint shining in her eyes, but she didn't say anything.

The seconds of silence stretched out, until finally, I sighed. "Alright, Nuin, what is this 'task' we came here to do?"

"Nekure," Nuin said with a nod.

Following Nuin and Aset's lead, I looked at Nekure. His eyes were closed, and his hand was outstretched in front of him, like he was waiting to catch something dropping from the ceiling.

Without warning, his eyes opened, and his hand closed. When he uncurled his fingers, a tiny, crystalline butterfly rested in the center of his palm.

My eyes widened. "What . . . is that made of *At*?"

Nekure nodded.

I glanced at Nuin, then back at the other Nejeret. "And *you* just made it?"

Again, he nodded, and as he did, the little butterfly evaporated in a poof of colorful mist.

"But . . . how? You are just a Netjer-At." I shook my head slowly and focused on Nuin. "*You* could do that, but a Netjer-At . . . ?"

"Ah . . . but Nekure is not *just* a Netjer-At," Nuin said, his colorful eyes glittering even in the dim light of the sanctuary.

Confusion creased my brow. "He is not?"

"He is my son," Aset said.

I blinked in surprise and stared at Aset. Her *son*? "That is impossible. Female Netjer-At are physically incapable of having children."

"*After* manifestation," Nuin said. "Which is why, from the moment my first Netjer-At offspring was born, I forbade any female Netjer-At to lie with a man, Netjer-At or human, prior to manifestation. The resulting offspring would prove to be too powerful of a vessel for Apep, should he come to know of its existence." Nuin shook his head slowly, regret filling his eyes. "I underestimated my counterpart's determination . . . and depravity." He sighed.

"I do not understand." I stared at Aset. "So . . . *how*?"

Aset sighed. "I was taken shortly after my twentieth year, just when I started to show the first signs of pre-manifestation. He was a possessed Netjer-At from the lands to the north who had offered his body to Apep willingly, and he stole me away from my mother's home, wounding Heru in the process. He intended to take me away, to the cold lands, but before he could, I was saved and he was"—her lip curled—"no longer a problem."

I glanced at Nuin for the briefest moment, and based on his stony expression, concluded that he'd been the one to rescue Aset.

"But I was not saved before *he* could have his way with me." I met Aset's eyes, her hard, challenging stare, and realized that she'd told me about this once before, when I was in the hospital after waking from a coma that resulted from an attempted date rape—"*It was a long time ago and no longer has a hold over my life, but I understand the terror,*" she'd said.

I reached for her hand and gave it a squeeze. "Aset, I am so sorry for what you went through."

She offered me a tight smile. "I have made my peace with it." She looked at Nekure, her eyes suddenly shimmering with unshed tears. "And now I have my son, the only child born of two Netjer-At, though only we four and Heru know of his true nature."

I shook my head and fixed my gaze on Nuin. "But why does that make him anything different from a regular Netjer-At?"

"Because such a union not only generates a child," Nuin said, "but a new sheut—not nearly as powerful or multifaceted as the one you currently hold within you, but it does give the Netjer-At some unique talents. Nekure is a special case, but aside from him, such a being cannot be allowed to exist."

"Because it is too risky?" I said.

He nodded.

"So . . ." I looked at Nekure. "Your unique sheut talent is being able create things from the At," I said, and he nodded. My eyes narrowed, and focusing on Nuin, I switched to English. "How do you know he's the only one? I mean, think about how many people are alive in my time . . . people who might manifest . . ."

"Ah, but it is a simple task to see who will manifest by searching the possible futures in the At."

"Except nobody knew *I* was going to manifest."

"Because *I* was cloaking any such futures. I could not let Heru prevent your birth because he saw that you'd eventually manifest and bring about the prophecy. All that has happened *had* to happen exactly as it did so ma'at can be restored." Nuin shook his head, frowning just a bit. "Come now, dear Alexandra, you already know this."

My fingers clutched the linen skirt of my dress. "You're right, I do. But what I don't know is *how* ma'at will be restored. What will I have to do?"

He held my gaze but said nothing.

"How will I get rid of this damn power that's *killing* me? I need to know, Nuin."

He interlocked his fingers and rested his hands over his ankles. "In time . . . when you are ready."

I clenched my jaw, closed my eyes, and took a deep breath, and when I raised my eyelids, I spoke very softly, enunciated very clearly, "I'm willing to trust you because of everything we've been through together, and because I know you play the long game and you must have some reason I couldn't possibly comprehend for not filling me in, but only so long as you swear to me that there really is a way for me to survive this . . . for *Marcus* to survive this." I stared at Nuin, watching him *not* respond. "*Swear* to me, Nuin. I *need* this . . ."

He blinked twice, one corner of his mouth lifted in that insanely irritating half-smile he favored, and finally, he nodded. "I swear to you, dear Alexandra, that there is a way both for you and Heru to survive this *and* restore ma'at to the universe."

I exhaled and rubbed my hand over the lower half of my face. "Fine. That's good enough for now." I paused, hesitating. "So . . . you've been extra diligent about checking the At to prevent Nejerettes from getting pregnant before they've manifested . . . except for Aset. Why'd you let it happen to her? Why'd you wait until *after* she was raped to rescue her? Why didn't you—"

"I was away, Alexandra, and the Nejeret Apep had possessed was very good at cloaking, so no others detected his intentions before he could carry out the act."

"You were away," I repeated, not appeased one bit.

"Yes, Alexandra, I was away . . . searching for a Nejeret and Nejerette who could restore balance to the universe." He paused, and I dreaded what I knew was coming next. "I was searching for you."

12

NOTHING & SOMETHING

Nuin stared at me, his blank expression combined with the passing seconds making me a little uncomfortable. But he'd knocked me temporarily speechless with the bomb he'd just dropped.

"May we proceed, dear Alexandra?" Nuin said, once again speaking in the original tongue. "I still have much to do before we depart."

A little numb, I nodded.

"I am going to release your power now," he said, and he slowly raised his hand and touched his first two fingertips to my forehead.

Closing my eyes, I felt . . . nothing. I raised one eyelid, peeking at Nuin. "Was something supposed to happen?"

"Something did," Aset said and reached behind her. Seconds later, she handed me a small, several-inch-wide polished gold disk. "Look at your eyes."

I raised the mirror. "Whoa . . ."

They weren't exactly like Nuin's, which swirled with luminous colors spanning the entire visible spectrum, but they were close. My irises shone with a fiery maelstrom of reds, yellows, and oranges.

"When you triggered the anchor woven into the statuette and traveled back thousands of years, you enabled the power to fully integrate with your physical form," Nuin explained. "The evidence of it will be displayed in your eyes when the power is not shielded." He gave me a meaningful look. "This must be avoided at all costs."

"Apep," I said numbly. "He would know what it meant, that your sheut is within me . . . and that you are pretty much just a regular Netjer-At now. He would come after us, right?"

"He would," Nuin said.

"So is that my first lesson? Learning how to stop my eyes from glowing like a bonfire?" I frowned. But that wouldn't save Marcus, and Nuin had claimed *that* was our main purpose for coming here, for meeting with Aset and Nekure.

"No." Nuin patted my knee. "I will reestablish the inner shield when we are finished, and teach you how to do so yourself once you have more control." He looked at Aset. "I do not believe you are aware of the full extent of the relationship between Alexandra and the future Heru."

She tilted her head to the side.

"They are bonded, fully and completely."

Aset sucked in a breath and stared at me, her eyes wide. "But that would mean . . ."

"Neither will last long in the other's absence," Nuin said.

"Marcus—Heru, he was away from me for a few months after we first bonded, and he was in pain, but he didn't die . . . obviously."

"You were still *there,* even if your ba was not. Your body gave off enough residual bonding pheromones to keep him alive . . . for a time," Nuin said. "Had you not returned when you did, and fed the bond . . ." He shrugged. "It is impossible to say how much longer he could have lasted, what with the Nothingness clouding the futures."

"How do you know we fed the bond when I—" I squeezed my eyes shut, feeling heat flush my neck and cheeks. "You did *not* watch . . . did you?"

When I reopened my eyes and met Nuin's, he looked completely unrepentant. "As I have told you before, I had to determine the path that would lead to Heru's perfect match, to the bonded pair who, together, could restore ma'at. How could I accomplish such a task without knowing whether or not the two of you would be reunited in time to alleviate his withdrawals before they killed him?"

Nekure chuckled, and mortification saturated every fiber of my being. "I would very much appreciate it if none of you ever spoke of this again."

Nuin's lips quirked, but he nodded without comment, as did Nekure and Aset.

Aset cleared her throat, and we both looked at her. "This is all very fascinating, and I understand that Nekure is here to help Lex learn to use part of her power, but why am *I* here, grandfather?"

"You are here, my dear Aset, to deliver that which Lex is about to create out of the fabric of the At—the means by which Heru can survive in a world where his bond-mate no longer exists, however temporarily."

Again, Aset's eyes widened. "You want me to hold onto something for thousands of years, then give it to him once she"—Aset flicked her eyes to me—"leaves her own time to travel here?"

Nuin nodded.

"But what if I lose it? And how will I know when to give it to him?" she asked, sounding a little frantic.

"You will *not* lose it," Nuin said, his gaze steady on hers.

With a gulp, Aset nodded.

"And you will know when to deliver the object of Heru's salvation because you will be the one to see Lex off on her temporal journey."

"But—"

"Lex is here, now, dear granddaughter, which means you succeeded in the future. You and Nekure—you will make sure that everything works out."

I stared at them, first at Nuin, then at Aset, then at Nekure. "So . . . possible problem." I hunched my shoulders. "I have no idea how to make something out of At."

Nuin bowed his head toward me. "Nekure will guide you through the process."

I flashed Nekure a quick, grateful smile. "Yeah, but how does something like that save Heru from bonding withdrawals?"

Nuin smiled the knowing smile of a man who contains all of the most precious secrets in the world, past, present, and future. *Not all,* I reminded myself. "Because," he said, "within that object will be a supply of your bonding essence."

I opened my mouth, then shut it again when I couldn't formulate a response.

He turned his attention to Aset and Nekure. "We shall return shortly." Capturing my hand, he looked at me. "Let us enter the At together, my Alexandra. We will harvest the raw material, then return. I think you will find this portion of the task quite simple."

"And the other portion?"

"Extracting your own bonding essence will be taxing . . . and it will take time and immense mental focus. To be safe, you will have to do it every morning and every evening in order to store up a large enough supply." As he finished speaking, Nuin pulled my ba into the At.

The dizzying array of colors danced around us, though they seemed somehow more substantial than usual. "Alright, ye mighty god of time," I said with a heavy dose of sarcasm, "what do we do now?"

Nuin leveled an unamused stare my way.

"What?"

"I must admit, I do find your lack of deference toward me refreshing at times."

Grinning, I gave him a thumbs-up.

His expression didn't change. "This is not one of those times."

My smile slipped, and I lowered my hand to my side.

Without warning, Nuin's stern mask cracked, and he started to laugh.

Rolling my eyes, I said, "Wow, I can see that living for thousands and thousands of years has really made you mature. How old are you, anyway?"

Eyes that matched the churning rainbow surrounding us twinkled, and Nuin grinned.

"Fine, don't tell me." I exhaled in a huff. "But really, what do I do now?"

Nuin clasped his hands in front of him and rocked back on his heels. "Simply take a handful of the At, and we'll return to our physical bodies. Nekure will help you with the rest."

I pursed my lips, eying a reddish-purple tendril that was currently wrapping ethereal wisps between the fingers of my right hand. "It can't be as simple as just grabbing it," I said, closing my hand as I spoke.

"Oh, but it is." Nuin pointed to my right hand. "Look."

I glanced down and was more than a little surprised to find that the burgundy tendril of At was still there, and appeared to have solidified into long, taffy-like strands. "This is . . ." I searched for the right word while I stared at the fabric of the At . . . which I was currently holding in my hand. "This is weirdly awesome."

"Yes, yes . . . now grab a good handful so we can return."

I tugged on the purplish strands and started reeling in more of the stringy, stretchy substance. "How much do I need?"

Nuin flicked a hand my way. "That should be sufficient. Roll it up into a ball. It will be easier to work with in the physical plane that way—more like clay and less like that odd, fluffy confection you have in your time."

"Cotton candy?" I clarified as I worked on wadding my handful of what was essentially the fabric of space and time into a softball-sized clump.

"Yes, and I don't know how you can stand it. It's far too sweet."

I snorted. "As I remember it, when we went to that carnival that one time, you ate a pink and *a blue bag of cotton candy . . . then spent the rest of the night complaining about being jittery." And that was what made my relationship with Nuin unique—I'd grown up with him popping in for regular cross-temporal visits, watched him experience modern life, and laughed, cried, and snuggled with a man everyone else perceived as a god. Really, compared to everyone else, he* was *a god.*

So what did that make me, *now?*

Nuin crossed his arms and shrugged. "I no longer care for the confection. Are you done?"

I held up my harvested At for him to see. It was mostly purple and red, but had some veins of bright green and an orange-yellow that resembled baby poop. "I guess so."

He nodded and reached for me, wrapping long, strong fingers around my wrist. "Hold onto it."

And then we were back in the physical world, Nuin's hand on my knee and a warm, quicksilver mass undulating in my hands.

"Uh . . . this is *not* what I gathered back in the At," I said, holding the odd substance further away from my body. "Why does it look like this? And why is it *moving?*"

"It is the substance of the At . . . taken *out* of the At," Nekure said, procuring his own wad of silvery goo in the blink of an eye. "It is time given form. If you were to return it to the At, it would regain its former appearance, and if you were to stop touching it"—he turned his hand over, dropping the shimmering mass, which evaporated in a flurry of colorful mist as he finished speaking—"it would return on its own."

"But I have seen things made of At, and they do not look like *this*." I raised my hands a few inches. "They looked like your butterfly."

"Those were already set," Nekure said. "You must first mold it into the desired shape with your hands—though with time and practice, you should be able to do it with merely a thought—and then you must set it."

"Well, how am I supposed to do that? I just think, 'I am done,' and—"

Nekure nodded. "Essentially, yes. When you are certain that your creation is complete, it will be as though you have fired a clay pot in a kiln."

"Alright . . ." My gaze fixed on Nuin. "What exactly do I need to shape this writhing mass of At into?"

"It will need to be worn against Heru's skin," Nuin said, "so a hollow medallion, much like the ankh-At, should suffice, but with a stopper at the top so you can add more of your bonding essence to it with ease. It need not be very large."

I studied the substance in my hands while I started making an attempt to shape it into something resembling a medallion, but every time I started working on a new part, the bit I'd just formed reverted to its original unruly, quicksilver nature. "It . . . is not . . . working," I said through gritted teeth.

"Try closing your eyes," Nekure suggested. "Doing so helped me when I was first learning."

I glanced at him.

He nodded in encouragement. "Continue shaping the At substance, imagining how you would like the end result to look."

I did as Nekure instructed, imagining instead of a medallion, a smaller version of one of the perfume bottles that littered

Grandma Suse's bathroom counter. It was one I'd always admired—a slightly opaque bottle shaped like an elongated teardrop with an old-fashioned glass stopper that, as required by its lack of a flat bottom, was set on its own, unique silver filigree stand. It was so elegant and luxurious that I now realized it must have been a gift from my over-two-thousand-year-old grandfather.

"Very good, my Alexandra," Nuin said. "Do not forget to make the stopper."

Biting the tip of my tongue, I focused on fashioning a delicate piece that fit snugly in the opening at the top of the little vessel. I pressed my lips together and took a deep breath. "Okay, I think I am done."

"Oh!" Aset exclaimed at the same time that Nekure said, "Nicely done."

I snapped my eyes open and was stunned by the object in my hands. It was almost an exact replica of my grandma's perfume bottle, except my version appeared to be made of some form of quartz rather than glass and was much smaller, about the size of my thumb. It looked fragile enough that the barest of taps might shatter it, *looked* being the operative word. As far as I knew, objects made of At were virtually unbreakable.

"It is lovely," Aset said.

"I have no idea how that just happened." I shook my head and winced, unable to ignore the increasing ache. I looked at Nuin. "What do I do with it now?"

"Nothing for the moment," Nuin said. "We must return to the villa and take care of a more pressing matter."

"But . . . what about my bonding essence? Do I need to extract it now?"

Nuin reached out and touched his fingertips to my forehead, and I assumed he was resealing the sheut within me. "Not in your current state, no. The withdrawals have weakened you too much. Perhaps this evening, perhaps in the morning, depending . . ."

I arched my eyebrows. "Depending . . . on *what?*"

Nuin rose and nonchalantly brushed off the back of his linen kilt. "Depending on Heru's mood."

13

QUEEN & BLADE

From my shaded perch on one of the built-in benches around the villa courtyard, I spent several hours watching the household staff go about their midday tasks. Most came and went through the heavy wooden doors, carrying baskets and rough-hewn sacks that were empty when they left the villa but overflowing with goods—food, cloth, ceramic jars—when they returned. My only companions were the young woman and middle-aged man who were in the courtyard, tending the garden and cleaning and tidying after the previous evening's feast. They offered me smiles every now and again, which I returned easily, but no words passed between us.

The man, a slender, dark-skinned fellow with gray streaking his shoulder-length black hair and deep lines marking his weathered face, was pruning a fig tree a few yards away from my perch. He didn't seem to mind the relentless beat of the sun on his tanned shoulders and back. I minded, and I wasn't even *in* the sun. I couldn't imagine standing out there for minutes, let alone hours.

He reached up and plucked one of the few figs left on the lower branches, then held it out to me and said something I didn't understand. Smiling, I uncurled my leg from under me and stood.

I'd only taken a few steps when two men pushed open one of the wooden doors barring the gateway out to the street. It was Heru and Set.

Heru waited by the gate while Set shut the door, continuing the conversation they'd been having as they'd entered the villa. Set shook his head and laughed, turning to pat Heru on the shoulder. In my own time, Marcus once told me that he and Set had been incredibly close before Set *changed*, but hearing the seemingly impossible and seeing it with my own eyes were two entirely different things.

As they started up the center of the courtyard, I accepted the fig from the gardener, offered him a nod and another smile, and retreated back to my shaded nook. I held the fig in my palm, careful not to squish it, and watched the two men who would, in the distant future, have an unimaginable impact on my life—my father and my bond-mate. But not yet.

As I watched them together, I couldn't help but notice how much they contrasted one another. Where Set was pale and bore the lean, toned body of a runner, Heru was golden-skinned and more heavily muscled, resembling a prize fighter in the prime of his career. Which wasn't too far from the truth; I'd seen him fight off four human attackers in my tiny Seattle apartment. He'd taken them down within seconds with knives as his only weapons. And then there was the encounter we'd had in Florence a little over a week ago, where he'd taken out nearly a dozen humans and Nejerets in a museum, some of whom had been carrying handguns. To say he was formidable would've been a gross understatement, and to say he might just be the deadliest man alive might not have been an exaggeration.

"Hat-hur!" Set called, altering their trajectory to follow the limestone path that led directly to my hideaway. A broad smile spread across his face, though Heru's expression wasn't so welcoming. In fact, he appeared somewhat doubtful, with the faint crease between his eyebrows and the slight thinning of his lips.

Halfheartedly, I raised my fig hand and waved. My heartbeat sped up at the sight of Heru approaching, despite my silent admonitions to myself that this wasn't the person I really yearned to see. That person wouldn't exist for another four thousand years.

I shut my eyes in a protracted blink. Knowing that this wasn't my Heru also didn't prevent me from feeling the desperate urge to throw myself into his arms and beg him to hold me, kiss me, make love to me—to do anything that might ease the incessant ache of bonding withdrawals even a little. Because I knew that in his core, this *was* my Heru. *Any* Heru was *my* Heru.

"My queen," Set said with a dramatic flourish as he neared my bench. "You are far too lovely to be relegated to the lonely shadows like this."

I offered him a tight smile. "I am no queen, and you know it."

The two Nejerets stopped in front of me, blocking my view of the courtyard.

"On the contrary," Heru said, "you are the first Netjer-At wife Nuin has ever taken, and as the Great Father is the ruler of our people, that makes you our—"

"Great Mother?" Set finished, laughing.

Heru shot him a sideways glance. "No. Our queen, especially since Khessie has insisted that she is a *princess* for so long."

I lowered my eyes and toyed with the fig's stubby stem. There was a tiny tear in the skin of the fruit, and its sticky, opaque juice oozed onto the tip of my thumb. I quickly licked it off. "I have no desire to be a queen." I'd had enough of being a leader in my own time as the Meswett, the prophesied savior of our people in the future, and I had no interest in taking on such a role here and now.

When I raised my eyes to Heru's face, his liquid amber gaze was dark and intense. "Perhaps you should not have become the Great Father's wife if you were not interested in all that the role entailed," he said, a slight edge to his words.

I clenched my jaw and tried to hold in my instinctive reaction, but arguing with this man was part of who I was. You had to grow used to standing up for yourself when your significant other was a five-thousand-plus-year-old "god" of time. Despite the effort, I was on my feet within seconds.

"That is not fair," I said, taking a step closer to Heru and pointing my finger at his chest. "I had no choice. You do *not* know—"

Black spots spread across my vision, working their way in from the outer edges, and the blood rushing to my head roared in time with my heartbeat, growing as loud as a raging river. "Whoa . . ." The fig dropped from my loose grasp, and I could feel myself swaying, though I couldn't seem to stop the unwanted motion.

Heru grabbed my elbow to steady me, his grip sure and strong. "What is wrong, Hat-hur?" He stepped closer, lifting his hand. "Are you unwell?" He touched the crook of his index finger to my chin and tilted my face upward. The dizziness was fading, but I was suddenly weak in the knees for a reason that had nothing to do with my current affliction.

I was so close to him, to the smooth skin of his sculpted torso. As I looked into his golden eyes, as I watched his pupils slowly dilate, I could practically feel my body greedily soaking up every ounce of naturally produced bonding pheromone within him.

"Alexandra?" Set said, my name—my *true* name—heavily laden with concern. He touched my shoulder. "Does this have something to do with what Nuin told Aset and me?"

"Yes," I whispered.

Heru blinked, seeming to wake from a somewhat dazed state, and I wondered if *he* was soaking up *my* bonding pheromones, too. A horrifying thought began to erode the edges of my temporary bliss. *If we bond in this time, and I leave . . . he'll die.* That could *never* happen.

Shaking his head, Heru blinked several times in rapid succession. His focus shifted so he was looking over my shoulder. "Who is Alexandra? And what are you talking about, cousin?"

I sighed, not wanting the moment to end, but knowing it had to. Sure, I literally *had* to be around Heru to keep myself alive, but there was no way I could allow any form of physical intimacy between us—not if such a brief touch could trigger the initial stage of bonding on his part.

"It is what she is called, where she comes from," Set said. "Now take hold of her. We must bring her to Grandfather."

My entire body tensed as Heru's arms started to slip around me. "No," I told him. "There is no need." I pushed against him weakly.

"Don't be ridiculous," Heru said. "You are barely staying upright."

I pushed against his chest harder. "I am fine. Let me go!"

"As you wish," Heru said, releasing me as I shoved one final time.

I stumbled back several steps, and when the backs of my legs hit the inset bench, I plopped onto my butt and the back of my head smacked against the wall. "Ow," I grumbled, rubbing the tender spot at the base of my skull. The plaster covering the mud-bricks hadn't done much to cushion the impact.

When I glared up at Heru, I found him standing where he'd been, arms crossed and a spark of amusement lighting his eyes. His expression, however, was completely bland.

Straightening my back, I stood. "I thank you for your help, but as you can see, I am fine, now. I should return to my"—I swallowed roughly—"my husband." *Which is supposed to be you,* I thought as my eyes lingered on Heru.

He nodded, showing no signs of making any further move to help me. I met Set's eyes, and he offered a conciliatory smile and a shrug.

I was only a few yards past them when I heard the sound of their footsteps behind me. I stopped immediately and turned around.

Heru and Set halted as well, only a few feet in my wake.

I narrowed my eyes but said nothing as I spun back around and continued on my way. Until my hand brushed against Heru's in a backswing. Again, I stopped and faced them. Both men were inches from running into me. Set took a step backward, but neither Heru nor I did.

Pursing my lips, I tilted my head back to look up at him. "What are you doing?"

"Following you," he said with an innocent smile.

I glanced at Set, but again, all he did was shrug. I returned my focus to Heru. "Why?"

"To make sure that if you collapse again, someone will be there to catch you." There was a challenging glint in his eyes.

"I didn't collapse."

"Because I caught you."

I took a deep breath, then another. "You—" I snapped my mouth shut and shook my head, suppressing a weak laugh. "Whatever floats your boat," I said in English. Turning on my heel, I headed around the corner and into the hallway leading to Nuin's private rooms, voicing no further complaint as the men shadowed me.

A few seconds later, Set laughed. "Whatever floats your boat," he repeated. When I glanced over my shoulder and caught his eye, he added, "This language has amusing sayings."

I raised one shoulder, part of me expecting Heru to comment on Set's use of my unfamiliar, foreign language. I knew he'd heard me speak it with Nuin, but he had to be wondering how Set knew it as well, especially considering that Set, Nuin, and I were the only people in the world who *knew* English. Heru, however, remained silent until we reached Nuin's sitting room. Only then did he speak.

He strode across the room to where Nuin was seated in what seemed to be his favorite chair against the far wall, on one side of the senet table, albeit it wasn't like he had a lot of seating options. The only other chair was the one opposite his across the table. There was also a very uncomfortable-looking wooden settee placed against an adjacent wall, but that was about it.

"Those meetings you and Set have been having; they have been about her"—Heru pointed haphazardly in my direction—"haven't they?" He sounded neither accusatory nor angry, simply matter of fact.

Nuin rubbed his face, almost looking exhausted, and I wondered if he'd been waiting for this confrontation. After the expectant silence had grown to an uncomfortable level, he nodded.

"You taught him that guttural language—no doubt confided in him about her—for what reason?" Heru asked. "Is he replacing me as your Blade?" I didn't know what it meant exactly, but "Blade" was clearly a title.

"For a short time, yes," Nuin said, absolutely calm.

"Why?"

"Set is replacing you as my Blade because I trust none more than I trust you," Nuin told him.

"That makes no sense," Heru said.

"Ah . . . but it does when you consider that I shall be entrusting you with the life of my beloved."

Heru shot a wary glance my way. "You mean Hat-hur?"

"You may call her Alexandra . . . or Lex. She prefers those names."

"Then why did you introduce her to everyone differently?"

Nuin stood, and even drained of most of his sheut, he still outshone Heru, both in his sheer presence and in the amount of power emanating from him. "My decisions are *my* decisions, and they are final. Think carefully, Grandson, before you question them."

Heru's head bowed, but Nuin's words didn't cow him for long. His neck straightened, and he held his head high. "She is unwell."

Again, Nuin nodded. "She is."

"How is that possible?" It was an honest question. As a Nejerette, I should have been all but indestructible, outside of violent physical harm.

Nuin patted Heru's shoulder, the picture of honesty and friendship. "You must trust me in this—she needs fresh air, exercise, and companionship to maintain her health."

"That seems wise . . ."

"And I am entrusting *you* with the task of keeping her healthy." Nuin paced away from Heru, rubbing his chin ponderously.

"I am right here, by the way," I said with a weak wave. "No need to talk about me like I am not." Set was the only one to look my way.

"So . . . what? You are making me her nursemaid?" Heru said.

Nuin paused, then pivoted to face Heru, his posture tense. "I am making you *her* Blade."

Heru's hands balled into fists. "For how long?"

"For the rest of today, and then we shall see."

"Is this a punishment?"

My heart sank at hearing Heru's words.

Nuin shook his head slowly. "Punishment? Are you so eager to insult my lovely wife?"

Heru's head swiveled in my direction, and when his eyes met mine, I caught a flicker of shame.

I swept my gaze back to Nuin in time to catch his wink.

"No," Heru said, almost pleadingly. "It is just . . . I would like to know what I must do to regain my former position."

Nuin expelled a puff of breath. "Exactly the opposite of what you are doing right now. *Be* her Blade." He glanced my way and smiled. "Look out for her. Protect her." Something he saw on my face altered his expression, and his gaze sharpened, becoming hawkish. He shifted his glare to Heru. "Do *not* leave her side. She is more precious to me than anything else on this earth."

Heru bowed his head. "As you say, Great Father. What would you have me do with her for the remainder of the day?" I could barely believe the subservience I was hearing from him. I'd never seen Marcus acquiesce to anyone, but then, Nuin didn't exist in my time.

"We are leaving in the morning. I am entrusting you in making sure that she has everything she needs for the journey."

Heru inhaled and opened his mouth, then seemed to think better of whatever he'd been about to say and breathed out heavily. "Gather your things," he said as he brushed past me. "I will be waiting in the courtyard."

I watched him stride toward the curtained doorway. "What 'things'?" I muttered under my breath, fairly certain I owned nothing but the clothes on my back, and even my dress was borrowed.

But as it turned out, I did have "things." Nuin retreated into the bedroom for the briefest moment, then returned, carrying a flat wooden container about the size a small jewelry box. It was crafted from some dark reddish-brown wood and inlayed with another wood almost as pale as ivory in a simple geometric pattern. Two bulbous knobs no larger than the tip of my pinkie protruded from one of the longer sides, directly opposite each other on either side of the box's seam. A thin leather cord twined between and around the knobs in a tight figure eight, ensuring the box stayed shut. Something within rattled as I accepted the small container.

I raised my eyebrows. "What's this?"

"The remainder of the turquoise beads that formerly made up your dress"—Nuin looked down at the turquoise, quartz, and silver belt around my waist—"other than those you are wearing, of course." He laughed suddenly. "What is it they say in your time . . . you are an independently wealthy woman."

I accepted the box, shaking it gently. "Thank you for this, Nuin. *Really*." I smiled wryly. "And that term comes from a slightly earlier time than mine."

Nuin waved his hand dismissively. "Go, my Alexandra. Have fun. The time in Heru's presence will do you good. You will feel much better when you return."

I let out a soft laugh. I already felt better after the brief contact with Heru in the courtyard. It was impossible not to imagine actually *being* with him again. I opened my mouth, then hesitated.

Nuin tilted my face up with a finger under my chin. "What is it?"

I cleared my throat. "Is there, um, any way for something to happen between us—Heru and me—without risking bonding on his part?"

"There is not," Nuin said, and my heart sank.

"I see." Looking down at the box, I started to turn away.

Nuin grabbed my arm just above the elbow. "However, there is a way to place a sort of block once a bond is established, much like a memory block."

My mouth fell open. "But—but . . . why did you not just do that for me?" It wasn't that I didn't want to spend time with Heru—the opposite was true—but not having to worry about feeding the bond would give me more time to focus on learning to control my borrowed power so I could return to *my* Heru, who I wanted to see even more than his ancient counterpart.

Nuin was shaking his head. "I no longer contain the power to do such a thing."

"But *I* do?"

"No," he said, again shaking his head. "Even with my sheut, you cannot create such a block within yourself."

My shoulders sagged as I grumbled internally about why he'd even brought it up.

"Now, dear Alexandra, go find Heru and enjoy your day of shopping."

I perked up a bit, and not because of the word "shopping," but because I was about to experience what it was like to trade and barter in an Old Kingdom marketplace. It was an archaeologist's dream.

"And be careful," he added.

I eyed him.

"I meant what I said to Heru, dear Alexandra. His new position as your Blade is far more significant than being *my* right hand. The moment you arrived in this time, you became the single most important person alive."

14

LOVERS & WIVES

When I entered the courtyard, a small crowd of young men were milling around Heru near the gate, their skin tones varying from Heru's golden tan to the darker brown of my gardener friend. Each was lean and fit, obviously well fed, and dressed similarly to Heru in above-the-knee, white linen kilts. And every eye watched my approach.

Self-conscious, I tucked my hair behind my ear and offered the group a hesitant smile as I neared, stopping a few feet from Heru. "What are they here for?" I asked, sweeping my gaze around the crowd of young men. They were quiet, watching us both.

"They are our porters for the day," Heru told me.

My eyes widened—there were so many of them.

Heru tilted his head to the side ever so slightly, studying me. "Or did you think you and I would lug back all of the merchandise ourselves?"

"I, um . . ." My neck and cheeks flushed, but I kept my gaze steady on him. It wasn't difficult; Heru's eyes had always captivated me, and they weren't disappointing at the moment. "I suppose I did not give the matter much thought."

"Evidently."

I fought the urge to grind my teeth. I wanted to shout at him that I wasn't really an idiot, that I was only acting like one because in my time *everything* was done differently. But I couldn't; I'd barely known *this* version of Heru for a day. I took a slow, calming deep breath. "I was not aware that so many young men were employed in this house."

Heru broke eye contact, doing a visual assessment of the group. "They are not, but I tasked a few of our own to find a few more who were willing to help out this afternoon, and now we have attained more than enough helpers." He hesitated, his attention returning to me. The path his eyes trailed over my face was almost palpable, tracing my nose, my cheekbones, my jaw, and my lips before returning to my eyes. "It would seem that word of Nuin's queen has spread."

I ran my hands down the front of my dress, smoothing the soft linen skirt unnecessarily. "What do you mean by that?"

Heru shook his head. "Nothing. Forget I said anything." He gripped my elbow and guided me through the gate, releasing me as soon as we were walking along the street's slightly uneven paving stones. Unlike the previous day, when the roads had been all but empty, there were now people everywhere—rushing around or pausing in front of tall mud-brick walls to chat. There was even a pair of men repairing a portion of a villa wall that had collapsed.

We headed in the opposite direction of the canal docks. Heru's strides were long and nothing close to leisurely, and the pace wasn't overly conducive to casual conversation.

"Are we walking the whole way?" I asked.

Heru glanced at me like I was dim-witted.

"Instead of taking a canal boat . . . ?"

"Yes."

"Is it very far?"

"Not too far."

"How long will it take?"

"A quarter of an hour," he said, his words clipped. Lucky for me, the ancient Egyptian's divided their day into twenty-four hours much like the people from my time—twelve hours of day and twelve hours of night. A quarter of an hour was a period of time that had genuine meaning to me. Finally, *something* was familiar.

For several minutes, neither of us spoke. Our small parade of porters chattered away behind us, but the silence between Heru and me thickened until it was almost choking. Unable to stand it any longer, I blurted, "Listen, Heru . . . I feel awful about you losing your usual position as Nuin's Blade. I completely understand if you blame me for—"

"Did you ask Nuin to order me to be your companion while you traded at the markets?"

"I—no, I did not."

"Then I have no reason to blame you."

I took a few breaths, willing myself to hold my tongue. I failed. "But you *do* blame me. You will barely even look at me, let alone speak with me. You must think—"

"I do not."

I curled my fingers into fists and growled in frustration. "Why are you always so—"

"You speak as if you know me," Heru said. "You do not." His words were as effective as a slap.

I stopped walking and stared at him as he continued on. The porters stopped as well, fanning out behind me. It only took Heru a few seconds to catch on, but he was already a dozen feet ahead. He slowed, stopped, and turned.

I looked away, watching a pair of women who appeared to be in their mid-thirties chat in front of a two-story building. Clearing my throat, I swiped my cheeks with one hand. I refused to let Heru see the devastating effect he could have on me. He wouldn't—*couldn't*—understand the reason why.

Out of my peripheral vision, I watched him retrace his steps until he was standing in front of me. He raised his hand and gently touched my shoulder. "That was unduly harsh. I apologize."

I swallowed and cleared my throat again, but I said nothing as I continued to watch the women. They were arguing in hushed tones. *About what? Their children, maybe? Or possibly some gossip gone bad?*

Heru slid his hand down the length of my arm to my hand. He held my fingers, not entwining them with his own as I was used to, but just held them. I choked back a convulsive sob. *I miss you so much.*

"You are alone and far from your home," he said softly. "For whatever reason, you have abandoned your former life to come here and be with the Great Father." He sighed and ran his free hand over the closely shaved black hair on his scalp. "Secrets surround you, and Nuin has chosen to confide in Set rather than in me. *That* is what is bothering me, not you."

I finally looked at him.

"You appear surprised."

I bit my lip, unsure how much I could safely tell him, and averted my gaze. The two women had abandoned their argument and were now watching us. I met Heru's golden tiger eyes once again.

"Why do so many secrets surround you?" he asked.

"I cannot tell you that," I said softly. "And even if I could, you would not believe me."

"You do not know that, Hat—" When I flinched at the near use of my misnomer, he amended what he'd been about to say. "Alexandra. You do not know what I will and will not believe." But I did, because I *knew* him. I knew this man as well as I knew myself.

A tear snuck out of the corner of my eye before I could blink it away. I hated it . . . all of the crying . . . the lying . . . the pretending. "Please just trust me when I say that I cannot tell you," I implored, my eyes pleading.

Heru raised his hand, almost like he intended to wipe away that rogue tear, but stopped himself halfway and lowered it back to his side. "This morning, when I asked you about Ankhesenpepi and how you had made an enemy of her so quickly, why did you say that it was because of me?"

I squinted up at the clear afternoon sky. The sun was still blazing high overhead. "Are you sure you want to know?"

"Yes," he said, the single word a cross between a growl and a hiss.

I inhaled slowly, considering how to tell him. "She threatened me last night." I lowered my gaze, leveling it on him. "She cornered me during the feast, berated me for 'stealing' her power, and told me that she knew about our conversation in Nuin's chambers—when we were alone together—and that if I did not stay away from you, she would tell everyone that we had been"—I cleared my throat—"intimate."

Heru's face darkened.

"So, you are really only part of the issue," I said, offering him an apologetic smile. "She thinks I want to take her power from her, but honestly, I do not."

Heru returned my smile, his warm and familiar in a way that ignited so many intense feelings within me. "Because of what you are and who you are wife to, in time, you will have more power than any other woman who has ever lived."

An unexpected, slightly hysterical laugh bubbled up from my chest, and I wrapped my arms around my middle. "I never wanted any of this—being Netjer-At, having a life that could span eons, being married to a man who is the ruler of his people . . ." . . . *absorbing a foreign power, having to abandon my love, living four thousand years before my mom was born* . . . "I just wanted to live my life and—" I shrugged and shook my head. "I just wanted to live my life."

Much to my surprise, Heru chuckled. "Now *that* is something I can relate to." I had no idea what he was talking about. Marcus loved being Netjer-At and thrived when he was in control; power was his bread and butter. "I will speak with Khessie, tell her to cease this cat crawl."

"Cat crawl?"

Heru stepped closer and placed a hand on the small of my back, urging me to resume walking with the faintest pressure. "You are unfamiliar with the expression?"

I nodded and smiled, letting him lead me.

He retracted his hand, his fingertips skimming along my lower back before they were gone completely. *It wasn't intentional,* I told myself. *It didn't mean anything.* But my racing heartbeat and electrified nerves weren't overly receptive to logic.

"It is when two cats circle one another slowly, clearly antagonistic, but neither attacking."

"Oh, I see." Again, I nodded. "That makes sense."

We rounded a corner, and the paved street gave way to sandy, hard-packed dirt, crowded with people. The buildings ahead were far less sprawling and grandiose than the villas and temples of the previous lane. These, if I was interpreting them correctly, were the conjoined, two-story townhouses common to the majority of the Egyptian populace during this era. They were akin to the mud-brick brethren of San Francisco's famous terraced homes, minus the intricate moldings, glass windows, and bright paints.

"How is the kitten?" Heru asked. "What are you calling him?"

"Horus—I mean, Rus," I said, half-expecting him to shout, "Ah-ha! You named him after me!" Which was silly. The name Horus hadn't been used for the god Heru until the Ptolemaic period, when the Greeks ruled Egypt. "He seems to be enjoying his new home." I glanced at Heru. "Where did he come from?"

"He is from the latest litter of my local wife's favorite cat."

I choked on my own saliva as he spoke. "Your *local wife*?" And here I'd thought knowing he had some sort of a relationship with Ankhesenpepi would be the extent of the torture I would have to endure in this time. I should have known better.

At his curious expression, I offered him a pathetic attempt for a smile. "Pardon me, please. I—" I frowned and shook my head. "What with your relationship with Ankhesenpepi . . . I suppose I did not consider that you would have other wives, as well."

Heru's expression hardened. "Khessie is not one of my wives, and she never will be."

"But you—you—she . . . why not?"

Heru looked affronted. "Why would I *ever* take her as a wife? Khessie is Netjer-At—what would be the purpose of such a union, other than to increase *her* power and standing? There would be no benefit to me."

I almost couldn't believe the words I was hearing pour out of his mouth. "And your wife—"

"Wives. I have three." Heru focused on the way ahead, and I had the impression that he was avoiding looking at me.

My eyes widened. "Your *wives* . . . you married them because doing so benefits you in some way." I blushed. "Other than the obvious . . ."

Heru chuckled, but it sounded forced. "Children, of course . . . and affection."

I felt a sick sort of curiosity and couldn't help myself. I asked, "What are they like—your wives?" Because the only two women I'd met who he'd been involved with—Ankhesenpepi and a human woman from my time, Sarah—were pretty despicable examples of my gender, and I wasn't sure I wanted to think too much about what that said about me.

"Meryet is the only one who resides in Men-nefer," Heru said. "She is where Rus came from."

I squeezed my eyes shut in a protracted blink. *What is it with the Netjer-At men and their need for multiple wives?* It wasn't like polygamy was widely practiced in ancient Egypt; that was only a misperception held by many people in my time. "And there are two more . . . ?"

"Yes . . ." Heru sounded hesitant. "You speak of them like such a thing is strange. Is it not a common practice among the male Netjer-Ats of your homeland to take multiple wives?"

I imagined Marcus politely requesting permission to take a human wife. "No, it is definitely not." I cleared my throat for what seemed like the dozenth time in only a few minutes. "And, I suppose, considering I now have my own sister-wives, I would like to learn more about how it works between a man and his wives." After I replayed my words in my mind, my cheeks burned again. "I did not mean *how* it works; I know *that*, but, um . . ."

Heru chuckled, and the sound set me aflame—soul, heart, and libido alike. I hoped, desperately, that he wouldn't sense my reaction.

I swallowed. "Please, forget I said anything about it."

He ignored my request. "I maintain my wives' accommodations, and they provide potential new Netjer-Ats. Meryet resides in Men-nefer permanently, along with our three surviving children." He continued, but the one word—*surviving*—resounded in my head, drowning out whatever else he was saying. Heru and Meryet had buried at least one child. *Heru* had buried children, his own children. I'd known that; I'd known he'd watched countless of his descendants be born, grow to adulthood, and eventually die. I just hadn't thought . . .

"I am so sorry about all those you have lost. I cannot imagine how hard that must be," I told him, my words laden with sympathy. But not empathy—I'd never lost a child, and I never would. Nejerettes' bodies—or rather, *manifested* Nejerettes' bodies—rejected any fetuses almost immediately after fertilization due to our hyper-regenerative abilities. It was only reproduction through the males of our kind that we were able to carry on as a species at all.

"I am grateful for those who have survived," he said, and I caught his wayward glance; it was filled with pity, of all things. "I cannot imagine what it would be like to have never had any children at all."

I let out a breathy, bitter laugh. Even if I'd eventually wanted children, that avenue was permanently closed to me. "It is better to have loved them and lost them, than to never have loved them at all," I said, quoting Tennyson in the original tongue as best I could.

Squinting thoughtfully, Heru nodded. "I have not heard it phrased as such, but yes, I think you have captured my meaning."

"More than you know," I said under my breath.

Heru didn't respond, so I pretended that he hadn't heard me. He had, and we both knew it.

15

SUPPLY & DEMAND

Heru and I rounded a corner and walked into a throng wilder and louder than any farmers market I'd ever seen. A seemingly endless sea of people were hawking their wares under brightly dyed canopies, haggling relentlessly with their potential customers. And beyond the crowd stretched a glittering blue-gray mass sprinkled with a smattering of white specks. The Nile. The ancient, beautiful Nile, teeming with vessels. It was such a chaotic, wondrous scene that it was almost magical.

I snagged Heru's wrist, drawing him to a halt. "Give me a moment, please. I just need a moment to take it all in."

Heru barked something at our young porters, and they circled around us, creating a barrier between us and this wild, exotic marketplace.

"Oh," I said with a low laugh, "there is no way you are keeping me separated from this. You have no idea how long I have dreamed of . . . to see this with my own eyes . . . to experience it . . ." I tore my attention away from the miasma of commerce and pinned Heru with my gaze. "How does this work?" I raised my little box of turquoise beads. "How do I barter?"

Heru glanced down, but his eyes quickly returned to my face, where they lingered. "I will guide you to the stalls of the merchants who are the fairest and have the best merchandise. You will tell me which items you favor, and *I* will barter *for* you." He held out his hand, palm up. "Give me a few of your beads so I have something to show the vendors. Are they all turquoise, or are any of the quartz or gold or silver pieces in there?"

I raised my eyebrows, wondering just how closely he'd examined my dress; knowing the man Heru would one day become, pretty damn closely.

I started unlooping the leather cord securing the box, suddenly grateful for my ring of young, sturdy porters. I didn't think waving money around was wise in *any* time period. "It's just turquoise," I said once I had the box open. I plucked out a few pieces to hand to Heru, then resecured the leather binding. "Is it of high enough quality? Will we be able to get everything we need?"

"And then some," Heru murmured. He scanned me from head to toe, then back up again, and his black-rimmed gold irises swallowed me. "Though I do miss the dress."

My heart skipped a beat, and the corner of my mouth quirked up. This Heru was as much my perfect match as mine was, there was no denying that . . . not for either of us. My mood sobered. Our compatibility just meant I had to be that much more careful around him. If we bonded . . .

"You probably should not say things like that," I told him.

"Because of Nuin . . ."

"Because of Ankhesenpepi," I countered, and it *was* partially the truth.

Heru's eyes darkened. "You do not need to worry about Khessie. I told you I would speak with her."

I snorted. I was fairly certain that dear Khessie was a tenacious little Nejerette, and I didn't think a scolding, especially not one from Heru, would do any good at all. "And I wish you the best of luck with that." Before he could respond, I grabbed his forearm and yanked him out of our protective ring. "Where shall we start?"

"You need clothing . . . additional clothing," he said, briefly glancing down the length of my body. For once, he didn't pull away from my touch, and we walked arm in arm past several stalls. "Kelain is the seamstress favored by Aset and Meryet, so let us begin here," he said, stopping in front of a stall that wouldn't seem out of place at an arts and crafts fair.

Woven reed mats had been set out on the ground, creating a cleaner setting for the vendor's goods. Which was important, considering that the baskets arranged around three sides of the stall were filled with piles and piles of pristine white linen. Above each basket, on something that reminded me of the old-fashioned coatrack in the entryway of Grandma Suse's house, hung several garments. The vendor's way of displaying what was in each basket, I supposed. Each was a dress of some sort, hem-lengths ranging from just below the knee to just above the ankle and with several variations on the two-strip bodice similar to that of the shift I was wearing.

There were several women in the stall—two conversing, and one kneeling while she held up a thin ribbon of linen to various parts of another woman's body—her *nude* body. I hastily looked away.

One of the women deep in conversation noticed us, glanced our way briefly, and then did a double take. She touched the other woman on the shoulder, murmured something, and nodded, and the other woman slipped away with a polite smile for Heru and me.

"Kelain," Heru said as the remaining woman approached us. He said something to her in the common tongue.

Kelain clasped her hands together in front of her and

lowered her head in a slight bow, murmuring what I assumed was a polite response to Heru's greeting. When she raised her head, her eyes slid to me. She scanned me slowly from the feet up, more of a mental measurement than the sizing-up I'd received from Ankhesenpepi. Her lips spread into a broad smile when she reached my face, and she said something I couldn't understand.

I caught Heru's eye and raised my eyebrows in silent question.

"She says she heard that Nuin took a divine wife, but she did not believe the rumors until now," Heru translated.

The dressmaker watched our exchange curiously, waiting until we fell silent to speak again.

Heru responded to her incomprehensible words with a slight nod. "I am letting her know that I will be translating your exchange with her to ensure you get everything you need."

I leaned in closer to Heru and kept my voice low. "I have no idea *what* I need . . . just so you know."

Heru stared down at me, the corner of his mouth curving upward. Apparently I'd amused him. "I shall let her know that you need a full wardrobe."

I smiled. "Thank you."

Heru continued to stare down at me for another few seconds, his eyes turning troubled before he blinked and looked away. He passed the message on to Kelain, who promptly took my hand and guided me further into the alcove that made up her stall until we were standing near the other two women. She grasped the skirt of my shift on either side of my hips and began to raise it.

I clasped her wrists, holding her hands and my dress in place. "What are you doing?" When she shook her head, I looked at Heru. "What is she doing?"

"I believe she is attempting to unclothe you."

My eyes bulged, and I swung my head around to look at him. "*Why* is she trying to unclothe me?"

Heru frowned. "So she can determine which garments fit you best." His voice had taken on the I'm-talking-to-an-idiot tone I was growing used to.

I pressed my lips together. Public nudity wasn't nearly as taboo to these people as it was to those of my time. I'd known it prior to traveling back here, but looking around, it was an unavoidable fact. Many of the women were walking around only in skirts, breasts exposed, and some were wearing only skimpy linen loincloths.

"I am *not* taking this dress off out in the open where everyone can see me," I said.

Heru raised one eyebrow. "Are you ashamed?"

I opened my mouth, then closed it, unsure how to respond. "No, but . . . where I come from, being naked is a private matter."

He shrugged. "Very well." He said something to Kelain, who frowned but released her hold on my dress. She turned away from me, speaking to Heru while she rummaged through her stock. She pulled a few garments from each basket, holding each item up against my body and tossing a few back into their original containers. The rest she placed in a tall, oval, woven reed basket.

By the time she finished, I had several dozen new dresses, some as light and sheer as silk chiffon, which I was definitely relegating as sleepwear only, and some thick enough that they almost made up for my lack of bra or underwear. Going commando all the time was going to take more than a day to get used to.

Watching a slender young servant girl pass wearing only a delicate golden circlet around her neck and a black loincloth that resembled modern bikini briefs, I had a brilliant idea. Maybe I *could* find some underwear. I tapped Kelain's arm and pointed to the girl.

Kelain shook her head, clearly not understanding my request.

I exhaled heavily and strode over to Heru. "Do women ever wear something under their dresses like what that young woman is wearing?" I asked, again pointing to the nearly naked servant.

Heru's brow furrowed. "Would that not be a bit confining?" He shook his head. "No, it is better to let everything breathe."

I glanced down the length of hard-packed muscle that covered his body, lingering on his kilt. Due to the way it was wrapped around his body and knotted just under his navel, the linen garment hung longer around the back and sides, and pulled up to above mid-thigh in the front, with a longer flap hanging down the center. I knew exactly what those linen folds hid, and thinking that he wasn't nearly as concealed as I'd assumed was going to drive me just a little bit mad.

"So you just walk around, letting it all hang out?" I asked.

Heru fought it for a moment, but his lips spread into a wide grin and he laughed out loud. "Let it all hang out," he repeated. "Indeed I do, as does your husband. How do you not know this?"

"I . . . well . . ." I shrugged.

"You should pay more attention next time you and he—" Awareness dawned on his face, and he leaned in closer, his nostrils flaring as he inhaled deeply. When he pulled away, his eyebrows were raised and his golden irises were bright. "Except it would not be a 'next time,' because there has been no *first time*."

"We are not talking about this." I spun away from him.

He caught my arm, holding me in place long enough to whisper, "He is a fool," then released me.

My heart was pounding and seemed to have relocated to my

throat. Heru thought Nuin was neglecting me, and he felt sorry for me. I longed to tell him the truth, that the marriage was a farce and that I was from the future and truly bonded to *him*, but that wasn't an option.

While I watched Heru complete the transaction with Kelain, I remained silent, my expression guarded. I paid her a small handful of turquoise beads when Heru directed me to do so. He sent two porters back to the villa, one carrying the basket filled with the dresses we'd purchased and one carrying a thick bundle of several different types of linen, all folded and rolled tightly and wrapped in a protective reed sheath that reminded me of a sushi roller.

Each stop after that was much the same, aside from the vendors *not* attempting to strip off my clothes. We spent some time at a stall that offered a wide assortment of containers. Most were a variation on the lidded basket Kelain had packed my purchased clothing in, but there was a smattering of wooden boxes and chests as well. Heru selected several baskets of different sizes, then helped me pick out a cosmetic chest, the ancient Egyptian version of a vanity. I only had three options, so it wasn't like the decision was excessively difficult.

I settled on a piece much like Nuin's, constructed from a polished, brownish-red wood and inlaid with ivory in geometric patterns around the border of each face. After we paid, Heru removed a dozen more beads from my little treasure box and handed them to the last of our porters. The young man listened to Heru's instructions, then trotted off into the throng of shoppers, traders, and other porters.

I watched as the crowd swallowed him up. "Where is he going?" I asked Heru.

"He can gather the amenities you will need to fill out that chest easily enough on his own."

I cocked my head to the side.

"We are running out of daylight, and I dislike the idea of

keeping you out on the streets once the sun has died." Not *set*, but *died*—which seemed appropriate, considering the sun, symbolizing the god Re, was believed to enter the land of the dead every night as it sank into the western horizon, then reemerge into the land of the living as it rose each morning in the east. "The jeweler will be our last stop today. If there is anything else you need, we can send someone out tomorrow morning before we depart."

"Okay . . ."

He placed a hand on the small of my back and remained close as he guided me through a crowd that showed no signs of thinning. We were nearing the Nile's western bank, and the people bustling around us were becoming more unseemly looking, their linen clothing dirtier and tattered and their bodies in need of a good wash.

I tilted my head so my mouth was angled up toward Heru's ear. "Is this the bad part of the market?"

He kept a wary eye on the crowd. "It did not used to be, but with the droughts . . ."

"There have been droughts?" I asked, my curiosity piqued. Years of back-to-back droughts that devastated the agricultural industry was another unproven—and mostly unprovable—theory for the fall of the 6th Dynasty and the Old Kingdom of Egypt. I was seeing firsthand that it might not be *just* a theory.

Heru nodded. "This is the eighth consecutive year with an insufficient Akhet." Akhet being one of the three seasons the ancient Egyptians divided their year into, along with Peret and Shemu, it translated, more or less, to "inundation." It was a several-month period during which the Nile would flood, inundating the floodplains with silt and leaving behind incredibly fertile black soil once it receded. One of the ancients' names for their land was "Kemet" which literally meant "black," in reference to the silty soil . . . their lifeblood. If this was the eighth year in a row with a poor inundation, then food yields would be nearly nonexistent.

"They're starving," I said, a lump forming in my throat as I observed the people around me through this new lens. There were mothers carrying crying babies, bartering with grain vendors at a near shout while children old enough to walk clutched their legs, most nude and little more than skin and bones. Even I could hear the mothers' desperation, though I couldn't understand their words.

Please, my babies are starving! They'll die! We'll make payment next week, I swear. Please!

"There must be stores of food, or maybe . . ." But I didn't know enough about ruling an ancient civilization to suggest anything beyond that. I looked up at Heru, my eyes wide with horror. "The Netjer-At must have seen this coming. You could have stocked up . . . prepared . . ."

"We did what we could. It is why Khessie has been stationed by the Pharaoh's side for the past several generations," he said, sliding his hand along my back and curving his fingers around the side of my waist to pull me closer. One glance up at his face told me he wasn't doing it out of a desire to cuddle. There was a dangerous glint in his eyes, a promise of death for any who even considered attempting to steal from me.

"You did not do enough," I murmured. I may not have known exactly *why* the story ended the way it did, but I knew the end of the story. This civilization, these people . . . they were dying.

Heru's hand clenched on my waist. "The drought was not supposed to last this long. In all of the possible futures, the previous Akhet was normal, making this Shemu"—which was a time of harvest—"plentiful." He shook his head, almost in disbelief. "None of us saw this."

An icy chill washed over me despite the stifling heat.

"Because of me. You could not see this possible future, because of me. It is my fault."

Heru glanced down at me. "What?"

"The At . . . it does not act normally, where I am concerned," I explained carefully. "If you look for me in it, you will not find me, not in the past, the present, or the possible near futures. You could not see this devastating possibility, because *I* am in this future . . . this *present*."

Heru was shaking his head. "I do not see how such a thing is possible."

I flashed him a small, sad smile. "I know. It is one of those secrets I told you that you would not believe."

Heru pressed his lips together and didn't respond.

On our left, there was a doorway. Two burly men stood on either side, holding long spears with stone spearheads and wearing leather belts around the waists of their kilts, a heavy mace hanging from a loop on each man's hip.

"Armed guards?" I said, looking at Heru. "Is this the jeweler's?" I wasn't positive, but I was fairly certain there hadn't been actual jewelry shops in Old Kingdom Egypt.

Heru shook his head. "This is the residence of the dockmaster. I know him well." He nodded to each of the guards and led me through the narrow doorway. It was short enough that he had to duck to make it past the threshold. "I did not wish to alarm you, but we are being followed. You will be safe here while I take care of it."

I grabbed his arm with both of my hands, feeling the play of muscles under his skin as he attempted to pull away. "You will simply leave me here, alone? But—"

Heru gently peeled my fingers from his arm. "No, I will leave you here with Weni, and once the issue has been dealt with, I will return." He turned away from me and called out, "Weni!" He said more, but as usual, I couldn't understand him.

Weni's voice preceded him as he appeared in the back doorway. He looked to be in his late twenties and was lean, though not scrawny like most of the people milling around near his residence, and as was the fashion, his sleek black hair was parted down the middle and nearly reached his shoulders. His skin was a few shades darker than Heru's, and his face was pleasant, if not exactly handsome, though the roguish glint to his eyes weighed in his favor on the handsome scale.

He looked from Heru to me, then back to Heru, his lips spreading into a decidedly lascivious grin. Whatever he was saying to Heru as he approached and embraced him, I had the distinct feeling it would have made me blush profusely had I been able to understand him.

Heru laughed and shook his head, glancing back at me a few times while he spoke to Weni. After a short exchange, he clapped his friend on the back and returned to me. "I will not be long. Weni does not speak the original tongue, so you do not have to worry about conversing with him." He raised his hand a few inches, almost as though he were reaching for me, then seemed to realize what he was doing and let it drop back to his side. "Do *not* leave this building."

"But what if something happens to you?"

"Ah, I would be offended had we not met only yesterday." He grinned, but it wasn't a friendly expression. "There is no man—or woman—in this city who can best me."

I didn't doubt it; I'd seem him fight. "But what if—"

Again, his hand rose, and this time he didn't stop himself. He touched my shoulder, then slid his hand down my arm to give my fingers a squeeze. "I shall return soon." He strode toward the doorway.

I watched him leave, then turned to face Weni and nearly jumped out of my shift. He was standing right there, barely a foot away. Apparently I'd been too distracted by watching Heru's backside to hear Weni approach.

He still wore his friendly expression, but as I looked into his brown eyes, something darker coalesced, seething just under the surface.

Only one being had eyes like that.

I started backing away and opened my mouth, but faster than was humanly possible, Weni struck, wrapping one long-fingered hand around my neck.

16

GRAB & SMASH

My attempted scream died out in a strangled gurgle.

"Quiet now, chosen of Re," Weni said in the original tongue. Or rather, Apep said in the original tongue. He tilted his head from side to side, stretching his neck. It was as though Apep was trying to make himself fit more comfortably in Weni's skin. "I am going to release you. If you scream, those human guards will come in here and I will kill them, and then I will kill you. If you are quiet, I will let them live. Do you understand?"

I made a choking noise, which was as much as I could manage with him cutting off my air supply.

"I will take that as assent." Apep-Weni loosened his hold enough that I could breath, but he didn't let me go. He walked me backward until my back was pressed against a rough wall. The uneven bricks jabbed into me, but that was the least of my problems.

"You said you would release me." My voice was little more than a hoarse whisper.

"So I did." He removed his hand from my throat with a flourish and rested his palms on the wall on either side of my head. When he leaned in, my whole body stiffened, and when he ran his nose down one side of my neck and up the other, I squeezed my eyes shut and held my breath. Not crying out for help was one of the hardest things I'd ever done.

"The mighty prince did not lie," Apep-Weni said. He pulled away just enough that I could see his eyes. They were entirely black now, the inky darkness that signified Apep's presence sliding around the surface of his irises like oil on water. "I thought surely he had sampled what the new Netjer-At queen has to offer, but it would seem you are as yet untouched . . . both by the prince *and* the king."

My heart was racing, and I attempted to take regular, even breaths to slow it, but it only beat faster. "What—what do you want?"

He leaned in slowly, and I turned my face away as much as possible. Stopping just short of my cheek, he inhaled deeply. "What do you think I want?"

Nuin's sheut . . . your *sheut* . . . "I—I do not know," I said, watching him out of the corner of my eye.

"Much as I might enjoy taking your body, we do not have time for that." Flashing a smile that held no warmth, he pushed off the wall and turned away from me. "Weni is very upset in here." He tapped the side of his head. "You should hear him screaming away. He thinks Heru will kill him."

"Why would Heru kill him?"

"For what he is about to do," Apep-Weni said, still wearing that grin. It was a grin of warning, a grin of pure malevolence.

I swallowed, my saliva feeling too viscous. "Why—why would you want Heru to—to kill Weni?"

Apep-Weni scanned me from head to toe, slowly. "I do not care either way, but it will happen nonetheless. A mere by-product of what I am going to do to you . . . to send a message. He will have no choice."

I blinked rapidly, forcing back tears and wishing my

borrowed powers hadn't been locked away. If I'd been able to shift spatially, then I would have been able to save my own damn self, except . . . then Apep would know that either his or Nuin's sheut was in me, and he would tear it out.

"There is no need to do anything to me. I—I will pass on whatever message you wish. Please . . ."

"Ah . . . but I feel the message will be much clearer with your heart torn out of your body."

I gulped.

He took a step toward me. Another. I glanced at the doorway open to the busy street, then at the doorway leading deeper into the home. "Nowhere to run, lovely Netjer-At queen." He was only a step away.

Holding my breath, I reached for his shoulders and kneed him in the groin as hard as I could. Had Apep been possessing a Netjer-At body, he probably could have evaded the strike, but Weni was a regular human.

Apep-Weni hunched over, and I took the opening to bolt for the exit. I only made it two steps.

He snagged my ankle, tripping me. I skidded to the floor, my palms and knee taking the brunt of the impact. I kicked backward to break his hold on my ankle, but his grip was solid. He yanked me closer. The skirt of my dress caught on the edges of the mud-bricks, twisting around me and hiking up my legs while Apep-Weni flipped me over onto my back and pulled me closer still.

"Nuin took what is rightfully mine," he said, trying to hold my legs down as I kicked at him. "Until he gives it back, I will continue to take what is his. I will destroy every single thing he holds dear, starting with you."

"Heru!" I screamed. "Heru!"

Apep-Weni's face contorted with rage. "You stupid whore!" He snagged my ankle again, this time with both hands.

I kicked my other foot, aiming for his face, but he moved

aside and caught my leg under his arm. He twisted my ankle sharply, and my bones responded with a sickening crunch. A bright wash of agony surged up my leg, making me instantly nauseated and filling my vision with stars.

"Heru!" I cried out again.

And then the guards were there, trying to pull Apep-Weni away from me. But he maintained his hold on my ankle, and a second wave of agony washed through me, eclipsing the first. My succeeding cry sounded barely human.

"Alexandra?" It was Heru. "What—"

He came into view in a blur, grabbing Apep-Weni's wrist and twisting it in a way that jarred my ankle again before forcing him to release his hold on me. Snarling something at the guards, Heru wrapped a hand around Apep-Weni's neck and lifted him, slamming him against the nearest wall.

The guards rushed out of the building so quickly that I wondered whether Heru had threatened them or sent them for help.

I squeezed my eyes shut, fighting off waves of nausea. "Heru," I rasped, "You have to stop." But when I opened my eyes, the scene was the same; he was still holding Apep-Weni in a death grip. It wouldn't be long until Weni's body ran out of air. "Let him go, Heru! You cannot kill him! He had no control over what he was doing."

I might as well have been talking to a statue.

"You do not understand, Heru . . . it was not Weni! He was possessed!"

Heru flinched, but he still didn't let up, like he couldn't hear me through his rage. He was about to kill his friend; Weni was about to die for something he hadn't even done, not really. I couldn't let that happen.

I scooted closer and, leaning on my hip, sat up as much as I could. I raised my hand, trailing my nails down the skin on the side of Heru's torso. I knew how much Marcus loved that, so I was betting on his earlier counterpart being equally receptive to a gentle touch on that sensitive flesh.

He raised his free arm, and I thought he might actually strike me.

"Heru," I said softly.

He froze mid-swing and looked down, his eyes wide with horror at what he'd almost done.

"You have to let—" My words caught in my throat as an inky mist darker than pitch started seeping out of Weni's mouth, nose, and ears. It was Apep, leaving Weni's body.

Heru released him, immediately crouching down to scoop me up with an arm under my knees and one behind my shoulders. By the time his friend sank to the floor, slumping over onto his shoulder, we were on the opposite side of the room. And darkness still poured out of Weni.

"What is that?" Heru asked, his voice harsh.

I wrapped my arms around his neck and pulled his head lower so his ear was near my lips. "It can still hear us," I whispered. "I will tell you once we return to the villa."

I heard a cough, and loosened my hold on Heru's neck so we could both watch Weni. The darkness was fading as it oozed out one of the open-air windows set high in the wall, and Weni was leaning on his forearms, hacking up nothing but air. He glanced at us and reached out a hand for the briefest moment, then continued dry heaving on the floor.

"It was not *Weni* who hurt me. He was not in control," I told Heru. "We need to get him a healer."

"Your ankle is broken," he said, ignoring my demand. "We need to get you back to the villa so it can be set before it heals incorrectly and must be re-broken."

I cringed, hoping that wouldn't be the case, but considering the residual kick Nuin's powers had given to my regenerative abilities, if we waited even ten or fifteen minutes, it would start to heal. I wasn't a big fan of the re-breaking of any part of my body.

"Do you know how to do it?" I asked him.

"I do, but there are others who are far more skilled, so—"

I looked into the golden and black depths of his eyes, working up my courage. "You have to do it . . . right now."

Heru started shaking his head. "I do not think—"

I cut him off, "I regenerate faster than most."

Still holding me close against his torso, Heru studied me. Finally, he said, "Nuin is the father of our kind. Are you the mother?"

"I . . . I am unsure of your meaning."

"Are you as ancient as Nuin? Are you one of the first of our kind?"

I scowled. "Do I look as ancient as him?" I said, knowing full well the ridiculousness of the retort—to most, Nuin and Heru would appear to be identical twins in the prime of their lives, early thirties at the oldest, regardless of the fact that Nuin was far, *far* older—but pain was clouding the part of my mind that thought logically. "Do not answer that," I said with a sigh. "I am young . . . in fact, *you* are ancient compared to me."

His eyes widened, then narrowed. "And yet, you heal more quickly than those who are far older?"

I gritted my teeth and squeezed my eyes shut. "Yes, consider it another one of those secrets you are so desperate to learn." I opened my eyes and focused on his. "And if you continue to delay setting my ankle, it *will* have to be re-broken, and then I will hate you forever."

For some reason, that earned me a half-smile. "I doubt you would hate me forever."

I responded with raised eyebrows and a pointed stare.

"Or perhaps you will . . ." He took a deep breath, then exhaled heavily and did something that both shocked and delighted me: he pressed his lips to my forehead in the tenderest of kisses. "I apologize for the pain I am about to inflict," he whispered.

"I forgive you," I breathed. My pulse had reverted to a pace nearly as quick and erratic as it had been when I'd been grappling with Apep. I knew Heru could hear the change and hoped he attributed it to fear.

Gently, Heru set me on the floor and knelt at my feet. He tore a wide strip from the bottom of my dress, twisted it into a short strip of makeshift rope, and handed it to me. "You will want to bite down on this."

"Tell me when you are going to do it," I said before placing the rolled-up linen in my mouth.

Holding my gaze, Heru tugged on part of my foot.

The pain was mind-shattering; it became my whole world. I screamed.

And then I passed out.

17

ONE & ONLY

The dazzling rainbow of colors swarmed around me, a chaos of reds, blues, greens, golds, and everything in between. The At was so brilliant, so much brighter than it was in my time period, and I couldn't help but wonder why—because the Nothingness had dimmed it in my time? Something else?

Everything—the At, my ba, the nonexistent ground beneath my nonexistent feet—lurched, and the colors wavered, shimmered like I was viewing them through water, and faded to the less intense colors I was more familiar with. Apparently Nuin's block didn't work on my ba when it was outside of my body, because I was fairly certain I'd just jumped through time. Or rather, like being yanked by a bungee cord, my ba had returned to its own time . . . Marcus's time. It didn't matter, not at the moment. There was no way I was about to waste this opportunity.

Whether it was because I was a product of two of the most powerful Nejeret lines, or because I'd grown up with a sliver of Nuin's sheut tucked safely inside me, I was capable of doing pretty much anything any other Nejeret or Nejerette could do. And this included "tracking," the ability to hunt down the ba of any other Nejeret. If Marcus was in the At, I could find him . . . if *he was in the At.*

I closed my eyes and thought of him and only him. Marcus . . .

. . . Marcus . . .

. . . Marcus . . .

. . . Marcus . . .

"Is this real?"

My eyelids snapped open.

Marcus, wearing his usual, immaculate charcoal slacks and white button-down shirt, looking so beautiful and perfect and exactly what I needed to see at that moment, was standing right in front of me, surrounded by the dulled colors of the At. His eyes were round, his lips parted, his unbreakable composure shattered.

Hesitantly he raised his hand, almost like he thought trying to touch me would break the illusion. "Dom told me—but I didn't believe him. Are you really here?"

"Yes . . ." I lunged forward, throwing myself at Marcus.

His arms wrapped around me, so warm and strong, so comforting . . . so right. I inhaled his spicy scent and lifted my face to his, not willing to waste any time on teasing kisses.

Apparently, Marcus was of the same mind, because he crushed his lips against mine, devouring me with a kiss filled with need and desperation. A kiss that I thought, just maybe, could pull me all the way back to him, utterly and completely.

Breaking the kiss, I gasped for air and looked into his eyes, drowning in those golden pools filled with so much warmth and love. "How long?"

Marcus rested his forehead against mine, breathing just as hard as I was.

I fisted my hands in the back of his shirt. "How long have I been gone, Marcus?"

He closed his eyes. "A little over a day."

Which fit with how long I'd been in ancient Egypt, confirming Nuin's claim that my body, my ba, would remain anchored to its native timeline. "Did Aset—"

The At started shimmering.

"No . . ." I didn't want to go back. I wanted to stay with Marcus, to remain in this placeless portion of the At forever.

Marcus's fingers clenched on either side of my head, and once again, he brought his mouth down to mine.

The At lurched, and he vanished.

His voice drifted through the momentary fissure of time, a distant echo trailing after me. ". . . love you, Little Ivanov . . . always . . ."

I came back to consciousness lying on something as hard as stone, my head resting on something warmer and softer. A lap, I realized. A single, shallow breath identified the owner of the lap: Marcus. Ever so softly, he was brushing his fingers through my hair. Contentment filled me, and I smiled.

I opened my eyes and drank in the sight of him as I raised my hand. I skimmed my fingertips over the barely-there stubble shadowing his jawline, then over the velvety softness of his lips. "Do you have any idea how much I love you?"

Desire darkened his eyes, but he pulled my hand away from his face. "You know I do not speak your language," he said in Nuin's tongue.

"What?" I asked, automatically switching to the same language.

"You are confused." He smiled faintly, and there was sadness in the expression. "I think you have mistaken me for your husband."

I blinked several times.

"I am Heru, not Nuin."

"Nuin," I repeated, and like a dam had been broken in my mind, my wits rushed back to me. "Nuin . . . is my husband."

"He is," Heru agreed, still caressing my hair. "Though I cannot say I lack envy for his position." Before I could formulate a response, he said, "You were right, you do heal more quickly than most. After you lost consciousness, I had to re-break several areas multiple times to set your bones in the correct alignment." A shadow of a smile crossed his face. "I am just grateful that you did not actually feel most of it."

"How long was I out?"

"Less than a quarter of an hour. The swelling has gone down some. Soon, it should be stable enough that I can carry you back to the villa without risking unsetting anything." He placed his palms on the floor on either side of him, and his arm muscles bulged as he tensed to move out from under me.

Before I realized what I was doing, my fingers wrapped around his nearest wrist. I glanced at the place where I was holding onto him, then up at his face. "Please. Stay."

There was a moment of indecision before he relaxed back against the wall.

"Thank you." I wished he would continue stroking my hair, but I was pretty sure requesting as much would put an end to this stolen moment. "How is Weni?" I turned to look across the room. The dockmaster was still passed out on the floor near the opposite wall, unconscious but, thankfully, not dead. "Oh."

"Can you tell me what happened now?" Heru asked, drawing my attention back up to him. "What was that—that *smoke*?"

"Look at me," I said.

Heru muttered something in the common tongue, then sighed and gazed down at me. There was no oily darkness, only the usual black-banded gold. A Nejerette could get lost in those eyes. Heru cleared his throat.

"You can tell when the spirit is possessing someone by looking into their eyes. The darkness swims around just below the surface."

Heru's brow furrowed, but he remained silent.

I lowered my voice. "The spirit is called 'Apep,' and—"

Heru's eyebrows rose. "Apep?"

"Shhh!" I hissed, placing my hand over his mouth. I could feel his lips curve into a smile, and laughter danced in his eyes. "Stop it, Heru. This is serious!"

The teasing light in his eyes faded. "I know," he said against my hand.

I pulled it away from his mouth.

"Again, apologies. Forgive me?"

I crossed my arms over my chest and scrunched up my face, pretending to think really, *really* hard.

"Oh," he laughed. "Who is not taking the matter seriously *now?*"

Lips pressed together, I smiled up at him. I held his gaze for several seconds before sighing. "Apep is the disembodied spirit of a being of equal power to Nuin—"

"And to you," Heru said, his expression intent.

"I—yes, and of equal power to me." I took several breaths to collect my thoughts as I decided how to proceed. "Apep is capable of possessing the physical form of a human or Netjer-At . . . or any being, for all I know."

"Why did he not possess you?" Heru asked. "Would it not make sense for him to seek out the most powerful host?"

"It would," I said slowly. "But the full extent of my power is somewhat, er, hidden. He did not know."

"But still, you are Netjer-At, where Weni is merely human." Heru frowned. "For that matter, Apep did not try to possess *me,* either, and either of us would seem to be a more desirable host . . ."

I mirrored Heru's frown and shook my head. "He had other plans for me, but why he did not attempt to possess *you* . . . that I do not know." I made a mental note to ask Nuin about it once we returned to the villa.

"Why does he do it—possess people?"

I was quiet for a moment. "Nuin has something that once belonged to him, but Apep abused it, so he lost the privilege to retain it. Now he wanders around from body to body, seeking out a way to make it his again."

"Is that what he was doing here—trying to make you his again?"

My eyebrows rose. *"Me?"*

"It is you, is it not, this 'thing' Apep is after?"

"No. Apep is after his sheut." As soon as the words left my mouth, I scowled. "I should not have told you that. You must un-hear it."

That earned me another tantalizing half-smile. "So why did he come after you?"

I looked away, unable to meet Heru's intense eyes while I told him. "He said I was a message. He said, 'Nuin took what is rightfully mine. Until he gives it back, I will continue to take what is his.'" When I returned my gaze to Heru's, his jaw was clenched and there was death in his eyes.

"Did he"—he swallowed roughly—"*violate* you?"

I shook my head, and a tear escaped as I replayed the horrifying minutes in my mind. "He told me he would kill the guards and then kill me if I screamed, so I kept quiet until I knew for sure what he was going to do. He told me he was going to—" I took a deep breath. "He was going to tear my heart out of my chest. So I fought, and when that proved futile, I called out to you." I cleared my throat, remembering the all-encompassing fear, closely followed by the nauseating pain. "That was when he broke my ankle."

"So much courage," Heru murmured.

Not enough courage, I thought as I stared up at him. Electricity seemed to arc between our gazes.

A groan came from the opposite side of the room, breaking the mounting tension.

"See," Heru said, clearing his throat. "He did not require a healer after all."

"Why did you not send somebody for one once I was unconscious? He could have died!"

"Weni? No . . . he is too stubborn to go like that."

Weni grumbled something, and Heru laughed, but when Weni's words gained more coherency, Heru's expression sobered. He spoke to his friend, concern evident in his eyes.

"Is he okay?" I asked.

"He is apologizing . . . and ordering me to beg you for your forgiveness . . . praising your unmatched beauty—"

I rolled my eyes.

"—and professing his eternal loyalty." Heru frowned for a moment and said something to Weni in a harsh tone.

"Stop being mean," I told Heru.

He returned his attention to me, his eyebrows raised. "I thought you did not understand the common language."

"And I do not, but even *I* can tell you are being a butthead."

For a moment, Heru said nothing. Then he was laughing, full and booming. "A 'butthead'? That may be the most ridiculous thing I have ever heard. Ever."

"Well, some things translate better than others," I muttered.

"So it would seem."

"I do not blame you," Nuin told Heru.

Heru continued pacing back and forth across Nuin's sitting room, exactly as he'd been doing ever since he and I returned at dusk. I was settled in the chair opposite Nuin at the senet table, petting Rus, who was sound asleep on my lap, and watching Heru like he was a one-man tennis match.

Heru looked at me, then shot a scathing glare at Nuin. "Who you blame is up to you. As is who *I* blame. Do you have any idea what almost happened to her?"

"I take it that you blame me?" Nuin said.

"How could I not?" Heru snapped. "You should have told me of this enemy. Had I known the potential danger that stalked her, I never would have left her side!"

"And how would you suggest I protect her in the future?"

Heru said nothing, just continued pacing.

"Would you stay by her side at all times, if it meant she would be safe?"

"I would," Heru said without hesitation.

Nuin nodded. "Done."

Finally, Heru's pacing faltered, and he faced us. "I do not understand."

"You will stay by her side."

Heru shook his head. "I thought you were asking what I would do if I were *you*. I did not mean—" Heru looked at me, and whatever he saw on my face—possibly the hurt in my eyes, or maybe the defiance at his rejection—stopped him from finishing what he'd been about to say. He stared at me for a long moment, then bowed his head. "I would gladly accept this duty."

"Very well," Nuin said with a note of finality. "You will be Alexandra's Blade, both her companion and her protector, at all times unless I am with her and give you leave. You will teach her to defend herself, and if she still desires it, to speak the common tongue. You will be responsible not only for her safety, but for ensuring that all her needs are tended to."

I nearly choked at the double meaning behind Nuin's words. There were a few needs Heru most certainly couldn't tend to, not without signing his own death warrant. Bonding between us wouldn't happen; it *couldn't* happen.

"You can have tonight to take care of those matters that will be neglected during your time with Alexandra." In other words, I thought, Heru had tonight to put a stopper in his relationship with Ankhesenpepi.

"Understood," Heru said, then turned his attention to me. "I will return at the sun's rebirth." He bowed his head to me and to Nuin, and left the room.

I watched him stride away, then shifted my focus to Nuin. I

studied his face, a niggling feeling worming its way into conscious thought. It wasn't a good feeling.

I narrowed my eyes. "You knew," I said in English.

Nuin blinked and returned my stare, his expression completely blank. "I'm not quite sure I know what you're talking about, dear Alexandra."

"You *knew* Apep would come after me . . . or at least, you suspected." I leaned forward, pressing my palms onto the tabletop. "That's why you sent us out of the villa in the first place; shopping was just the most convenient excuse. You *wanted* Apep to find me. You *wanted* him to attack me so you would have a carrot to dangle in front of Heru to get him to fall in line."

Nuin smiled serenely. "Perhaps. And my plan worked quite well, did it not?"

I'd let myself be lulled by Nuin's sometimes playful demeanor into thinking he was like me, like the rest of the Nejerets, that there was something of humanity left in him. But I'd been a fool. The other Nejerets had all *been* human at one point. Based on everything I'd learned about Apep and Re-Nuin, I was starting to doubt whether Nuin had ever lived as anything other than what he was—a god.

"Apep could have possessed me, Nuin . . ."

He nodded. "He could have, but there was never any danger that he *would* have."

"You don't *know* that."

His grin would've given the Cheshire Cat a run for his money. "But I do. Apep is able to move in and out of any human he wishes to possess at a whim, but he would not risk possessing a Nejeret." I opened my mouth, but Nuin raised a hand, cutting me off before I could even *start* to protest. "He would not risk it because if he possessed a Nejeret, he would be stuck in that single body until it perished. And that Nejeret could fight against Apep's ability to control his borrowed body for a very long time indeed. If he possessed you, you could fight him for years, centuries even, and he would be trapped within you, unable to leave. Eventually he would take over, but it would not be immediate, not unless you *let* him control you."

"Why didn't you tell me any of this before?"

Nuin shrugged. "It never came up."

"Bullshit."

He smiled.

"But what about—Apep was able to leave Set's body to possess Marcus." I raised my eyebrows. "So clearly he *can* leave a Nejeret's body . . ."

"Ah . . . but that is a special case. Apep's sheut, something he is linked to even if it is no longer fused with the rest of his being, forms something of a bridge between Heru and Set in your time. Apep may use that bridge to move between them, but only sparingly, as possessing Heru's less familiar body would be quite draining on Apep's energy reserves."

After seconds of staring at Nuin and mulling over his words, I exhaled heavily. As usual, he'd made the right choice; his plan had worked. It had hurt like hell, but in the long run, it had worked. "You know . . . I love you, Nuin, I really do, but you sure can be a sneaky bastard." Sitting back in my chair, I crossed my arms.

"Flattery will get you everywhere, dear Alexandra."

"It wasn't a compliment."

He shrugged. "Are you ready to begin?"

I cocked my head to the side. "Begin?"

Nuin produced the tiny bottle I'd created from the fabric of the At and handed it across the table to me. "Extracting your bonding essence. Your time with Heru has strengthened you, and now you're ready to learn how to save his life."

PART III

Cairo, Egypt
Present Day

18

KAT & JENNY

Dear Lex,

It's Kat, BTW. You've been gone for hours, and Marcus is seriously starting to lose it . . . just so you know. He DESTROYED your suite. Like, complete and utter destruction. If that's what "true" love looks like, I'm definitely not ready for ANYTHING close to that.

But anyway, Dom said he saw you in the At, and he thought you were trying to tell him that you're in another time. I'm writing this to you on the chance that you time-jumped into the future. If you're reading this, please, just come back. Neffe's been monitoring Marcus, and she said his withdrawals have already started. She and Dom were talking super quietly, but I think they forgot that my Nejerette traits are starting to kick in and, you know, that I could hear a little better. Anyway, I overheard them saying that they didn't think he'd last more than a week without you. Which means YOU won't last a week without HIM.

You HAVE to come back. We're all so worried about you. Please, just come back.

Your half-sis,
Kat

"Kat!" Jenny called from the bathroom. "Do you want me to leave the straightener on?"

Jenny wasn't *really* my sister, but she was sort of like my sister, since she was Lex's half-sister, and Lex was *my* half-sister . . . whatever. It didn't matter. All that mattered was that Jenny was as freaked out about Lex's disappearance as I was, and in my book—which is *the* book—that made us family.

Abandoning my notebook and pen, I rolled off the ginormous bed and headed toward the bathroom door. "Nope. Not like it'll do any good in this heat." The straightening iron hadn't tamed my dark, frizzy curls in Florence, and I doubted it would do any better in Cairo.

Jenny and I had been sharing a room since the *Set incident*, as we've been calling what happened in the underground temple. I'd tried staying with my mom, at first, but she was still pissed at me about risking my life—eye roll—for Lex, so I'd asked Jenny if I could stay with her for a while. *It* is *weird that Mom didn't even argue, though . . .*

I leaned my shoulder against the doorframe and watched Jenny stare at herself in the mirror, her mouth open as she put on mascara. "Are you sure that's such a good idea?" I asked. We'd both been a blink away from crying like two-year-olds since Dom told us about Lex's disappearance.

Jenny offered me a watery smile in the mirror. "It's a deterrent; if I know my mascara'll smear, I won't cry." She crossed her fingers. "I'm hoping."

I looked at my naked wrist. "J, it's, like, four in the morning, and we're all gonna look like crap from being up all night anyway. Why even try . . . ?"

Jenny lowered her mascara wand and sighed. "Grandma Suse—that's Alexander's wife—she always says that the best way to get through the worst times is to do normal things: go to work, clean, get ready . . ." Jenny shrugged and looked away, but I could see her chin trembling in the mirror. She cleared her throat. "So that's what I'm doing," she said as she returned her attention to her reflection and raised the mascara wand to her other eye. "Normal things."

Pushing off the doorframe, I stepped into the bathroom to stand beside her. I reached for the straightening iron and moved it closer to me before finger-combing through my long, frizzy curls and picking out a section to start with. I raised the straightener to my hair. Normal things.

My eyes flicked down to the reflection of Jenny's belly; she was just starting to show under her sweater. "Is that how you've been dealing with . . . you know . . ."

With another sigh, Jenny jabbed the mascara wand into the tube and turned to face me, resting her hip on the edge of the pale granite counter. "At first, yeah. But not anymore." Looking down, she touched her barely-there baby bump. "It's not the baby's fault, and I'm going to love him or her no matter how psychotic their dad is . . . because you and Lex and Dom . . . you're all Seth's—Set's—kids too, and there's nothing wrong with you guys."

I looked at my reflection in the mirror and ran the hot iron down the length of my hair. Every day, I saw more and more of my dad in my face, like his sharp features were taking over—or maybe it was just an illusion caused by my paling skin. *So* annoying. I'd worked *really* hard to build up a tan this summer, and now my Nejerette regenerative abilities were wiping it away like it had never existed. I glared at my reflection. *I hate you, Set.*

And I couldn't help but wonder if maybe Jenny was wrong. What if Set's evilness would somehow spill over into their kid? What if it had spilled over into *me*? "Did you ever consider, um, not, um, you know . . . *having* the baby?" I asked her.

Jenny laughed softly. "You can say *abortion*, I won't freak out." She touched my shoulder and headed out of the bathroom. "But no, I didn't. I guess it's just not something I could bring myself to do." I could hear her rummaging around in the wardrobe. "Lex would, I think. She never really wanted kids anyway. She's always had a one-track mind, and up until she met Marcus, that single track was all about Egypt. Which could be *so* annoying, let me tell you." She was quiet for a moment, and there was the sound of more rummaging. "Ah . . . there they are. But maybe, now that Marcus is in her life, she'll change her mind about starting a family . . ."

She doesn't know . . .

"She can't," I said softly.

Jenny appeared in the doorway, slipping on some sky-blue ballet flats. "What was that?"

I swallowed and met her eyes in the mirror. "Lex can't have kids."

"Why? Because of her position as the 'Meswett' or whatever?"

I shook my head and refocused on my own reflection, moving on to a new section of hair. "Nejerettes can't have kids once they manifest. It's impossible."

Jenny's eyes went wide, and she brought her hand up to her mouth. "Oh, I—I didn't know." She frowned and looked down at the floor. "I'm sorry, that's—that must be so *awful*. I can't imagine . . ."

I shrugged. "I've known for pretty much *ever*, so it's no biggie for me. It's normal, just the way it is, you know? But for someone like Lex, who wasn't raised knowing *what* she might be . . . yeah, finding it out would suck balls." I rolled my eyes and exhaled heavily. "I bet *that* was a fun convo for Alexander . . ."

Jenny continued to stare at the floor, but she brought her arms up to her belly and wrapped them around her middle. Her shoulders were shaking.

I set down the straightener and turned to her. "Hey . . . J . . ."

I rubbed my hands up and down her arms, crouching down a little so I could see her face. "It's cool, really. I'm fine with it."

Jenny shook her head. Dark smears of mascara bled from her lower lashes. "I'm just so scared for Lex . . . I mean, I just got her back, and now—" A hiccupping sob cut her words short, and her shoulders shook even harder. "Now . . . I don't know if . . . I'll ever see her . . . again . . ."

I wrapped my arms around Jenny and held her tightly while she cried, fighting tears of my own. Some people sympathy-vomit or sympathy-yawn, but I'd *always* been a horrible sympathy-crier. Of course, the fact that I was afraid of the same damn thing didn't help one damn bit. The tears broke free. Damn.

Someone started knocking on the suite door. Knocking and knocking and *knocking*.

Growling under my breath, I released Jenny and stomped to the door. "What?" I said as I yanked it open.

Dominic was standing in the hallway with his fist still raised. I studied him with scrutinizing eyes. For once his prim and proper shell seemed to be cracked. His normally slicked-back hair hung in dark ribbons around his face, his eyes were shadowed, and his shirt was untucked, the top few buttons undone.

"You look like crap," I told him, gaining at least a teensy bit of pleasure from seeing him so out of sorts. He was my usual instructor in how to use my new superpowers, and sometimes he could be such a . . .

"Neffe has need of you and Jenny in the lab," he said, rubbing his face with his knocking hand before lowering it down to his side. His accent was heavier, which meant he was really freaking exhausted.

"The lab? What lab?" I cocked my head to the side. "There's a *lab*?"

"It is underground, in sub-basement two."

I held up my hand. "Hold on a sec, here, buddy—this place has an *underground*?"

"What does she need?" Jenny asked from behind me.

I glanced over my shoulder to find that she'd wiped the dark smudges from under her red-rimmed eyes.

"She thinks she may have come up with a way to decrease the severity of Marcus's withdrawal symptoms, but she needs both of you in order to test her theory."

I huffed out a breath. "Geesh, Dom—why didn't you just say so in the first place?" I pushed past him through the doorway and headed down the hall toward the nearest set of stairs.

"I *did*."

"ARE THERE GOING TO BE NEEDLES INVOLVED?" I asked Neffe as I sat on a metal stool beside Jenny.

We were in "the lab" in "sub-basement two," having taken somewhat hidden elevators from the ground floor. Where the aboveground parts of the Council's Cairo palace were very antiquey and low-tech, the underground was about as ultra-modern and high-tech as I could imagine. Everything was stainless steel or polished white or pristine glass. And with the lack of windows, I felt like I was on some sort of futuristic spaceship.

When Neffe didn't respond, I added, "'Cause I'm not a big fan of needles . . ."

Neffe paused in prepping her microscope slide and met my eyes, looking bored. She took a deep breath, exhaling heavily, then returned her attention to her equipment.

"Okay . . . never mind. I didn't want an answer anyway," I muttered.

Neffe stilled, closing her eyes for a moment. "You are a

saint," she said, glancing at Dominic, who was standing opposite her at a high, stainless steel table.

Jenny coughed, and I was pretty sure she was masking a laugh.

I glared at each of them in turn.

Finally, Neffe gave Jenny and me her full attention. "Are you sweating?"

My eyebrows knitted together. "Uh . . . no. Why?" I looked at Jenny, who shook her head.

Neffe waved her hand at the open floor space in front of our stools. "Do some jumping jacks."

Jenny and I exchanged a look as we stood and moved a couple steps away from each other. Halfheartedly, I started hopping and flailing my arms, looking anywhere but at Dominic. I hated that he was watching me look so stupid.

"How long"—feet together—"do we have to"—feet apart—"do this?" I asked. Feet together . . . feet apart . . . feet together . . .

Neffe offered me a tight smile. "Until you sweat."

I bared my gritted teeth to her. "Great."

She looked at Dominic. "Will you please hunt down my father? I will need him to be present to test the effectiveness of the synthesized pheromone cocktail."

Standing, Dominic nodded. "I will send him right down." He started toward the door.

"Thank you, Dom," Neffe said. She glanced at me. "And please hurry."

Five minutes later, I was most definitely starting to sweat. I stopped doing jumping jacks and plopped down on my stool. Jenny did the same.

Neffe planted herself in front of us. "You are sweating?"

Jenny and I both nodded.

"Good. Take off your shirts."

We stared at her for a few seconds. "Uh . . ." Jenny said in chorus with my indignant, "*What?*"

Exhaling heavily through her nose, Neffe pressed her lips together. "I need access to the sweat on the skin of your underarms; it is the easiest way for me to gather a sample of the various pheromones given off by your bodies." She held up a long cotton swab and tilted her head to the side. "I'm trying to save my father's and your sister's lives, so your unhindered cooperation would be appreciated."

With another exchanged look, Jenny and I pulled our shirts over our heads. Luckily, Neffe had her samples and we were back to being fully clothed by the time Marcus pushed the lab door open. 'Cause him walking in when we were topless would have be *mortifying* . . .

"I still think this is a waste of time, Neffe," Marcus said as he strode over to Neffe's workspace and eased down onto a stool. He looked awful, or as awful as *he* could ever look.

I sighed and rethought what I'd written to Lex. True love, at least with someone who looked like him, might just be worth all the trouble . . .

We sat and watched Neffe work for what felt like hours. I tried to make small talk with Jenny, but she looked almost as haggard as Marcus, and I didn't feel far behind. Neffe was the only one of us who didn't seem to be wilting under the weight of exhaustion and dark emotions. No, Neffe was handling the situation in an entirely different way; she was focusing on a problem she *could* solve. Maybe.

The door opened, making all of us jump, but only Jenny, Neffe, and I actually looked at it; Marcus simply stared at the metal tabletop like he wasn't even there. Which, I realized, might actually have been the case—nothing was stopping him from spending his time searching the unstable At for Lex.

Dominic came into the lab ahead of a petite Nejerette with a dark bob, bronze skin, and pixie-like features. "Marcus, I'm sorry," Dominic said. "She demanded to see you right away." He stopped several paces away from Marcus, holding out his arm to block the woman from reaching him. "She claims to know you . . . and to know how to help you."

When Marcus still didn't turn around, Dominic glanced at Neffe, who frowned and shook her head. It looked like she didn't know the strange Nejerette either.

"Heru," the woman said. "Please . . ."

Marcus lifted his head and, ever so slowly, turned around on his stool. "Aset?"

19

FRIEND & FOE

Marcus stood and approached the Nejerette like he was moving through tar. When he reached her, he raised his hand and touched the side of her face. "You're real," he whispered. "Aset . . . how are you real? You died . . . I saw—"

"But you didn't see, did you, brother?" the woman—Aset—said with a hollow laugh. "Set blinded you, and you only *thought* I'd been killed. You *all* thought I'd been killed, because you had to think that."

"But—"

"You never saw my body, dear brother." She covered his hand with her own, leaning her cheek against his palm and closing her eyes. "Feel me, Heru, I am real." She opened her eyes and smiled up at him. "I'm real."

A choking sob escaped from Marcus, and he moved so quickly, raising his other hand and lowering his face to Aset's, that it took me several seconds to register what he was doing. He was *kissing* her. My eyes bulged. It was nothing crazy, and there was clearly no tongue or anything like that, but still . . . he was *kissing* someone who was definitely *not* Lex.

"Hey!" Jenny stood and took a few steps toward them, but

Neffe caught hold of her wrist before Jenny could get past her.

"Don't," Neffe hissed.

Jenny threw her free hand out toward Marcus and Aset in an almost violent gesture, just as the pair broke apart. "But—"

"She's his *sister* . . . his *twin* sister," she said. "It's nothing like what you're thinking."

There was only one thing that I was thinking—*Ewwwww* . . .

Aset took a step back from Marcus and looked past him, her eyes settling first on Jenny, then on me. "Don't worry. I have nothing but the utmost respect for your sister. I would never do anything to hurt her, and my love for Heru is purely that of a sister."

I remained on my stool, bug-eyed as I watched the scene before me.

"Lex . . . you know Lex?" Marcus said. "How? Do you know where she is?"

Aset nodded, her lips curving into a sad smile. "I do, dear brother. I know where she is . . . and *when*."

A collective, heavy exhale filled the room.

"So you were right," Marcus said to Dom, who only nodded and continued to stare at Marcus's no-longer-deceased sister.

"Yes, yes . . . he was right, Lex is safe, blah blah blah . . ." Aset shifted her canvas shoulder bag and started digging through it. A moment later, she pulled out a small, carved wooden box. She handed it to Marcus. "For you, from Lex."

"She gave this to you?" He accepted the tiny container, but hardly looked at it. "So you've seen her since I—since the incident last night?"

Aset smiled. "Who do you think drove the getaway car?"

My mouth fell open. *Heru's sister kidnapped Lex?* I stared at Dom and Marcus, not understanding why they weren't hauling her away to interrogate her.

"Long story short—"

"I want the long story," Marcus said.

Aset pursed her lips. "And I'll give you the long story once we're on our way."

"Where are we—"

She raised one hand in a sharp motion, cutting him off. "Lex is with Nuin—and with you and me—in Men-nefer, a month or two before Nuin's death . . . I don't remember how many days, exactly."

"She traveled back over *four millennia?*" When Aset nodded, Marcus shook his head. "That block of time has always been a bit of a fuzzy spot in my memory."

"And now you know why."

"Because Lex tapped into the power Nuin gave her and made me forget . . ."

"Actually, she made you remember a slightly altered version of events, but essentially, yes, she sealed your true memories away." Aset touched the side of the box. "She made this for you, so you would be able to survive while she's gone."

My eyes could have been tricking me—I mean, I hadn't blinked for at least two minutes, so it was entirely possible—but I thought I could see Marcus's hands tremble as he opened the box. He pulled out a tiny crystal bottle attached to a silver chain heavy enough to not look too girly on a guy, but not thick enough to look like a ridiculous "gangsta" chain. He held the bottle up in front of his face. "This isn't quartz, is it?"

Aset shook her head. "It is made of the At itself." She took it from his hands and lifted it, standing on tiptoes to raise it over his head. She settled the chain around his neck, tucking the tiny bottle into his shirt. "And *inside,* it is packed full of Lex's bonding pheromones. All you have to do is have it touching your skin, and you should be fine . . . for a while. But you must not open the bottle, or the pheromones will float away."

Marcus touched his fingertips to the little lump under his shirt.

"Better?" Aset asked, studying his face.

He nodded and took a full, deep breath. "Much. And . . . what about Lex?"

Her eyes most definitely twinkled. "Trust me when I say that Lex is doing *just* fine."

Marcus shook his head. "How—"

"You forget, dear brother"—she touched her fingertips to his chiseled cheek—"Lex has *you*."

Marcus said nothing for several seconds. "You mentioned going somewhere?" Already his voice sounded less tight, less strained, and he stood a little taller.

"Yes," Aset said, readjusting her shoulder bag. "We must leave for the Netjer-At Oasis immediately. Lex has left you something there that I think you'll be eager to see."

"She left me something . . . from the past?"

"Yes, and only once we've gone to the Oasis and explored what she left behind will she return." She nodded once. "This I know."

"Very well." Marcus strode toward the door, Dom and Aset close on his heels. "During the journey, you will tell me everything you know of what is going on with Lex," he said to Aset over his shoulder. He opened the door and held it for the other two to pass through the doorway.

"I will tell you what I can," Aset said as the door swung shut.

Stunned by pretty much everything that had just happened, I stared at the door.

Until Neffe clapped her hands repeatedly. "What are you just standing around for? Go make yourselves useful. We're leaving soon."

For once, I had no retort. I hopped off my stool and hurried to the door.

"Go!" Neffe repeated, and I heard Jenny rushing along behind me.

I stuffed my favorite pair of jeans into my duffel bag, which also happened to be the only pair of jeans I'd packed from Seattle—which, honestly, I thought was showing a *ton* of restraint—then pulled them back out and tossed them on the bed. Skinny jeans and the Sahara did *not* seem like an epic combination. But just as I was zipping up the bag, I stuffed them back in.

Dominic barged into the room. No knock. No apology. Just barging. "Why aren't you ready yet?"

"I could've been naked," I said, crossing my arms over my miniscule chest. "You really should've knocked."

He stood in the doorway and stared at me. "But you weren't."

"No, but I could've been. It's about respect, you know?" I quirked my mouth to the side.

He furrowed his brow, looking, of all things, confused. *Men . . .*

"You would've knocked for Lex."

"Lex would already have been packed and downstairs." Dom raised his eyebrows lazily. Who even *does* that? "I would not have had to retrieve her."

I rolled my eyes. "Well, in case you haven't noticed . . . I'm. Not. Lex."

"I have, but *I* am not the one who keeps comparing you to the Meswett."

I rolled my eyes again and hoisted my duffel bag onto my shoulder before reaching for the messenger bag containing my more personal items. "So what's this oasis place like anyway? Is it filled with springs and palm trees and camels that spit and—"

"You've watched too many movies."

I approached the doorway and the new-door-formerly-known-as-Dominic, stopping in front of him to show him my "ha ha, you're so funny" face. "I'm eighteen—which means I'm still a *teen*ager, note the *teen*. That means watching movies is practically part of my job. It's like school."

Dom stared down at me, those dark eyes seeming to dig into my soul and to weigh its worth. He didn't look impressed. "You received your diploma; you no longer attend school."

Only because Marcus's people had arranged it right before we left Seattle. "Whatever. Move?"

He didn't.

I batted my eyelashes at him and smiled sweetly. "Please . . ."

Dom sighed and stepped out of my way.

I paused in the hallway to wait for him as he shut the door. *Such a gentleman, my big, stuffier-than-an-antique-shop brother.* "You never answered my question. What's this 'Netjer-At Oasis' like? And how come I've never heard of it, if it's, like, a *thing*?"

Dom smoothed his hair back and started walking toward the stairs, and I fell in step beside him. "We don't speak of it," he said.

"Why not?"

"Because the Oasis is where the Great Father's body lies."

I stopped dead in my tracks in the middle of the hallway. "Wait, *what*? We know where Nuin's body is and it's not a sacred place? How is this Oasis not our Mecca?"

"A great disaster befell it thousands of years ago, immediately after Nuin's death, and the desert reclaimed it. And since then, it has not been spoken of except amongst the closest of friends. It is somewhat of a taboo topic." He continued on down the hall, and I had to speed-walk to keep up.

"But, *why*? Why all the mystery and secrecy and stuff? Why don't we ever talk about it or what happened there?"

Dom shrugged. "It is simply our way. It is tradition. You should respect it."

I could almost hear him silently saying, *You should respect* me.

I rolled my eyes. Again.

DOZENS OF US STOOD IN THE CAIRO PALACE'S MARBLE and gold grand entryway, all of our attention on Marcus and Aset, who were posted before the doors. Marcus was making his final announcements and doing a half-assed job at taking roll call.

"We're leaving in fifteen minutes," Marcus said. "If you see that someone is missing, find them before we leave. We're going with or without them." Clearly, solving the problem of his withdrawal symptoms hadn't improved his mood much.

I glanced around the cavernous space, scanning the backs of heads and faces of each person. I reached for Dom's sleeve and gave it a tug. When he shot me a sideways glance, I said, "My mom's not here. I've got to go get her . . ."

Pressing his lips together, Dom shrugged.

I dropped my bags on the polished marble stairs and turned to run back up, but a hand latched around my elbow before I'd made it up two steps. I turned. "Dom, wha—"

"Hurry," he said, his dark eyes intense. Sometimes, he looked so much like Set, it was creepy.

"Um . . ." I nodded, and when he released me, I raced up the stairs that much faster. I ran down the hall past the room I was sharing with Jenny, skidded around a corner, heading for my mom's room, and lunged forward the last few steps, falling to my knees. Because there, on the floor in front of her door, was Jenny, blood seeping through the crotch of her khaki pants.

I didn't even hesitate. "DOM!"

20

DEATH & THREAT

"DOM!"

He rounded the corner at a near sprint and seemed to assess the situation in a matter of seconds. "Neffe," he called over his shoulder. "We need you. It's Jenny. Something has happened."

I reached for Jenny's hand, squeezing it, but not too hard because it was limp and felt so fragile, and I didn't want to break her. And there was so much blood . . .

Neffe glided around the corner, Aset and Marcus close on her heels. "What is it?" she said, but she didn't wait for an answer. She shouldered Dom out of the way as she crouched on the other side of Jenny, reaching for her wrist. "Her pulse is weak." She focused on the blood seeping through Jenny's pants, staining the fabric crimson, then shifted her focus to me. "You've been spending a lot of time with her. Has she complained of any discomfort? Cramping? Bleeding?"

"I—I—" Swallowing and unable to tear my eyes away from the blood, I nodded. "My mom . . . she—she . . ."

Neffe reached across Jenny's body and closed her hand

around my wrist, her nails digging into my skin. "Your mother *what?*"

Eyes wide, I shook my head. *So much blood . . .*

It was only hours ago that Jenny had been talking about the baby, about how she was going to love it no matter what . . . and now . . . now . . . what if she was losing it?

"Kat!"

I blinked but couldn't look away.

Dom knelt beside me. "Let go, Neffe." As Neffe released my wrist, Dom captured my hand. "Look at me, Kat." His voice was gentle. "Look at me."

I did, and it was like I'd been underwater but had just broken through the surface and could breathe. I stared into his dark eyes, thinking they weren't nearly as cold and boring as I'd thought. They were guarded. They held secrets. They were filled with emotion—turmoil, desperation, anger—not devoid of it like I'd pretended.

"You mentioned your mother, Kat. Why?"

I rubbed my thumb over the back of Jenny's hand. "Jenny—she started feeling nauseous . . . like all the time. I told her she should tell Neffe, but my mom stopped by our room before she could and started asking Jenny about her pregnancy and how she was feeling." I frowned. "I remember thinking it was weird that she was being so chatty with Jenny, because she hadn't said much to me since I switched rooms . . ."

"And what happened next?" Dom's voice was coaxing, his accent soothing rather than irritating, like I used to think.

"And my mom told her she'd felt the same when she was pregnant with me, and then said that nothing the doctors gave her had helped, but that Marcus showed her how to make an ancient Nejeret medicine . . . that it was the only thing that helped her. She told Jenny that the nausea was only the beginning, and that cramping would soon follow, but that if Jenny took the medicine my mom made for her, she'd avoid the worst of it."

"I never showed Gen how to make anything like that," Marcus said, a razor-sharp edge to his voice.

"How long has she been taking this 'medicine'?" Aset asked.

I looked at her. "Um . . . since we got to Cairo." I shrugged. "So, like, four or five days." I started shaking my head. "But my mom would never—"

"The concoction could have been tainted with a bacteria," Aset said. "Maybe E. coli or listeria . . . the girl likely would have assigned any symptoms caused by the infection to her pregnancy."

"You have medical training," Neffe said. It wasn't a question.

"I do." Aset glanced at Marcus. "I was the doctor who treated Lex last year, after . . ."

Marcus clenched his jaw so hard that I was surprised I didn't hear the sound of his teeth breaking. "Did you know what that piece of shit would do to her?"

Aset didn't even blink an eye at his seething tone. "I did."

"And you didn't try to stop it?"

And . . . I was starting to worry about Aset's safety as Marcus glared at her. If looks could kill, she would have died, like, eight thousand times in a few seconds.

Aset pursed her lips and raised her eyebrows. "Lex is the one who told me when and where I had to be so she and I would meet when she first woke in the hospital. *She* told me it had to happen that way."

"Um . . . guys . . ." I stared down at Jenny's washed-out face. "Shouldn't we be doing something to help Jenny and the baby . . . ?"

My words seemed to shake Marcus out of his outraged trance, and he started barking orders. "Neffe, do what you need to do for Jenny, and when you know more, let me know what kind of delay we're looking at."

Neffe bowed her head. "Yes, Father." She looked at Aset, who nodded and moved closer to her, and the two Nejerettes started speaking in hushed tones.

"Dom," Marcus said. "Arrange a team to search for Gen. *Find* her."

Dominic was up and running down the hall as soon as Marcus's order was voiced.

Marcus turned eyes that burned like the sun on me. "*You* don't leave my sight."

I gulped. It was all I could do to make myself nod.

"Gen's gone," Dom said as he strode into the sitting room next to the entryway, where Marcus, Aset, and I had been waiting, surrounded by Lex's full retinue of guards. In my opinion, it was less of a sitting room and more of a ballroom, with fancy things like "settees" and "chaise lounges."

Dominic stopped on the enormous, intricately patterned rug in front of the armchair where Marcus was sitting. "The security cameras caught her sneaking away last night, during the chaos after you—" He cleared his throat. "After Lex vanished. I have our people working on tracking her down."

Aset said something to Marcus in a language that sounded a little bit like the Nejeret language, but whatever they were speaking was different enough that I couldn't understand them. But I *could* understand their tones: snippy. *Just like a brother and sister should sound,* I thought.

"So she left to go do something." I shrugged nonchalantly, feeling anything but nonchalant. "I don't see why you guys are so hell-bent on finding her. I mean, it might all have been an accident . . . and Jenny and the baby are *fine,* Neffe said so. So she didn't *actually* hurt anyone . . ." It wasn't that I was an idiot —at least, not most of the time—but this was *my mom* they were hunting down. My *mom*. She wasn't the kind of person who would do something like poison a woman in an attempt to make her miscarry. She was the type of person who *helped* people, not hurt them.

Yeah, if you looked up *denial* in the dictionary . . .

"Only the guilty run," Dom said. "She ran."

"But . . ."

Marcus straightened in his chair, stretching his back. Leaning forward, he rested an elbow on his knee and rubbed his hand over his short hair. "That's not *always* true, Dom." He exhaled a heavy sigh. "Pull our people back in. We'll need all the trustworthy help we can get at the Oasis."

Dom bowed his head, then turned and walked toward the doorway.

"Wait." Marcus lifted his head to look at Dom. "I want Lex's parents and grandmother here before we leave."

"Are you intending for them to accompany us to the Oasis?" Dom asked.

"I am."

Dom's eyes narrowed the slightest amount. "You understand that by doing this, you'll likely have to reveal the truth about us to Alice and Joe."

Marcus nodded. "It was bound to happen eventually."

"Lex will not be pleased . . ."

"Lex isn't here," Marcus snapped, earning mutters from the guards stationed around the room and a "tsk" from his sister. "But she will be *more* displeased if she returns to find them dead." *That* shut everyone up. "They're coming with us. Work out the details with Alex—he's upstairs with Neffe in Jenny's room."

Again, Dom bowed his head and walked toward the doorway.

I licked my lips and switched from watching Dom to looking at Marcus. "If you ever do find my mom . . ." I hesitated. "What are you going to do to her?"

Marcus stared at me for a long time, his face tense. "Alex is demanding Nejeret justice, but . . ." He sighed. He'd been doing that a lot lately. "I've loved Gen like a sister for a long time." He shook his head. "I won't sanction her death until we know everything—her guilt, her motivations, her accomplices—and only if her overall intent was malicious."

. . . sanction her death . . .

I swallowed. Cleared my throat. Licked my lips. Swallowed again. There was a metallic taste in my mouth, and I wondered if I might vomit. "And . . . what about me?"

"You will swear an oath, just as Dom did centuries ago—just as all of Set's children must do—and be adopted into my line. It would have been required of you upon full manifestation anyway."

"And if I don't?" My voice was tiny, too high.

His eyes burned into me. "You already know the answer to that question."

He was right, and I nodded. All of Set's children were given a choice: swear an oath to obey Marcus absolutely and completely —and Nejerets took oaths *very* seriously—or die. It was by the Council's edict, and was only by Marcus's tireless arguing on our behalf that we weren't all put to death immediately. Everyone knew it.

"Lex didn't have to swear the oath." *Shut up,* I screamed at myself. But for some idiotic reason, I just kept on blabbing. "She's Set's daughter, too, but—"

"She's also my bond-mate." Marcus's lips spread into a cruel grin. "*You* are not." He leaned forward, resting both of his elbows on his knees. "I'm not known for my patience and mercy, Kat. Be careful."

"Be careful of w—what?" I hated myself for stuttering, but sometimes Marcus could be really effing scary. *How does Lex do it?*

"Of everything."

A breath.

Five.

A dozen.

"Okay," I said, nodding. "I'll swear the oath."

21

SAND & STONE

Katarina, my dearest daughter,

I know what you must think of me, but I had to do it. And I had to run . . . to leave you behind, for now. I'm doing this for you—for <u>*us*</u>*. There is a group who can help free you. You'll be able to be your own person, free to make your own choices instead of being a slave to Nejeret hierarchy. The Council of Seven will not be in charge forever. A revolution is coming. I only wish I'd caught wind of it before you were forced to manifest. I'm so sorry I couldn't save you this eternal pain.*

So you see, I had to accept this task. I had to do what must be done to protect us once the revolution happens. By harming the Meswett's sister and getting rid of Set's unborn offspring, I'm proving that my loyalty doesn't lie with Set or with the Council, that I'm trustworthy and capable, and that I'd be a worthy member of the opposition.

I'll send for you as soon as I know it's safe for you to join us. It's possible that you will be required to prove where your loyalty lies as well before you'll be allowed to join me, but I know you'll do the right thing. I'll keep you updated.

Destroy this letter and do not, under any circumstances, tell anyone about what I've told you. If the wrong people find out, we're both dead. Remember, it's always been you and me, Kat, and it'll always be you and me. I love you, sweetheart. I'll see you soon.

Love,
Mom

"Kat?" Dom knocked on the bathroom door. "Are you alright? Are you sick?"

"I'm fine," I said weakly. "Just—just a little—a little overwhelmed . . . that's all."

I stared at the single, crinkled piece of paper I'd found balled up and stuffed into one of my sneakers when I'd been repacking my duffel bag, watching it shake in my grasp. Something was crushing my chest, making it impossible to draw a full breath.

She was delusional. *My mom* was delusional. These were my people, my family, and she wanted me to betray them . . . to help some group of crazy people start a *revolution* and overthrow the Council?

But she *was* still my mom . . .

I tore the letter into tiny pieces and dropped it in the toilet, flushing without hesitation. I wouldn't betray Marcus and Lex and the others, but I wouldn't betray my mom either. After taking a deep, steadying breath, then another, I opened the bathroom door.

Dominic was leaning against the side of the wardrobe only a few steps away, his arms crossed over his chest and his eyebrows drawn together. His expression smoothed as I emerged. "Are you alright?"

I nodded.

His eyes scanned my face, almost like he was searching for

something. He frowned. "Aset came by while you were in the bathroom. They're ready to depart."

I glanced at the bed, where Jenny lay, sedated and unconscious, but healthy enough. "Do I have time to say goodbye?"

Dom nodded and moved across the room toward the foot of the bed. I followed, moving around the side to sit in the chair I'd been using for the past few hours.

"Do you think she'll be able to hear me?" I asked, taking hold of her cool hand.

Dom shrugged. "Perhaps. Perhaps not. But there is no harm in believing it."

Swallowing roughly, I stared at him. "You'll keep her safe?"

"I swear it," he said with the slightest bow of his head.

"Okay, good. That's good." Because not much terrified me more than the thought of my mom returning to finish what she'd started. I gave Jenny's hand a squeeze and leaned in closer to whisper my goodbyes.

"It's so . . . sandy," I said, staring out the passenger window of the Jeep I was sharing with a Nejeret named Carson. Dom, Neffe, and Alexander had remained back in Cairo, giving Jenny time to recover and regain her strength while also waiting for Lex's parents and grandma. They wouldn't be arriving for another week, so I'd been handed off to someone else for the trip west into the Sahara.

Carson laughed. It was a low, gentle sound. A soothing sound. I decided I liked his laugh. I just wished I felt like laughing, too. "Your first time out in the Red Land?"

I glanced at him, frowning. "Huh?"

Carson smiled at me, risking looking away from the caravan of other Jeeps stretching out ahead of us. It wasn't like he was going to veer off the road or anything—there *was* no road, just an endless sea of sand—so it wasn't really that risky. And I was glad he did it, because when Carson smiled, he was ridiculously hot. Like, superstar hot. Like, A-list-actor heartthrob hot. *Hot.* It was a nice distraction when thoughts of my mom threatened to consume me.

Carson's eyes were a deep blue, I just wanted to swim in them, and his hair was brown and tousled, like maybe he just got out of bed, or maybe he'd spent fifteen minutes arranging it just so. I sighed. Maybe I would never know, but I'd sure like to . . .

His smile became lopsided, and he returned his eyes to the dune we were cresting. "The 'Red Land' is what the ancients called the desert. You've never been out here, huh?" Unlike most Nejerets, Carson spoke like a real person, not like he'd just walked out of some period movie. I decided I liked *that* about him, too.

Once again, I looked out my window and sighed. *It's not like I've got a shot with him anyway . . . not now that I'm the psycho traitor woman's daughter . . .* "Nope, never been out in the desert before, never been to Egypt before, never been out of Seattle before, never had a wanted mom before . . ." I snapped my mouth shut and glanced at him. *Why'd I have to say that last part?*

Carson met my eyes for the briefest moment. "Seattle, huh? Cool place. I spent the last few years there myself."

I perked up a little in my seat, grateful he'd ignored the whole "wanted mom" slipup. "Really?"

He nodded slowly.

"Where?"

"I lived in the U District . . . in a house with some guys."

"Nejerets?"

"Yep."

"Were you going to school?" I asked, hopeful; if he had been, then it was likely that he wasn't really that much older than me. *Which would be* awesome . . .

"Sort of." He flashed me his killer smile again. "I was stationed there . . . to watch Lex."

I slumped a little in my seat. "Oh. Did you, um, go to school somewhere else before that?"

"Oxford, a few years back."

I bit my lip, my hopes plummeting. "And before that?"

"Oxford was my first—and was just undergrad. Marcus stationed me and the other guys at UW because we were actually interested in grad school, me specifically because I was able to get into the archaeology program."

My eyebrows rose, and I looked at him. "So you *worked* with Lex, you didn't just watch her?"

"Yep." A small smile touched his lips. "We're friends, actually." His smile widened, and he shook his head, laughing softly. "The last time I saw her, she'd won a bet on who'd get published first. I had to give her a hundred bucks."

"So she knows you're a Nejeret?"

Carson shook his head, and his brow creased.

"She's big on trust, you know . . . on not lying . . . since everyone pretty much lied to her *forever* . . ."

Taking a deep breath, he flicked his eyes my way. "I know, which is why I asked to be stationed down in Edfu, so she wouldn't have to cross paths with me and feel even *more* betrayed—especially after what happened at the trial with her friend, Cara . . ." He shook his head. "Did you hear about all that?"

I snorted. "Are you kidding me? I watched it on the news." I gritted my teeth. "I hope someone cuts off that Mike guy's balls."

Carson let out a breathy laugh. "You and me both, sister. You and me both."

At the word "sister," my stomach twisted. "Wait . . . you don't mean that literally, do you?"

"I'm pretty sure I do. Mike looks like he could stand to lose a ball or two."

I laughed. I almost couldn't believe it, but I really laughed. "No, you geek . . . the sister thing. Set's not your—"

"My dear old dad?" He shook his head. "Nah . . . my dad was a great-great-great-great-great-great-*great* grandson of Marcus's."

"Was?"

He nodded. "He was gone before I was even born."

My fingers clenched around the seatbelt crossing my shoulder. "Was it—was it Set?"

"In a way." His hold on the steering wheel tightened, making a creaking noise. "Listen . . . about your mom . . ."

Here we go . . .

"I understand what it's like to feel betrayed by your parents."

I stared at him. "You do?"

"I do." He met my eyes, then looked ahead. "I really do." After a moment's pause, he said, "Just remember that you aren't your mom. You're *you*. She made a choice for herself, not for you, so don't feel like you have to punish yourself or, I don't know, feel like it's inevitable that you'll follow in her footsteps. Just be your own person. Make your own choices."

Make your own choices . . . be your own person . . . I smiled, really liking the sound of that. "I took the oath the day before yesterday."

Carson's hands tightened on the steering wheel again. "Oaths are important," he said, his voice flat, almost distant. "A few words can change your life forever."

"Yeah," I said, returning my gaze to the endless expanse of

sandy dunes and feeling a little less lost than I'd been feeling a few minutes earlier. "They really can."

We reached the "oasis" late that afternoon, and everyone hopped out of their Jeeps and hustled around, setting up a city of tents that reminded me of the one I'd lived in for months during the excavation. It sort of felt like coming home. Especially the part where *everything* was sand or rough limestone and just so . . . blah.

"I thought an oasis was supposed to be, like, green and lush and stuff . . ."

Carson looked around, frowning thoughtfully as we hauled a heavy-duty chest of I-don't-know-what from one of the Jeeps and started carrying it toward the center of camp. "Legend goes," he said in a woo-woo ghost-story voice, "it was this crazy crystal city in the middle of the desert, surrounded by enormous walls of limestone, but because it was linked to Nuin's ba, when he died, the walls collapsed in on the city and the desert reclaimed it."

I gave him a sideways glance. "And Dom says *I* watch too many movies . . ."

Chuckling, Carson shrugged. "I didn't make up the legend." He squinted conspiratorially. "You could always ask one of the ancients for the truth. I've heard some people say that Marcus was even *there* when Nuin died . . . like, *by his side*."

My eyes widened. "Really?"

Carson shrugged again. "I don't know. That's just what I heard."

Brow furrowed, I considered his words. Marcus wouldn't tell me anything, I knew that. But, if Aset really was his twin sister, then she was just as old as him. *I wonder if* she *was here back then, too.*

My mouth fell open as I considered another, much more chilling possibility. *What if* Lex *was here*—is *here*—*back then . . .*

Tiny, invisible ghost spiders were suddenly crawling all over me.

PART IV

Sahara Desert, Lower Egypt
6th Dynasty, Old Kingdom

22

COMPARE & CONTRAST

"Do you have any idea how much I love you," Heru said in barely intelligible English; it had the sound of something memorized by rote.

I grabbed his wrist and stared at him as we continued to walk alongside an ambling line of donkeys packed with the belongings and traveling supplies of nearly two dozen people. "What did you just say?"

Heru met my eyes for a moment, curiosity filling his. "Do you have any idea how much I love you." He switched back to the only language we shared, the original tongue. "That is what you said to me yesterday, after regaining consciousness, is it not?"

"Yes . . ." How he'd remembered the sounds almost perfectly when he had no idea what they meant was beyond me. I returned my outward attention to the way ahead, a seemingly endless sea of sand with more swells than I could count without going cross-eyed. Inside, I was completely focused on a single thought: *Please don't ask me what those words mean.*

"What does it mean?"

I rearranged the white linen wrap draped over my head and

around my shoulders. The hood blocked the unrelenting glare fairly well, and the matching robe hung nearly to my ankles, just long enough to protect most of my body from the direct sunlight without me constantly tripping over the hem. Heru, along with all of the other Nejerets and humans, was wearing a nearly identical garment.

I shifted the purring little furnace that was Rus, curled up in his linen sling, to the left side of my body and stared at the sand a few steps ahead. "I would rather not tell you."

Heru bumped my shoulder with his arm. "Why not, little queen?" I didn't need to catch a glimpse of his face to know that he was smiling. "Are you so ashamed of your feelings for the Great Father?" Which cut right to the heart of the issue; he thought I'd mistaken him for Nuin in my delirium. I hadn't.

"Something like that," I mumbled. "So, how far is it to this Netjer-At Oasis?" We were heading into the Sahara on the west side of the Nile, and based on the sun's midday location, I could tell we were heading in a generally west to slightly southwesterly direction.

Heru chuckled. "Very well, I shall let the matter go. We should arrive at the Oasis in just over a week." And an ancient Egyptian week was ten days, so closer to two weeks to me. I was *not* looking forward to ten days of trekking through and camping in the unrelenting desert.

"Are we *absolutely* certain we won't run out of water and die of dehydration . . . and have our dried-up husks uncovered by humans in thousands of years?"

Laughing out loud, Heru assured me of our safety. "We've traveled this route hundreds of times. After all, the Netjer-At Oasis is our home. Wherever else we go, we always return there."

Not in my time. I'd never heard of this secret oasis that was apparently the ancient Nejeret headquarters, and I was not only bonded to a member of the Council of Seven and the great-granddaughter of the leader of the Council, but I was the Meswett, the prophesied savior of our people and an honorary member of the Council. That alone had made me a leader in my own right, whether I'd wanted to be one or not. It just seemed so odd that I hadn't heard *anything* about the Netjer-At Oasis before traveling back four millennia.

I heaved a deep, resigned sigh. I doubted I would ever catch up on Nejeret trivia—though living out our people's past *was* turning out to be a good start.

"What troubles you now, little queen?"

Our past . . . our future . . . you . . . "I wish you would not call me that."

"Would you prefer '*big* queen'?"

"No," I laughed. "I cannot say that I would."

"Ah, then you shall forever be little queen to me."

Blushing for the lamest reason—*Heru gave me a nickname . . . yippee!*—I cleared my throat. "Why are we returning to the Oasis right now? Is it because of what we saw at the market . . . how bad things are getting with the drought?"

"In a way. It is many things: Pepi's death, the droughts and famine, Khessie's inability to help the land any further by continuing to rule the mortals, and the increasing power the Nomarchs are gaining." Mention of the Nomarchs piqued my interest. They were the regional governors of ancient Egypt's twenty-plus different nomes, or territories. Yet another theory in my time claimed that the slow transfer of power from the Pharaoh to the regional leaders during Pepi II's rein was what had led to the demise of the Old Kingdom. A shift of power on top of droughts and famine sounded like a perfect recipe for revolution to me.

"Has there been much unrest? We thought—" I shook my head, rephrasing what I'd been about to say. *We thought the downfall of the 6th Dynasty was caused by . . .* was hardly an appropriate way to talk to someone who was currently living *in* the 6th

Dynasty. "In my homeland, we heard rumors of rebellions and regional leaders gaining power, but we were unsure how much truth there was to those rumors."

"You heard correctly." Heru's linen cowl flapped as he shook his head. "Had Khessie taken care of this latest Pepi as she was supposed to, this all might have been a little more manageable, but . . ."

"But what? What do you mean 'taken care of'? He lived until he was in his nineties." I shrugged. "That seems pretty taken care of to me."

"She led him on too well, and he loved her too much." Heru laughed, but it was a bitter sound. "He refused to lay with any of his other wives, and for whatever reason, Khessie manipulated the At, hiding for some seventy years the fact that none of the few children born to his wives had been fathered by him . . . possibly because she fed on his adoration for her. She should have told us of his refusal and sent him on to the next life so a ruler with the will to produce an heir could be appointed. But . . ."

He took a deep breath, exhaling a tired sigh. "She did not, and Pepi spent the last twenty-five years of his life more or less an invalid with Khessie ruling in his stead. And now, not one of the bastard children born to his wives survives." He shook his head slowly. "I still do not understand why she would do such a thing, risk the people of this land so recklessly . . ." He shook his head. "Nuin was not pleased, as you can imagine, but she is his daughter, and he has long favored her."

"I think she was afraid," I said, hoping my words were quiet enough that the woman in question wouldn't overhear me. I was pretty sure she was somewhere up ahead, but with the desert cowls, everyone looked alike from the back.

Catching my reluctance to speak at a full volume, Heru moved closer and leaned down so his head was nearer to mine. "Please explain what you mean," he said softly.

I hesitated, unsure how open I could really be with Heru regarding Ankhesenpepi. "She seems like a woman who would do anything for power, and I would bet that losing power is her greatest fear . . . along with the reason she dislikes me so much."

Heru made a rough noise low in his throat. "That, and her misperception of our relationship."

Right . . .

"But I think you may be correct," he said. "She is devious and conniving, and would likely trade anything short of her life to be in your position—the Netjer-At queen. Even as Nuin's eldest daughter, she has never been considered such."

I was shaking my head in disbelief, and the words were out before I even knew what I was saying. "If you think so poorly of her, then why do you—" I snapped my mouth shut.

"Why do I . . . ?"

"Nothing." I stared at the rear end of one of the donkeys up ahead. "Forget I said anything."

"If that is what you truly desire."

I was standing in a shallow valley of sand, surrounded on all sides by rounded dunes. The sky overhead was red and orange, and I thought this might be what it would be like to stand on the surface of Mars.

Heru and I had both stripped off our desert cowls once the sun set, starting its nightly trip through the underworld, and now stood barefoot in the sand, facing each other. Heru was wearing nothing but his usual linen kilt, and I had on a decidedly thin slip of a dress. The yellows, oranges, and reds bleeding across the sky set Heru's skin aglow and his golden irises ablaze. He was stunning . . . and more than a little distracting, with all of that skin and muscle and . . .

"Hit me," Heru said.

"What?" My eyes widened, and I took a step backward. "No."

Heru exhaled heavily, a sound that could be mistaken for nothing other than annoyance. "Hit me."

I shook my head. "I will not. I might hurt you . . ." I fully understood that Heru training me to be less of a defenseless wimp would require me to actually practice defending myself against other people—him, for starters—but I just couldn't bring myself to actually *hit* him.

Heru laughed, the sound low and velvety. "Trust me, you could not possibly hurt me."

Taking a step closer, I gave him a chummy punch on the shoulder. It was pathetic. Even more so because it wasn't like I was incapable of hitting him. I'd done it before, once; I'd slapped him, but I'd been seething with anger. And, damn it, he'd deserved it. He'd abandoned me in a compound filled with Nejerets during the scariest, most confusing time of my life—other than now, which was decidedly scarier and *more* confusing. But *this* wasn't Heru's fault. I had no desire to hit him.

"You stare harder than you hit," he said, settling a level gaze on me.

"'You stare harder than you hit,'" I repeated in a snotty, singsong voice. "I do not want to *hurt* you." I held up a hand, stopping him before he could reiterate how impossible it was for me to hurt *his mightiness*. "Regardless of whether I even could, why would I try if I had no desire to cause you pain?"

Heru studied me, pursing his lips the faintest amount and narrowing his eyes. The protracted moment of silence started to grow uncomfortable, and he crossed his arms. "If I asked Khessie to hit me, *she* would do it . . . *could* do it."

Jealousy and rage flared to life, intense and uncontrollable. I acted on pure instinct. Clenching my jaw, I pulled my arm back and swung. My palm struck the side of his chiseled face with a smack, stinging instantly.

"Ow . . ." I said, shaking out my hand.

Heru was grinning, his eyes shining. "It would seem that you found sufficient motivation to want to hurt me."

I mirrored him, crossing my arms over my chest, and started digging the toes of one bare foot into the sand. "If I promise to try to beat you senseless, will you promise to never compare me to her again?"

"So . . . I would not be allowed to say that she is shorter than you?"

I smiled, just a little. "Heru . . ."

"Or that her feet are much more masculine than yours?"

I couldn't help but laugh. I relaxed my arms at my sides. "You are making fun of me."

"Clearly *those* comparisons are not driving you to fulfill your promise to try to 'beat me senseless.'" He grinned wickedly. "Until you show me that you intend to fulfill your side of the bargain, I see no need to fulfill mine." He tilted his head downward, tucking his chin closer to his neck and watching me with a dangerous glint in his eyes. "The curve of Khessie's hips is enough to make a man—"

"Stop, Heru," I said, my voice low and even.

"—want to take hold of her and—"

"Be quiet!" I shouted, slapping my hands over my ears.

The dangerous glint in his eyes intensified. "Make me."

I shivered, partially from the rapidly cooling evening air, and partially from the challenge issued by every inch of his body. Glaring, I stepped closer, stopping when I was only inches away from him and had to tilt my head back to meet his eyes.

He raised one eyebrow. "As intimidating as your very presence is . . ."

Staring into those golden pools, I slammed the heels of my

hands into his abdomen. I skittered away as he doubled over, momentarily breathless, then lunged at him, leaping onto his back, wrapping my legs around his middle and hooking my feet together. I snaked my right arm around his neck, squeezing in what I hoped was an effective choke hold—not that I had any clue how such a thing was actually done—and brought my lips to his ear. "How am I doing?"

Apparently not that well, because Heru straightened and peeled my arm away from his neck with little effort. Luckily, my other arm was hooked over his shoulder, my fingers clutching one very well-formed pectoral, so I managed to stay on his back. Besides, I wasn't going anywhere with the death grip my legs had around his hips. In fact, I only had to scoot a few inches lower for my heels to dig into his . . .

"You would not dare," Heru said between heavy breaths, and I gave myself a mental pat on the back for making him breathe so hard.

"I would not?" I continued my slow slide down his body.

Heru dropped to his knees, and leaned back until I was sandwiched between him and the hot sand. The weight of him was enough to steal my breath, and I was certain he wasn't even trying to hurt me. If he had been, he would have slammed me backward into the sand while he'd still been standing rather than slowly lowering us to the ground. No, he just really didn't want me shoving my heel into his tender man parts.

I unhooked my feet and slapped his chest with both hands. "You . . . win . . ."

Heru rolled off me and crouched on his knees beside me, helping me up to a sitting position while I coughed and gasped for air. He even tugged down the skirt of my shift for me.

"I believe we have come to an agreement," he said, meeting my eyes. "If you continue to show that much enthusiasm when I am training you to defend yourself, I will refrain from even mentioning *her*."

"Deal." I held out my hand to shake on it. When he didn't show any sign of extending his own, I grabbed his wrist and guided his hand to mine. Gripping his tightly, I shook for both of us.

Heru looked down at our joined hands, then met my eyes, his expression bewildered.

"It is a custom from my land. We shake hands when we have come to an agreement."

Heru's smile was slow to come, but it grew to something radiant. He tightened his grip and shook back. "We have an agreement," he said with a nod. His smile faltered. "How long is this custom supposed to go on?"

I laughed. "Only a few seconds."

"Ah . . . I see." He stood, easily pulling me up to stand in front of him. "And now, little queen, I will teach you how to focus your excessive enthusiasm so you *may* have a chance to hurt me."

23

PAIN & GAIN

Aset and I walked arm in arm alongside the caravan of burdened donkeys, Heru, my ever-present sentinel, following several paces behind us. All three of us were bedecked in our linen desert robes and cowls, as was everyone else, making us look like a procession of overheated, sweaty Halloween ghosts.

It was our fourth day on the hot, dry trek through the Sahara toward the Netjer-At Oasis, and I was fairly certain I had sand pretty much everywhere. The ceaseless hours of hand-to-hand defense lessons Heru required every night ensured that, as did the literal hole-in-the-sand latrines.

Aset glanced over her shoulder at her brother, then leaned closer to me. "He is taking this task of watching over you very seriously, is he not?" she whispered. There was a suggestive twinkle in her eyes.

"Trust me, Aset, *nothing* like that has happened," I told her just as quietly, keeping my eye on Heru's expression to gauge whether or not he could hear what we were saying. "And nothing like that *can* happen . . ."

"I suppose . . ." A wistful sigh escaped from her. "But you are feeling better with the withdrawals, yes?"

I nodded.

She was quiet for a moment. "You could still tell him . . . about the two of you in the future, no? Even if you do not act on your feelings . . ."

"He does not even know that I am *from* the future. I really do not think—"

Aset tutted me. "You will have to block everyone's memories of you when you depart anyway . . ."

Everyone's except yours and Nekure's, I thought, which she was perfectly aware of.

". . . so why not at least be honest with him? He will not remember until your time, and you will feel less burdened in *this* time."

I chewed the inside of my cheek. "I am afraid."

"Of . . . ?"

I sighed. "I fear he will think I am insane . . . and that I will drive him away."

"If you had told him when you first arrived, perhaps, but he knows you now. And he knows that you are a little different . . ." She paused. "I think you should tell him."

I sighed.

"What does Nuin think?"

Glancing back at Heru, I found his eyes on me. I offered him a quick smile, then leaned closer to Aset. "He agrees . . . or at least, when I first arrived, he *agreed* that I should not tell Heru, that he found the idea of bonding—of being tied to someone so completely—distasteful, and that telling him *we* were bond-mates in the future would only make him avoid me. But we have not spoken of it since then. In fact, we have not spoken much at all." I exhaled in exasperation and shook my head. "Maybe I should tell him, maybe I shouldn't . . . I just don't know."

An almost electric thrill washed over me, and I stumbled. Only my link with Aset's arm kept me on my feet.

She halted beside me as what felt like a burst of lightning pulsed in my chest, and I doubled over. "Lex?" Aset's voice sounded panicked. "Lex? Heru!"

But there was no need for her to call to him. He was already there, right behind me, one arm wrapped around my shoulders and crossing my chest, the other clutching my waist. Were it not for him, I would've collapsed onto my hands and knees.

"What is it?" Heru said, his breath brushing my cheek. "Is this the same ailment as before?"

I clutched his forearm. "No," I breathed. This felt nothing like bonding withdrawals; this felt so much worse. I looked at Aset, who was standing in front of me, her awestruck face mere inches from mine.

"Your eyes . . . they are—"

Another burst of electric power exploded from my chest, and the agony reached all the way to my fingertips and toes. Smoky wisps of every shade of red, orange, and yellow pulsed from the exposed skin on my hands. I was betting the same was visible on my face.

"Get . . . Nuin," I managed to say through gritted teeth.

Aset nodded, her face ashen. She turned and sprinted away, tripping over her robe only once.

I groaned under the sheer force of the next wave of power. My breaths were quick and shallow, and I could hear others around me, some murmuring, some shouting. Rus, bundled in his linen sling, yowled and dug his needlelike claws into my chest. I somehow managed to dig him out from under the layers of linen and hand him off to the nearest person—Denai, I thought.

"Heru," I gasped, "Get me away from everyone. They cannot see this. They cannot see what I am." *If Apep is riding along inside one of them . . .*

Heru didn't hesitate in scooping me up. Cradling me in his arms, he broke into a run, calling over his shoulder that only Nuin, Set, Nekure, and Aset were allowed to follow, adding in a warning that he would personally eviscerate any others who dared to defy him. He sprinted over a low dune, then around a taller one, skidding several times on the descent but never coming close to dropping me.

When we reached a deep valley between several sand dunes, he fell to his knees, still cradling me. He was looking at my face, into my eyes, when the next wave of power broke free.

His lips parted as he stared at me, wonder altering his every feature. For seconds, or maybe minutes, we stared into each other's eyes.

"Thank you, Heru, but you have to release her now," Nuin said, his voice calm and sure.

Heru tightened his hold on me. "No."

"Alexandra? Can you hear me?"

I could feel the pressure building again, and I whimpered.

"Heru, you must release her and return to the others."

Heru's eyes finally left mine, and the look he turned on Nuin was filled with defiance.

"Go," I whispered, squeezing my eyes shut. It was about to happen again, and this time I was certain it would be way more than a burst of power; this was going to be an explosion, and I feared it would tear apart anything near me. I feared it would tear *me* apart.

"Go!" I howled, my voice filled with desperation . . . with agony . . . with power. "GO!"

Heru finally heeded my demand, handing me over to Nuin.

"Go," I repeated. "Go . . . go . . . go . . ."

"He is gone, dear Alexandra. It is just the two of us now." Nuin's voice was soothing.

He will make it better. He will make me *better.* I was so sure.

"I'm going to remove the shield, and we will both be

surrounded by the outpouring of excess power for a short time, but the sheut will expend itself, and you will be okay again." He hugged me against him, and I realized I was crying—sobbing. The force of the convulsions wracking my body was making him shake as well.

Unable to respond with words, I nodded.

"Alright, child, just breathe," Nuin's voice resonated with power. "Breathe." I had no choice but to follow his command. He pressed his lips to my forehead, pulling down the block.

And I screamed.

I felt like I'd been lit on fire. The desert and clear blue afternoon sky disappeared, and in their stead, our own private aurora borealis burst into life, countless rainbow tendrils snaking around us. They were alive. They were feeding off me, consuming me.

Again, I screamed, and it was the sound of a soul dying.

With a whoosh, the colors retracted, imploding until they once again fit snugly inside me.

"Breathe, my Alexandra," Nuin told me, a hint of strain marbling his calm tone. "Breathe."

I sucked in a breath of air.

"Good. Again, breathe. Good girl."

"What . . . the hell . . . was that?" I asked between gasping breaths.

"That," Nuin said, raising his eyebrows, "was entirely my fault."

I closed my eyes and focused on taking long, steady breaths. "Meaning?"

"Meaning it's time for us to start your training in earnest."

24

OATHBOUND & AWESTRUCK

If Heru'd had his way, he would've carried me like a helpless baby the final few hours of the afternoon's journey. I was starting to think Heru would prefer to just stick me under his arm and cart me around in general, if only to keep me out of harm's way.

Though he may have had a point on this one occasion. Once I convinced him to put me down—about fifteen minutes after the caravan had resumed its slow but steady parade across the desert—I proceeded to stumble and trip over basically nothing for the *next* fifteen minutes. I was bone weary, but at least it was a weariness that wore off fairly quickly. By the time we made camp beside an enormous, rocky outcropping, I felt more or less normal, if a little jittery. Not even the wary glances sent my way were overly bothersome.

Nothing seemed unsettling in comparison to Heru's silence all afternoon. He stayed by my side, ready to reach out and steady me if I needed him, but he said nothing. And every time I met his eyes, I saw questions and fear, and worst of all, accusation.

"What is wrong with her?" he asked as we approached Nuin,

who was standing with Set at the very edge of camp.

Nuin didn't answer. He simply looked past us, nodded at someone behind us, and started walking along the perimeter of the outcropping, away from camp. "Come with me."

Heru, Set, and I exchanged a confused look. I shrugged, then started after Nuin, and Heru and Set had little choice but to follow. Hearing footsteps crunching in the rock-strewn sand behind us, I looked over my shoulder. Nekure was trotting to catch up.

Nuin led us around a jutting cliffside, up a narrow path that passed between the face of the cliff and a huge, natural monolith, and finally, toward an uneven break in the cliff's wall.

I picked up my pace to catch up to him, but Heru caught my wrist. When I looked over my shoulder, meeting his eyes, my breath hitched. Because I knew the man he would one day become so well, I knew what those desperate, golden eyes were asking. *Will you stay where I can see you? Will you let me protect you? Will you let me know your secrets? Will you let me know* you?

Will you trust me?

I stopped trying to pull my wrist free of his grasp. "I would tell you everything, Heru, I really would . . . if I thought you would believe me."

He simply stared down at me, his eyes demanding answers I wasn't willing to give him.

I touched my free hand to the one he'd wrapped around my wrist, pushing it lower so our fingers could link together. "I have a feeling that what you are about to see is going to give you some of the answers you seek."

I continued on to the opening in the cliff's wall, Heru right behind me. Our fingers were still linked.

He squeezed my hand when I pulled too far ahead, and again, I looked back at him. "Netjer-At—we pretend to be gods," he said, stopping just before the opening. "We *pretend* to be gods, but . . ."

I turned to face him.

"Are *you* a true Netjer? A true goddess?"

I smiled, laughing softly, and raised my hand to trail my fingertips down the side of his face. His stubble felt rough and a little sweat-dampened. "Sometimes I still feel like a regular old human, and other times I feel like a young Nejerette who is drowning in events and powers that are so far beyond her comprehension . . ." I sighed. "But most of the time I simply feel lost. I honestly do not know what I am anymore."

Heru's jaw tensed under my fingertips, but those liquid gold eyes softened. "I see you. I know what you are."

A halfhearted laugh bubbled in my chest. "And what is that?"

He smiled, and my soul sang. "My little queen . . ." He lowered himself to his knees and gazed up at me, those eyes no longer warm, but hard and determined. "I live to serve, Alexandra. My life is yours, Alexandra, may you live forever."

I stared down at him, dumbfounded. He'd attempted to pledge an oath to me once before, and I'd denied him. And now, though he'd spoken in a completely different language, the words were essentially the same. Tears welled in my eyes. It was so hard to treat him like he was a different person from Marcus when he did things like this, proving that he truly was the same man.

A smile touched my lips as the tears broke free. I placed my hands on his shoulders, sliding them up his neck until they were on either side of his head. "I would rather have your friendship than your obedience, my Heru." Because this Heru *was* my Heru as much as Marcus was.

"You have both," he said, his voice rough.

My heart seemed to clench, and the tears only increased. Catching movement out of the corner of my eye, I glanced away from Heru. Set and Nekure were hanging back near an outcropping in the cliff's face, giving us privacy.

Heru stood, and my hands slid down the front of his body. I

closed my eyes, enjoying this single, lone chance to feel that soft skin, that hard muscle beneath my fingertips. His hands were on my face, his thumbs wiping away my tears, and I so desperately wanted to lean into him, to kiss him, to feel his soul merge with mine . . .

Which would *kill* him.

I opened my eyes and pulled my hands away from his abdomen. Clearing my throat, I took a step backward. "I shall test your claim right now, then."

He stared at me, his face unreadable.

I held my arm out toward the opening in the cliff's wall. "Please, join Nuin. I just need a moment to collect myself, and then I will join you."

His face hardened into a recognizable expression: defiance. "I would prefer not to leave you alone out here."

I offered him a weak smile; it was the best I could do. "I will not be alone." I nodded at Set and Nekure, who were heading toward us.

Heru hesitated, but after a few heartbeats, he stepped around me. A few seconds later, he was gone from my sight.

I sat on a small boulder, waiting for the urge to cry to pass and wiping the remainder of my tears from my cheeks.

"You have made mess of your kohl," Set said in his broken English as he neared. Nekure passed me, heading through the break in the rock wall, but Set hung back.

I laughed dryly. "What I wouldn't give for some waterproof kohl . . ."

"A product available in your time?"

"Something like that."

Set crouched in front of me and tore a small piece of linen from the hem of his kilt. "I offer to help"—he raised the cloth, bringing it close to my face—"if you will allow me to?"

I smiled and nodded, and he touched the cloth to the skin under my eyes, wiping gently. Unlike Heru, whose two identities had now merged in my mind—a dangerous reality—I saw this Set and the one from my time as two distinctly separate people. This Set was kind, generous, and exceptionally thoughtful—none of which were words *anyone* would use to describe Apep-Set.

"I have question for you, as well, and hope you will give honest answer."

I licked my lips and swallowed. "Ask away . . . I'm all ears."

"'All ears' . . ." He laughed. "Your language has such strange sayings."

I grinned. "I think *every* language has strange sayings . . ."

"This is truth."

"So, what did you want to ask me?"

Set hesitated, frowning the slightest amount. "When first we meet, you had fear in your eyes . . . fear of me." He was quiet for a moment as he continued to wipe the tear-smudged kohl off my face. "I have hurt you, in your time, I think. Is this truth?"

It was my turn to hesitate. But considering that I was going to wipe his mind of all memory of me when I left this ancient time, I figured I might as well tell him at least some of our shared history. I captured his wrist and pulled his hand lower, holding it in both of mine. Looking into his warm, coffee-brown eyes, I said, "Yes, Set, you did hurt me." At his crestfallen look, I added, "But you didn't have a choice, and it wasn't your fault. I know this now."

"I do not understand." His brow furrowed, and he shook his head. "Why would I do such a thing?"

I shrugged. "It's complicated . . ."

"We are related in some way, no?"

I blinked, and my mouth fell open. "Why—what makes you think that?"

He smiled, just a little. "The resemblance is impossible to miss, I think. Aset and Nekure have commented on this to me, as well."

Well, they didn't say anything to me . . . I cleared my throat. "Um . . . yeah, we're related."

A pregnant silence hung between us, waiting . . . expanding . . .

"Are you my daughter?"

A breath I hadn't realized I'd been holding whooshed out of my lungs, and I closed my eyes. I nodded.

Suddenly, his arms were around me, and I was sobbing, and I didn't understand why.

Set rubbed my back as I clung to him. "I am here, my daughter . . . I am here . . ."

By the time Set and I made it through the break in the cliff's wall and into a wide cavern lit by periodic cracks in the stone overhead, my eyes were dry and my makeup was as tidy as it could've been after the repeated waterworks. The floor was soft sand, cool through the bottoms of my leather moccasins, but overhead, the ceiling was dripping with stalactites, some long enough that I had to be careful as I walked around to avoid bonking my head. Nuin, Heru, and Nekure were standing in the relative center of the space, speaking in hushed tones.

"Come, dear Alexandra," Nuin said, holding his hand out to me.

I approached him. "What are we doing in here, oh he who loves mystery above all things?"

Nekure made a choking noise, and I glanced at him. He was trying not to smile.

Nuin narrowed his eyes, but I thought I spotted a tiny sparkle of amusement. He looked at the three Nejerets, who were standing side by side. "As you witnessed today, Alexandra is not merely Netjer-At . . ."

Nekure and Set already knew what Nuin was sharing, but Heru didn't. I focused on Heru's face as Nuin spoke. His eyes, too, stayed locked on mine.

". . . just as I am not merely Netjer-At. But my time in this body is coming to an end, and it was essential that I pass on my power, my sheut, to another. I chose Alexandra as the recipient because it is what had to be." He paused for a moment, and I thought he must've been considering what other half-truths to share.

"But Alexandra is still physically Netjer-At, and as such, her body is not able to fully handle the power I have given her, just as no other Netjer-At would be able to do. She must learn to control it and regularly expend it so it does not overwhelm her and quite literally explode out of her, as it did today. Doing so will extend the time she has to complete the tasks she is destined for before the sheut destroys her completely."

Heru's eyes snapped to Nuin, and his entire body went rigid. "*Destroys* her?"

Nuin laughed softly. "I tell you that my own life is coming to an end and you say nothing, but I mention that Alexandra is in danger and you react quite differently." He grinned. "This pleases me. It makes me think that you must be taking *very* good care of my beloved wife."

I stared at Nuin, my eyes narrowed. I hadn't the slightest clue why he would say something like that—and say it teasingly, not accusingly. It was almost like he *wanted* Heru and me to have a physical relationship. Which he knew was impossible.

Heru clenched his jaw. "I would never dishonor either you or her in such a way."

Nuin made a noncommittal noise, and I was pretty sure he winked at me.

Cheeks flaming, I shook my head and forced myself *not* to

look at Heru. I had no clue what Nuin was thinking. Did he *want* me to doom the timeline by bonding with—and killing—Heru?

"Now, dear Alexandra," Nuin said, "I will teach you how to stop time and to jump from place to place at will, and *tonight,* I will teach you how to use some of your more subtle, mental abilities." He touched my forehead, and based on the sudden widening of the three Nejerets' eyes, I was betting that my own eyes were on fire with power.

I looked at Nuin, waiting for instructions.

"Set," he said, pointing to the cavern wall on my left, "go stand over there." He turned his attention to Heru and pointed to the opposite wall. "Over here, Heru." Nekure, he directed to the cavern opening. All three moved quickly, and once they were standing in their assigned spots, facing us, Nuin smiled at me. "Go to Heru."

The corners of my mouth tensed as I took my first step toward Heru, and when Nuin grabbed my arm, holding me back, I frowned. "What—"

Still smiling, Nuin shook his head. "Using the sheut, go to Heru."

I took a deep breath. "I have never been able to control it at will. It only happens when I feel a strong emotion and *need* to be somewhere."

"Very well." Nuin moved so swiftly, I didn't realize what he was doing until the crystalline dagger was already flying through the air toward Heru.

"No!" I shouted.

Time stopped, and misty tendrils of color surrounded me. One moment I was standing beside Nuin, the next, I was in front of Heru, staring at the dagger. It was a beautiful piece of craftsmanship, clearly made of At, and its point was barely a foot from Heru's shocked face.

I shot Nuin's frozen form a scathing glare, then wrapped my

fingers around the dagger's hilt, thinking it would be so easy if the thing would just cease to be.

My fingers started sinking into the hilt, and I watched, amazed, as the entire dagger reverted to its original state, a liquid hunk of quicksilver goop. I released it, and it dissolved into a colorful mist and was gone.

"Whoa . . ."

Heru's arm was suddenly swinging through the air, and I barely had time to duck before his attempt to swat the no-longer-existing dagger away struck *me* instead.

"Crap," I hissed as I fell back on my butt. At least the sand was soft.

It took Heru several seconds to process what had just happened. As his eyes settled on me, sprawled on the ground, they widened, his lips parting. "How . . . you were there"—he pointed in Nuin's general direction—"but now you are here . . . and the dagger . . ."

I tossed another glare at Nuin over my shoulder, and when I looked back at Heru, he was kneeling on the sand before me.

"Are you alright?" he asked.

"All but my pride." I accepted his hand and stood, brushing off my backside and shooting several more glares Nuin's way.

Heru stared at me, his eyes filled with awe. "It is true . . . you *are* a goddess."

"For the moment, yes, that term is very appropriate for her," Nuin said. "Very good, Alexandra. Now jump to Set."

I let go of Heru's hand and, planting my hands on my hips, turned to face Nuin. "Are you going to throw a knife at him, too?"

Nuin grinned. "Only if I must. Once you are able to use the power at will, I will not have need of such motivations."

As it turned out, he had three more At knives secreted away in his kilt. He only had to use two.

25

REVELATIONS & RESERVATIONS

I was exhausted by the time Nuin said I was finished practicing spatial shifts. Each successive jump took more concentration, and the lag time between jumps increased steadily until Heru, Set, and Nekure had to steady me with sure hands when I appeared before each of them. Only when I lost consciousness for a few seconds, awakening with Heru's arms holding my slumped body tightly against him, did Nuin relent.

"Was it really necessary to push her so far?" Heru said.

I patted his sides. "I am alright. I can stand."

He helped me get my feet securely under me and released all but my elbow, which he held onto with a firm grip. I was grateful; I wasn't sure I could balance on my own.

Turning away from Heru, I watched Set approach Nuin. "Surely you did not need to make Alexandra—"

Nuin cut him off with a hard look. "I am doing what is necessary to keep her alive."

"To prolong her life, you mean," Set countered.

Clasping his hands in front of him, Nuin took a deep breath, giving off an aura of placid unconcern. "Until she may complete her tasks, yes."

I exhaled heavily. "Nuin . . . how am I supposed to complete these 'tasks' if I don't even know *how* I'm supposed to complete them?"

Nuin stared at me for a long time, his expression turning considering. Finally, he nodded. "I will tell you part of what the future must hold for you. I had intended to save this information until the final moments before you departed—to avoid complicating things for you here, you see—but . . ." He shook his head serenely. "I suppose I do not see the harm in it." His eyes flicked to Heru, then settled back on me. "And considering the unexpected restraint you have been showing, I think only good will come of telling you now, dear Alexandra, so I shall . . . in private." He glanced at Heru, Set, and Nekure. "You may return to camp."

Heru released my elbow, lingering near me for a few seconds, probably to make sure I wasn't about to collapse. I wasn't; I already felt notably steadier. At the sound of his retreating footsteps, I had to force myself not to turn around and follow him.

Nuin held his hand out to me. "Come, my Alexandra, sit with me."

I approached, keeping a watchful eye on him, and accepted his hand when I reached him. It was finally starting to sink in that my knowledge of this man—this *god*—barely scratched the surface. Proceeding with caution seemed like a really good idea at the moment.

With a sigh, Nuin drew me down to the sand. He sat cross-legged, and I knelt on the ground in front of him. He studied me with somber eyes, their swirling colors appearing a little duller than usual. "I've relied on the knowledge I gain from the At for too long," he said in English, "and it would seem that I no longer have a knack for doing things the old-fashioned way."

"Doing things?"

"Yes, you know . . . living . . . making decisions . . . confiding in others . . ."

Frowning, I shook my head. "So, what are you saying?"

"I assumed that certain personal matters would progress differently—*naturally*—and far more quickly than they have, but my assumption was clearly false," he said with another sigh. "And now I see that I am at fault, because I have not been open enough with you, dear Alexandra."

"Personal matters—are you talking about Heru and me?"

Nuin nodded. "Your connection to each other is quite strong, and it grows stronger every day. I assumed your relationship would have developed into something more physical at this point, considering . . ."

Again, I was shaking my head. "But we—I—we *can't* have a physical relationship. If I bond with Heru and then"—I snapped my fingers—"poof, I'm gone . . . he's *dead*."

Nuin narrowed his eyes, and his lips curved into a secretive smile. "Ah, and now I see where I have erred. I thought I'd explained something far better than I had." Laughing quietly, he shook his head. "If you and Heru bond in this time, he won't die when you leave."

"But—"

"Because *you* will save him."

I searched Nuin's face, his mesmerizing eyes, trying to understand. "But . . . *how*? By extracting a bunch of my bonding pheromones for him to keep until we meet in four thousand years?"

"No, dear Alexandra. You could not extract enough to last so long. No, I am speaking of a different matter entirely. Don't you recall my mentioning that you could use the sheut within you to create a block within another that would forestall withdrawal symptoms indefinitely?"

I blinked several times, searching my memory, then slapped my palm to my forehead. I felt like such a blind, bumbling idiot. "You said I couldn't create something like that within *me* . . . but you never said I couldn't create a block for Heru." I laughed out loud, not quite ready to let myself believe that bonding with Heru *in this time* was really possible. "I can't believe I didn't understand what you meant."

Nuin smiled broadly, but his expression quickly sobered. "There is one caveat that you must be *very* conscientious of . . ."

I raised my eyebrows.

"Once the block is in place, the next time you and Heru have intimate contact—"

"Define 'intimate contact.'"

Nuin laughed softly. "Sexual intercourse, Alexandra."

My eyes widened, but I nodded for him to continue.

"The moment the two of you achieve a fully realized union of your two bas, the block will be shattered, and Heru will once again be subject to the regular onset of bonding withdrawals should the two of you be separated again and the block *not* be reset again."

I chewed on the inside of my cheek. "But it could be—reset again, I mean, right?"

Nuin nodded. "As many times as is necessary."

"So . . . it's really possible? Heru and I can really be *us*?"

Nuin nodded and clasped his fingers together, resting his hands on his ankles. "In fact, I believe it may be essential that the two of you truly be together during your time here."

I tilted my head to the side. "Essential? To what?"

"To your survival, dear Alexandra. You see, the only way to purge the sheut from your body and have you survive is for it to be naturally siphoned into another being, binding with another ba . . . within you."

My brow furrowed. "Huh?"

Nuin smiled. "Once you've returned to your time, you must bear a child."

My mouth fell open.

"Two, in fact. One to bind with the sheut within you, and one to bind with the sheut within the Heru of your time."

"*What?*" I was shaking my head and staring at him with widened eyes. "But—but . . . I *can't*. It's not physically possible."

"But it *is* physically possible."

I snapped my mouth shut.

"Bonding has many side effects, one being the increased dependency between the bond-mates on each other's bonding pheromones, another being the triggering of a rare, dormant fertility hormone in the Nejerette's body. Once activated, this fertility hormone suppresses the Nejerette's regenerative abilities for the duration of the pregnancy."

He paused, then explained, "Only once the Nejerette's system is saturated with enough of the combined bonding pheromones of both bond-mates will the fertility hormone be triggered, regeneration suppressed, and successful conception a possibility." He smirked. "Which is why it is my belief that you and Heru must achieve a physical relationship in *this* time—it will take much more intimate contact between the two of you to exchange enough bonding pheromones for your body to reach that critical saturation point."

I'd started shaking my head again, and forced myself to stop. Taking deep breaths, I released my skirt and pressed my hands against my knees, trying to make Nuin's words make sense.

He reached out and touched the back of my hand. "And when your body finally *does* reach the critical saturation point and the fertility hormone *is* triggered, both Apep's sheut—assuming it's whole within Heru—and the sheut within you will naturally gravitate toward the newly forming ba within your uterus, safely separating from your own ba and Heru's. And the two sheuts will cause this new ba, and therefore the embryo, to divide into two separate beings, and you will carry twins." Nuin smiled, and his face lit up with so much wonder and glory that some of it should have spilled into me. It didn't.

"Twins," I breathed.

He nodded. "And they will be more than human, more than Nejeret—"

"Twins . . ." I cleared my throat. "Like, two of them? At once?"

Nuin chuckled. "Yes, my Alexandra. And as I said, it will take a while to reach the critical saturation point, so if you want your body to be anywhere near close to that point by the time you return to your own time, I'd highly suggest that you—how do you say it?" He squinted thoughtfully. "Ah, yes . . . *clear the air* with Heru—and soon, lest you run out of time before the sheut destroys you."

I swallowed roughly. Suddenly, my heart rate sped up as I realized that if I wanted to *be* with Heru in this time, if I wanted to prevent my own impending death, I would have to tell him. Everything.

26

WILL & WON'T

I rushed back to camp, Nuin a short ways behind me. I was practicing some pretty impressive repression skills; of all that Nuin had just revealed, only a single thing had truly sunk in: if I bonded with Heru in this time, bonding withdrawals wouldn't kill him when I left. We could have this much more time together. I could really share part of Marcus's ancient past with him, and when I returned to my own time, I could unblock his memories of us *now*, and together, we could revel in the experiences we'd shared millennia ago.

And we're going to have children . . . twins . . .

Nope, I definitely wasn't ready to deal with *that* little revelation yet. Absolutely, definitely not. I was ready to think about *anything* but that.

What I needed was to find Heru. I was resolved to finally tell him the truth, to finally confess everything about where I came from, who I was, and who *he* was to me.

His tent was my first stop, closely followed by the one I shared with Denai and the other two priestesses who'd chosen to accompany me to the Oasis, which was sandwiched between Heru's and Nuin's tents. Both were empty, so I wandered from tiny cookfire to tiny cookfire—there were only three of them, each manned by cooks under Heni's guidance—but Heru wasn't posted around any of them. Frustrated, I headed for the edge of camp, intending to walk a circle around the perimeter to see if I could spot him among the limestone cliffs and sand dunes surrounding us.

But I didn't spot him; I *heard* him.

His voice lured me in, harsh and clipped, and though I couldn't understand his words, I could hear how impassioned he was. I followed the sound toward a lopsided monolith near the rock outcropping. And when I saw him—with *her*—on the other side of the monolith, I froze.

Ankhesenpepi's back was to the tall stone, and Heru's body was flush against hers, his hand gripping her neck and his face mere inches from hers.

I wanted to scream, to shout for him to release her, to will her into nonexistence. I *needed,* with every fiber of my being, to warn her off him . . . to claim him, just as I'd done in my own time. But this wasn't my own time. I clenched my hands into fists, my nails digging into my palms, and I kept just this side of losing control.

A desert wind picked up around me, gusting in their direction.

Heru snapped his head my way, and suddenly I was a deer and his eyes were headlights and I had to run, to escape, if I was going to have any chance of surviving some imminent collision. I spun around and hurtled toward the nearest possible safe haven—the huge rock outcropping—no thought for the wind whipping through my hair or snapping the fabric of my dress.

I wasn't a slow runner. But Heru was faster. If Nuin hadn't reset the block cutting off my access to his sheut, I could have jumped to any place I desired. But he *had* reset the block, and I was just me, Lex, Nejerette, and all I could do was run.

I made it a few hundred yards, out of sight of camp and the

monolith I now wanted to demolish because to my mind it would forever carry the impression of his body pressed against hers.

Heru's hand curled around my arm, gripping it tightly, and he jerked me to a halt. He stepped in front of me, his face hard and tense and very clearly livid.

"What were you thinking, running away on your own like that? Where would you go? Wha—"

I slammed my palm into his abdomen, just under his ribs, like he taught me to do if I wanted to knock my opponent temporarily breathless. Twisting my arm, I yanked it out of his grasp and sprinted away. The wind was roaring in my ears.

"Alexandra!" Heru shouted, but I ignored him, immersing myself in the howling of the wind, in the abrasion of sand against my skin.

I ran as fast and as hard as I could along the rock wall, staring down at the sand and focusing on putting one foot in front of the other.

An arm hooked around my waist, and my back slammed against a hot, hard body, and I was suddenly having a really hard time inhaling anything but sand. I was dragged closer to the rock wall, and then there was only stone and darkness met by a jagged sliver of muddled light and what appeared to be a living wall of sand.

I'd run straight into a sandstorm.

"Are you alright?" Heru asked, his voice harsh. Like it had been when he'd been with *her* only moments ago.

I elbowed him in the abdomen, and he released me, not that I had anywhere to go. We were standing in a crevice in the cliff's wall wide and deep enough for *maybe* four people, and there was a sandstorm screaming just beyond the opening, only a few feet in front of me.

"Did you get sand in your eyes?"

Scrubbing my hands over my unscathed face, I shook my

head and turned to him. I had no choice but to remain mere inches away from him. "I did not realize there was a storm." I looked down, avoiding his shadowed features and feeling like I'd just earned the grand prize for world's most moronic Nejerette. "Thank you for pulling me in here."

He made a rough, dismissive noise. "Why did you run away?"

I clenched my jaw. "I would think it obvious, at this point."

I listened as he inhaled and exhaled several times. When he finally spoke, his voice was quiet, just audible over the howling storm behind me. "What we both want, Alexandra . . . that can never be. You are wife to the *Great Father*."

I squeezed my eyes shut. *Here goes* . . . "Only in name."

Several more breaths. "What are you saying?"

I sighed. "Nuin and I will never be a true husband and wife. We will never have a true marriage . . ." I paused, working up the nerve to tell him about *us*. "Nuin and I will never have that because I am already attached to another." Behind me, the wind howled, but it was nowhere near as intense as the lightning storm standing before me. I took a deep breath. "Heru . . . Nuin named me his wife to protect me while I am here . . . *now*. I am not from *this* time, and my true husband waits for me in *my own* time."

Heru shook his head, his features too shadowed for me to make out his expression clearly. "I do not understand. Such a thing is not possible . . ."

"You saw me jump from one place to another a little while ago . . . you *saw* the power I carry explode out of me . . . how is this any less believable?"

Again, he shook his head. "It is not—"

I huffed out a breath. "Just as the power Nuin gave me enables me to shift through space, I can do the same through time." I pressed a hand against Heru's chest, stopping his unvoiced questions or any further protestations. "You have seen me manipulate time already; when Nuin threw that first dagger at you, I stopped time as well as jumped from one place to another."

Hope filled me when my words weren't met with a shake of his head.

I looked up into his shadowed eyes. "Do you believe me? Do you believe it is possible that I can move through time? That I *did* move through time to be here?"

His chest rose and fell against my hand, and after a moment, he nodded.

I exhaled in relief.

"And this other man you are attached to . . . ?"

Swallowing, I licked my lips. "It is you, Heru. Thousands of years in the future . . . *you* are my husband." I held my breath.

The wind moaned in the opening behind me.

My heartbeat whooshed in my ears.

Heru breathed in and out. In and out. In and out.

Seconds passed, possibly minutes, and neither of us said anything. We simply stared at each other.

Finally Heru covered my hand with his own, molding it against his chest. "What you witnessed with Khessie just now . . . it was nothing."

I shook my head, my brow furrowed. It had certainly looked like something.

"She followed me away from camp, and I was giving her a warning to—"

"A warning? It looked more like a promise." I met his eyes, and at seeing the intensity burning in their golden depths, even in the heavy shadows, I looked away.

"A promise . . ." The hand Heru had placed over mine shifted, moving slowly along my forearm and over my elbow, until his fingers curled around my arm. He pulled me close enough that our chests were touching and wrapped his other arm around my back, splaying his hand on my hip possessively.

"Yes . . . a promise." He chuckled, low and rough. "A promise to ruin her if she ever speaks ill of you to me again."

My lips parted, and my breaths came faster. I raised my eyes, once again meeting his. "I see . . ."

Heru slid his hand further up my arm and ran his fingertips over my shoulder, along my collarbone, and up the side of my neck. He curled his fingers, tilting my chin higher. "So tell me, little queen, how do I claim you in the future? Do I battle another for the right to call you wife? Do I—"

I cleared my throat. "Actually, I claimed you . . . or *will* claim you." My voice was breathy.

Heru laughed. "These things you say . . . I take one step toward believing you, then one step away."

My eyes narrowed. "What is it that you find so hard to believe—that I would claim you, or that you would accept?"

Heru lowered his head, bringing his face closer to mine. "Claim me and find out, little queen."

My breath caught. He smelled too good. He felt too good. Being so close to him felt too *right*, like as long as we were together, we could take on anything. I bit my lip.

"Or has this all been an elaborate ruse?"

"No, I—" I pressed my lips together, feeling more than a little embarrassed. I didn't actually know *how* to claim him. "You have to understand that I was not raised Netjer-At. I did not know our ways, so when I claimed you, I acted on instinct." I shifted my gaze to the side, studying the rough limestone wall. "There was a woman, and when I found her in your tent with you, I threatened her, warning her to stay away and never come near you again . . . and claimed you as my own." I almost rolled my eyes at myself, it sounded so primitive—*Heru, mine . . . you, go away . . . urgh . . . garr . . .*

But Heru didn't look amused; he looked enthralled. "Tell me," he said. He was breathing harder, like me, and the hand on my hip moved, tracing languorous designs on the linen of my dress. "Tell me what you will do to any female Netjer-At who attempts to slip into my bed. Tell me I belong to you and you alone. *Tell me*."

"I—" I swallowed. "I—"

I couldn't do it, not when I knew—I *knew*—that certain things had to happen during the millennia between now and the moment I claimed him, certain people had to be born to him and other women, people like Neffe, who would one day save his life.

Biting my lip, I shook my head, my eyes stinging. "You do not understand. I cannot—"

"Then *I* will, because I cannot bear this agony any longer," he said as he leaned in closer. He brushed his lips along my jaw ever so slowly before pressing his cheek against mine. "I will gut any man who even attempts to lay with you. I will tear him apart, because you are mine." His breath was hot against my ear. "What say you, Alexandra? Do you accept my claim, or will we be strangers from this day forward?"

My heart felt so full, beat so fast, I was fairly certain it was about to explode. "I—I accept your claim," I whispered. In any time . . . in any place . . . I would always accept this man. I might not get to keep him forever, but I *would* be his for as long as I was in this time.

His lips traced the hollow below my cheekbone, and I closed my eyes, basking in the glow of sensation such a gentle touch elicited. A sweet ache swelled low in my abdomen, and I moved my hands to his sides and pressed my body against his, needing to be as close to him as possible.

"Heru . . ."

His mouth covered mine, and I moaned as I opened up to him. It was our first kiss for him, and about our millionth for me, but everything felt brand new. I was beginning to think that everything between us would *always* feel brand new.

His tongue caressed mine with a slow, sensual promise, and

his hands encased the back of my head, allowing him to maintain control of the intensity of the kiss. His lips, his hands, his sounds—*oh God, his sounds*—all contained subtle demand, a slow burn that could so easily spread into a roaring inferno of desire.

I wanted more. I wanted everything his kiss was promising, but I didn't want to wait. I wanted to be claimed by him, bonded to him, joined with him. I wanted to feel whole again, because kissing him, feeling my body flush against his, made me realize that I'd been a fractured being since the moment I arrived in this time. I no longer had the luxury of existing as just me, a single entity, but was part of something greater—*us*. I needed to feel *us* again.

Moving my hands down the outsides of his thighs, I started gathering up his kilt. I could feel him, so swollen and needy under that fabric, and at that moment, removing that barrier was the single most important thing.

He sucked in a breath when I finally found him, when my fingers finally encircled him. His hand was suddenly wrapped around my wrist, preventing my hand from moving, and his other clasped the back of my neck. He broke the kiss, his breaths hard and heavy.

Leaning his forehead against mine, he said, "Answer me this, Alexandra, and do not lie . . ."

I pulled back, searching his eyes and shaking my head. "Answer *what*?" I didn't understand his sudden mood shift. He was still pulsing with desire—we both were—but there was something else, an underlying current of accusation, of anger.

"In the future, are we bond-mates, as well?"

"I—" Had I left that part out? Things had happened so quickly . . . "Yes, Heru, we are. I meant to—"

"I will not be trapped like this." His voice was hard, and definitely contained a thread of accusation.

I released him, but he maintained his hold on my wrist and

neck, and my stomach twisted with dread. "It was not meant to be a trap. I just—"

"I have known you barely six days," he said, his harsh words cutting through mine. "Why would you think that was enough time for me to bind my life to yours?"

My blood heated, but I refused to let him see how much his words hurt me. Keeping my expression blank and staring into his smoldering eyes, I said, "Remember that I have known you for much longer than that. I was not thinking . . . I apologize." My eyes stung with unshed tears, but I gritted my teeth and held them back. I'd cried far too much since arriving in this time. I was done with it. "Please release me."

Heru pulled me closer and searched my eyes. His outrage at nearly being "trapped" melted away. "You must give me time, Alexandra . . . time to know you better . . . time to decide for myself."

I licked my lips, fighting the urge to raise my face those last few inches to once again feel the soft pressure of his lips against mine. "I understand." I swallowed back a sob. "I understand, I do, it's just . . ." The sob fought back up and broke free despite my best efforts to keep it contained. And damn it all to hell, I started crying. "It is so difficult, Heru . . ."

With a sigh, he wrapped his arms around me.

I clung to him, my hands clutching his sides as I gave in to the sorrow, the desperation, the heartbreaking longing I always felt around him. "I miss you so much . . . and being around you . . . but not being *with* you . . . it is the most difficult thing . . ."

Heru didn't respond, didn't console me with words. He simply held me and rubbed my back, giving me as much of himself as he could.

It was almost worse than if he'd given me nothing at all.

27

ALL & NONE

I wandered away from camp amid an ocean of sand dunes, seeking solitude. I crested the nearest and started down the other side, looking back over my shoulder every few steps. Once the clusters of long, pale tents and the glow of tiny cookfires were no longer visible, I lowered myself to the ground and bent my legs, hugging my knees to my chest.

I glanced back at Heru, who was standing sentry on the dune's peak, his hands clasped behind his back. His attention was everywhere, listening, watching, waiting for some imminent attack I didn't think would ever come. "There is nobody but our people out here," I said with a sigh. "I think you can leave me alone for a short while, at least."

Three days had passed since our near-bonding encounter during the sandstorm, since I'd learned that one day, in the distant future, we would have children—or we would perish—and Heru had been keeping his distance, or as much distance as one could keep from another person when one was sworn to protect that person and refused to be released from one's oath. Of course, he didn't know about the children thing, but still . . .

Being around him all day, every day, when he was so clearly

afraid to touch me, to even move too close to me, was exhausting; he'd even recruited Set to help me practice my slow-to-develop hand-to-hand combat skills. I constantly felt like I was on the verge of tears, and I wanted to punch Heru for being able to do that to me. I'd never been a crier . . . not until I met him.

Healthy, Lex, that's really, really healthy . . .

But honestly, most of those tears had been caused by Apep-Set, and Heru's presence had merely been a coincidence. Even my current situation could be laid at Apep-Set's feet. Thinking *that* made me feel a little better.

"Well, Heru, if you insist on remaining, at least come sit with me. It makes me nervous to have you standing there."

"I am watching over you."

"Perhaps, but you also might be making silly faces at the back of my head, or—"

His lips quirked. "I have not, and I would not. I swear it, little queen." It was the first time he'd called me that since the sandstorm.

I smiled weakly. "Come sit with me, Heru. Please . . ."

He relaxed his stance and released his hands, letting them hang at his sides as he started down the sandy slope toward me. He sat on my right, keeping a few inches between our hips, and stretched his legs out in front of him. The distance made my heart clench, just a bit.

Taking a deep breath, I forced myself to smile and turned my face up to gaze at the night sky. It was so different than the one I was used to, dimmed by city lights and viewed through a haze of pollution. This ancient, pristine night sky stole my breath every single time I saw it. The stars were brilliant and too many, bleeding together like freckles after too much time in the sun. And then there was the Milky Way, sweeping across the sky in a nebulous arc.

According to one ancient Egyptian creation myth, the goddess Nut would swallow the sun, Re, every evening and give birth to him the following morning, over and over again. I'd read in a book once that the ancients believed the arc of the Milky Way to be Nut's body, arching over the earth, sheltering us all while we waited for Re to be reborn.

"Does it give you peace?" Heru asked.

"Hmmm . . . ?"

"Staring into the heavens." He cleared his throat. "You do it so often, I can only assume it brings you some manner of peace to see something familiar in a place that is clearly so strange to you."

I raised my eyebrows and looked at him, taking in the sharp edges and hard planes of his face, the silvery sheen of starlight in his eyes, the lush curve of his lips. "I see something familiar every time I am around you." The words were out before I could stop them.

Heru frowned, and averted his gaze. "But seeing me does not bring you peace."

"Perhaps not, but it does keep me alive and healthy." I hugged my knees more tightly.

Heru was silent for a long time. "This will make me sound quite dense, but I have to admit that I did not consider that you would be suffering from bonding withdrawals were you to be away from me for too long." He shook his head. "I cannot imagine what that must be like."

"No," I said, "you cannot." And to ease the sharp edge to my words, I offered him a smile, albeit a sad one. "But one day, you will understand."

Heru's eyebrows drew together, though he didn't respond.

I returned my attention to the stars. "Do they bring *you* peace?"

"They trouble me."

Surprised, I lowered my eyes to him again. He wasn't looking up at the sky, but at me.

"I do not understand them," he said, "and things I do not

understand trouble me." I wasn't sure if he was talking about the stars anymore.

Swallowing, I forced myself to look away. I lay back on the sandy slope and stared up at a scene more beautiful than any piece of art. "In time, people will come to understand the stars better, and then they will start to explore them, much as they will explore every part of this world."

"Explore the heavens?" I could see him out of the corner of my eye, staring down at me while I gazed up at the night sky. "How could we explore something that is not of this world?"

"Because it is of this *universe,*" I said, laughing softly to myself. To be the one teaching *him* something . . . it was pretty damn fun. "The stars are . . . they are like our sun, for the most part, huge orbs of burning gas. But some are like our own world, with lands and seas, and others are giant balls of ice, and others are . . ." Glancing at him, I felt a flush spread up my cheeks and down to my chest. "Sorry . . . I got a little carried away."

Heru merely continued to smile his small, secret smile and stare down at me.

I sat up. "That probably did not make any sense anyway. An astronomer I am not."

He tilted his head to the side. "What is 'astronomer'?"

"I guess you could say it is a person whose job is to study the heavens."

"Why would anybody make this their job? For what purpose?"

"To learn . . . to understand . . ." I shrugged. "I suppose it serves the same purpose as what I do in my time . . . uncover what ancient people left behind—artifacts, ruins, their bodies—to understand them better."

"And what do you call someone who does what you do?"

"An 'archaeologist.'"

The corners of Heru's mouth twitched. "So even though you were unaware of our people, that you might one day be able to view times long past in the At, you found your own way to peer into the past." His eyes squinted as he smiled. "You intrigue me so very much, little queen."

My receding blush flamed back to life, and I picked at a pulled thread in the skirt of my dress.

"I would like to hear more about these other worlds that are like our own."

My gaze snapped to his. "Really?"

He nodded.

"Um, okay . . ." I curled my legs under me so I was kneeling, facing him, and started drawing in the sand between us. "So, this is the sun, and—"

"Did you know that when you are excited, you sometimes slip into your native tongue?"

I offered him a small smile. "Sorry." Returning to my drawing in the sand, I told him about the solar system, providing those details I could about each planet and some of the moons.

Heru found earth's moon and the sun the most intriguing, likely because those were the two most present in his everyday life. He was fascinated by the fact that the sun was so much larger than the moon, but didn't appear so in the sky, which only amazed him further because it made him think about how far away the sun really was.

I'd expected him to fight me on the whole "the earth is round" concept, but he merely nodded, his eyes narrowed in thought. Just because he was a younger version of himself, his intelligence was no less sharp, his focus on a subject no less intense.

I was just diving into a diatribe about Pluto, arguing that it didn't matter to me if there were a million hunks of ice floating around out there just like it, Pluto would always be a planet in my mind, when Heru shocked me speechless.

"Do you have any idea how much I love you," he said in heavily accented English.

My mouth fell open, and I snapped it shut before I could look like a buffoon for too long. I stared at him, searching his eyes.

"Will you tell me what that means now?" he asked.

I looked down at my fairly elaborate sand drawing of the solar system, poking little craters into Mars with the tip of my pointer finger. "I do not think I should . . . it will make you uncomfortable."

"Because you did not mistake me for Nuin," he said. "Because you were speaking to me, were you not?"

I added a flying saucer near the moon.

"Please, little queen—Alexandra." Heru captured my hand and started rubbing his thumb against my palm. "Tell me."

Staring down at our joined hands, I swallowed roughly. And then I told him.

"But you were not really speaking to me . . . you were speaking to who I will become."

I nodded, and hated myself just a little bit for doing it. "Marcus—it is your name in my time. My ba traveled to my present while I was unconscious—it does that sometimes—and I found you there." My voice grew thick. "You wrapped your arms around me and kissed me and . . ." Blinking, I took deep breaths. "And you told me you loved me, and then I was waking up, and you were right there in front of my eyes." I looked into his eyes, searching those shimmering silver-gold depths. "I said it to Marcus and to you . . . and to every version of you between then and now."

"I think that if I were him"—Heru smiled ruefully—"which I am, what would upset me the most about this situation would be not knowing what you were going through . . . not being able to do things like this, to sit and stare at the stars or to know what you were doing all day. Even now, even unbonded, it pains me to think of . . ." He clenched his jaw. "The thought of not knowing . . . I think that would be utter misery."

I shook my head, heart swollen with hope despite my mind not entirely understanding his point. "What are you suggesting?"

"Why not leave something behind for me to find in the future—a record of your time here? It will give you something to do once we are at the Oasis . . . other than training with Nuin, and with Set, Nekure, and me, of course."

My lips parted and I grinned. "I think that is a wonderful idea." My excitement was short-lived, and I bit my lip, feeling the need to keep our budding proto-relationship based on honesty. I gave his hand a squeeze. "I have to tell you something, but I need you to promise to listen . . . to not say anything until I am finished."

Heru eyed me, his expression contemplative, his eyes wary. "Go ahead."

I took a deep breath, and then I dove in. "I cannot stay in this time. I—there will come a day, maybe in a few weeks, maybe in a few months, when I must return to my own time."

He shook his head violently. "No, I will not allow—"

"Be quiet! You promised . . ."

"I did not."

I rolled my eyes. "Just let me finish," I said. "When I leave, *if* we have bonded—if you decide that is what you want—then I will be able to create a shield within you that will prevent the withdrawals—"

"But *I* will know you are gone, and—"

I shook my head. "No, Heru, you will not know, because I will lock those memories away in your mind."

He withdrew his hand from mine. "I see." He seemed on the cusp of saying more, but instead, he pushed off the sand and stood.

His sudden distance, sudden coldness, shredded my heart. “Heru—”

“Let us return.”

I sucked in a breath to protest further, but exhaled instead of saying anything. Deflating, I stood and walked with Heru back to camp. Neither of us uttered another word.

PART V

Netjer-At Oasis
Present Day

28

SEEK & HIDE

"So it's true then—you *were* there when Nuin died," I said to Aset during one of my how-to-be-a-*real*-Nejerette lessons. The blood running through my veins felt as electrified as it did when I was around Carson. For nearly a week, we'd been camped beside the jagged, sand-swept rocky lumps that had supposedly been part of the Netjer-At Oasis thousands of years ago, and I'd finally worked up the nerve to ask Aset if she'd been at the Oasis when Nuin died and the whole place collapsed in on itself. Or so legend said . . .

Aset smiled, making her cheeks rounder, which only made her prettier. She was one of those gorgeous people who I just couldn't hate, even though I really wanted to—*I mean, really, who looks like that?*—because she was just too effing nice. I supposed it made sense that she would be perfect-looking, since she was Marcus's twin sister and all, and really, *nobody* could deny that *he* was drool-worthy to the *n*th degree. I also supposed that Marcus must've missed out on the "nice" gene . . . or maybe Aset stole his.

"I was there—here—at the Oasis," Aset said, "but I was not present for the Great Father's death, no." She was sitting across from me at the top of a sand dune near camp, her legs crossed and her hands clasped in her lap. "Are you ready to try again?"

I bit my lip. I really wanted to ask her more questions—*Are the legends true? Was the Oasis home to a city made of crystal? Did the whole thing collapse when Nuin died? Is that why it looks like a big ol' pile of rubble?* But I was practicing using restraint, hoping doing so would make people stop treating me like a pre-manifestation teen and more like a full-fledged Nejerette.

And I was grateful to Aset, because she treated me like I mattered, like I could help, like she actually gave a shit about me. With Dom, Jenny, Neffe, and Alexander still in Cairo, waiting for Lex's parents and grandma, and everyone else pretty much expecting me to turn traitor like my mom, Aset was one of two people I could call a friend right now, Carson being the other. I didn't know why she treated me so well, but I was really grateful she did.

Exhaling, I nodded. "Yeah, okay, let's check again. Last time it seemed sort of stable . . . or *more* stable, I guess, and the twenty-third time's the charm, right?" I smiled at her nervously. Ever since the *Set incident*, the At had been unstable—damn Nothingness. It definitely wasn't the best time to learn how to navigate the At, but I'd had some of the best teachers available —first Dom, then Aset—so I'd say I was pretty lucky. "You really think having me with you in there is helping? Or, at least, isn't hurting?"

Aset met my smile with a kind one of her own. "If you were hurting my progress in this search for a stable portion of At, I would be conducting it on my own," she said matter-of-factly. "And more importantly, you proved your devotion to Lex when you sacrificed the chance to ever reach full maturity in order to rescue her. Because of that, I know I can trust you, and I would not enter the At with one I could not trust."

"Yeah, but everyone here is devoted to Lex," I said, glancing behind me at the camp of almost a hundred Nejerets; it grew every day as more of Marcus's people trickled in.

"Everyone but one," Aset countered. "There is a traitor here, this I know."

I opened my mouth to assure her that it most definitely, absolutely, in *no* possible way was me. At all.

She silenced my unvoiced words with another smile. "Not you, this I *also* know."

I frowned. "*How* do you know? Or is this another one of those things you can't tell anyone?" Along with getting to know how dang nice Aset was, I'd also learned that she carried more secrets than anyone I'd ever met—*ever*.

She nodded.

"Does Marcus know there's a traitor?"

Again, she nodded. "But there is little he can do about it. What will happen will happen." She held out her hand to me. "Come, now, let us link and make one final attempt to find stability." Her eyes sparkled with some of those secrets. "I've got a good feeling about this one."

Brow furrowed, I placed my palm against hers and curled my fingers around the back of her hand. "Here goes nothing . . ."

We lurched into a tidal wave of At, rolling around and around as the psychedelic colors stuttered, flashing in and out like they were being broadcast with a crappy signal. Honestly, not the most comforting situation to be in . . .

"It is better, yes?" Aset practically shouted.

I nodded as my stomach lurched. How I seemed to have developed motion sickness when I didn't technically have either a stomach or an inner ear—I mean, I was *a disembodied ba at the moment—was beyond me.*

"Concentrate on finding stability, Katarina." Aset's voice was smooth and calm, and her incorporeal hand was firm in mine. "Think only about

finding the nearest pocket of stability." She'd repeated the same words, over and over again, throughout the lesson.

I squeezed my fake eyelids shut, blocking out the here-one-moment, gone-the-next swirling colors, and concentrated. Stability. Stability. Let's go, stability . . . show me the stability . . . give me stability or give me—

"Open your eyes, Katarina," Aset said, giving my hand a squeeze.

I did, only to find myself exactly where I'd started: sitting on the top of a sand dune beside the enormous jumble of wind- and sand-eroded, crumbling limestone that was all that remained of the Netjer-At Oasis. Except I was still in the At.

"We've done it." She grinned. "We've finally found a bubble of stability."

I stared around at the pristine, unwavering *scene for all of two seconds, then released Aset's hand, jumped up to my feet, and started dancing around with hops and kicks and flailing arms and possibly a few stumbles. "We* did *it . . . we* did *it . . . we* did *it," I sang, over and over again. Not even Marcus had been able to enter a stable portion of the At since we'd arrived at the Oasis. It was like this place in particular was even more affected by the unpredictable Nothingness in the At than everywhere else, like it was the Bermuda Triangle of the At . . .*

"Yes, we were lucky," Aset said as she stood and brushed off her pants. She started down the dune. "Come along, Katarina. We don't know how long this pocket will last, and who knows when we'll get another shot."

I jogged down the slope to catch up with her, having a much easier time moving across the sand now that it was locked in place in an echo, making it more like concrete. "Omigod, can you imagine Marcus's face when we tell him we found a stable spot? Can you?" I clapped, giggling and cackling, then linked my arm with Aset's and picked up the pace, pulling her at a part-walk, part-jog to the edge of the rocky rubble that had once been the Netjer-At Oasis.

Aset slipped her arm free from mine and, once again, clasped my hand. "Whatever you do, Katarina, do not let go." There was a distinct thread of warning in her voice, making me uneasy. "Linked as we are, it should be much easier to maintain this pocket of stability—now that we've actually found one—until we can find what we're looking for."

"We're looking for something?" This was news to me. I'd thought it was just another lesson in how to use my new powers. "What are *we looking for?"*

Aset closed her eyes, and her grip on my hand tightened. "We're going back to the moment immediately after Lex leaves the past, shortly after Nuin's death and the collapse of the Oasis, and finding the place where the survivors emerged from the rubble, as it is the only way back in."

I continued to stare at her. "People were in there *when it happened? And they survived?"*

"They did. Now, hush, dear . . . I must concentrate."

As she spoke, the golden sand and clear blue sky and jagged rocks dissolved into a rainbow mist that glided past in vertical lines. With a flash, the colors were gone, and we were once again standing in the desert, except now the stars glittered overhead like an ocean of diamonds. Before us, the eroded rocky rubble had been replaced by a mound of craggy, crunching stone.

A short ways away on the right, there was an arched opening in the mass of limestone, like the mouth of a tunnel. And covering the opening completely was an opaque, almost shimmering slab of . . . well, I didn't actually know what it was, but it was definitely acting as a door, blocking the tunnel.

"And there, Katarina, is our way into the Oasis," Aset said.

Once again, the colors of the At surrounded us, and when they flickered away, we were back to standing before the eroded, sand-covered rocks in the present time. Aset moved closer to the general location of the opalescent door, but all that was there now was a patch of sand in front of a tall-ish boulder.

The echo started to flicker, and both Aset and I stared around as it faded away into Nothingness.

"We lost it . . ."

Aset turned bright eyes on me, and her lips spread into a victorious grin. "It doesn't matter; I found what I was looking for."

29

OVER & UNDER

Marcus was sitting behind the folding desk in the "office" in the front half of his two-room, canvas tent, Aset and me standing side by side opposite him. We were all using the equipment left over from the excavation a few weeks ago, and though the location had changed, the layout was more or less the same . . . except for the bathroom and shower trailer. That hadn't made it across the miles of desert. Which sucked. In my opinion, a five-gallon jug of water per person per day was *not* enough water to stay both hydrated *and* clean . . .

"You're certain?" Marcus studied Aset and me, his eyes seeming to pick apart and weigh each tiny little nuance of our expressions and stances. "And you really think there's some part of the Oasis under there?"

Aset maintained her smile, though it was starting to wilt, and nodded for the thousandth time. "Yes, I'm certain. Why don't you believe me when I say that *I* remember all?"

"Because *I* don't," Heru said, not taking his eyes off her.

"And we've discussed this, dear brother. It is what had to be . . ."

I sighed. My feet were getting tired from standing—we'd

been there for nearly an hour—and I was starting to feel a little light-headed. "Look, Marcus. I saw it, too. Not inside or anything, but the huge slab of whatever it was—"

"At," Aset clarified.

"—was definitely blocking the mouth of some kind of tunnel."

Marcus stared at me for a moment, then shifted his focus back to Aset and squinted the barest amount. "Alright." He nodded. "We'll start digging tonight, while it's cooler. Hopefully we'll be done by morning." He paused, hesitated. "And you're sure that whatever's left under there is safe? That it's not going to collapse on our people?"

Aset's smile regained its brilliance. "Few places have ever been safer."

Yeah, she was super nice and sweet and stuff, but holy hell, could Aset be mysterious when she wanted to be . . .

Marcus pointed to the arched, opaque slab that had been uncovered by the seventh rotation of Nejerets just as the sun peeked over the dunes to the east. "So you're telling me that *that* is made of 'At,' like this"—he touched the small lump under his shirt, which I assumed to be the bottle Aset had delivered to him when she'd first shown up nearly two weeks ago—"and that Lex made it?"

Aset nodded.

Carson and I stood behind them a few feet, sneaking glimpses between shoulders when we could. His fingers brushed against the back of my hand, and my eyes snapped to his face. He was watching me, not the "door," a shy smile curving his lips. My heart melted into a puddle of heart-shaped goo. His smiled widened, his blue eyes sparkling, and he took hold of my hand, slipping his fingers between mine. Yeah . . . complete and utter heart goo.

" . . . the rest of the city was made of," Marcus said. "I lived here for over a thousand years before the collapse. How did I not know the Great Father built the whole place out of At?"

"He did not want you to know. It was a dangerous thing, knowing what he was capable of."

Marcus was quiet for a long time, standing beside his sister and staring at the tall door of quartz-like At. "Do you think Apep will return?" he asked her quietly.

She shrugged. "Eventually."

"Then perhaps I shouldn't enter . . . shouldn't learn Lex's secrets. If he returns, and—"

Aset touched his arm. "He *will* return, and there is only one place where you will be safe from possession . . . for now." She nodded toward the door. "He cannot possess you when you are surrounded by so much At. Besides, just because he's possessing you, that doesn't mean he has access to your thoughts. He'll only know what you choose to share with him."

Marcus shook his head. "How could you possibly know—"

Aset laughed, a cheerful, chiming sound, and linked her arm with his. "In time, all will make sense, dear brother—for you sooner than for most, I think. You shall see." She guided him forward, ignoring his obvious hesitance. "Come on."

I exchanged a look with Carson. "So we found the door to get inside . . ." My brow furrowed. "How do you think we get *through* it?"

Carson shrugged and returned his gaze to the slab of At, and his eyes bulged at the same time as murmurs and whispers broke out among the dozens of Nejerets standing around the sloping hole, watching the siblings approach the door. He tugged on my hand. "Look, Kat . . . look!"

I did, and my mouth fell open.

The door was *glowing*, just like the At-chest had done when Lex had approached it back in Senenmut's underground temple. Marcus and Aset were dark silhouettes against the bright, iridescent glow of the door. I could just make out her profile as she looked up at her brother. She started nodding, and Marcus extended his hand toward the glowing slab of At.

With a sizzling sound, it dissolved into a myriad of colorful, misty tendrils. They slowly expanded upward, outward, fading until they evaporated completely and the slab of At was gone. Through the opening it left behind, there was nothing but absolute darkness.

Marcus looked over his shoulder, snapping orders to whichever Nejeret or Nejerette was closest. "Bring the LED rope . . . flashlights . . . headlamps . . . anything that'll provide light." He glanced around. "Carlisle!"

"Yes, Sir," said Marcus's "man" who handled pretty much everything as he brushed past my right shoulder and made his way down the ramp of sand toward Marcus and the doorway. Whenever I heard Carlisle speak, his words very proper and British, I dubbed him "Jeeves" in my mind.

"Call Dom or Neffe," Marcus told him. "They should be leaving Cairo with Lex's family in a few hours."

"I'm aware, Sir."

Marcus raised one eyebrow. "Tell them to procure generators, LED ropes, and whatever else you think we'll need to light up whatever's left in there." He pointed toward the mouth of the tunnel with his chin.

"Very well." With a slight bow of his head, Carlisle turned and started walking away from Marcus. He pulled one of the über-high-tech satellite cell phones all of Marcus's top people seemed to have out of his back pocket as he walked.

A skinny, blonde Nejerette I'd mentally labeled as one of Marcus's *minions*—one of the many of his people who weren't old enough, powerful enough, or useful enough to warrant a seat at the grown-ups' table, where all of Marcus's plans were discussed and put into action—ran past Carlisle at a jog, her arms filled with flashlights and headlamps. She skidded to a halt beside Marcus. "Here you go, Heru." She lowered her eyes in deference, but I just thought it made her look weak. With a wet-mop attitude like hers, she'd never climb high in the Nejeret ranks.

"Thank you, Amelia," Marcus said, fishing a headlamp out from the tangle and handing it to Aset before taking one for himself.

After he had his headlamp situated on his buzzed head, looking pretty silly, in my opinion, he selected a flashlight—one of the enormous ones that shone as brightly as a spotlight. Without another word, without even a glance around to see if anyone else was ready to follow, Marcus plunged into the darkness, quickly becoming little more than two retreating beams of light.

Aset selected a flashlight of her own and started looking around, scanning the faces like she was searching for someone. When her eyes landed on me, she grinned and waved me over. "Come on, Katarina. You're just as responsible for finding this as I am, so you must explore with me." Her smile was so genuine, her eyes so warm, that I thought, had she been human, she would've made an excellent mother. She *wouldn't have betrayed us all and abandoned her own daughter,* I thought bitterly.

I took a step toward her, but hesitated, glancing back at Carson. I bit my lip.

"Go," he said, smiling and shaking his head in a way that made me weak in the knees. He laughed, making his bright blue eyes sparkle in the morning light. "This is a once-in-a-lifetime opportunity, Kat. You *cannot* miss it. *Go.*"

I grinned, feeling silly. "Okay," I said, and before I could lose my nerve, I stepped back to him and lifted my face to his, pressing my lips against his cheek. "I'll tell you all about it," I called over my shoulder as I jogged toward Aset.

"You'd better!"

"Ah . . . Ma'am," Carlisle called just as I reached Aset.

"Pick out a headlamp and flashlight, dear," Aset said to me, then looked up at Carlisle, who'd hustled over to stop at the lip of the ramp. "Yes?"

He is such a Jeeves, I thought, smiling to myself as I pulled a headlamp with a lime-green band onto my head. I was pretty sure it was the same one I'd used before.

"Would you please let Heru know that Alexander is on his way and should arrive within the hour, but that Dominic will make the arrangements requested before picking up the Larsons and Susan Ivanov from the airport, then bringing them here along with Neffe and Jennifer Larson?"

Smiling, Aset nodded. "Yes, of course. And I'm sure my brother would appreciate it if you had Alexander join us in here as soon as he arrives . . . and no others until then."

"As you wish, Ma'am." He bowed his head to her.

"Thank you, Carlisle." She wrapped her tiny hand around my arm just above the elbow and started leading me into the opening. I couldn't see the light from Marcus's headlamp or flashlight at all anymore.

"And, Ma'am . . ."

Aset paused and glanced back at Carlisle.

"Alexander informed me that he's picked up another Nejeret . . . a man who goes by the name of Nik and claims to be one of your people. He knew enough about you and our plans that Alexander decided to grant his request to join him on his journey out here." Carlisle attempted a smile, and a muscle in his cheek twitched. "Though Alexander should have informed Heru before deciding to bring him, I thought it prudent to verify his identity with you before they drew much closer."

"Ah, yes . . ." Aset offered Carlisle a smile much more

genuine than his own. "Nik is mine, and I apologize for any confusion. He was supposed to meet us in Cairo, but he was held up and must've decided hitching a ride would be the easiest way to catch up to me." For once, she was the one to bow her head to him. "I should have informed you, and I apologize for that oversight. I hope you'll forgive me."

"Of course, Ma'am." Carlisle turned away.

Before he could take a step, Aset said, "And Carlisle . . . if you hear word of anyone else claiming to be one of 'my people,' I assure you they are lying and should be handled accordingly."

"I understand." Carlisle nodded before continuing on his way.

"Shall we?" Aset pulled me toward the opening again, releasing my arm as I matched her slow steps into the darkness.

It didn't remain dark for long. Under the assault of both of our headlamps and flashlights, the darkness gave way to curved, silvery walls. A closer look showed me it was less silvery and more like seamless, barely opaque stone. I followed the wall on the right upward, until my headlamp showed it arching overhead before cascading down the other side. I peered closer at the floor, but as far as I could tell, it was made of the same stone, though it was flat. My skin tingled, the hairs standing on end, as I realized something I should have from the moment we entered the tunnel—it wasn't made of stone; it was made of At.

"Honestly, if I wasn't seeing this with my own two eyes, there's no way I'd believe there was an entire tunnel built of effing At," I said as I continued to focus on the tunnel floor a few feet ahead of us. "I mean, really? *Really*? It's crazy, right?"

Grabbing my wrist, Aset tugged on my arm, and I ceased my meandering pace onward. "Look," she said, slowly scanning her flashlight beam across the way ahead.

The combination of my increasingly sensitive Nejerette vision and our meager artificial light enabled me to see at least some of what lay ahead—a ghostly ancient city of large, graceful structures composed of narrow archways, elongated spires, and fluted columns. A sinuous darkness curved lazily between the buildings, drinking in the light, and I assumed it was some sort of spring-fed underground stream . . . snaking through an underground city . . . that appeared to *also* be made of At. *Un-freaking-believable . . .*

"It seems so impossible," Aset said, her voice filled with longing and loss. "It feels like it was just yesterday that I left her in here . . ."

Her words shocked me out of my stunned state. "Her? Who? Lex?" I touched Aset's shoulder, and when she didn't seem to notice, I gripped it and gave her a hard shake. "Aset, are you talking about Lex? Are you saying you left her in this—this *crypt*? Did you leave her in here to die?"

"No!" Aset stared at me, her eyes wide and wild and glistening in the pale, artificial light. "No, I—she made me. She told me—she—" Aset turned me to face her and gripped my upper arms so hard that I winced. "I left because she told me to, and when I returned, the door was sealed . . ." She shook her head, her shimmering eyes boring into me. "It *had* to stay sealed." She released me, but continued to shake her head. "We will know her fate not long from now, I think. We will know all of our fates . . ." She forced a smile. "All will work out; you will see."

I blinked, narrowed my eyes, and crossed my arms, shrugging to escape her talon-like grip. "Just so you know, you sound like a total crazy person."

Aset let out a breathy laugh. "I would imagine so, Katarina." She smiled and sighed. "Come. It is too dark to make much out right now, and I have a feeling that I know where Heru went."

"Where?" I asked, following her down a barren slope toward the stream.

"Home."

30

DEATH & DECAY

Aset led me across a narrow, arched bridge bordered by delicate, At-filigree railings. The stream definitely had to be fed by a spring, because I could hear it burbling. A slow brush of my flashlight beam showed me that the "stream" was lined by what appeared to be paving stones, making me think it was actually more of a canal.

"How is this even here?" I whispered, afraid that speaking too loudly would cause it all to come crashing down around us.

"Heru's home is just this way," Aset said, flicking her flashlight along the path lining the opposite side of the canal. She waited for me at the foot of the bridge, and once I was across, started walking along the edge of the canal. "Nuin is responsible for creating the Netjer-At Oasis—or *Cavern,* I suppose it might be called now," she said with a roundabout glance. "It has been here as long as I've been alive, though I suppose the Oasis did grow over the years, but Lex is the one responsible for concealing it, for keeping it out of the spotlight, for protecting it from the desert . . ."

I looked at Aset, watching her delicate features as we walked.

"But how did she do all of that? How is this not buried in, like, a mile of rock?"

Aset paused and raised her flashlight beam to the cavern's ceiling. "Look up. What do you see?"

I followed the light, but couldn't tell much other than that the cavern's ceiling was high overhead. "So a cave popped up around this place at just the right time?"

"You're funny," Aset said, her tinkling laugh making me smile. "It didn't just pop up—*Lex* did it. She erected a dome of At just as the limestone cliffs shielding the Oasis came crashing down on top of us." Aset's gaze became distant, and all remnants of her momentary humor disappeared. "The ground shook . . . the screams . . . you cannot imagine the terror."

It was clear from the tense set of her features that she didn't actually want to talk about whatever she was reliving in her memories, so *I* gave *her* a gentle tug to keep going. "Sounds scary. You said Heru's place is this way?"

Aset cleared her throat. "Um, yes," she said, veering to the right, down a narrow alleyway between two rows of crumbling two-story buildings that appeared to be constructed from regular old stone, not At. "It's just this way, across the orchard and gardens."

I raised my flashlight, shining the beam along the way ahead. One of the more fanciful buildings sat on the opposite side of the "orchard"—more like a haunted forest with its sparse, skeletal trees—its face composed of three graceful archways, two smaller ones flanking a larger, which appeared to be an open doorway. As we reached the opening, I saw that there was no door at all.

"I guess there wasn't much crime here . . . ?"

Aset stepped through the threshold and into what I could only describe as a small palace. It was more than a little haunting in the dim light. "There was no need for doors," she said. "Nuin forbade us from willfully harming one another, and nobody would dare defy him. At least, not until the end . . ."

I followed her into the palace. There were piles of unidentifiable things on the dust-covered floor here and there; what was left of the furniture after it rotted and collapsed in on itself, I supposed. As we moved from open space to open space through successive archways, my cursory inspection showed me that only a few pieces remained intact, all apparently made of some stone or another. It was *so* eerie. If ever a place was haunted, this one would be.

Aset led me through one final arched doorway and stopped, staring at the man kneeling on the floor on one side of the room. There was more stone furniture in here, what appeared to be three beds arranged against three of the walls. Two were empty; one was covered in something that looked an awful lot like a glass coffin.

Aset grabbed my wrist, preventing me from moving further into the room.

Marcus's head was bowed, his forehead leaning against the "coffin." He had to have heard us enter, and if his eyes were open, he would see our headlamps and flashlights illuminating the eerie space, but he didn't raise his head. He didn't appear to be moving at all. I was starting to get the sick feeling that the thing he was kneeling beside didn't just *look* like a coffin. It was cool in the At-cavern compared to the desert overhead, but the chill washing over my skin had nothing to do with the temperature.

"Heru . . ." Aset's voice was gentle.

"I don't remember this," Marcus said, his own voice a quiet rasp. "I remember her dying from a fever . . . but I don't remember *this*."

Her dying? I looked from Aset to Marcus and back. *Are they talking about Lex?*

"I was here with you when it happened . . . as was Lex." Aset sighed as she released my wrist and moved further into the room to stand beside Marcus. She gazed down at the *thing* and reached out to brush a thick layer of dust off the top. "She loved little Tarsi very much, I think."

"She was my favorite . . ."

"I know, Heru. I know."

Feeling like an intruder, I snuck closer. I just couldn't help myself.

The coffin was mostly opaque—thank *God,* because dead bodies are so *not* my thing—and I could just make out the shape of a person inside. A very *small* person.

Aset placed her hand on Marcus's shoulder. "Come, dear brother, there is more you must see."

It took him a moment, but after a sniff and a throat clearing, Marcus stood and looked at his sister. "Did you know it would be like this, under the rubble?"

Aset tilted her head to the side. "In a way, yes. This is how it looked—though with less dust and rot—when we left." She glanced around the high-ceilinged room. "It is very strange to be back, and for the city to be so . . ." She hesitated. "So dark, so empty . . . so dead." She took hold of Marcus's hand and led him back out the way we'd come in, through a half-dozen archways and rooms of various sizes, and out to the empty space that must have once been a garden.

I followed, hanging back to give them their privacy. I considered retracing my steps and finding my way out of the fantastical ghost town, because it was starting to seriously creep me out, but the thought of getting lost creeped me out even more, so I opted to stay with Aset and Marcus.

We wound along curving paths paved with worn limestone between more of the "regular" two-story buildings—some of which were little more than piles of crumbled stone—and around a few more of the graceful At structures similar to Marcus's home. We only stopped after we'd rounded the largest, most graceful and fantastical of them all and reached what looked to me like a mausoleum from a century-old cemetery.

Turning away from the underwhelming little structure, I looked at the At palace. My eyes followed it as it flowed upward; a few of its sleek spires actually punctured the cavern's ceiling.

"I am not sure exactly how much of your memory she altered," Aset said behind me. "You and Lex spent much time in here together. Do you remember this place at all?"

"No." Marcus's voice was rough. "Is it *his* tomb?"

"It is, and more. Lex built most of it during her time here . . . and you carried Nuin's body here, so she could inter him within, along with her story."

Her story? I glanced over my shoulder to see them standing side by side, facing the mausoleum.

Marcus was shaking his head. "I don't remember any of that. I thought—I thought we left him in his bed when the walls came crashing down . . ."

Aset nodded. "Set remembered much the same. Lex had so many memories to alter. I'm sure she would have left you with more complete, more settling alternate memories if she could have, but . . . she'd already been through so much, expended so much power . . . she did what she could."

Marcus looked at her. "Was she alright?"

Aset shrugged. "More or less. She experienced much during her time here—*then*—changed, grew . . . you will be quite amazed when she returns, I think. Amazed, and proud to call her your bond-mate." She raised a hand, touching his arm. "She is a remarkable Nejerette, and both Nekure and I were sorry to have to say goodbye to her when we did."

"Nekure . . ." Heru shook his head. "I completely forgot—where is he?" He paused. "Is he still—"

"Alive? Quite," Aset said. "He's on his way." She laughed. "He's changed much over the years. You'll barely recognize him." She pointed to the mausoleum, to what appeared to be a door set in the front between two slender, grooved columns. "It is like the other—attuned to your and Lex's combined bonding pheromones. You must touch it . . ."

Marcus stepped forward and reached out his arm. Like before, the slab of At barring his way dissolved into a colorful mist before disappearing completely. He shone his flashlight in the opening, revealing a steep stairwell that descended into darkness. And also like before, he plunged onward without hesitation. Part of me wondered if he thought he might actually find Lex down there, like she'd been waiting for him to find her for millennia.

Biting my lip, I shivered, awash in dread. *What if she* is *down there . . .*

"Come along, Katarina. There is nothing to be afraid of." Aset held her arm out to me, and together, we descended the stairs.

"What the—"

Aset rushed forward a few steps, "Oh my God . . ."

Marcus was standing beside another coffin, only this one was as clear as glass and most definitely occupied. And the body it contained looked like it had stopped breathing only seconds ago.

Mouth hanging open, I made it down the final few steps and, dazed, walked toward the coffin. I stood on the opposite side from Marcus and Aset and stared down at a face that was almost as shocking as the body's pristine state.

"It's you," I said, raising my eyes to Marcus's face.

"It's not," he said. "It's the Great Father."

"Nuin . . . ?"

Ignoring me, he tore his gaze away from Nuin's peaceful face to look at Aset. "Did you know about this, as well?"

She shook her head, her eyes wide, containing equal parts wonder and horror. "He looks exactly as he did when we left him down here. How—" She looked at her brother. "How is this possible?"

"How should I know?"

I cleared my throat and licked my lips, my eyes flicking down to the man who only appeared to be slumbering beneath that thin barrier of At. "I, um, don't mean to be rude or anything, but are you sure he's dead?"

"Yes," Aset said softly. "It was what had to be . . ." Both she and Marcus returned to staring down at the over-four-thousand-year-dead body.

"Okay . . ." Suddenly, the idea of getting lost as I tried to find my way out of this underground funhouse of WTF *wasn't* the creepiest option; continuing to stare at Nuin's dead, unrotted body *was*. I backed away from the coffin and turned around to study the walls. Walls were definitely a better, less creepy choice.

There were hieroglyphs inscribed in neat columns on every available surface, though I had no clue what they said, and a single, arched doorway set in the center of each wall. I made my way toward the one opposite the stairs and stood on its threshold while I scanned the space beyond with the beam of my flashlight. The ceiling was high, and like the doorways, arched, and the walls were covered with writing as well, though this script was flowy and cursive . . . and, as impossible as it seemed, written in English.

Lips parted and eyes wide, I stepped closer to the wall on my right and studied the words.

. . . sandstorm, and we almost bonded again. But I screwed up. I didn't tell you everything, and once you found out that we're bonded in the future, well, let's just say that things went downhill from there. You weren't too excited about the idea of . . .

There was no doubt in my mind that these were Lex's words. I stopped reading, feeling like I was peeking into her diary, and swept my flashlight beam over the rest of the room. When the light touched the far wall, maybe twenty paces away, I yelped and dropped my flashlight.

Someone was standing in a recessed part of the wall.

Heart racing and fingers shaking, I fumbled to pick up the flashlight and retrain its beam on the person. She was standing exactly where she'd been, exactly as she'd been. "Because it's a statue, moron," I muttered to myself.

I took a deep breath, then another, and started across the room. The closer I drew to the statue, the wider I opened my eyes.

She was tall and slender, wearing a simple, sleeveless dress that almost reached her ankles. One foot was placed ahead of the other, like she was stepping out of the alcove, and her left hand was raised, the fingertips touching the pendant hanging around her neck, which I was positive would be a thumb-sized falcon. Marcus had given its likeness to Lex a few weeks ago, when we'd still been in Florence. She was smiling, just a little, in a way that made me think she knew something, a secret or a joke or the truth about everything, but her eyes were sad, filled with longing as she gazed downward.

"Marcus," I whispered. I cleared my throat and tried again. "Marcus . . ."

"What?" His one-word response echoed around the room.

I spun, fully expecting to find him standing right behind me, or at least in the doorway, but there was no sign of him. He was probably still staring at Nuin's not-decayed-even-for-a-second body.

"You should see this," I said. "You'll *want* to see this."

"She's right," I heard Aset say. "You *will* want to see what awaits you in the other chambers. Go, dear brother."

Marcus appeared in the doorway, his flashlight beam hitting me directly in the eyes.

I raised my hand to shield my vision. "*Dude . . .*"

"What is it that I *need* to see?" he said as he strode into the room.

I blinked, confused. It seemed pretty obvious to me. But then I realized I was standing in front of the statue and probably blocking his view entirely.

It didn't matter; he was sidetracked by the writing on the walls after barely two steps. He moved closer to the left wall and murmured something in another language while he traced Lex's letters with his fingertips.

"Marcus, you should—"

"Not now, Kat," he said softly.

"Marcus—"

"I said not—" His words cut off abruptly as he spun around, facing me and finally catching sight of the statue. I moved away from it as he approached, his steps slow and almost hesitant. He stopped directly in front of her and raised his hand to trace his fingertips over every part of her face, just as he'd done with her words.

With a harsh, choking noise, he fell to his knees and rested his forehead against the front of her skirt. His hands clutched the sides of her dress as his whole body shook. Marcus Bahur, Heru, former leader of the Council of Seven, General to our people, and one of the most ancient and powerful Nejerets alive . . . was breaking down before my very eyes.

I jumped at a gentle touch on my shoulder. "Come, Katarina. Let us give him some time alone."

Nodding and numb with shock, I let Aset guide me back into Nuin's burial chamber and up the stairs.

"Ah, yes," she said as we emerged from the mausoleum. She pointed across the cavern, where tiny points of light were bouncing and shooting around haphazardly. "I thought it was about time for them to show up." She waved her flashlight in their direction and, raising her voice enough that Nejeret ears *might* hear her from that distance, said, "Meet us at the main bridge." It was far from a shout.

One of their beams of light waved back in response, but if they said anything, my ears weren't good enough to pick up on it.

Aset started walking, and I jogged a few steps to catch up to her.

"But . . . how will they know *where* the main bridge is?"

Aset glanced at me, her eyebrows raised. "Because Nik is there."

"And that makes a difference because . . . ?"

Aset smiled, like she only just understood my confusion. "Because Nik is from here."

31

WARN & WORRY

Staring up at the words Lex had somehow inscribed into the solidified fabric of space and time, I sighed. I'd been sitting cross-legged on the floor—also made of solidified At, along with pretty much every part of pretty much every other building in the oasis-cavern-*thing*—a notebook on my lap and my pen scratching against the paper as I copied down Lex's words, for hours. There were dozens of underground rooms like this, all with two-inch-tall words covering every available wall and ceiling space. Some rooms had arched ceilings, others just regular ol' flat ceilings, and the largest of all had a dome. I got the impression that Lex had been enjoying experimenting.

I set down my pen as a thought struck me—*what if that was the point, or at least* part *of the point? What if she created this place for practice?*

I could only assume that practicing her ability to make things out of the At was part of the reason she created the "Hall of Lex," as Carson and I'd started calling it. He'd thought he was *so* clever when he came up with the name, since "lex-" was also an ancient Greek root meaning "word" and there were words filling this place. I rolled my eyes, but I also smiled.

In the six hours since Marcus, Aset, and I first stepped into the tunnel, Marcus's minions had set up lighting throughout the Hall of Lex and in the half of the "city" on the tunnel-side of the canal. They'd even laid out LED ropes, creating a path from the Hall, across the bridge, and up to the tunnel that was about a half-mile long.

Not that I'd had much of a chance to look around the place now that it wasn't eerily empty and quiet and dark, but filled with Nejerets bustling around to move everything into the cavern and re-set up camp. Once the task of recording Lex's words in an easier-to-read format was decided, Aset suggested that only people who knew Lex well should be allowed in the subterranean Hall, which meant the job of scribe went to Aset, Alexander, Marcus, Carson, and me . . . and *Nik*.

I shivered, thinking about Aset's ancient, trusted companion. To say that Nik was *different* would be an understatement; *scares the crap out of me* would be more appropriate.

And it wasn't all the piercings or the black eyeliner, making his crazy-pale blue eyes look almost white, or the myriad of tattoos covering every visible part of him besides his face, all in various stages of fading as his body rejected them through regeneration . . . it was *him*. There was something about him that was more than a little unsettling, about how the air pressure shifted whenever he was in a room and goose bumps covered my skin.

Taking a deep breath, I shook myself in an effort to expel some of my Nik-inspired nervous jitters and returned my focus to my job. I stared at the wall and copied down Lex's words.

Nuin says that I'm picking up on how to use his sheut pretty quickly. I've grown so used to being able to do unbelievable things—alter memories, share my own memories, shift from one place to another, create a sort of bonding pheromone "plug" that protects you from withdrawals, transform things into At, create something from seemingly nothing—that doing those things just seems . . . normal. I bet you can't guess what your favorite is to help me practice . . . did you guess? Guess, Marcus, or I won't tell you! Just kidding. You can't get enough of me creating the bonding block, mostly because you LOVE shredding it to pieces. I kind of love that part too. I love you. I love every version of you, and getting to know ancient Heru has been . . . I don't even know how to describe it. I just love being able to know YOU better. If I could spend the thousands of years between now and when you're reading this by your side, growing and experiencing the centuries with you, I would. I really, truly would. Regardless, know this, Heru: however much time stands between us, however much distance separates us, I will find my way back to you. I will return to you . . . one way or another.

"Hey."

I jumped, unintentionally flinging my pen against the wall, and turned to glare over my shoulder. My glare withered the moment I laid eyes on *him*. Nik was standing in the archway connecting this room to Nuin's burial chamber, leaning his shoulder against the side and looking at me. *More like staring at me,* I thought. *Creep . . .*

I cleared my throat and reached for my pen. "Uh . . . hey."

"I heard about your mom—Genevieve."

I offered him a none-too-friendly tight-lipped smile. "Good for you." When he didn't say anything for several heartbeats, simply continued to stare at me, I added, "Did you want a trophy or something?"

His eyes narrowed, and he straightened, taking slow steps into the room. He wasn't walking strangely, not hunched over or anything, but something about the way he moved, the controlled, withheld intensity, reminded me of a stalking lion.

Setting my notebook and pen on the floor beside me, I slowly got to my feet, keeping Nik in my direct line of sight. As he came nearer, I backed up a step. Another. My back touched the grooved wall, and I glanced past him, staring longingly at the doorway.

I licked my lips and attempted a weak smile. "Listen . . . I'm sorry. That was, um, rude . . ."

He was only a few feet away. He took another step and seriously invaded my personal bubble, staring down at me with those eerily pale eyes.

I gulped, and my fingers searched the wall behind me for a way out, though I knew they would find nothing but Lex's words. "What—what do you want?"

Nik's eyes narrowed to slits, and he pressed his lips into a thin, flat line. He inhaled, and, closing his eyes, grinned.

Sensing that this might be my only chance to escape what was quickly turning into a totally freaky situation, I took a lurching step to the side, intending to sprint toward the doorway.

Nik slammed his open hand against the wall, blocking my escape. "You're afraid of me. Good." He leaned in closer, and I pressed my back against the wall as hard as I could to keep his body from touching mine. "That will make this so much easier."

"W—what?" I hated my stupid eyes for tearing up, and balled my hands into fists to help me hold the tears in.

Nik chuckled, the sound low and smooth. "I don't trust you," he said, and I couldn't help but stare into his ice-blue eyes. They were alight with fanatical intensity. "If you're hanging around here just biding your time . . . if you're planning on following in your *mother's* footsteps, I'd rethink those plans. I haven't spent over four thousand years doing everything I can to keep Lex safe just so some barely manifested Nejerette brat could fuck it all up."

My eyes widened, and a few of those traitorous tears escaped. I shook my head vehemently. "I—I—"

He leaned in closer, and there was no way to avoid it; his jeans brushed against the bare skin just below the hem of my shorts, and his black T-shirt pressed against my tank top. My already too-fast breaths sped up. I felt claustrophobic, trapped as I was between Nik and the wall.

Nik grinned again, his eyes filled with warning. "Don't even think about doing anything that would hurt Lex or hinder what she has to do. Do you understand?" His face was so close, I could see the individual flecks of blue, silver, and white in his irises. "Do you?"

Swallowing compulsively, I nodded.

"Hey!" Carson said from the doorway. "Get away from her!"

Nik's lips spread into that predatory grin, which I was starting to suspect was his go-to, scare-the-crap-out-of-people expression, and he glanced over his shoulder. "Two birds, one fucking stone," he said so quietly that I doubted Carson heard him. He pushed away from the wall, from me, and stalked toward Carson.

Pride welled in me as I watched Carson stand his ground. He stood taller, straightened his shoulders, and trained a steady glare on Nik. "Don't you ever lay a hand on her, or—"

"Or you'll what?" Nik stopped in front of Carson, blocking my view of him. It wasn't that he was enormously tall or thick or anything like that—he was actually pretty trim and of average height for a guy—but that Carson was kind of small. We were pretty much the same height.

"I'll—"

Nik pretended to lunge forward, and Carson jumped. Laughing softly, Nik stepped to the side and turned so he could look from me to Carson and back. "I think you need a new boyfriend, Katarina. Next time look for someone with a spine."

"I'm not—he's not . . ."

While Nik's attention was on me, Carson threw himself at Nik, who spun, took hold of Carson by the throat, and slammed him back against the nearest wall. Carson spluttered and kicked and clawed at Nik's arm, but none of it did any good.

Nik glanced at me. "Like I said . . ."

"Let him go!" I shrieked, finally breaking out of my terrified stupor. I took several lurching steps across the room toward them. "Why are you *doing* this?"

"Why?" Nik returned his focus to Carson. "Because there's a traitor among us, and I want to make sure he"—his eyes flicked to me—"or *she* doesn't fuck up what has to happen." He seemed to catch himself. "I've been watching you, Carson, ever since you got that position as one of Alexandra's monitors. You disappear in the At, sometimes, and I can't break through the cloak . . ." He cocked his head to the side. "What are you hiding?"

When Carson didn't respond, Nik squeezed his neck, and Carson's eyes bulged.

"Nekure! Release the boy!" Aset said, her words slicing through the tension. She was standing in the archway, her hands on her hips and her expression thunderous.

Nik leaned in closer to Carson, growled something unintelligible, and, letting go of the younger Nejeret, stepped backward.

"Go find Heru," Aset said to Nik as she stepped into the room. "He's up top with the others—Lex's family has arrived with Dominic and Neffe, and he may need assistance."

To my surprise, Nik bowed his head and strode out through the arched doorway.

Aset looked at Carson, who was gasping and clutching his neck as he leaned against the wall. "You go as well. I need to speak with Katarina alone."

Carson shook his head. "I'm not . . . leaving her . . . to—"

"Go!" I almost couldn't believe Aset was capable of sounding so harsh, so commanding.

With a reluctant look at me, Carson walked away, too. I watched him leave, wishing I could chase after him.

"You should be careful of him."

I nodded vehemently. "I didn't even *do* anything to provoke him. Nik's just so—"

"I wasn't talking about Nik."

"What?" I blinked at Aset, scrunching my brow and shaking my head. *Be careful of Carson?*

"Nik was not lying. Carson is cloaked during brief, almost undetectable moments in the At, and we can't figure out why . . ."

I was still shaking my head. "I'm sure it's just an, I don't know . . . a misunderstanding or something."

"Perhaps," Aset said. She closed the distance between us and wrapped a comforting arm around my shoulders. She smiled, but it didn't quite banish the hard glint in her eyes. "I sincerely hope you are right."

I searched her eyes. "Nik—he thinks *I* might be a traitor, too . . . like my mom." I looked at the floor.

Aset gave my shoulders a squeeze. "Nik takes his duty very seriously, and all he knows of you is that your mother betrayed Lex by harming her sister." She nodded, more to herself than to me. "I'll speak with him . . . clear things up. He won't bother you again."

I smiled at her weakly. "Um, okay . . . thanks."

"Now, come." She guided me through the archway and into Nuin's burial chamber. "You're missing all the fun. Lex's mother fainted as soon as she saw Alexander, launching the grandmother into giving Alexander the scolding of a lifetime, and when I left, Lex's father was giving Heru a piece of his mind, and Heru was *barely* holding his tongue . . ." She laughed softly, the sound echoing off the solidified At like hundreds of tiny bells. "It is a scene I shall watch over and over again in the At."

PART VI

Netjer-At Oasis
6th Dynasty, Old Kingdom

32

WIVES & CHILDREN

I stared at an enormous and rather unremarkable rock outcropping, wondering if, once again, something had been lost in translation. Maybe the word I'd thought meant "oasis" actually meant "huge mesa." Personally, I preferred *my* translation, and I really hoped it was still, somehow, accurate.

I wasn't built for desert excursions; under my protective linen robe and cowl, I was hot, sweaty, and pretty ripe, and I'd been looking forward to glassy pools surrounded by palm trees, where I could take more than the barely useful sponge baths I'd grown used to over the past week and a half. Hearing that the rocks ahead were, in some way, supposed to be the "Netjer-At Oasis" had been a needle to my hopes, poking them and causing them to deflate in an instant.

Heru was walking beside me, as usual . . . and was silent, as had *become* usual. The cold shoulder mixed with his near constant close proximity was exhausting, and I'd had enough. It was time to break the silence. Plus, I needed some clarification on the whole "oasis" thing.

I said as much to Heru, adding, "So tell me, how is *that* the Netjer-At Oasis?" I studied his profile as we crossed the final stretch of windswept sand separating us from the mammoth rock outcropping, along with the rest of our Nejeret, human, and donkey caravan.

Heru continued looking ahead. "The rocks surround the Oasis in a ring, like a protective wall." He sent me the briefest sideways glance, and whatever he saw on my face—a thousand shattered dreams, a you-kicked-my-puppy expression, absolute and utter disappointment, something along those lines—caused him to chuckle. "I do not wish to spoil the surprise, little queen, but do not fear; you will not be disappointed for long, I think."

I pursed my lips and narrowed my eyes. "I hope you are correct, Heru . . . I really do."

When we'd crossed half the distance and were several hundred yards away from the tall wall of rock, a dark sliver came into view—an opening in the wall's face. The closer we drew, the taller and wider it seemed. Only when the first set of people and pack animals reached the opening did I realize just how big it was—wide enough for a half-dozen people to walk side by side, and at least twice their height.

I figured Nuin was in that first group, as he'd taken the lead almost every day, while Heru seemed to prefer bringing up the rear. At the moment, only Aset, Nekure, Denai, and the other priestesses were behind us.

Rus, who'd been sleeping in his little sling, snug against my chest, awoke with a squeaky meow-yawn and proceeded to stretch with such intensity that his little furry body shook.

I pulled out the collar of my robe, peeked down at the kitten, and spoke to him in English. "Hey, little guy."

He stared up at me with sleepy, squinted eyes and yawned again.

"I think you're gonna get to stretch your legs soon . . . maybe chase some bugs . . . how's that sound?"

He started purring that loud, overenthusiastic purr that belongs solely to kittens. It wasn't my words that were making him so happy; it was the hand I'd tucked under the layers of pale linen so I could scratch under his chin.

"But you have to promise to leave the scorpions alone, okay?"

His eyes closed, and he tilted his chin back, stretching out his neck.

"I'll take that as a 'yes.'"

We were nearing the opening in the wall of rock; it was too symmetrical to be natural, and inside, the walls and floor were far too smooth. My heart rate picked up as my excitement made a resurgence. A nice, polished tunnel through a wall to *somewhere* was a lot better than a giant, solid rock.

"You speak with little Rus quite often," Heru said.

I glanced at him. "I have to speak to *someone* . . ." It was an unnecessary jab, and I wished I could suck the words back in as soon as they flew out of my mouth. I was far from companionless—Aset, Nekure, Set, Denai, the priestesses, Nuin—but the one companion I desired above all others was out of my reach. And I *knew* he had a pretty damn good reason to hold me at arm's length, even if, with every breath, I wished he would pull me close, hold me tightly, and promise to never let me go.

Heru didn't respond. He did, however, take hold of my arm and pull me to the side of the tapered opening before I could enter the tunnel. My hasty words must've irritated him as much as I'd feared they would.

"Apologies, Heru. I know this situation is difficult . . ."

He led me closer to the rock wall and stopped, stepping in front of me and watching the final few stragglers disappear into the tunnel. After a quick nod at someone behind me, he pushed his cowl back, and all of his attention was focused on me.

Those molten, golden eyes stared down at me. That chiseled jaw clenched. Those high cheekbones seemed sharper in the afternoon light, making him appear more wild and fierce and ancient—more *other*—than usual. His appearance was a stark reminder that, even now, thousands of years in the past, it had been a long time since he'd been human.

I fidgeted under the intensity of his stare, pulling both of my arms into my robe and petting Rus. I met Heru's eyes, but looked away almost immediately. Growing irritated at my deferential reaction, I forced myself to lock gazes with him. "What? What is it? Why are you looking at me like that?"

Shaking his head, Heru let out a heavy sigh and *almost* smiled. "I would speak with you now, and I would have you say nothing until I am finished."

My eyebrows rose.

Heru pushed back my own cowl, and I squinted as I lost the only thing shielding my eyes from the sunlight. He trailed the backs of his fingers over my cheek before pulling his hand away. It had been days since he'd touched me outside of training, and his fingers left behind a trail of tingles on my skin.

I swallowed roughly, doing my damnedest to hide my reaction to that simple, restrained touch. My heart was racing, but I kept my breaths as even as I could.

"There is much I would have you understand of my life here . . . of my life in general, and why the choice you have given me is such a difficult one," he said. "But I fear that much of what I have to say will upset you, and whatever you may think of me, upsetting you is the last thing I want to do."

I could think of one thing he wanted to do less—bond with me. But I held my tongue.

A humorless smile curved his lips. "Ah . . . but I see you do not believe me." He shook his head again, laughing softly. "I cannot say I blame you . . . and now I shall risk driving you away completely. But I would have there be honesty between us, however bitter that honesty may taste."

I pulled part of my bottom lip between my teeth, and Heru's eyes flicked lower for the briefest moment. Honesty—I wasn't sure it was something we *could* have, not completely. I wasn't sure if I could tell him that Nuin would die before I left this ancient time, or that Set would be possessed by Apep, and the possession would last millennia. And then there was the whole *twins* issue . . . how would he react to finding out that thousands of years in the future, we would—*had to*—have children? And our children *wouldn't* exactly be normal. I'd already turned his life upside down. I wasn't sure either of us could handle any further upsets, not yet.

Heru cleared his throat. "My other two wives—they are here, as are our children and many of my aging human descendants from past unions. I would have you meet them, have you learn something of the sacrifice I—and others—would be making should you and I truly be together."

I was shaking my head before he'd finished speaking. There was no reason for him to give up any kind of relationship with his children, and where his wives were concerned, as much as it pained me to admit it, relations with them would return to normal as soon as I was gone. It would be as though I'd never existed in this time. It had to be that way.

"But—" I stopped myself and squeezed my eyes shut in a protracted blink. "Please, continue," I said and reopened my eyes.

The faintest hint of a smile turned the corners of Heru's mouth upward. "Many Netjer-At men value human women for one thing alone—their ability to bear our children." He paused, his stare turning challenging. "I am not among them. I only take wives I genuinely care for . . . I genuinely desire . . . and I love them as best I can during the short time I have with them." He did smile this time, a sad, wistful expression. "Their lives are so fleeting, but it is that very quality that helps me remember that every day matters, that every moment deserves my full attention."

As he spoke, I realized that, while I still felt extreme, wrenching jealousy toward every single woman he'd ever been with, I also felt gratitude toward them for helping to shape him into the man I loved so desperately, a man who'd been hardened by time, but who wasn't oblivious to its passing like so many of the ancients of our kind.

His eyes searched mine. "Bunefer has been my faithful wife for fifty-seven years, and in that time, she bore me eight children. Five survived to adulthood, the youngest of which manifested two years ago; she is the first child of mine to do so in over a century. Bunefer is quite elderly now, and though our relationship has changed over the years, I still hold great affection for her and consider her one of my closest friends. I will mourn her passing for centuries." His eyes shone with the love he felt for Bunefer, and tears pricked in my own eyes. "I believe she will like you very much—she and Aset have always been very close."

My eyes widened.

"And then there is Seshseshet." He exhaled heavily. "Sesha is . . . well, she is much like you in many ways—pensive, guarded, filled with single-minded determination"—he smiled, and for once, the expression touched his eyes—"and quite beautiful. We have been together for nineteen years, and during that time, she has given me six children, four of which remain with us." He paused, but his eyes never left mine. "I would have you stay in my home with my family . . . with me."

Stunned, I opened my mouth but couldn't seem to find *any* words. All I could manage was to slowly shake my head. *Stay in his home . . . with his family . . . his* wives?

"I have already spoken to Nuin about this, and he is amenable, so long as you are. You would have your own private sleeping chamber, but this would also give us a way to come to know each other better . . . to understand how our lives and the lives of my family would be changed if we bonded." Again he paused, and the skin around his eyes tightened minutely. "What do you say? Are you willing to try this?"

I inhaled and exhaled several times, pondering how to respond while I studied every angle, every line of his face. On my fifth inhale, I did the unthinkable—I nodded. "Very well . . . I am willing to try."

Relief filled Heru's eyes and visibly altered his stance; his shoulders relaxed, his chin lowered, and his lips curved into a genuine grin.

What did I just agree to? I adjusted Rus's weight in his sling, anxiety already rising. I wasn't ready for this, for meeting *them*. I felt the desperate need to delay and said the first thing that came to mind. "But I would like to clean myself up before you take me to meet them."

"There is a small bath house in my home. We could—"

"*Before* I meet them, Heru . . . and I need to fetch a fresh dress—"

He didn't miss a beat. "Your priestesses will no doubt be waiting for you on the other end of the passageway, in the Oasis. We will gather a clean dress from them before sending them on to my home with your belongings—"

I felt my eyes go wide and my heart flutter wildly. This was all happening too fast. "But—"

"And then I will take you to a small, secluded pool where you may bathe under the sun, and—"

I shook my head, feeling my chest tighten with rising panic. "Heru, I—"

"Bunefer and Seshseshet will love you," he said, reaching up to run his fingertips along my jaw and down my neck, curling his fingers around the back of my neck. And though his eyes were usually filled with a gleam of repressed longing when he looked at me, he was now letting the emotion show in his open expression.

My breath hitched.

"And my children will love you," he said so very softly.

Part of me expected him to declare his own feelings, to put

my mind at rest by telling me, once and for all, he'd decided to bond with me. It was the selfish, hopeful, and apparently, delusional part of me.

Ever so slowly, he leaned in, bringing his face closer to mine. His lips brushed across mine with the faintest pressure, just enough that I could feel them curve into a smile.

I was afraid to move, afraid to breathe, afraid to do anything that might shatter this moment.

Heru pulled away just as slowly, the slight smile still curving his lips. "Come, little queen." He stepped around me, pausing at the mouth of the tunnel and looking back at me while holding out his hand.

I maneuvered my left arm through the folds in my robe until my hand was free. Tentatively, I approached Heru and placed my hand in his.

He grinned, his eyes crinkling at the corners and his irises sparkling with genuine pleasure. I'd never thought of the skin between my fingers as an erogenous zone, but the slow, sensual way his glided between mine changed my mind completely. His grin turned sly, knowing, and just the tiniest bit wolfish. Oh, he knew exactly what he was doing and could read the effect he was having on me as clear as day. Even though he wasn't bonded to me, I was still fully bonded to him, and that made even the most benign touch feel decadent and rouse more than a hint of desire.

Heat flooded my neck and cheeks even as things low in my abdomen tightened in misguided anticipation. I licked my lips, unable to break eye contact with him.

Heru's pupils expanded, dilating with desire that mirrored my own, even if it was paler on his end due to our one-sided bond. His eyelids slid closed, and he inhaled deeply. He said a word I didn't know, but based on his harsh tone, I assumed he was cursing. When his eyes snapped open, his irises were almost entirely black; just the thinnest circlet of gold surrounded his pupils.

"You enjoyed teasing me in my time as well," I said, allowing a small smile. I raised my chin a little. "Be careful, Heru. Your self-control may be strong, but it is not limitless . . ."

His eyes narrowed, holding a glint of challenge. "Perhaps you overestimate my desire for you."

I cocked my head to the side and *barely* held back a smirk. Mutual desire was one thing that had *never* been lacking between Marcus and me, and Heru being a younger Marcus, well . . . "Perhaps, but I do not think it would be a wise theory to test."

Heru pressed his lips together in a thin line and made a rough noise low in his throat. "Perhaps you are right," he said, starting toward the passageway and pulling me along beside him. "Perhaps . . ."

33

OVER & OVER

As we plunged into the shadowed tunnel, I couldn't help but laugh, just as my heart couldn't help but beat too quickly. Cooler air enveloped me, and I sighed in relief. Shade, like water, was a rarity in the Sahara, and I basked in the momentary lack of sunshine.

Up ahead, the other end of the passageway was a point of brightness that expanded quickly as we walked. Through it, I could see sunshine and greenery and, as Heru had predicted, the silhouettes of three women—the Hat-hur priestesses who'd all but begged to stay with me, despite claiming to believe that I wasn't actually their goddess. I still wasn't completely convinced . . .

I couldn't see much beyond the shield of date palms and low, desert shrubs that sprouted a few yards beyond the tunnel's exit. It was almost like they'd been planted there on purpose to block unwelcome, unexpected visitors from catching a glimpse of whatever lay beyond them in the Oasis. Knowing Nuin and his slight flair for eccentricity, I figured the Netjer-At "homeland" would be populated by structures at least as unique as the people who inhabited them.

I nodded to myself, certain that the thick shield of palms had been placed strategically.

As Heru and I emerged from the passageway, Denai smiled and bowed her head. "We will accompany you to Nuin's residence, Alexandra. I am sure you wish to bathe and rest." Her eyes slid to Heru, lingering on our joined hands, and she arched an eyebrow. "And you must wish to return to your home, Heru."

However loyal she was to me, she didn't wholly approve of all the time I spent with Heru. I thought it was less because I was being potentially unfaithful to my "husband," and more because of Heru's past relationship with Ankhesenpepi, who Denai seemed to despise—as did almost every other woman I'd spoken with, aside from Nuin's primary human wife, Ipwet, who I tried to avoid as much as possible.

I offered Heru a weak smile. "Actually, Denai, I will be staying at Heru's home."

Denai's face transformed, going from disapproving to flabbergasted in an instant.

I choked on a laugh, coughing and barely holding back a grin. "I just need a clean dress . . ."

Straightening her back, Denai held her head high. "I see. And what of us? Where would you have *us* stay?"

Heru cleared his throat. "You are more than welcome to stay in my home as well." The corner of his mouth twitched. "That way you can continue to protect Alexandra's virtue."

Denai ignored his barb and returned her attention to me. She'd relaxed, and the usual, good-natured sparkle had returned to her eyes. "Would this please you, having us remain there with you?"

"Very much, Denai." I scanned the two other young women, Sia and Kemi, and smiled. "Very much, indeed." And I meant it. I was nervous as hell about moving in with Heru, two of his wives, and his brood of kids, and having the priestesses' familiar faces around would do a lot to ease my nerves. Plus, I simply enjoyed their company. They were loyal, trustworthy, and kind women I'd come to consider close friends.

Sia, who as soon as I'd requested fresh clothing had started rummaging around in a bundle attached to one of the three donkeys lounging nearby, handed me a rolled-up dress of fine, white linen. A moment later, she added the belt Denai had made from some of the turquoise and quartz beads that had come from my destroyed bead-net dress and my pair of turquoise- and gold-embellished leather sandals.

Kemi fished through another bundle, pulling out a jar of the paste that passed as soap in this time—a mixture of natron and ash very similar to what I used every morning and evening to clean my teeth.

I accepted the offerings with a smile and murmured thanks.

"Are you certain you do not want to accompany us and wash up there?" Denai's hands were on her hips, and she was making a really valiant effort not to eye Heru suspiciously.

"Yes, Denai, I am sure," I said, laughing softly. "I would very much like to make a good first impression."

She sighed dramatically. "Very well. We shall inform Heru's wives of your imminent arrival and aid them in setting up our quarters." She bit her lip. "But I hope you will not take too long . . ."

"She will take as long as she takes," Heru said, tugging on my hand as he stepped toward a down-sloping, palm-lined path that ran along the rock wall.

My kitten chose that moment to start kneading my chest.

I slipped my hand free of Heru's, earning raised eyebrows and parted lips, and looked at Denai. "Will you take Rus? I am certain he is starving, not to mention dying to run around."

Denai grinned. She loved the little furball almost as much as I did. We made the exchange with a lot of help on her part, considering everything I was holding, and I gave her my thanks before rejoining Heru.

He watched me with guarded eyes as I approached.

I stopped in front of him, studying his face and trying to puzzle out the reason for his sudden reticence. Behind me, I could hear the priestesses and donkey making their way along another of the paths leading away from the mouth of the tunnel. "So . . . where is this pond you mentioned?"

Heru continued to stare at me, a million thoughts seeming to whirl around in his eyes.

"Heru?" I touched my fingertips to his forearm. "Is something wrong?"

Exhaling, he shook his head. "I thought . . ." He cleared his throat. "For a moment, I thought, perhaps, that you changed your mind . . . that you would choose to stay at Nuin's residence instead. I have never felt so—" Again, he shook his head, his brow furrowed. "It does not matter."

He took hold of my hand once more, the gentle slide of his fingers between mine just as sensual as it had been before. "Come. I will show you the most perfect, hidden pool for washing . . . you will love it, I think."

At this point, a tub of water behind a boulder would've looked like the most perfect, hidden pool for washing. I snorted as he led me down a path lined with limestone reaching up toward the clear blue sky on one side and a mass of date palms and shrubs on the other. But my mouth fell open as we rounded a curve and the secluded hideaway came into view.

Heru had brought me to a small spring surrounded by limestone boulders that seemed to have been artfully arranged around the water and the tiniest burbling waterfall trickling into a wide pool that glittered with sunlight. It really *was* the most perfect, hidden pool. It looked like it had been relocated from some fairytale land into the heart of the Sahara.

"How is this real?" I said, laughing in wonderment as I stared around. He'd been right; I loved it. And if it was any indication of what the rest of the Oasis was like, I was almost tempted to forgo washing up in favor of getting a good look at the rest of the place. *Almost*.

I tore my eyes away from the delicate waterfall and looked at Heru. "It *is* perfect . . . this place . . ."

He smiled, genuine pleasure gleaming in his eyes. Releasing my hand, he reached for the items I was carrying and set them on a low, flat boulder beside the pool. And then he returned to me and started unwrapping the thin fabric looped loosely around my neck. He tossed what had been my cowl onto the ground before taking hold of the sides of my multi-layered linen robe.

My hands found his wrists, gripping them tightly as I held them in place, and I looked up into his darkening eyes. "What are you doing, Heru?"

He raised his eyebrows, feigning casual unconcern, but nothing could hide the desire—the challenge—in his eyes. "I am merely helping you disrobe so you may bathe."

Staring at him, I held his wrists for a moment longer. And then I let go.

My robe, more a sun- and heat-protectant than anything else, was pulled over my head and had joined the cowl on the ground within seconds. I stood before Heru in a thin, white linen shift that had been clean when I'd donned it that morning and the supple leather slippers I'd been wearing throughout the eleven-day journey, wondering if he would attempt to remove the rest of my clothing as well.

He took a step backward and started attending to his own over-layers. They landed on the rocky ground beside mine, but he didn't stop there. He toed off his own hide moccasins as he worked on unknotting his linen kilt.

I couldn't move, couldn't tear my eyes away from him. I could barely breathe. Watching him was the only thing I was capable of at that moment. My breaths came too fast, like I was doing something strenuous instead of just standing there, staring at him as he undressed and loving every single nanosecond.

Not that he seemed to mind. His eyes never left mine, never judged . . . only promised.

At least, I *hoped* they promised.

He dropped his kilt on top of the pile of discarded linen garments and stood before me, completely nude. And he said nothing. He watched me watch him, watched me taking in the sight of him. His expression went through a play of emotions, starting with curiosity and eagerness only to move on to excitement and desire . . . to *need*. His chest, like mine, was rising and falling too quickly.

"Alexandra . . . please . . ." His voice was hoarse, asking, demanding.

Returning my gaze to his, I removed my shoes, then crossed my arms in front of me and gathered my shift at my hips. I pulled it over my head in one smooth motion, eternally grateful to the priestesses for being so gung-ho about hair removal. The ancient Egyptians were *not* fans of lice, and made sure to eliminate as many habitats for the little buggers as possible. What had been a few moments of stinging pain led to a shorter, if more memorable moment of absolute glee. The gleam in Heru's eyes as he scanned me . . . his body's response . . . at this point, I was ready to kiss all of the priestesses, I was so grateful.

I raised my chin and squared my shoulders. Oh, he definitely seemed to enjoy that. "Are you going to get into the water?"

Heru's lips twitched as his gaze heated. "After you . . ." He held out his arm toward the crystalline pool.

Smirking, I shrugged and showed him my backside, slowly making my way to the pool. It was nothing he hadn't seen before . . . or rather, wouldn't see later.

The water felt heavenly, the perfect Goldilocks temperature, and I groaned as it reached my hips. My smirk grew when I heard the water splashing behind me. I stopped when it was waist-high but didn't turn around.

"Perhaps you were right about my self-control," Heru said, his voice rough.

"Perhaps . . . ?"

The water lapped against my back as he moved closer. "Perhaps that is your intention . . ."

Laughing, I shook my head. "Bathing here, like this—that was your idea. Do not presume to blame me—"

Suddenly Heru's hand was on my hip, sliding to my stomach, and the front of him was pressed against the back of me, and damn me to an eternity of torture by Apep-Set if I didn't almost lose myself to pleasure in that moment. I could be *so* pathetic sometimes . . .

"But I do blame you, little queen." His breath was hot against my ear just as he was hot against my backside, making the water feel cool in comparison. "I blame you for invading my every thought . . . my every dream. I blame you for making me desire what only you can give me more than I have ever desired anything from another being, Netjer-At or human." His other hand slipped up my ribs until he cupped one of my breasts.

I gasped as his finger pulled and twisted tender flesh without mercy.

"I blame you for making me want to know your mind as much as I want to know your body."

I reached behind me, taking him in hand and savoring his sharp inhale as my thumb slid along his hard length. I closed my eyes, thinking nothing had ever felt so good. I was so very, wonderfully wrong.

Heru's hand glided lower on my abdomen, moving completely underwater, finding my most sensitive places for the first time. I gasped and moaned in his hold, and for minutes, he did the same in mine. It was the most intimate we could be without actually initiating full-on bonding.

"Heru . . ." I reached up with my free hand, hooking it around the back of his neck. "Heru, you have to stop . . . you have to stop this before it goes too far . . ."

"*You* stop it," he said, his voice barely a rasp, and I melted completely.

Pleasure overwhelmed me, and based on his sudden rigidity, overwhelmed him as well. For dozens of breaths, we stood in the water, clinging to each other, until finally our bodies went limp and boneless.

I arched my back against him as I felt his arousal resurge, and I forced my fingers to unclench from around him. "Let go, Heru."

"What—"

"This will continue, over and over again . . . you must let go." I squirmed in his hold, flailing a little.

"This is—I've never—how long does it go on?"

"It never stops," I said.

He still held me, my body tensed, my muscles ready to flee. His voice was barely audible when he spoke. "Never?"

I shook my head.

"How do you handle it . . . the wanting . . . ?"

I laughed hoarsely. "How do you think?" There was only one thing that made it bearable, and it was the one thing he wasn't ready to give me.

His answering groan, his clenching hands, were enough to make me melt all over again. "We should finish washing up," he said.

"Yeah," I rasped. "We should."

34

CAN & CAN'T

"Do you feel better?" Heru asked as he rewrapped his linen kilt around his waist.

I nodded and wrung out my hair one final time, then pulled my clean shift over my head. "Remarkably so, thank you." His hawklike gaze burned into my skin, and I averted my eyes while I affixed my belt around my waist. "I wish you would not look at me like that."

"In what way am I looking at you?" He finished tying the thinner ends of the kilt into the intricate knot men of this time used to "keep their pants up."

My lips curved into a wry grin, and I glanced at his face. "Like you are imagining what it would be like to truly be together."

His eyes heated even further. "But I *am* imagining what it would be like."

My cheeks flushed. I was fairly certain my whole body blushed. Again, I looked away, focusing on the pile of dirty linen, and cleared my throat. "We should gather our things and—"

In three long strides, Heru was in front of me, his hands

gentle under my jaw, tilting my face upward. His eyes searched mine. "I was imagining what it would be like to be inside you, and I was imagining what *our life* might be like in your time . . . to be as unified as a man and woman can be . . . to have our livelihoods intertwined for all eternity . . . to have *chosen* that."

"I—" I licked my lips. "With Nuin's sheut, I have been improving my control over memories." I bit my lip. "I could show you some of my memories of us . . . if it would not seem too strange to you, I mean."

I could see in his eyes that he wanted to say yes, wanted to experience what he could of our future together, but he shook his head. "I will stick with imagining . . . for now."

"Oh." I looked down at the rocky ground.

Heru slid his hand down my neck, over my shoulder, and down my arm to twine our fingers together. "Come, little queen. I am eager for you to meet my family." He grinned, but there was a hint of worry in his eyes. Probably because there was more than a hint in mine. "And I know that you are eager to see the rest of the Oasis."

I finally managed to return his smile.

Heru led me back up the path to where we'd split off from the priestesses and through an overlapping break in the date palms. It gave way to a narrow walkway paved with what I thought was brick-shaped paving stones arranged in a zigzag pattern—at first—but they glinted too much in the afternoon sunlight to be stone.

"Heru," I said as we stepped onto the pathway, my eyes glued to the ground. "The paving stones are made of *At* . . ." And then I looked up, at the way ahead, and my mouth fell open.

Stretched out before me was a small city of graceful, opalescent buildings composed of elegant domes and arches and sleek colonnades and spires, all gleaming in the bright sunlight. There were other, smaller and boxier structures that appeared to be made of regular limestone bricks clustered around the more grandiose buildings—*palaces, they* must *be palaces*—along with copses of tall date palms as well as small orchards of other fruit trees. But those elegant, shimmering buildings . . . they were like something from some distant, alien world, almost too beautiful to exist here.

I shook my head. "It is *all* made of At." I glanced at Heru, but quickly turned my attention back to the walled-in city.

Each palace appeared to function as the center of its own little neighborhood, surrounded as it was by a starburst of the more mundane buildings as well as orchards and gardens. From my vantage point, it seemed that each "neighborhood" merged together to form a cityscape more awe-inspiring than any cityscape of my own time. And weaving a sinuous path through it all was a sparkling stream, crossed by bridges lined with railings of At filigree.

"I did not know such a thing was possible . . ." Again, I shook my head. "Did you know what it was . . . that it was constructed from *At*?"

Heru shrugged, giving my hand a tug to move me forward along the path. "I knew that Nuin had built it long ago, before I was born . . . but until I met you and saw firsthand the wonders a wielder of sheut is capable of, I did not know *how* he had built our people's home or *what* he had used to make it."

I stared at the fantastical palaces juxtaposed with the more ordinary structures as we neared the edge of the first cluster of buildings. There was a single palace of At, smaller than some and larger than others, and what appeared to be a well-tended orchard and garden surrounded by dozens of the smaller, stone buildings.

"This is where my family resides," Heru said, pointing ahead. He shifted his arm, indicating the highest-reaching At palace at least a half-mile off to the left. "That is Nuin's residence, in the center of the Oasis, and near it is a bridge I think you will find quite beautiful." He looked at me, his lips spread into a broad grin. "After you have settled in, I will show you everything."

"Father!" It was a high-pitched shriek. "It is Father! Father approaches!"

More high-pitched shrieks joined the first as three small children emerged from a narrow alley between two of the stone buildings and sprinted toward us. The youngest was a girl who looked to be around four years old, the oldest, a boy around nine, and the other, a girl somewhere in between. They all had black hair and bronze skin, just like their father, and they were all ridiculously adorable.

Heru released my hand as the smallest flung herself at him. Laughing, he picked her up under her arms and swung her around, seeming to revel in her squeals and giggles. When he stopped spinning, she wrapped her tiny legs around his waist, her arms around his neck, and buried her face against his shoulder. He patted her back gently, meeting my eyes for a moment before the other two kids reached us. They, too, practically attacked Heru with hugs, though their feet remained more or less on the ground.

The elation, the pride—the *love*—that had shone in Heru's eyes in that brief moment when he looked at me was seared into my memory. It stole my breath and made tears well in my eyes, my heart desiring something I'd never yearned for before, something that, until a week ago, I'd thought was an impossibility. For the first time, I truly wanted this with him—a family. I wanted *our* family to be a real, living thing. And it would be. It *had* to be. But not yet . . . not for thousands of years.

"I think you have been gone too long this time, husband," a woman said, "and the children have turned rabid." The voice was rich and a little husky.

My attention shifted away from Heru and his trio of children, and I watched a woman approach from the same alleyway. She had dark hair that she wore longer than was fashionable, cascading in waves over her shoulders, and she was more handsome than pretty or beautiful. And she was very, *very* pregnant.

She called Heru "husband" . . .

My mouth was suddenly as dry as the desert surrounding the Oasis, and my heart beat too heavily in my chest. *His wife . . . pregnant . . . their children . . .*

I swallowed thickly, unable to stop thinking about what we'd just done back at the pool and feeling like a conniving homewrecker. Heru had been right to show me this, to show me *them*, and he'd been right to do so before we did something that couldn't be undone, at least not while I was still in this time. His wife was *pregnant*.

"Sesha," Heru said, extracting himself from his kids and setting the little girl on the ground. He held his arms out to his wife, cupping either side of her face in his hands and bending his head down to brush his lips against hers in a brief, tender kiss.

I couldn't breathe. I couldn't find enough oxygen in the hot air. And I couldn't tear my eyes away from the expecting parents. Jealousy and shame and self-disgust consumed me.

Heru moved his hands down to his wife's rounded belly and smiled. "I did not know you were with child again."

"But she is," another woman said. Her voice was raspy and weakened by age. She hobbled closer, hanging on the arm of a strapping teen boy who was unmistakably another of Heru's sons. "And you did not listen last time, but you must now. This will be her final child, husband, unless you wish to send her to the gods before her children are grown."

Heru's glee evaporated off of his face, and his hands fell away from Seshseshet's belly. He looked from her face to the old woman's, who I realized had to be Bunefer. "There have been problems?"

"Yes," Bunefer said. "As there were last time, though much

worse." She shuffled a few steps closer and stared up at him, waggling one arthritic finger under his nose. "No more, Heru. You know what you must do, now."

"Please, Bunefer, enough." Seshseshet smiled kindly, and her eyes settled on me. "We have a guest, and there is plenty of time to discuss these matters later."

"Oh . . . yes. I forgot." Bunefer hooked her arm through Seshseshet's, and together, they ambled toward me.

I could feel my eyes widening, my heart racing. I wasn't sure I could actually *talk* to them, not now that I'd seen *her*, seen how gentle and loving Heru was with her.

"I was worried she was that awful Netjer-At woman who has been clawing at Heru for ages," Bunefer said to Seshseshet, squinting her cloudy eyes at me. I wasn't sure she could actually see anything. "Even with the way those Hat-hur priestesses were going on about her . . . well, I cannot tell. *Is* she . . . ?"

Seshseshet laughed softly and shook her head. "No, Bunefer, she is not Ankhesenpepi, thank the gods." Both women stopped a few feet in front of me, Seshseshet's full lips spreading into a smile once again. "I am pleased to welcome you into our home," she said, bowing her head a little.

"I—I—" I looked into her warm, brown eyes, then over her shoulder at Heru. His face was a mask of wariness, like he could sense what I was about to do. "I am sorry," I blurted. "I cannot do this." Turning on my heel, I took one lurching step after another until I was all-out sprinting away, toward the only sanctuary I could think of—Nuin.

I was about halfway there when Heru caught up to me. He took hold of my arm and dragged me into a small copse of squat date palms. His expression was filled with so much concern, so much torment.

"What is wrong, Alexandra?" He shook his head, staring down at me with liquid gold eyes. "I do not understand—"

I tore my arm free of his hand and, without thinking, slapped his face. "How dare you! How dare you turn me into some—some sleazy—"

"You do not understand—"

"Seshseshet is *carrying your child,* Heru, and she welcomed me into her home . . . *me*! After what we just did"—I looked up at the clear blue sky—"I have never felt dirtier in my entire life. Marcus would never ask me to do this . . . would never put me in this position, never make me feel like a *whore.*" I leveled an angry glare on him. "You may be a younger version of the man I love, Heru, but you are *not* him."

Heru stared at me, stunned.

Holding my head high despite wanting to collapse onto the ground and weep, I turned away from him and marched out of the copse of trees. I wore mental blinders the rest of the way to Nuin's, not seeing people or buildings. And with each step, I felt more and more despicable.

35

WILL & WAY

Nausea roiled in my belly, regret curdling on my tongue. I'd spoken rashly, lashing out like a wounded animal, and the words I'd thrown at Heru, however much I regretted them, could never be unsaid. True, I could make him forget them, but doing so would've made me an even more despicable person.

When I reached Nuin's palace, I found my "husband" standing out front in the dead center of the largest of five gracefully curved archways, his hands clasped in front of him and a pleasant smile curving his lips. My hurried pace slowed as I approached. I climbed up three shallow, broad steps and threw myself into his arms.

"What have I done?" I bemoaned against his shoulder. I knew Nuin had heard; he heard *everything*.

"You were hurt, dear Alexandra." Nuin rubbed my back gently and rested his cheek on top of my head. "I'm sure that all will work itself out. Just give it some time."

I sighed heavily, swallowing the urge to whine about how I wanted things to work themselves out *now*.

"Several days ago, you and Heru spoke about creating something to leave behind for the future Heru to find," Nuin said, changing the subject as he pulled away. I was eternally grateful. "I believe I have just the thing. It will—what is the saying in your tongue—*kill two birds with one stone*. You will leave something for future Heru *and* expend some of the built-up energy from my—*your*—sheut, thus prolonging your life."

Nuin captured my hand. "I started the project years ago, before I knew all of the details of who would end up carrying the burden that is now yours . . . and it has been sealed up ever since."

He guided me around the corner of the palace to a circular patch of soft sand that appeared to be some sort of a rock garden. In the center of the garden stood another At building, this one looking more like a tiny temple sanctuary, much like the Hat-hur inner sanctuary back in Men-nefer, except there was no obvious entrance. We stopped before the face of one smooth outer wall, and Nuin released my hand.

"You must unmake the door, dear Alexandra," he said, holding his hand out toward the wall. It was well over head-height and as wide as three people.

My eyebrows rose. "But I've never handled that much At before."

Nuin waved a hand dismissively. "The big things are easy; it is the tinier amounts that are harder to manage. All you must do to maintain control over the physical At is touch some part of it. Unblock your access to the sheut you hold within you, like I taught you, and try it. You'll see."

Brow furrowed, I frowned, but I didn't argue. I let down the block inside me, stepped forward, and touched my fingertips to the solidified At. Closing my eyes, I thought, *unmake*.

The At softened until it felt almost liquid against my fingertips. I opened my eyes and pulled my hand away, watching the quicksilver mass dissolve into a colorful mist before it evaporated completely, and in its place was a wide doorway displaying a broad set of stairs—also made of At—that led downward, underground.

Nuin brushed past me, descending the stairs, and I followed. Enough daylight spilled in through the wide doorway behind us that the chamber at the bottom of the stairs was dim, though still visible to my Nejerette eyes. It was about the size of the average modern living room, and the walls were covered with neat columns of hieroglyphs, but they were slightly different from any I was familiar with. More ancient, I realized, giving Nuin a sideways glance. And a rectangular At altar had been erected in the center of the space, waist-high—just the right size for a person to lay on.

Nuin reached the foot of the stairwell ahead of me, and I jogged the last few steps to reach for him. He looked over his shoulder as my fingers latched around his arm.

"You created this to be your tomb, didn't you?" I said, glancing at the altar. There was a reason it was just the right size for someone to lay on . . . because it was *meant* to hold a body.

He smiled his favorite, mysterious Nuin smile and pointed to three false doors creating impressions in the opalescent walls ahead and on either side of what could only be called a burial chamber. "You must leave my words unharmed, but you may expand through each doorway as far as you wish."

"Uh . . ." I gave him another sideways glance. "But we're underground. Wouldn't I have to dig into the ground first? You know, so there's space to put whatever I 'build'?" Doing so would take *ages*.

Nuin shook his head. "As the At expands in this plane, it does not displace matter, but *re*places it."

I narrowed my eyes. "That doesn't make sense. Matter can't be created or destroyed. It's a thing we know in my time . . . a universal law of physics."

Nuin frowned and cocked his head to the side. "I said nothing of creating or destroying."

"But, you said—"

Nuin turned to face me and rested his hand on my shoulder. "Think of it like this, my Alexandra. When I first created the door that had been sealing this chamber, the matter that had been there—the different atoms making up the air—*transformed* into solidified At, and when you unmade the door, the solidified At reverted back to the types of matter it had originally been, in the *exact* state it had been in when originally transformed. It is as though you are transposing that alternate plane onto this one, but only in a delineated place, and while the At-matter is *here,* whatever it is displacing is frozen in time."

I shook my head, getting it and not getting it at the same time. "Clearly, a Nejerette does not a physicist make." I cleared my throat and pointed to the false door on the opposite wall from the stairwell. "So, do I have to hop into the At to grab more raw material, or can I just use what the door's made from?"

Nuin's face lit up. "Very good! Yes! You can be so bright sometimes, my Alexandra."

I eyed him, totally confused. "Um . . ."

"Simply touch the door and unmake the portion of solidified At you wish to unmake, then will it into whatever new shape you wish. More At will be pulled in as needed without additional guidance from you. It's really quite intuitive . . . just think of what you would like to happen, and it will happen." He held up a finger. "So long as you're touching the At."

"Alright . . ." I made my way around the altar and stopped in front of the false door. I raised my hand, touching my fingertips to a portion near the edge. "Here goes nothing."

Honestly, I just hoped I didn't cause the whole underground chamber to come crashing down around us . . . or to be *unmade,* leaving us encased in earth. I shuddered and took a deep breath, forcing myself to concentrate.

I pictured a simple room, about the same width as the burial chamber and twice as long, but with an arched ceiling instead of a flat one. I figured I might as well toss some architectural variation in to amuse myself. I felt the solidified At liquefy and readjust, slowly expanding outward. The earth didn't shake, the ceiling didn't shatter. I simply continued to picture that arched room, gleaming with its opaque, quartz-like walls and floor.

"Oh . . . oh dear gods . . ." The voice was husky and female and definitely *not* Nuin's.

My eyelids snapped open as I set the At with a thought, feeling it solidify into a smooth, cool surface under my fingertips. I turned around slowly, hoping I'd misheard. But I hadn't.

Seshseshet stood on the bottom stair, her elbow linked with Aset's. Both women's eyes were wide, but Seshseshet's mouth was hanging open as well.

"Uh . . ." I looked at Nuin, hoping for guidance. Only a select few had ever seen me use my borrowed powers, including Aset, and we'd intended to keep it that way. It was why I was *extremely* careful about where I practiced using the sheut, and why the block shielding my power—and my glowy, rainbow eyes—remained up at pretty much all times. If Apep discovered that Nuin was no longer at full power . . . if he learned that *I*, a mere Nejerette, held the sheut . . .

"I think I need to sit down," Seshseshet said. Aset helped ease her down to sit on the second-to-last stair, but Seshseshet continued to stare at me with wide eyes. "You are a true goddess? Is this why you have rejected my husband?"

I shook my head, taking several steps toward her. "No, I am—"

"She is, and will continue to be," Nuin said, and I shot him a surprised look. "For a while. In time, she will return to being a regular Netjer-At, like Aset or Heru. You cannot speak of this,

Seshseshet, of what you have witnessed . . . not to anyone, not even Bunefer."

Seshseshet blinked slowly, and I was pretty sure it was the first time she'd blinked since seeing me work my *magic*. "Of course. I will speak of this to no one."

Aset cleared her throat daintily and addressed Nuin. "Seshseshet wished to speak with Lex, Great Father . . . in private."

"Ah, yes." Nuin walked past the altar and started toward the stairs with a nod. "Very good." He held out his arm to Aset, who accepted, resting her hand on his forearm like a dignified Edwardian lady, and together, they ascended the stairs. And left me alone with Heru's *pregnant* wife.

I glanced around the underground chamber, searching the inscribed walls for some hint of what to say. I didn't find a single thing.

Seshseshet laughed quietly; it was a soothing sound. "I apologize for my reaction just now." She shook her head. "It is only —I have never seen the like . . ."

I exhaled a weak laugh. "Not many have."

Smiling, she patted the stair beside her. "Please, sit with me. I would speak with you about your relationship with my husband."

My stomach soured, but I couldn't bring myself to deny her request. She deserved my cooperation after what I'd unintentionally done to her, attempting to steal away a man who wouldn't be mine, not really, for over four thousand years; *right now* he was hers. I moved the rest of the way around the altar and sat beside her on the step.

"It is complicated, loving him," she said.

Watching her out of the corner of my eye, I shook my head. Complicated didn't even come close.

"But I believe you already know this." Her smile widened a little. "In the village where I grew up, it was not a normal thing for a man to have more than one wife"—she met my eyes, a sparkle in hers—"or a woman to have more than one husband. But my village was near Men-nefer, and the Netjer-Ats and their ways are well known there." She paused. "One day, Bunefer walked into my father's villa and demanded to see me. She was hunting for Heru's next wife, she told me, since she'd been unable to be a complete wife to him for many years, and he'd refused to search for another—"

I shook my head. "A 'complete wife'?"

"They had not lain as husband and wife because doing so would risk Bunefer becoming pregnant—her last child died before it was born, nearly dragging her into the land of the dead as well." A wistful smile spread across Seshseshet's face, and I was starting to think she rarely went without a smile of some kind. "Bunefer was so petite, but so dignified . . . I was in awe of her. She told me she needed to find a woman who could keep Heru away from the—I apologize—*Netjer-At whore* in Men-nefer and make him want to return to the Netjer-At Oasis on a more permanent basis to be with his family."

I frowned. Seshseshet's tale was not painting the prettiest picture of Heru's character.

"As I came to know him, I learned that it was Nuin, not Ankhesenpepi, who was keeping Heru away from the Oasis and his family, and it was the duty he felt as Nuin's Blade that kept him in Men-nefer so long as Nuin was there."

"What did you do?"

"I spoke with Nuin, requesting permission to be an annoying shadow to Heru day and night to ensure *Khessie* had no chance to corner him alone." Seshseshet nodded. "It surprised me how pleased I was to find that Heru never ordered me away and only laughed every time *she* was put off by my presence. And then one night . . ." There was a knowing glint in her eyes, making my stomach lurch.

I swallowed a burst of jealous nausea and clenched my jaw.

"I was with child not long after, and Nuin ordered Heru to

take me to the Netjer-At Oasis and to remain here until I'd born him three children." She sat up a little straighter and started rubbing her bulging belly. "He did not leave again until I'd given him *five* children." She sighed. "But now it is too dangerous for me to continue being a complete wife to him, and he must find another." She met my eyes. "Or at least a Netjer-At woman who will love him and care for him in ways that I no longer can, not merely wish to use him to gain more power."

After a deep breath, Seshseshet said in a rush, "I came here to ask you to reconsider becoming a part of our family."

I stared at her, my eyes opened wide in surprise.

"The priestesses who serve you adore you, as does Aset, and now that I have seen how truly powerful you are, I know that you would never use Heru for self-serving purposes." For once, her smile slipped, and her gaze bored into me. "You will love him and support him and be a true partner to him in a way that only one of your kind can be. You *must* do this. You must keep *her* away from him . . . from our family. I beg of you."

I opened my mouth, then shut it again when I realized I had no idea how to respond.

Seshseshet reached for my hand. There was fear and desperation in her eyes. "You do not know how horrible she can be . . . what she is capable of . . ." Shaking her head, she squeezed my hand. "Please, at least consider it."

I shook my head slowly, recalling the last things I'd said to Heru and feeling sick to my stomach. "Seshseshet—"

"Call me 'Sesha,' please," she said.

"Sesha . . ." I cleared my throat. "It is not that I do not wish to try to be Heru's true partner, but that I think it may be too late for us . . ." . . . *at least, in* this *time.* "I said something cruel to him, something unforgivable."

Seshseshet furrowed her brow. "I have not seen him since he ran after you, but I will send the children out in search of him, and when they find him and bring him home, I will speak with him. I am certain he will understand that you did not mean what you said, and all will be forgiven." She squeezed my hand again, her eyes searching mine. "You will be here?"

I shrugged, then nodded. It wasn't like I had anywhere else to go. Not really.

Seshseshet started to stand, or at least *tried* to stand. I hopped to my feet and helped her up, and when she patted my hand, letting me know she was fine, I let her go.

"I will send him to you, here." She smiled her increasingly familiar, warm smile. "I do not think it will be long." But I didn't share her confidence.

I accompanied her to the top of the stairs, not completely convinced of her ability to balance. She looked like she might topple forward at any moment.

Aset appeared in the doorway, holding out her arm to Seshseshet and looking at me. "Nuin left to attend to something, I do not know what." Concern shone in her eyes. "But he told me about your argument with my brother."

Fantastic . . .

"Are you alright to be alone? Do you want me to return after I accompany Sesha home?"

"No, no . . . I am fine," I lied. I wasn't fine, but I also didn't want to be around anyone. When my mind was troubled, solitude was my preferred coping mechanism.

"Very well . . ." Aset studied my face for a moment before turning to walk away with Seshseshet.

I watched their retreat until they rounded one corner of Nuin's palace and were obscured by a series of delicate columns, then trudged back down the stairs to study my new creation more closely. It was the only thing I could think of doing that had even a remote chance of distracting me.

Denai and the priestesses visited after a couple hours, bringing me food and lingering around the mouth of the stairwell, but I didn't invite them down to what I'd started to consider my private sanctuary. Set stopped by, as well, and after him, Nekure, with a wineskin, which I didn't turn away.

I sat with Nekure on the outer steps as the sun dipped behind the western rim of the cliffs walling in the Oasis, neither of us saying much. I found unexpected comfort in his silent presence, and appreciated that he didn't feel the need to corrupt that silence with words.

The evening passed without any sign of Heru, and by the time full dark blanketed the Oasis and I was once again alone in my sanctuary, I sat on the floor, my back against the smooth At wall, and spoke to Marcus the only way I could. I inscribed my words on walls that I'd willed to glow, telling him about what I'd experienced so far.

I was just starting to describe our eventful trip to the marketplace when my eyelids drifted shut, and I slumped against the corner of my sanctuary, sound asleep.

36

GIVE & TAKE

I came awake with a gasp. The semiopaque walls of my sanctuary still glowed with a gentle incandescence, and there was a crick in my neck from sitting curled up in the corner for so long. But none of that mattered at the moment.

Somebody else was in my sanctuary. I could hear the intruder descending the final few stairs into the altar room.

I held my breath. The colors of the At-mist curled around me, preparing to whisk me away to safety . . . but I didn't want to retreat; I wanted to fight. This was *my* place, *my* haven, and someone else, some *intruder,* was violating it. A not-so-tiny, not-so-quiet part of me hoped it was Ankhesenpepi, so I would have an excuse to see how well my exhausting training with Heru, Set, and Nekure was paying off . . . and beat the crap out of her.

I grinned, and the At-mist surrounded me in a burst of rainbow colors. I exited time and space, only to reemerge in the altar room a few yards away, directly behind the intruder. As I reformed, a mere thought brought an At blade into being in my hand. I pressed it against the front of the intruder's neck—a *man's* neck—at the same time that I pressed myself against his back. His spicy scent filled my nostrils.

Heru. *He* was my intruder.

He grunted, his fingers wrapping around my wrist. "Do it, Alexandra." He pulled my knife hand closer to his neck, forcing the blade to slice into his skin. "The pain will be a relief compared to that caused by your last words to me. You want to hurt me, so do it."

"No!" I shrieked, unmaking the knife.

Maintaining his hold on my wrist, Heru twisted around to face me. The full moon bathed the side of his face in shadows and silver, while the soft iridescent light spilling through the doorway to my sanctuary made the other side seem to glow from under his skin.

He took a step forward, pushing me backward. He took another. Another.

My breaths were coming faster. "What are you doing here?" When my butt hit the edge of the altar, my heart gave an extra enthusiastic thump.

Heru stared down at me, his eyes just as shadowed and silvered by the combination of diffused moonlight and glowing At walls as the rest of his face. His jaw clenched, and his nostrils flared once.

He was so close. Only inches between us. I took a shaky breath. "Did—did Sesha talk to you? Is that why you are here?"

His eyes tensed, and he shook his head. Why that made me feel relieved was beyond me, but it did. "I followed you," he said, his voice quiet and silken. "I watched you with Nuin . . . watched you come down here. I watched Sesha and Aset and Denai and the others visit . . . watched you sit with Nekure under the moon . . ." There was a sharp edge to that final observation.

Tilting my head to the side, I narrowed my eyes. "Did you listen when Sesha was here?"

"I did." He glanced around, but only for the briefest moment. "Little sound comes out of this place, much like how it is in the other buildings constructed from the At . . . but I did hear. None of my wives ever believed me, but I have never been intimate with Khessie. I find amusement in taunting her, like a trained cobra, but I would never let her close enough to bite; even I am not so ruled by my baser instincts that I could overlook her poisonous nature."

My eyes widened. I'd been so sure about his relationship with her . . . so sure. I shook my head the barest amount. These weren't lying eyes.

My wrist, still held in Heru's almost painful grasp, was the only thing separating us, and it felt as substantial as a brick wall and as flimsy as air. "If you do not believe me," he said, "then tell me to go. Say what you said earlier, tell me you meant it, and I will go."

Sucking in a breath, I parted my lips.

You may be a younger version of the man I love, but you, Heru, are not him.

I would never repeat those words. I wished I could erase those words from existence completely.

"Tell me," he repeated, his eyes searching mine. "Tell me, and I will leave you alone." He held his breath, tension tightening his expression.

Leave me alone? I shook my head, feeling the sting of tears. I didn't want him to go, to leave me alone. I didn't *ever* want him to do that . . . not in any time period, not in any place.

Closing his eyes, Heru exhaled, and his almost pained expression melted away.

Shakily, I raised my free hand and touched my fingertips to the side of his face. There was a hint of rough stubble. I brushed my thumb across his full lower lip, tantalized by the dual silk-and-sandpaper sensations on the pads of my fingers.

"You are trembling," Heru said, his eyelids slowly rising.

Despite my loose linen dress, I felt like I was wearing a corset; my chest didn't seem to have enough room for my heart and lungs to cohabitate in their suddenly hyperactive states.

Heru leaned his cheek into my hand, then turned his head to run his lips back and forth over my palm. The sensation—tickling and tingling—was almost too much, almost unbearable.

I sucked in a ragged breath.

"I have decided." His gaze locked with mine, heated and demanding. "No more imagining."

Licking my lips, I repeated his words. "No more imagining." The words were simple, but their meaning was so clear that us uttering them created an immutable verbal contract between us. We would bond in this time . . . in *any* time.

Heru leaned in until our lips were a hairsbreadth apart, but he didn't close that final distance. Instead, he made a rough, pleased sound low in his throat and angled his face lower to run his nose along the line of my jaw. "Your scent intoxicates me," he said, pressing a feather-light kiss to the skin just under my ear. "I can only imagine how you will taste."

My heartbeat stumbled over itself. "No more imagining," I somehow managed to say, though the words were breathy. I twisted my wrist free from his grip and moved my hands down to the front of his linen kilt. "And no more waiting."

Heru moved in that faster-than-humanly-possible way that was born of a combination of his Nejeret physiology and centuries spent honing his body's reflexes. He captured both of my wrists and pushed them away from his thighs with infuriating ease. His eyes glinted with challenge and promise. With desire.

"Taking our time . . ." He shook his head slowly. "That is not the same thing as waiting. It is savoring, and I intend to savor every inch of you with my hands." Those hands were sliding up my arms, over my shoulders, and back down the sides of my body until they gripped the linen on either side of my hips and pulled my dress up and over my head. "With my lips." Those lips were curved into a sultry, taunting smile. "With my eyes." Those eyes skimmed down the length of my body, their focus a searing brand on my skin. "And with my tongue." That tongue slid over his lips, wetting them with sensual promise.

"And only then, when I know your body better than I know my own, will I take you." That challenging glint flashed in his eyes again. "And I *will* take you, little queen . . . over and over and over again."

I swallowed roughly. My chest rose and fell. Rose and fell. Rose and fell. My heart galloped, each beat pounding against my sternum.

Lifting my chin and squaring my shoulders, I met Heru's challenging gaze with one of my own. I had no problem with any of his tantalizing promises, save for one; I wouldn't remain sane much longer if the ache of wanting, if the bond's mounting need to be completed, wasn't sated, and soon. He could have his fun—do his "savoring"—*after*. And because I was as familiar with his body as he promised to become with mine, I knew how to get my way. I knew his weaknesses. I knew *exactly* how to push him to the brink of control, to fan his need to an undeniable level just as he'd already managed to do within me.

Too quickly for him to stop me—and some of my borrowed power *may* have been involved—I dropped to my knees, shoved the linen of his kilt up and out of the way, and took him into my mouth. *All the way*.

He sucked in a breath, his fingers suddenly tangled in my hair. He seemed to be caught between pulling me closer and trying to push me away. I looked up at him, into his blazing gaze, and let him see just how much *I* was enjoying savoring *his body*.

I was shocked that he let me continue for as long as he did, let me remain in control for as long as he did. But when he did stop me, he made it very clear which of us was truly in charge.

With a hoarse growl, he gripped my upper arms, and lifted

me until I was sitting on the edge of the altar. There was the sound of fabric tearing, and then he was standing between my legs, his arousal, hot and hard, pressing against me. He claimed my mouth as he entered me, neither his kiss nor the joining gentle.

The single, urgent thrust shattered the pressure welling inside me, and I threw my head back and gasped, riding swell after swell of explosive pleasure. Sheer, physical relief washed over me, almost as enjoyable. Tension left my muscles in waves, tension I hadn't noticed until it was gone. Apparently being around Heru, even experiencing our fleeting dalliance in the pool—none of it had been enough—and the toll of not being intimate with the man who was quite literally mated to my soul, had been snaking through my body, creating fissures, widening them, and slowly tearing me apart. But not anymore.

Now I was whole; there was only peace . . . blissful peace.

Heru seemed to understand how badly I needed to bask in the nearness that came with such a joining, to satiate our broken bond. He wrapped his arms around me and simply held me against him for minutes while I gave in to the sensations caused by my fractured soul being slowly pieced back together.

When my breathing grew more regular, I raised my head and met his eyes, giving him a lazy smile.

He brought his hands up to my face and wiped tears from my cheeks. "I have never seen pleasure make someone cry such tears."

Laughing softly, I shook my head. "It was more from relief than from pleasure, I think . . . though there was *plenty* of pleasure."

He arched an eyebrow and slowly shifted his hips away from me. "*Was* plenty of pleasure?" He thrust forward without warning, earning a grunt from me. His eyes traced over my face as he repeated the motion, studying my responses closely. "If it is gone away, then I must chase after it." He increased his pace, his force, but his eyes never left my face. "I will chase . . . your pleasure . . . until I catch it again . . . and I will never . . . let . . . it go . . ."

Either he stopped talking or I stopped listening. It didn't matter either way, because he didn't have to chase either of our pleasures for long.

Sensation swelled inside me until it was too big, too full, too much, and then I was overflowing not just with ecstasy or relief, but with something that eclipsed mere physical pleasure, my ba merging with his. Our souls intertwined more deeply than our bodies ever could, uniting us in that single moment of eternal bliss that made everything else feel, smell, taste, and sound muted in comparison. I became fully aware of the universe in these moments, and oddly enough, never cared one bit. Marcus-Heru-my-bond-mate *became* my whole universe in these moments, just as I became his.

Breathing hard, Heru stared at me as his ba untangled itself from mine, settling securely inside his body. His eyes were wide with wonder. "I had no idea it could . . . that bonding would be so . . ." He shook his head. "I have no words to describe it."

I laughed weakly, not because I wasn't ecstatic, but because it was the most my temporarily spent abdominal muscles could manage. "I doubt there will ever be words that can describe it."

Heru's gaze changed, his eyes darkening with some heavy emotion. I just hoped it wasn't regret. He raised his hand, grazing his fingertips over my face, and my eyes fluttered closed. And then he spoke words that nearly shattered my heart. "If I asked you to stay with me, to live out the years between our two times by my side, would you?"

There was nothing I wanted more than to have a chance to grow and change over the millennia *with* him, to truly be his equal, the partner he deserved. But that could never be. My chin trembled, and clearing my throat, I shook my head. "I cannot . . . you know that."

He rubbed a slow, languorous line back and forth over my bottom lip. "Because of the sheut?"

I nodded.

"But if there was a way—"

"There isn't."

"But *if* there was . . . would you?"

I sighed, but it came out as more of a sob. "I wish, more than anything—" I shook my head, knowing that wishes never solved anything. "I love you. I will always love you . . . in any time. Is that not the most important thing?"

"I dislike that you must carry such burdens." Heru's fingertips continued to trace slow, gentle lines over my face, like he was trying to memorize what I looked like with touch alone. I didn't think he even realized he was doing it. "I dislike that the Great Father has put you in such danger. I dislike everything about this situation . . ."

I captured his free hand and pressed his palm against my chest, just over my heart. "I do not think you dislike *everything* about this situation."

Heru breathed out slowly.

Forcing a lopsided grin, I moved his hand a few inches until it was cupping my breast. "What about this?" I gazed up at him through my lashes. "Do you dislike this?"

His eyes narrowed.

"Or this?" I asked as I moved his hand down my ribcage and abdomen and guided it between my legs. "Do you dislike this?"

The corners of Heru's lips quirked, and he chuckled.

No more coaxing was needed on my part.

37

PRACTICE & PERFECT

"Tell me what you are writing," Heru said as he pressed himself against the back of my body, his heat burning through the thin linen of my dress, and wrapped his arms around my middle. He kissed my temple, keeping his lips pressed against that sensitive skin, his breath tickling the fine hairs growing there.

My shoulders tensed, and I laughed softly. I leaned my head back against his shoulder and sighed. "I am describing the sandstorm . . . and what we were doing—or *not* doing—while we were stuck together in that little cavern." I craned my neck so I could see his face. "And how angry you were."

Heru started tracing slow circles around my belly button with his index finger. "I was not angry."

I scoffed, or at least, I tried to. It came out as more of a shuddering exhale. "You were most certainly angry."

He stared into my eyes and shook his head. "I was not. I was terrified."

My eyebrows rose. "You? *Terrified?*"

"You are the most terrifying being I have ever met." His voice was soft, even.

"I doubt that."

The corners of his mouth twitched. "And yet it is still true."

He released me and captured my hand, guiding me toward the doorway to the altar room, where he'd laid out a small feast while I'd been working. A wineskin, fruits, cheeses, and flatbreads covered the altar itself.

Again, I raised my eyebrows. "How did you gather all of this so quickly?"

Heru frowned. "You were inscribing for nearly an hour. It was not done so quickly . . ."

"Oh . . . I did not realize it had been so long." I mirrored his frown and shook my head. "How strange . . ."

"Perhaps you should take a break for the rest of the night."

I glanced at the opening at the top of the stairs, where the first hint of dawn light shone through the doorway. "I believe it is already morning."

"Then perhaps you should take a break for the *day*."

Giving his hand a squeeze, I stepped closer, stood on tiptoes, and pressed my lips against his. "I will take a break to eat," I said when I pulled away, "but then I really want to finish this room and get the next one started. I do not want to forget anything . . . forget to tell *you* anything." I searched his eyes. "You would want to know everything, correct? That would set your mind at ease . . . ?"

"As much as anything could, short of seeing you, standing before me . . . of holding you in my arms." His hands settled on either side of my neck, his thumbs fitting perfectly along my jaw. When his lips touched mine, his kiss was deep and penetrating, and I melted against him.

"I will allow you to continue your work, but—"

"You will *allow* it?"

He ignored my question. "*But,* I will tell you what to write in this new room."

I pushed the upper half of my body away from him with

hands on his bare chest and eyed him. "You want to write a note to your future self?"

A tantalizing half-smile touched his lips. "Something like that." He held his hand out toward the array of food. "Come. Let us eat."

Not twenty minutes later, we'd both had our fill and were standing in front of the false door on the right side of the altar room. My hand was pressed against the smooth, solidified At, and my eyes were closed. I finalized my mental image of the structure I wanted to create—a simple, long hallway with plenty of space for many off-shooting rooms, should I require them.

With a single, focused thought, I unmade the false door and expanded the solidified At away from me for nearly twenty yards. When I opened my eyes, I found myself standing before the doorway to a gleaming, pearlescent hallway.

I stepped through the opening and made my way to the end of the hall, where I went through the same routine, except instead of another hallway, I formed a doorway that led to a circular, domed chamber. Glancing over my shoulder, I found that Heru was still standing in the altar room, his focus on me hawkish.

My nerves sprouted wings and fluttered in my stomach. "Is something wrong?"

Ever so slowly, Heru shook his head. "Do you have any idea what you look like when you do that?" He approached, his pace steady, his movements smooth.

I bit my lip and shook my head, watching him come closer. I felt like a cornered animal all of a sudden.

"Your skin glows, and your hair floats around you like you are underwater." He didn't stop when he reached me, but forced me backward into the freshly formed room with his body. "You are a goddess," he said, his voice husky, his eyes darkening with promise. "You are *my* goddess."

My butt and shoulder blades touched smooth, cool wall, and

Heru stopped, his body almost touching mine. Almost, but not quite.

"Make a door, little queen."

"Why?" I asked, even as I willed one into being and darkness engulfed us.

"Because I am about to help you learn how to remain more focused on your surroundings while you write, and I do not want anyone to interrupt such a valuable lesson. It is too dangerous for you to remain so unaware." He breathed in deeply near my neck, his exhale giving rise to goose bumps. But still, he didn't touch me. "Give us light, little queen."

I swallowed and did as he requested, making the walls glow with a soft luminescence. "How—how are you going to help me learn to be more aware?"

A promising grin spread across his face. "You are going to record everything I do to you—describe how each touch makes you feel—until I decide that you have practiced enough."

My breath hitched. The task sounded impossible. "I do not think I will be very successful . . ."

"I do not think you have much of a choice, because I am not stopping until every surface in this chamber is filled with your words . . ." He moved so his mouth was just hovering over mine.

"I could lie . . . write gibberish," I said breathily. "You would not be able to tell."

Heru pulled away, his grin turning wolfish. "In four thousand years, I would."

I imagined Marcus reading my descriptions of his past self making love to me, and my heartbeat faltered, then resumed beating triple-time.

"Begin writing, little queen. I believe today is going to be *quite* interesting . . ."

I licked my lips and raised my eyes to the very top of the dome. Letting out a shuddering breath, I started writing.

Your hands are sliding up my arms. Only your fingertips are on my skin . . . it almost tickles, but it feels too good. Goose bumps are spreading out from every place you're touching me . . .

You're holding my arms over my head, commanding me to keep them there. Your fingers are skimming down my arms, down the sides of my body. Your touch is so gentle . . . so light. I want you to tear off my dress, but you're only lifting my skirt . . . slowly . . . so damn slowly. Everywhere you touch, my skin feels like it's on fire. I need you to—Oh my God, Marcus . . . you're on your knees, and . . . and . . . and . . .

38

ROUTINE & DISTURBANCE

Living with Heru and his family wasn't nearly as awkward as I'd expected it to be. Days passed, filled with mornings spent helping Seshseshet with the two younger children while she did "around the house" things, afternoons spent working in my underground sanctuary behind Nuin's palace, evenings spent training with Nuin and usually some combination of Set, Nekure, and Aset, and nights spent with Heru. True, Heru was almost always around me during the day's activities, as well, but it was the nights that I treasured.

I would erect an At barrier in the doorway and windows of my sleeping chamber in his home, locking the two of us—and our sounds—inside until morning. And *every* morning, just as the sun was peeking over the cliffs surrounding the Oasis and Heru and I were dozing together, limbs tangled and minds lulled into contented sleep, a tapping would start on the other side of the At door.

And every morning, Heru and I would groan sleepily as we donned our discarded clothing before I willed the barriers to revert to their former state—air. Tarset, Heru's youngest daughter, a tiny four-year-old, would scamper in for some early morning snuggles. She was so obviously a daddy's girl, and I was just grateful that her love of her father hadn't resulted in jealousy for all of the time he spent with me. In fact, the reverse seemed to be happening.

Just before dawn two weeks after Heru and I first bonded, I lay facing him on one of the thin pads that passed for mattresses in this time. I'd grown accustomed to them, had even started to sleep quite restfully, though spending every night sleeping beside Heru might have had something to do with that. The barriers covering the window openings were gone, letting fresh desert air fill the room, and Heru was tracing symbols on my hip with his fingertips, his eyes lidded with morning languor.

My face scrunched as I concentrated. I stayed like that for several seconds while he ran through the series of symbols again, then shook my head. "It is too many . . . you do not play fair, Heru."

His lips twitched, but he held back a smile. "Hat-hur-Alexandra," he said, repeating the first symbol—a disc resting in the cradle of two curving cow horns, which had become his go-to symbol for me, since "Alexandra" was almost impossible to spell out phonetically using hieroglyphs. He moved on to the next symbols as he slowly uttered the rest of his tactile message, "is the goddess I will worship, the queen I will serve, the wife I will be faithful to, the woman I will love"—his gaze seared my soul—"for all eternity."

I blinked rapidly, fighting back the tears suddenly welling in my eyes. Leaning in, I pressed my lips against his, taking his mouth as tenderly as he'd taken my body only hours ago. "Heru is the god I will worship, the king I will serve, the husband I will be faithful to, and the man I will love for all eternity," I said a hairsbreadth from his lips.

"I am no king."

Not yet, I didn't say; I only smiled and stared into those molten, golden pools. One day he would be the leader of our people, elected by the Council of Seven after both Nuin *and* Heru's father, Osiris, the Nejeret who would take over after Nuin's death, were gone. But he didn't need to know that. Informing him of future deaths would only upset him, and causing him undue pain was the last thing I ever wanted to do.

Tap. Tap. Tap.

My eyes darted to one of the arched windows. The barest hint of golden sunlight was shining through the opening. As my lips curved into a smile, I held in a laugh. Based on the amusement sparkling in Heru's eyes, he was doing the same. How Tarset could time her demanding little knock so perfectly every morning was beyond me, but she could, and it was the most welcome joke. I was starting to fall in love with that little girl, just a little.

Tap. Tap. Tap.

After one final, short kiss, I sat up and glanced around the fairly large and relatively unadorned space in search of my dress from yesterday. The room didn't need decoration, not with the graceful swooping and swirling embellishments Nuin had worked into the solidified At when he'd created this palace, but I had added a few creature comforts in the form of a standing wardrobe, a couple chairs, a small, square table, a washstand, and a screened-off "toilet" area, all fabricated from solidified At as well. I found my dress hanging from the corner of the nearest chair by one strap.

I made my way across the room, knowing full well that Heru was watching my every movement from the bed, and slipped the dress over my head. By the time I turned around, Heru was already in the process of wrapping his kilt around his hips. He tied the intricate knot far more easily than I ever could, settled back on the bed, and nodded.

Tap. Tap. Tap.

Smiling, I moved to the At door and pressed my palm against its smooth surface. It dissolved into a quicksilver mass, and when I removed my hand, dissipated in a cloud of colorful, smoky tendrils, revealing a small girl with enormous, honey-brown eyes, chubby cheeks, and a mess of shoulder-length black hair haloing her head.

Tarset's eyes were huge circles as she watched the final tendrils of fuchsia and lime-green fade away. A broad grin spread across her round face, making her cheeks even chubbier. She giggled, then lunged forward, capturing my hand in both of hers and dragging me toward the bed.

"Alright, little fig, what do you command of me this morning?" I asked as I scooted onto the thin mattress after her. I turned onto my side and propped my head up with my hand, watching Tarset maneuver Heru's arms into a position she deemed acceptable.

Finally, she curled into a ball between us and sighed. "I want to know what Xena does next."

I suppressed a laugh and raised my eyebrows. "You like that story more than the one I told yesterday?"

Tarset's round face scrunched and she shook her head. "Why does the princess need a boy to save her? She should save herself."

I couldn't help it; I threw my head back and laughed. Pulling Tarset closer to me, I hugged her tightly. "You would fit in well where I come from, Tarsi."

She abandoned her father and snuggled closer against my torso, and I realized that I'd fallen in love with this little girl more than just a little bit. One day, in the distant future, it was practically ordained that Heru and I would have a couple children of our own—assuming my body ever reached the bonding pheromone saturation point—and the time I spent with Tarset made me yearn for that day's arrival. But it also set a deep-seated sadness further and further into my heart, because that day would only come after Tarset was a four-thousand-year memory.

Part of me longed to share my bittersweet torment with Heru . . . but doubt paralyzed my tongue every time I considered telling him. What if Nuin was wrong? What if it never happened? What if we failed, and the sheut tore me apart from the ba out, causing both my and Heru's deaths? What if . . . there were too many what-ifs.

Gazing at me with those big, amber eyes, Tarset said, "Will you take me there someday? I want to see where you come from!"

My throat constricted, and my heart lurched. When my chin started to tremble, I forced myself to take slow, deep breaths. I shook my head. "I wish I could, little fig, I really do, but . . . it is a place that only I can go."

"Because you are a goddess?"

"Something like that."

She touched the corner of my eye, where a tear was doing its damndest to break free. "Why are you sad?"

"Because, someday soon, I will have to return to that place."

She stuck out her lower lip in a pout, then smiled. "But you will come back."

My next deep breath was noticeably shaky. "I do not know if I will be able to, little fig."

"Then I will visit you."

"Tarsi . . ."

"You said that sometimes Xena goes to the places where only the gods can go. That is what I will do." Her eyes shone with fierce determination.

I forced a tremulous smile and nodded. "Okay," I lied. "I would like that very much, I think."

"Good." She rolled onto her back and stared up at the high, opalescent ceiling. "Now tell me what happens to Xena next."

Laughing a soft, miserable laugh, I met Heru's gaze. And my tears broke free.

I squeezed my eyes shut and cleared my throat. "When Xena found out what happened to her son . . ."

IT WAS MIDMORNING, AND NEKURE, TARSET, AND I were sitting in the flower garden in the center of the Heru household's private orchard, surrounded by date and doum palms, as well as fig, olive, and peach trees, and with the palace's At spires reaching high overhead, blocking the sun. Heru and two of his grown sons were clearing sand from the aqueduct's gutter—technology Nuin had stolen from a later time—while Nekure was helping me practice my ability to control small pieces of At more fluidly. Physically manipulating the At may have been the only "special" power he had access to through *his* sheut, but he'd had hundreds of years to perfect every minute nuance.

The flower garden was the only place outdoors where we felt comfortable using our unique abilities, since the orchards were completely surrounded by the stone buildings belonging to Heru's decedents, and none in his line would ever betray him by sharing our secrets.

Rus was frolicking among the poppies and rose bushes, chasing a delicate crystalline butterfly as it flew gracefully around the garden. Nekure had created the stunning little creature and was controlling its flight with the thinnest tether of At stretching from its tail end to his index finger.

Giggling, Tarset clapped as she watched.

Nekure's butterfly returned to him, landing on his open palm and falling still once again. "Now you try it again," he said, turning his pale blue eyes on me.

I blew out a breath and glanced down at my own, tetherless butterfly, then at Rus, who'd settled in the sandy dirt like a sphinx but hadn't taken his eyes off Nekure's butterfly. "It does not seem to matter how many times I try, Nekure . . ."

Nekure patted my knee with his free hand. "It took me nearly a month to learn to maintain the tether. You learned to do as much in two days." He smiled. "You doubt yourself too much, my friend."

I couldn't help but return his smile, though mine wasn't nearly as confident. I took a deep breath. "Very well . . . here goes."

I touched my index finger to the butterfly's tail and pulled my hand away, creating a thin thread of unset At between me and the figurine. Now came the hard part—willing each tiny movement into a seamless, flowing motion.

The left wing twitched.

The right wing stuttered open.

The left wing mirrored the movement a half second later.

Both wings glided upwards, closing together in a single, smooth motion.

I squealed, as did Tarset, and released the tether. "I did it!" My cheeks ached with the strength of my ecstatic grin, but as soon as my eyes met Nekure's, my excitement faded and my smile slipped.

His eyes were wide, his face even paler than usual.

"What?"

He pointed to my hand. "Look at your skin, Lex."

I did. It was glowing with a faint sheen of iridescence, shimmering with every color imaginable. "Shit!" I hissed just as I felt the telltale clenching sensation in my chest. For the second time, my borrowed sheut was overflowing with too much power.

I jumped to my feet. "Tarset, take Rus and run inside to your mother."

She stared at me with round eyes, her butt apparently glued to the ground.

"*Now,* Tarset!"

Her eyes widened even further, but she didn't hesitate. She scooped up the kitten and sprinted through the orchard.

I stumbled in the opposite direction, trying to think of the most remote place I could flee to in the shortest amount of time. If the power exploded out of me when others were too close to me, it just might obliterate them.

I'd almost reached the outer edge of the orchard when electricity thrummed in my chest, and my knee gave out. Catching myself with one hand on the sandy ground, I pushed myself back up to my feet and searched for a path that led away from the cluster of buildings that belonged to Heru's family. I had to get away before the power broke free, and I destroyed them.

Another pulse crackled out from my chest, a little bit more intense, and I doubled over. Someone grabbed my wrist—Nekure, I realized—hoisting my arm over his shoulders and wrapping his own around my waist.

"I have to get . . . out of . . . the Oasis," I told him between rapid breaths.

"This way." He started guiding me at a quick walk, though I couldn't say where he was guiding me *to,* since all of my strength and concentration was going into holding the destructive energy inside me. "Heru comes," he said.

Heru's scent surrounded me as his arm joined Nekure's, lending additional support. Together, they dragged me toward somewhere I could only hope would be secluded. Darkness surrounded us, and I realized we were in the tunnel that led through the limestone cliffs walling off the Oasis from the rest of the desert.

"How long can you hold it in, Alexandra?" Heru asked.

I gritted my teeth, the power expanding inside me in more frequent and more intense pulses. "Not . . . much . . . longer."

Suddenly, strong arms scooped me up, and I was being carried much faster than I'd been able to move on my own two feet. We burst back into the light, Heru carrying me out into the desert at a full sprint.

"Put me down, Heru." I was losing control. I could feel the electric power crackling over my skin. *"Now!"*

Gently, he set me down on the sand, and I curled my legs up to my chest and hugged my knees.

"Heru," I rasped, "Nekure . . . *run*!"

I clenched my jaw and took shuddering breaths. Wetness coated my cheeks as I held the expanding power in, hoping to give Heru and Nekure time to get far enough away from me.

I dug my nails into my palms.

I wedged my face between my knees.

I squeezed my eyes shut.

Throwing my head back, I screamed, and the power exploded from me in wave after wave of bone-shattering electricity. My flesh shredded. My muscles ashed away. I was unmade. For an eternity, I knew nothing but pain.

Between one breath and the next, the outpouring of power ceased, snapping back into me and quieting, and suddenly, I was whole again. I took harsh breaths, enjoying the feel of air whooshing in and out of my brand-new lungs, of my brand-new heart pumping oxygen-rich blood to my brand-new organs and muscles.

I could hear the faint swish-swish of footsteps in the sand, but my mind wasn't clear enough to make out where they were coming from. I just breathed. In and out. In and out. In and out.

Arms were around me, pulling me close to a hard body. That scent, spicy and intoxicating and comforting. Warmth. Happiness. Home.

"Is it done?" someone asked. *Nekure,* I thought somewhere in the back of my mind.

"It is," someone else said. The one who was holding me.

Heru. "Though with how much she has been using the sheut, I cannot imagine why it happened in the first place. She could not possibly use these powers any more than she already does . . . how could it build up to overflowing like that?"

"It did not last so long last time."

"No," Heru said. "It did not."

The fractured pieces of my mind rearranged, fitting back together. I sucked in a deep breath and clutched Heru. My fingers dug into the firm flesh on his back. "How long did it last?" I asked, my voice hoarse from that initial scream.

Heru's arms tightened around me, and he pressed his lips to the top of my head. "The sun is already beginning its descent." Which meant it was late afternoon; I'd been out in the Sahara, unrelenting power exploding out of me, for *hours*. I feared that we were running out of time . . . that *I* was running out of time.

I took a deep, fortifying breath and loosened my hold on Heru. Pulling my head away from his shoulder, I looked into his eyes. "We need to talk to Nuin."

39

DESTRUCTION & SACRIFICE

"Take the sheut out of her," was Heru's greeting to Nuin as the three of us barged past his guards—who never would have stopped me, in the first place—and into his private chambers, which were about midway up in his palace's tallest tower.

Nuin was in his compact, circular courtyard, sitting cross-legged at the head of a tiny pool filled with silvery fish, trailing his fingers through the water. It was where I usually found him. He'd once told me that the water helped him think, that its movement was so similar to the movement of time that it focused his thoughts, making the complex web of past, present, and future more understandable.

As we entered the courtyard, Nuin turned a steady gaze on Heru. There was something off about him, though I couldn't quite put my finger on it. "I cannot, and I will not," he said calmly.

Heru strode forward, leaving Nekure and me to watch from just inside the wide, multi-arched doorway. He stopped on the opposite side of the pool from Nuin and pointed back at me. "She had another of those attacks. It is *killing* her."

"I am quite aware. But if I tried to remove it, she would die instantaneously."

Heru's arm slowly sank.

"The only thing that surprises me," Nuin said, "is that this second attack did not happen sooner." He turned his attention to me, and it took me a moment to recognize what was different about him; his eyes were still brilliant, but they shone with a silvery opalescence, much like the default appearance of solidified At, instead of their usual rainbow hues.

I rushed forward to stand beside Heru. "Nuin . . . your eyes . . ."

Nuin gestured absentmindedly to his face with one hand. "While the presence of my sheut creates suffering for you, dear Alexandra, its absence does the same for me, it would seem."

I rounded the pool in three lurching steps, falling to my knees at his side. "I know pulling all of it out of me would kill me, but can you take *some* to save yourself?"

His moonlight gaze washed over my face, and he shook his head. "You must learn as much as you can, as quickly as you can, dear Alexandra, for I think this body is not long for this world."

My blood chilled as I wrapped my hands around his, demanding his full attention. "No, Nuin. Not yet."

"But I must . . . it is what has always been and will always be." His full, familiar lips curved into a smile. "That is what you had Aset tell me after you saved her so many years ago."

"I—" I reared back. "*What?* Nuin, what are you talking about?"

"Ah, long ago . . . it was how I knew you were the right choice." His eyes narrowed and he tilted his head to the side, studying me. "Long ago for me, at least. Still to come for you."

"You should not have chosen her," Heru said from directly behind me. "You should have chosen another."

Nuin blinked, his silvery eyes slowly angling upward. "But I did not choose Alexandra. She chose herself."

Heru's sharp stare shifted to me.

Eyebrows drawn together, I shook my head. I didn't think Nuin was all there at the moment, especially because I most certainly *hadn't* chosen this path for myself. I helped Nuin to his feet and guided him through the doorway that led to his crescent-shaped bedroom. Heru and Nekure remained in the courtyard.

I sat on the edge of Nuin's bed and, once he'd settled himself on the thin mattress, stared into those unfamiliar eyes. "Rest, Nuin, and I shall return for lessons in a few hours."

He peered up at me, his eyes regaining some of their usual sparkle, if not their usual rainbow brilliance, and he chuckled softly. "I see that you and Heru have been quite busy."

I shook my head. "I don't . . . what are you talking about?"

"The saturation point, dear Alexandra—you have reached it." He shrugged. "It is yet another sign that my time—and your time *here*—is coming to an end. Tonight, I believe I will explain to you how to use the sheut to travel through time."

I'd reached the bonding pheromone saturation point? What did that mean, exactly? "But I still don't know how to restore ma'at."

"Ahhh . . . but you do. The same thing that will restore balance to your body will restore ma'at to the universe." He paused, watching me closely. When I said nothing, merely stared at him in bafflement, he added, "When the sheuts that once belonged to Apep and myself are merged with brand-new beings, those beings will become the new Netjer, the next generation of true gods, the next guardians of ma'at in this universe."

And still, I stared at him, eyes widened by shock. "My—my children?"

Smiling kindly, he nodded.

"Heru and me . . . having kids . . ." I shook my head slowly. "*That* is what's supposed to save the universe?"

"Indeed it is, dear Alexandra."

"I don't . . ." I continued to shake my head. "That doesn't . . ."

"I knocked the universe out of balance when I stole Apep's sheut and stored it within this body, along with my own. Your children must be kept safe long enough to come into their power . . . they must be protected from Apep."

I nodded, more than a little numb. "Of course."

Nuin closed his eyes for a moment. "I am so very weary."

"Oh, um . . ." I cleared my throat. "I'll let you rest and come back later."

Before I could stand, Nuin's long fingers wrapped around my wrist. "But you cannot kill Apep."

I eased back down onto the bedframe and shook my head, my mind taking a moment to catch up to Nuin's abrupt change of topics. "But then he'll always be a threat . . ."

"No, my Alexandra, I mean that *you* are incapable of killing Apep. Only I could do that—but I never would, because to kill Apep would destroy ma'at completely. Apep *is*. What *is* cannot *not* be. The universe is part of Apep, just as it is part of me—or the *Re* part of me—and it cannot exist without either of us." Nuin exhaled heavily.

Again, I shook my head. "But . . . how am I supposed to protect—*what* am I supposed to do, then?"

"You must trap him in a Netjer-At's body, then trap that Nejter-At as well."

"Set . . ."

Nuin nodded, his eyelids drifting shut. "If Apep roams free, he will possess one of your children; he will use them to destroy ma'at . . . and then the universe will unravel until nothing *is*." He said nothing more for several heartbeats, and I thought he'd fallen asleep.

Until his eyelids fluttered open. "If Apep becomes free before you can trap Set's body, then you must seal him inside a prison of solidified At. It is the only other thing that can contain a being such as him." Nuin's odd, moonstone eyes locked on mine. "You *must not* let him possess you or Heru. Your bond is the key, and it will unlock either a future of balance, or a future of destruction . . . of nothing."

His eyelids slid closed again, and he sighed. "If he possesses you while you still contain the sheut—or Heru, for that matter, once his sheut is made whole within him—then you must give the sheut to another . . . must sacrifice yourselves . . . for a chance . . ."

Dropping Nuin's hand, I stood and backed away. "No . . ." My head turned from side to side slowly. "We won't—I will *not* kill myself. That was never part of the deal."

Nuin opened his eyes and speared me with his sharp gaze. "There is no deal. There is only truth."

"I am no martyr."

"No, dear Alexandra; you are no martyr. You are the Meswett, the girl-child, the messiah of all that ever was, is, or will be. You are far from a martyr." His eyes closed, and his chest rose and fell several times, until his eyelids opened one final time. His irises were dulled, but once again shimmering with swirling colors. "You are a god."

I backed away another step, shaking my head more adamantly. *I'm no god,* I thought. *I'm no god!* But what came out was, "Gods don't die." The words were barely a whisper.

"All things die."

40

LIFE & DEATH

Heru and I returned to his home shortly after leaving Nuin's palace, Nekure having already split off to alert Aset of Nuin's sudden decline. I didn't tell either of them about the disturbing information Nuin had relayed—that Heru's and my children would be destined to a life of near-absolute power and crushing responsibility—or about his haunting final remark.

All things die.

And I refused to consider that such a sacrifice—my life, or Heru's—would be the culmination of Nuin's grand machinations. I'd never been idealistic, and I didn't host any romantic notions about my true nature. I was not a martyr; I was a survivor, and suicide by sacrifice didn't fit in with my survival instincts.

The grounds were eerily quiet as we approached the familiar cluster of buildings belonging to Heru's family. My fingers were interlocked with Heru's, but my free hand was clenched into a tight fist. It would *not* come to that. *No. Way. In. Hell.*

I shook my head. It wouldn't come to that, because Nuin would recover from his temporary lapse into godly dementia, spend however long it took teaching me everything I needed to know to trap Apep—either in Set or not—and to return to my native time. And then I would figure out what to do about the whole "godly children" thing and everything *would* work out. Happily-ever-afters all around.

I clenched my fist more tightly, my nails digging into my palm painfully.

"Something is wrong," Heru said, stopping before the columned entrance to his palace. He gave my hand a squeeze, then released it.

I searched my mind for an excuse for my withdrawn mood. But when I looked at him, he was scanning the neat little gardens, the stone houses surrounding the palace, and even the path we'd walked. He wasn't talking about *me*.

Heru looked up at the sun, still hours from the horizon. "They never go in this early. There is still much to do . . ."

I frowned. "Maybe—maybe Sesha pulled everyone inside when Tarsi found her and told her about what happened?"

"Maybe . . ." Heru took the stairs leading up to the palace's arched doorway two at a time, me close on his heel.

The air was scented with vomit and sweat, and I had to suppress a gag.

"Sesha?" he called.

There was no response.

"Sesha! Where are you?"

A groan came from one of the back rooms, accompanied by the faint sound of weeping. Without our heightened hearing, I doubted that either of us would have heard it.

Heru made his way through several sparsely furnished chambers and down a long hallway filled with late afternoon sunlight that led to the back of the palace, to the cozy room where the three youngest children slept. Seshseshet was kneeling on the floor beside one of three polished, wood-framed beds carved to display a bevy of animals native to Egypt, her head resting on her curled-up arm on the edge of the bed and her body shaking with each of her faint sobs.

Tarset lay atop the bed, her skin pallid and coated in a sheen of sweat and her breaths quick and shallow. A brief glance at the other two beds told me they were occupied by the other two children, who also appeared unwell, but not nearly as ill as Tarset.

"Sesha . . ." Heru strode into the room and dropped to his knees beside his pregnant wife. When Seshseshet didn't look up, didn't show any sign of having heard him, he shook her shoulder. "Sesha."

She raised her head and turned red-rimmed eyes on him. With a wail, she threw herself into his arms and started crying in earnest.

I watched Heru attempt to comfort her—rubbing her back, murmuring soft, nonsensical words, rocking her—before making my way around the room, checking on the other two children. They were both burning up, but neither seemed to be having as much trouble breathing as Tarset was having.

I stopped at the head of Tarset's narrow bed and stared down at her. Her eyes were closed, her mouth open, and each ragged, rattling breath was clearly a struggle. My stomach knotted and fissures laced through my heart. *Not her . . .*

"What happened?" I swallowed roughly. "How—"

Without warning, Seshseshet spun on her knees and wrapped her arms around my thighs, hugging my legs and staring up at me with hope-filled eyes. "I beg of you, save her . . . please."

Slowly, I shook my head. "I do not know how to—"

"*Please,*" she repeated, desperation making her voice hoarse. "Please! You must be able to do something. This ailment already claimed Bunefer, and now it seeks my sweet Tarset. Whatever you say, you have the powers of the gods . . . I know you do.

Please, Alexandra! Use this great power you have. Save my little girl. *Please!*"

"I—"

"Do not drink any water—it's been poisoned," Aset said as she rushed into the room, Nekure close on her heels. She scanned the beds quickly. "Ah . . . but I see I am too late."

"Can you save them?" Heru asked his sister, his voice rough.

Aset approached the foot of Tarset's bed and shook her head. "I can do nothing for her, but the other two I may be able to save." She moved to Heru's youngest son's bed and bent over the boy.

My throat constricted. Aset—Dr. Isa, in my time—was a healer even now, but it would do no good for the little girl who'd snuggled her way into my heart. Aset couldn't help her. Tarset was going to die.

Not her . . .

"Please . . ." Seshseshet's hands were clutching the backs of my leg so hard that it was painful. "*Help her*, Alexandra."

I licked my lips, unable to tear my eyes away from Tarset's uncharacteristically pale face. "I cannot save her, Sesha, but I know someone who can . . . in my time, far in the future." Neffe was an even more talented healer than Aset, and with modern equipment, I knew she was the dying child's best chance. Plus, I had a moderately insane idea of a way to bring Tarset to her. Nuin's words replayed in my head:

As the At expands in this plane, it does not displace matter, but replaces it . . . it is as though you are transposing that alternate plane onto this one, but only in a delineated place, and while the At-matter is here, whatever it is displacing is frozen in time . . .

Frozen *in time . . .*

"You will take here there, to this future healer?" Seshseshet's eyes welled with a resurgence of tears.

I nodded, but my stomach churned with uncertainty.

"And then you will return her?"

"I—" Swallowing roughly, I shook my head. "Even I cannot do that. But she *will* have a chance to live her life . . . *there*."

"Then you will take care of her? You will love her and raise her as your own daughter? You will do this for me?"

I stroked Seshseshet's hair as my own tears welled. My saliva felt so thick, my mouth so dry, that I had to swallow several times before I could respond. "I will, Sesha, I swear it," I said, not adding, *if she survives . . .*

"Then do it, please, I beg of you. Just save her. Let her live. I have lost too many . . . just let her live . . ."

Heru stood, and I raised my eyes to meet his gaze. He nodded.

I returned the nod and leaned over the short headboard to place my fingertips on Tarset's forehead.

I concentrated.

Squeezed my eyes shut.

Took a deep breath.

And all at once, willed the At to replace every single cell of Tarset's body with solidified At.

There was a sharp gasp, and Seshseshet's arms fell away from me. "Is she—is she . . ."

"She is not dead." I opened my eyes and stared down at what appeared to be a perfect, quartz sculpture of a slumbering little girl. "She is frozen in time—in every time between now and the future, when I will return her to the way she was. To her, it should be only a blink," I said, hoping with every fiber of my being that I was right. I held my breath and glanced at Nekure; he had far more experience with this particular ability.

His lips were curved downward and his eyes were narrowed in thought, but ever so slowly, he nodded.

I exhaled in relief.

Seshseshet was running the backs of her fingers over her

daughter's stonelike face. "And your future healer will be able to save her when you wake her?"

I closed my eyes for several seconds. When I opened them back up, I met Seshseshet's watery stare. "If she cannot heal her, no one can."

Seshseshet bowed her head. "Thank you, Alexandra," she whispered. "Thank you."

Heru placed his hand on her shoulder and met my eyes, those liquid golden pools filled with more loss and gratitude and love than words could ever express.

I offered him a small smile and forced it to remain as a horrifying thought filled my veins with ice. Nuin . . . he hadn't been suffering from some godly form of dementia caused by missing his sheut; he'd been suffering from the effects of this poison, and the most likely culprit was someone who'd been possessed by Apep and was using poison to weaken Nuin enough that he couldn't fight as his sheut was torn out of him. Except his sheut wasn't *in* him; it was in *me*, leaving him all but defenseless.

I left Heru and Seshseshet to their mourning and crossed to the doorway, where Nekure still stood sentry. I grabbed his elbow and pulled him into the long hallway. He let me guide him away from the sickroom, and when I stopped and faced him, he watched me curiously.

"I think this is Apep's doing—all so he can distract the rest of us and weaken Nuin. Think about how Nuin was when we saw him . . ."

Nekure stiffened, his eyes searching my face but not really seeing as he processed my words. His eyes widened. "You must go to him. Now. Heru and I will only be minutes behind you."

The colorful, misty tendrils of At were already swirling around me when I heard my name. I looked at the doorway to the sickroom, where Heru was standing. His eyes met mine.

And then I was gone.

41

ASHES & DUST

I appeared in Nuin's tower bedroom in a silent burst of misty colors and found myself standing at the foot of his bed. A woman wearing the usual white linen shift was sitting astride him, her head bowed as though she were looking down and her shoulders and arms moving in a jerky motion. I could only see the bottom half of Nuin's legs, but based on the groans coming from him, I initially thought I'd made a mistake, he was fine, and I'd burst in on an amorous moment.

Until I noticed the cords binding his ankles together, pale against the bronze of his skin. I knew Nuin as well as anyone could know the Great Father, and I felt absolutely certain that he would never allow himself to be put in restraints. He was too important, his purpose too significant to *everything*, to place himself in such a vulnerable position.

My first inhale confirmed my worst fears. The tang of blood mixed with the foul stench of feces and a sharp sourness hung thick in the air.

A cold detachment cloaked me, and in another flash of colors, I shifted to the side of the bed.

The woman was Ipwet, I could now see, Nuin's primary

human wife. Her hands and wrists were coated in a crimson sheen as they worked a bronze dagger between Nuin's legs, and she seemed to be castrating him with excruciating slowness. The skin above his groin had been carved almost delicately, but the pervasive stench told me just how deep those cuts went into Nuin's body.

The coldness seeped further into me, taking root in the core of my being. I reacted without thought. On my next inhale, before Ipwet even had a chance to turn her head in my direction, my hand was around her neck. I watched, fascinated, as the At crept across her skin, overtaking her body completely in a matter of seconds. Her opalescent face was locked in a wide-eyed, open-mouthed expression that could have been permanent. Except, unlike Tarset, I didn't desire any sense of permanency for this woman . . . this monster.

Narrowing my eyes, I willed the atoms of At that had replaced Ipwet's physical body to separate, to shatter into a seemingly infinite cloud of solidified At. She exploded with a soft *poof*, and the particles that had once been *her* spread out and misted to the floor, until she was nothing more than a layer of imperceptibly thin dust.

I exhaled harshly and sucked in another, rancid breath. But in my cool, detached state, the stench didn't bother me.

I stared down at Nuin, my hands hovering over his ruined middle. Despite the chill in my soul, I couldn't help but choke on a sob. When I slid my gaze up his torso to his face, I saw that he was gagged, and his eyes, once again radiating their faded swirl of brilliant colors, were shifting focus back and forth between mine and some point behind me.

Because Ipwet hadn't been alone.

In the blink of an eye, I shifted to the other side of the bed and reappeared, facing my would-be attackers. There were three of them, all male, and all bigger and notably stronger than me, and all exuding an air of menace. And based on the way they moved, they were all Nejeret, which meant they were even stronger, even faster, even more highly skilled than any human. In the cool detachment, this was all so easy to see.

I grinned. *I* was more than a Nejerette. A foreign, alien power flowed through my body, wound around my soul. I was a *goddess*.

Who the hell did they think they were—Ipwet's minions . . . assassins . . . traitors to our people? Maybe. They may have been all of those things. But they were also dead; they were insects waiting to be squished under my heel. They just didn't know it yet.

Before the one in the lead could reach Nuin's bed, before he could even consider finishing the job Ipwet had started, I shifted. I winked into existence directly behind him, giving form to an At dagger in my right hand as I did, and slid the razor-sharp blade across the front of his neck. Taking hold of his shoulders, I turned and shoved him at my other two opponents. Dark, arterial blood sprayed their bare chests and stained their pristine linen kilts as he collapsed against them.

Mirroring each other, they sidestepped away, letting their companion's body settle on the polished floor. A glossy pool of blood spread out around his upper half, almost hypnotizing as it seeped from his dying body.

The two still standing circled around me. They kept their distance, but they watched . . . they weighed and measured me. They had knives, I noted, longer than mine and glinting copper in the late afternoon light that streamed through the tall, arched window openings. It didn't matter. Their knives wouldn't save them. Not from me.

"Go," I said as I turned in a slow circle to keep them in my sight. "Run from this place and never return, and I will spare you." I raised my hand, palm up. "I *would* run, if I were you."

The one on the left looked like he might bolt, but the man on the right laughed.

"So be it," I said. I created a sheet of At as thick as a single atom on my upturned palm and expanded it toward the Nejerets' necks with merely a thought.

Both sets of eyes widened for the briefest moment as the invisible guillotine sliced cleanly through their flesh before I retracted the sheet of At. Almost in slow motion, their heads slid forward while their bodies remained in place. Their fleshy skulls landed on the floor with a smack, rolling in haphazard directions while their bodies crumpled nearby.

Clap.

Clap.

Clap.

My gaze glided to the doorway, where Ankhesenpepi stood, one shoulder leaned against the grooved frame. "I honestly thought Heru was the one Re had given his sheut to, but you . . . that was an exquisite display of wielding the power."

I tilted my head to the side, watching the slender, beautiful woman. She seemed so much more brittle now—too severe, too harsh, too sharp.

Her lips spread into a wide grin. "I will put on an even more stunning display when I am wearing your skin." Her eyes were filled with a telltale inky darkness, slithering around on the surface of her irises.

I thought that should have elicited a reaction from me—a scream, maybe, or at least a shudder. But all I did was return her measuring stare. "Apep," I said with the barest nod.

Apep-Ankhesenpepi's lip curled into a sneer. "Heru's *whore*."

I raised one shoulder and let it drop, unaffected by her words. "I take it that this is all *your* doing." I gestured to Nuin, who was still gagged and tied to the bed a few feet behind me, his gut sliced open. His laborious breaths told me he was still alive. I drew on the coolness seeping into my soul from the foreign sheut I possessed. The inner chill helped me to maintain my composure while, inside, part of me was screaming in rage and agony and horror.

With a low chuckle, Apep-Ankhesenpepi pushed off the archway and took slow steps into the bedchamber. "Yes," she hissed, her eyes trained on me. "And imagine my surprise when I discovered only the tiniest slivers of sheut inside him. I let him keep those slivers, let it sustain him while Ipwet played. The old bag was so desperate for revenge . . . to make Nuin feel the pain she felt every time she gave birth to one of his little whelps."

When Apep-Ankhesenpepi was only steps away from me, she leered, her eyes scanning over me from head to toe. "Not quite as lush as this one—I've quite enjoyed the days I've spent in *Khessie's* body—but I think I will enjoy possessing that lithe body of yours as well . . . playing with it . . . with Heru . . ." Her next step brought her almost within arm's reach. "I do so prefer female bodies; there are so many more ways to possess them . . . to *invade* them . . ."

"You are boring me," I said as I took a step back and raised my hand. Vines of At sprouted from the polished floor, wrapping around her ankles and climbing up her legs, effectively restraining her. Another At dagger appeared in my hand, and I wrapped my fingers around its hilt.

Apep-Ankhesenpepi smiled. "Besides Nuin and Heru, how many other Netjer-At men have you let bed you, *whore queen*? Nekure and Set, I assume, since you spend so much time with them, as well. When I am wearing your body, I will take them all, over and over again." Her gaze flicked behind me, to Nuin. "Except for the *Great Father*." She cocked her head to the side. "Although I suppose we could engage in a little necrophilia, just this once . . ."

She was goading me, I realized. "You want me to kill you," I said, willing my dagger back out of existence. I narrowed my eyes. "Why?" Awareness dawned a moment later. "Ah . . . because you cannot leave that body while it still lives."

Behind me, Nuin said something incomprehensible against his linen gag.

I looked over my shoulder, and the moment my eyes landed on his savaged body, the cold, detached veil his sheut had settled over me evaporated, and panic surged in my chest.

"He is too far gone—"

"Shut up!" I snapped, flinging out my hand and erecting a glassy dome of At over Nuin's bed, sealing the two of us in our own, private world for however much time he had left.

I sat on the edge of the bed and reached for his gag. I sliced it off with a small, sharp At knife, then did the same with the cords binding his neck, arms, and legs. A film of tears coated my cheeks.

"My Alexandra," Nuin rasped as I finished cutting through his ankle bindings. He took a shallow breath. "Apep is . . . correct. I am dying."

I took hold of his hand with both of mine. "Let's go into the At. You won't feel the pain there."

He shook his head. "My body is . . . too weak. If I go into the At . . . it will fail . . . and I will not be able to . . . tell you what I must . . ."

I swallowed thickly, holding in a convulsive sob. I'd known this was going to happen, that he was going to die while I was in this time, but knowing it and *watching* it were two different things entirely. I *loved* him, and the thought of losing him . . . "Tell me what to do, Nuin. Just tell me what to do. There has to be some way I can use the sheut to—"

"No . . . my dear, sweet Alexandra." He laughed softly, but it quickly turned into a cough and a pained grimace. "I always knew . . . this would be *when* this body died . . . I just didn't know how . . . it would happen." He coughed again. "Quite painfully . . . it would seem."

My head was shaking from side to side, and my mouth was open, like I wanted to say something, but I didn't know what.

"You must be careful . . . of the oneness. Your mind is not capable . . . of continuing to function fully . . . when you've embraced the sheut . . . so completely."

"The 'oneness'?" I asked, wondering if he was referring to the cold detachment that had taken over, allowing me to kill four people without hesitation or remorse. I'd *killed* four people . . .

Nuin's eyes shifted to some point behind me, and before I could launch into a full-on breakdown, he said, "Ah . . . your boys . . . have arrived."

I glanced over my shoulder to see Heru, Nekure, and Set racing into the room. Apep-Ankhesenpepi appeared to be having some sort of a fit, flailing and shouting nonstop against the At vines binding her, though I had no idea what she was saying, and I really didn't care.

I met Heru's eyes through the barrier only briefly before turning my attention back to Nuin.

He swallowed, the action visibly difficult. "I thought . . . we would have a little more time . . . but we do not." Another shallow inhale. "Lower the barrier . . . Alexandra. My end . . . draws near and . . . there is something . . . I must do . . . before . . ."

I straightened, released his hand, and rose, moving to the place where Heru stood on the opposite side of the At barrier, his hands pressed against the glassy material. I raised my hand and placed my palm against his. The solidified At melted away in a colorful mist, and Heru's arms were suddenly around me in a brief but intense embrace.

When he released me, he took two large steps toward Nuin's bedside. "Great Father," he said as he knelt and bowed his head. "I have failed you."

"You have not." Nuin's voice was barely a whisper. His eyes met mine over Heru's close-shaven head. "Come here . . . my

Alexandra." He held up his other hand, and I moved around the head of the bed to sit on the opposite side.

I had a vague awareness of Nekure keeping Apep-Ankhesenpepi quiet and Set moving closer as I took hold of Nuin's hand. A tingling warmth engulfed my fingers, spreading up my arms and settling in my chest. "Nuin, what—"

"I have made . . . the sheut within you . . . whole." He smiled faintly, his eyes sparkling with unshed tears. There was no longer any hint of any shade of red, orange, or gold in his irises. "You must . . . be careful . . . of the oneness." A moment later, Nuin touched the fingertips of his other hand to Heru's forehead.

Heru closed his eyes and shuddered, and I assumed he was feeling the same odd sensation I'd just felt as Nuin implanted the last remainder of Apep's sheut within him.

Nuin removed his fingers from Heru's forehead and raised his hand to the side of my face. His skin was icy against my cheek. "You have a few weeks at most . . . before the sheut overtakes you. You know what you must do."

A chill enshrouded me, and shaking my head, I searched his face. Dread was a snake writhing in my gut. "But I don't even know how to get home." If he died, I *never* would. And in a few weeks, I would follow him to the grave, as would Heru.

Nuin's eyes held no hint of the rainbow shimmer at all, only a pale opalescence akin to moonstone, haunting in its unfamiliarity. "Simply enter the At . . . ba, sheut, and body . . . thinking of your time . . . and you should be transported . . . there."

I was still shaking my head. "But *how*?"

He took a slightly deeper, shuddering breath. "Remember when I . . . pulled you into a time . . . of my own making?"

I nodded.

"Just walk into a wall of At . . . *into*, not *through* . . . and you will enter . . . that plane." A cough wracked his body, and things in his ruined abdomen squished and squelched.

I swallowed a gag.

"Remember what must . . . be done if . . . Apep cannot be . . . trapped."

Eyes stinging with a resurgence of tears, I swallowed. "I am afraid. I am so scared of not *being*."

His gaze softened. "As am I . . . dear Alexandra. As am I."

Chin trembling, I turned my head and pressed my lips against Nuin's palm. "I love you, old friend."

"And I, you . . . my Alexandra," he said, his voice barely audible. "Now listen . . . closely. Unpleasant things . . . have happened . . . *will* happen. Let them . . . for *your* future . . . for *the* future." He paused. "You must save Aset . . . from her captor. Tell her who . . . you are . . . so I will know . . . to find you . . . to protect you." He exhaled completely and closed his eyes.

The three of us held our breath, waiting, hoping those eyes would open again. I bit my lip to hold in a convulsive sob.

Nuin's eyes opened and focused on me. He licked his lips, coating them with blood-tinged saliva. His faint smile was kind, and it broke my heart.

"I believe . . ." His fingers slid down the side of my face. ". . . in you . . ." His hand hit the thin mattress with a soft thud, and he exhaled again.

His eyes remained open, but they were no longer seeing.

42

DESTROY & PROTECT

Nuin was dead.

I felt a pulse of electric power in my chest.

Nuin, who'd been around my entire life, who'd watched over me, protected me, befriended me . . . was *dead*.

The power—coming from *Nuin's* sheut—pulsed again, thrumming in time with my heartbeat.

"Alexandra . . ." Heru's voice was barely a whisper, but the soft sound was overflowing with warning. "Your skin . . ."

I looked down at my hands, at my arms. Ribbons and tendrils of misty At thrashed around me, making it look like I was covered in flames of every possible color. I jumped to my feet and started backing away from the bed. I had to flee. I had to get away from these people that I loved before I incinerated them all. I had to—

The power spindled inside of me around the sheut, a tiny tornado of relentless, endless energy not of this world. This was different than before. *More*. I didn't have enough time. I didn't have *any* time.

"Shield them, Nekure!" I shouted, and the words were overrun by a scream. *My* scream.

The power broke free, a supernova of light and electricity and destruction. I had no choice but to throw my arms open, to let the fabric of space and time pour through me and expand in a world where it had no place, where all it could do was destroy.

The floor shook beneath my feet. Crackling and roaring and thunder filled my ears. I could hear screaming.

And laughing.

Apep-Ankhesenpepi was cackling joyously. "I was wrong about you," she said. "You are not Heru's whore; you are the mistress of death and chaos—of *me*—and you will kill them all *for* me."

. . . you will kill them all . . .

More of the At poured through me, invading this world. Expanding into its cracks. Tearing it apart.

"Kill them all. Let me taste their confusion. Let me feast on their horror. Let me bathe in their misery. Kill them all for me. *Become* me."

Kill them all for me.

Become *me.*

My eyes snapped open, and I speared Apep-Ankhesenpepi with a glare. "No. Way. In. Hell."

She was standing within a thin, semiopaque cylinder of solidified At with Heru, Set, and Nekure. All three men were on their knees, trying to keep from falling over completely as the palace shook, and Nekure's hand was pressed against the wall of At, feeding everything he had into it to hold it in place against the relentless onslaught of energy flowing out of me.

Some hidden history threaded through the sheut entered my awareness, and I understood. This moment, this choice—*my* choice—this was what had led to Apep's downfall to begin with. He—no, *it*, as I now knew that neither Apep nor Re, Nuin's true name, were of any gender—chose to let its sheut take control, to lash about, wild and free. *This* was what sparked the chain of events that led to Nuin—Re—tearing away Apep's sheut and hiding with it in an unborn human child. This unraveling chaos was the future Apep desired.

But it wasn't the future *I* desired.

I controlled the power; the power didn't control me. Screaming, I gritted my teeth and pulled the energy back.

It resisted.

I pulled harder. Dropping to my hands and knees, I dug my fingers into the solidified At floor like it was room-temperature butter, and heaved.

The unleashed power sunk hooks into the largest, sturdiest thing around—the limestone cliffs surrounding the oasis.

Using every drop of willpower within me, I yanked one final time.

The cliffs gave way, the power snapping back inside me with such an intense reverberation that I was knocked onto my side, momentarily stunned.

A deep rumble vibrated in the air. A monster, groaning as it opened its mouth to swallow us all.

Not a monster . . . the *cliffs* were groaning; they were collapsing. I could feel them. I could feel *everything*—every life, every ba, every stone and tree and molecule of At. Now that Nuin's sheut was whole within me, I was connected to it all.

And I was about to *destroy* it all.

"NO!" I pushed up onto my knees and thrust my hand over my head, willing the most enormous At structure I'd ever created into existence.

The dome slammed into place, surrounding every part of the oasis within the encircling cliffs. I could feel the rocks crashing against its surface, some as big as buses, some even larger. But I set the dome of solidified At, and it held. Even as my hand slipped away, as I fell back onto my side, as darkness seeped across my vision, it held.

PART VII

Netjer-At Oasis, Egypt
Present Day

43

KAT

. . . *And minutes later, when I woke, you were cradling me in your arms. And can I just say that nothing can give a hangover like a sheut explosion.*

I laughed out loud. Lex had been through so much, but it was like writing to Marcus was her outlet, the one way she'd learned to deal with all of the crazy without actually *going* crazy. My laugh faded quickly as I glanced down at the words filling the page. Marcus was going to be *pissed* when he found out about what Nuin told Lex—that she might have to sacrifice herself to give the rest of us a chance, and that, even if everything worked out, their kids would end up being god-slaves to universal order for, like, *ever*.

Lex had been gone for almost a month, and Marcus was slowly unravelling—not because of bonding withdrawals or anything like that, but because there seemed to be no end, no winding-down of her adventures in the past. I thought he'd actually started to think that his past self *had* managed to find a way for Lex to live out the thousands of years separating us from her, and that *this* Marcus would have to wait four thousand *more* years to ever see her again. It didn't even matter that it was impossible . . .

And I was pretty sure Marcus didn't give a flying crapola about any of this Apep-Set or ma'at stuff. All that mattered to him was Lex—Lex returning, Lex ridding herself of the sheut poisoning her, Lex having *twins* . . .

Staring at the words she'd inscribed so long ago, I let out a heavy sigh and stuck out my lower lip. Marcus might actually start caring about that "bigger picture" stuff now that both their fates—and their unborn kids'—appeared to be zooming toward a brick wall otherwise known as complete-and-utter-destruction if they failed. If they failed . . . we were all dead.

My chest clenched, and I felt something wet on my cheek and hastily wiped it away. I was *not* crying. I *wasn't*!

With a sigh, I turned the page and continued recording.

At least the dome really did hold, and I really didn't kill everyone. My God . . . can you imagine? I'm having a hard enough time dealing with the fact that I killed four people, and that I hardly cared that I was killing them while I was doing it. It's sick and twisted and totally creepy, and it's definitely something that's going to haunt my dreams for years . . . assuming we have years . . .

Anyway, after the sheut explosion, Nekure wrapped Apep-Ankhesenpepi's wrists in chains of At. He created an At dagger and held it flush against the front of her neck. Of course, when I opened my mouth to warn him that the threat of death was more like promising to fulfill Apep's deepest desires, Apep-Ankhesenpepi slammed her head forward and slit her own damn throat. We're just lucky that Apep hasn't been able to do the same with Set. If Set didn't have a will of iron . . . but he does, so it's no use worrying about something that won't happen.

Right, so, Ankhesenpepi bled out, right in front of us, and Apep oozed out of her in all of his inky, oily glory and started toward me. Nuin—or rather Re, who'd apparently been lying in wait in Nuin's dead body—rose up in a sparkling iridescent mist and rushed Apep, who chose to hide in the nearest person, Nejeret or otherwise, rather than be subjected to whatever Re could do to him in his now-incorporeal state. As I'm sure you've guessed by now, the person Apep hid in was none other than Set, who immediately passed out.

I frowned. I'd spent my whole life hating and fearing my dad. He was the monster under the bed, in the closet, *and* standing just outside, watching through the window. Hell, there were a bunch of times he probably *had* been standing just outside the window, watching me and mom. *He's always been such a creeper . . .*

Which made it so damn weird to think that my real dad, the guy who gave me his genes, wasn't actually a bad guy. According to everything I'd read of Lex's—and I'd read *a lot*—he was kind of a sweetheart. And Lex was going to trap him, hold him prisoner in his own body, for pretty much ever, as far as we knew. And that was the best-case scenario.

I swallowed repeatedly and cleared my throat. I. Would. Not. Freaking. Cry. I had a job to do, and it didn't include blubbering like a baby, damn it.

Taking a deep breath, I continued writing.

Re, having no body and no incorporeal enemy to contend with, changed direction. He hovered around Nekure, who was completely baffled as to why the shimmering mist was doing that until I told him that Re—well, I said "Nuin" to him, because I hadn't actually explained all that stuff about Nuin actually being Re, mythological archnemesis of Apep, blah blah blah—was probably waiting for permission. Once Nekure understood, his face brightened with a smile and he nodded. Personally, I wouldn't have been so eager to be possessed, but to each his own . . .

"Wait, whaaat . . . ?" I stared at the wall, at Lex's next words, my eyes wide and my mouth hanging open. "No effing way." I blinked several times, then read her words out loud. "*We watched as Re seeped into Nekure, and then he passed out, too.*" I licked my lips and shook my head at the wall. "Holy effing shitballs."

"I can honestly say that I didn't think it would be you," Nik said from the lone doorway out of the chamber.

I yelped and flung my notebook and pen in the air. They landed just beyond my feet as I spun on my butt to face the intruder.

Nik stepped into the room and raised his hand to the doorway. A sheet of what looked like liquid tin foil spread out from his palm, covering the opening in seconds. In a blink, it turned into pale, shimmering stone that matched the room's walls, ceiling, and floor. Not stone, I realized—solidified At.

I shifted so my feet were under me and rose, slowly, like not making any fast movements might prevent Nik from doing whatever the hell he was planning to do that required a door of At sealing us in. I backed away just as slowly, until my back hit a wall. My heart pounded in my chest.

He was still standing by the blocked doorway, watching me. His head was cocked to the side and a tiny smile curved his lips.

"What—what do you want?"

He shook his head and just kept on staring at me, wearing that knowing little smile.

"I won't tell anyone, if that's what you're worried about. I mean, if you want me to keep it a secret that you're, you know, possessed . . ." I cleared my throat. "I, um, will."

Nik's eyebrows rose, and he touched his fingertips to the front of his black T-shirt. "*Me?*" He shook his head, and the corners of his mouth turned down in the slightest possible frown. "I don't want anything from you. *He* does."

"He . . . ?" I blinked several times. "Nuin? I mean, *Re*? Why?" I shook my head. "I don't have anything. What could he possibly want from *me*?"

Nik grinned and closed his eyes for several seconds. When

he opened them again, they were no longer pale blue, but the color of glimmering opals. His expression changed, becoming warm and kind and making Nik's face seem far less menacing and far more handsome.

"Katarina Dubois," he said, bowing his head. "We have never actually met, though I have heard much about you, and I have seen you many times . . . through Nekure's eyes, of course."

"Uh . . ."

He held his hands up in a placating gesture. "I mean you no harm, I swear it."

"And Nik . . . ?"

He shrugged. "I do not know his inner thoughts, only those he chooses to share with me."

I swallowed. *How reassuring . . .*

"We do not have much time."

"What are you—"

"Alexandra will be returning in a matter of minutes."

"How do you—"

"A long time ago, she informed Nekure and myself of several occurrences that would herald her return to this time. Someone discovering the truth about me was the final sign, though she seemed to find great amusement in not telling us *who* that someone would be. I am certain that finding out that it's you will both disturb and intrigue Nekure greatly." He waved his hand dismissively. "But that is of no matter right now. Alexandra will arrive momentarily."

"So why are we—"

"You have a very important task," he said, interrupting me *again*. It was getting annoying. "One that the fate of the universe depends on."

I felt the color drain from my face. I was pretty sure I didn't have whatever it took to be one of those universe-depends-on-you kind of people; that was more Lex and Marcus's shtick, not mine. "Wha—what do I have to do?"

Re-Nik smiled blissfully. "You must find Heru, alert him of Alexandra's arrival, then hunt down Carson and—"

"Carson?" I frowned and tilted my head to the side. "Why?" I *may* have felt a teensy bit of pleasure in interrupting *him* that time.

Re-Nik's cheek twitched. "Because he is important as well. Together, the two of you will trigger a series of events that must be. Now, you must—"

"Does he know about you, too?" I couldn't hold in *all* of my grin at getting the chance to interrupt him again. "Is that why Nik sort of hates him?"

Re-Nik strode toward the door of At and touched his hand to its surface. It evaporated almost immediately. "There's no time to explain." He stepped to the side of the doorway. "Go now, Katarina."

Eyes wide and heart beating too quickly—*Lex is returning!*—I pushed off the wall and ran past Re-Nik toward the doorway. I wasn't sure if it was my imagination, but I may or may not have heard him murmur something that sounded an awful lot like, "I am sorry."

44

LEX

"There," I said as I pulled my fingertips from Heru's forehead. "It is done." I smirked, just a little. "And I promise to let you shatter the bonding block as soon as possible when I return to my time. I know how much you enjoy doing that . . ."

Heru didn't return my teasing smirk, and no mischief sparkled in his eyes. There, only sadness shone, pure and bright. He cupped either side of my jaw, tilting my face upward, and gazed into my eyes, searching, asking . . . pleading. "Alexandra . . . little queen . . ." His voice was soft, his touch tender. "You do not need to do this. The bonding block, that was necessary, but my memories of you . . . I *need* them. The thought of not knowing . . ."

We were surrounded by an ocean of sand, about a mile from the Oasis, which was now covered in an At dome and a mound of limestone rubble. The rest of our people awaited us just out of sight . . . or rather, they awaited *him*. I would not be returning with him. I would not be traveling back across the Red Land to Men-nefer with Heru and the rest of his family, would not watch his children grow up, would not be a part of his life for thousands of years.

I smiled the saddest smile. "But you do not *need* your memories of me, not yet. And you will not miss them, because you will not *know* of them."

"But I *want* to keep them," he said somberly.

My smile turned bitter. "There is a great difference between want and need," I said, echoing something he'd told me thousands of years in the future in Seattle, just before walking me home for the first time.

Heru's eyes were filled with a plea, but he didn't ask again.

Standing on tiptoes, I brushed my lips across his and whispered, "I love you, my Heru, so very, *very* much, and before you know it, I will be standing in front of you, unsealing your memories of my time here," right before I reached into his mind and locked every single memory of me—of all that had happened since my arrival—behind an impenetrable wall, replacing them with his own version of the same, vague recollections I'd given to everyone else. Everyone except Aset, Nekure, and the three Hat-hur priestesses, of course.

Heru pulled away and eyed me quizzically. "Apologies . . ." He shook his head, a tiny, confused smile tugging one corner of his mouth. "I do not know . . ." He cocked his head to the side. "Do I know you?"

"No," I said, taking a step back. The single word was thick with emotion, so I cleared my throat. "But one day, you will know me." My eyes stung with unshed tears as I pointed to a nearby sand dune. "Your family—Sesha and your children—await you just beyond the crest. You should rejoin them."

"My—my family . . ." Heru's eyes searched mine, and his face fell. "Bunefer . . . Tarset—they are *gone*."

I had to fight the urge to reach out to him, to comfort him. He no longer knew me, and doing so would only upset and confuse him further. "I am very sorry for your loss, Heru. I truly am." Swallowing roughly, I gestured toward the dune. "Your family needs you now. You should go to them."

"Yes . . ." Brow furrowed, he studied me for a moment longer, then turned and ascended the dune. At the top, he looked over his shoulder, meeting my eyes one last time, and then he was gone. I felt like my heart had been ripped out of my chest, just as Apep had threatened to do weeks ago.

I closed my eyes, allowing a single tear to escape, then took a deep breath and shifted back to just outside the broken Oasis, where Aset, Nekure, and the priestesses were waiting for me. I reentered the physical plane in a poof of misty colors directly in front of the mouth of a *new* tunnel, the only way through the rubble and into the covered city.

Aset and Nekure were standing off to the side, speaking quietly to the priestesses. From the snippets I caught as I approached, I surmised that they were solidifying *their* story of what happened over the past month, making sure everything was in sync so there wouldn't be any inconsistencies to raise eyebrows.

I reached into the folds of my desert robe as I approached them, pausing to scratch Rus's head before pulling a small, rolled up sheet of papyrus from the tiny drawstring purse tied to my belt. I handed it to Aset and met her eyes. "You must give this to me after you find me in Cairo. You will know when I need you by watching Set." I glanced at Nekure. "You are certain you can break through Set's cloak in my time . . . even when the At has been made unstable by the Nothingness?"

Smirking, Nekure nodded. "I have always been stronger than Set."

I frowned, worrying my bottom lip. "And you are absolutely certain that he does not know of *your* sheut? That Apep won't be able to glean that from his mind?" I'd blocked both Set's and Apep's memories of *me*, just as I'd done to everyone else, but I hadn't thought to search for anything relating to Nekure's unusual parentage.

Again, Nekure nodded. "He believes me to be Heru's first son . . . the product of a pre-manifestation affair with a woman from the cold lands while Heru and my mother were traveling in the north . . ."

I nodded once. "Good. It must remain that way." I turned my attention back to Aset. "I do not know how long it will take for Apep to take control of Set's body, so you must be wary of him. I believe Set will remain *Set* for quite some time, but when you see the darkness in his eyes, you will know that Apep is in control. And you must remember always that even when Apep is *not* in control, he can see and hear everything Set sees and hears."

"We understand," Aset said.

"Good." Again, I gave a single nod. "In the far future, when Apep leaves Set to possess Heru, then you must come to the location written here." I handed her a second piece of rolled-up papyrus. "It will not make sense to you yet, but in time . . . there is also a second place and time on there. It is when and where we will first meet in my native timeline. Before then, you must gain a position as a healer at the establishment I wrote down, and you must be there on the night listed."

Aset nodded. "I understand."

"And Aset . . ." I reached for her hand and took a deep breath. "I am going to ask you something, and I need you to answer honestly."

Her eyes widened the smallest amount.

"It was not Nuin who rescued you from Nekure's father, was it?"

The tiniest smile curved her lips. "It was not."

I released her hand. "Because it was me."

"Yes, dear friend." Her smile widened. "It was you."

And surprising me, she produced her own rolled sheet of

papyrus, no bigger than a cigar. "Directly before you return to your time, you must read this."

My eyebrows rose. "What is it?" I asked as I started to break the gold seal.

Aset placed her hand over the papyrus roll, stopping me. "Not yet—you must read this only when you are about to leave." She flashed her trademark warm smile. "Trust me." Only when I nodded did she pull her hand away.

"Okay . . ." I turned to Nekure. "Is Nuin—" I shook my head. "Is *Re* still out of commission?" Because I *really* would've preferred to speak to him before I left, but I supposed it didn't make much difference whether I spoke to him before leaving this time or right after returning to my own.

"So it seems," Nekure said. "I can feel him, but he has yet to attempt to communicate with me . . ." He shook his head. "I do not know how long it will take. Apologies, Lex."

I touched his arm and offered him a smile. "It is no fault of yours. What you did for him was very honorable." *And a great sacrifice,* I didn't say. Taking a step closer to him, I wrapped my arms around his trim torso in a tight hug, then did the same with Aset. "I will miss you both."

"Not as much as we will miss you, I think." Aset squeezed me back. "But we will meet again, this we know."

After we finished our goodbyes, I watched Aset, Nekure, and the priestesses walk into the desert, following the path Heru and the rest of the Nejerets and their families had taken only a few hours earlier. Aset was speaking animatedly to Denai, giving her instructions on what her new, secret Hat-hur cult must to do prepare for the events that would happen in thousands of years, leading to me coming here.

Only once they were out of sight did I retreat into the tunnel that led through the limestone rubble covering the dome. I sealed off the entrance with a door of At that could only be triggered by the combination of both Heru's and my bonding pheromones, then made my way down the tunnel and headed toward Heru's palace to say goodbye to Tarset.

The Oasis—more like a cavern now—felt like an eerie, desolate husk absent of the life it had teemed with only hours ago. But one day, in the distant future, I thought we might be able to resurrect Nuin's glorious city. It would be a fitting tribute to the long life Re had spent on earth as Nuin, the Great Father and creator of my people.

I moved through the empty rooms of Heru's palace like a ghost, touching nothing, feeling empty. When I entered the children's room in the back of the palace, Tarset still looked like a sculpture of a sleeping child lying on her bed.

Pulling a sleepy Rus out from his sling under my desert robes, I placed him on the bed beside the little girl. He stretched, yawned, and turned in a circle before curling up against her arm. I couldn't bring him with me—traveling through time would, quite literally, tear him apart—but I could offer him his own form of time travel, just as I'd done to give Tarset a fighting chance.

"See you soon, little guy," I said as I scratched the top of his head.

He blinked lazily, then rested his chin on his front paws and closed his eyes. A moment later, he was as still and solid—as *eternal*—as Tarset.

I smiled, finding comfort in knowing that Heru's youngest daughter wouldn't be alone during the long millennia. Glancing around, I imagined how the room might look in four thousand years, and all I could picture was inches and inches of dust and cobwebs . . . and I couldn't allow that—not on Tarset and Rus's stone-like bodies.

Leaning over the little girl, I pressed my lips to her forehead and whispered, "Sleep well, little fig." I cleared my throat roughly, tears welling in my eyes. "I'll see *you* soon, too." As I pulled away, I transformed the bed into solidified At so it wouldn't collapse over the millennia and spread a thin layer of At over it. No dust, no spider, or anything else would touch her or Rus while they lay there, frozen in time.

After leaving Heru's palace, I sealed myself in my underground sanctuary, spending a few hours adding one final room that described the events that had taken place the previous afternoon, sealing off the door to the scandalous domed chamber—I would let Marcus read those words once I'd returned—and creating a life-size statue of myself as one final gift to Marcus.

When I was finished, I stopped by the altar in the burial chamber—as it truly *was* a burial chamber now—and spent a few minutes fussing with Nuin's linen wrappings, making sure they were just so, before I formed a clear sheet of At over him as well. He was too wondrous to hide from the world, but too special to allow anyone to have free access to his body. And somehow, perhaps it was another of the strange snippets of information I was able to glean from the sheut now that it was whole within me, I *knew* that his body would remain as it was for all eternity. Time would not—*could* not—touch one such as him.

"I will see you again," I murmured, my hand pressed against the At just over his heart.

And then, turning away, I pulled my desert robe over my head, leaving the linen in a heap in the corner of the room, knowing it would be long gone by the time Marcus found this place, and removed Aset's note from my small purse. I broke the seal and started to read the precise hieroglyphs.

I fear you will be angry with me when you read this, but it is what must be.

That is all that matters. Know that because of what you are about to do, wherever you go, whenever you are, so long as Nekure and I are still alive, we will be there to help you along the way.

Before you return to your time, you must go back even further to rescue me and return me to my brother. And before you leave that time, you must give me this message to pass on to Nuin, as he will be in another time while you are there:

Great Father, my name is Alexandra Larson, the Meswett you seek. My mother is Alice, daughter of the Netjer-At Alexander and granddaughter of the Netjer-At Ivan, and my fathers are the Netjer-At Set and the Nejter Apep. I am Hat-Hur, your wife, and bond-mate to Heru. Find me, old friend, protect me, and ma'at will be restored to the universe, for this is what has always been and will always be.

I am not positive on the exact wording, but all of that must be said. Nuin receiving this message is the moment that sets the course for the next six thousand years, so make sure you do not err.

Good luck, my dear friend. I shall see you again soon.

I stared at Aset's words and shook my head slowly. She was wrong—I wasn't angry with her; I was stunned. Thinking about making my first, purposeful jump through time was intimidating enough, but now I had to do it *twice*, and I didn't even know *when* or *where* I was supposed to go.

My hands started to shake, making the papyrus rattle softly, and I knew myself well enough to know that if I didn't try *right now*, I'd lose my nerve and never try at all. And then this room would become *my* tomb as well as Nuin's.

"Get it together, Lex." I rolled up the papyrus and returned it to my little drawstring purse. "You can do this." I thought of Tarset, and of Marcus and my mom and dad and Set and Jenny and her unborn baby and all of the other people in my time who were depending on me. And then I thought of Aset, and what she was going through right now—in some distant, past time—and as my resolve solidified, my hands stopped shaking.

Holding my head high, I kept my focus locked on Aset, on saving her, and walked straight into the nearest wall . . . and out of time completely.

I re-entered time stumbling and gasping. Before I even had a chance to orient myself to the sudden silvery light or the rushing, roaring sound all around me, I ran into to a warm, hard, and oh-so-familiar-smelling body crouching directly in front of me.

"Shit!" I hissed as I tripped, skittered backward, and landed on my butt on soft, *wet* sand. The back of my head connected with a small rock with a sickening crack, and stars filled my vision, joining the brilliant night sky that blazed overhead.

Something cool and sharp was suddenly pressed against the front of my neck, and Heru's face appeared about a foot above mine. At least, I was pretty sure it was Heru. His spicy scent was exactly like Heru's, and his face resembled Heru's *almost* exactly, but not quite. He looked younger, softer . . . *more human,* I realized.

And then it dawned on me. Because *he was* more human; he had to be, if I'd really made it back to the time of Aset's attack and abduction. When Aset had been taken, she'd yet to manifest, which meant the same was true for her twin, Heru.

"Who are you, and what are you doing here?" he whispered in the original tongue, the low sound harsh. He shot a quick glance around. "And where did you come from?"

I rubbed the back of my head and slowly sat up, pushing against his dagger blade with my neck. He let up just enough to allow me to sit fully, and took a position squatting in front of me. When I pulled my fingers away from my throbbing skull, they were sticky with warm blood.

"Being assaulted by *you*, apparently," I muttered, only answering his second question, and even then only answering partially. Using a move he'd taught me, I took hold of his wrist and twisted sharply, forcing him to drop the weapon and knowing full well that, were he any older or more experienced, it wouldn't have worked. "And you do not need that, Heru." I released his wrist. "I am here to rescue your sister."

Heru moved away from me quickly, retrieving his dagger before standing. He eyed me warily.

Sighing, I touched the back of my head again and swept my gaze over the moonlit landscape. Ocean waves beat against sand a short ways to my right, the water as dark as midnight, and to my left, gentle slopes of pale sand spread out as far as I could see. The waves, at least, explained the rushing, roaring sound I'd heard. As far as I could tell, we were somewhere on the northern African coast, with the Mediterranean Sea to one side and the Sahara to the other.

Narrowing my eyes, I returned Heru's measuring stare. "What are *you* doing here?" At least the ache in the back of my skull was already receding.

He straightened. "Rescuing my sister."

"Hmmm . . ." I hadn't expected to find him there, despite it making sense that he would go after his sister. Recalling something Aset had told me when recounting her tale, I scanned Heru's body, not that I could see much under the ankle-length, black linen robe he was wearing. "You are injured. Where? Are you alright?"

Heru's eyes widened, and his free hand moved to touch the lower left side of his ribcage. "I am fine. How did you—" He shook his head. "How do you know who I am? How do you know about my sister?"

I exhaled heavily and pushed up to my feet. Brushing off my

backside, I met his eyes. "It is a long story . . . and one that we do not have time for now." I glanced out at the inky sea, then back at the endless desert. "Do you know where Aset has been taken?"

He nodded, his eyes flicking to some point behind me.

I shot a quick glance over my shoulder. A rocky outcropping jutted up toward the night sky several miles away.

"There is a cave. I believe he has her there."

I rubbed my hands together and stretched my neck from side to side, mentally preparing for whatever disturbing scene I might find inside this cave. "Is it just the two of them, do you know? Or are there others?"

Heru shook his head. "I took care of the others back at the Oasis—when he first took her."

"I see." Not willing to wait any longer, I said, "Wait here. I shall return with your sister shortly."

"What?" Heru started toward me. "But should I not—"

Before he could finish, the misty, swirling colors of the At surrounded me, and I jumped from the peaceful, moonlit beach to a cavern that could have been inhabited by the devil himself.

A single campfire lit pale, jagged walls with writhing streaks of orange and yellow, making the stone appear almost on fire itself. A sharp shriek cut through the crackle of burning wood, closely followed by a low, menacing laugh. On the cavern floor on the other side of the fire, a small, nude woman huddled, curled in on herself, and a larger, masculine figure loomed over her, his back to me.

"Please," Aset gasped. "No more." She hugged her knees to her bare chest in what was clearly a desperate attempt to protect herself.

Rage boiled my blood, and my hands curled into fists. "Your depths of depravity never cease to amaze me," I said through gritted teeth.

Aset's captor spun around, pulling an obsidian dagger from

his woven leather belt and licking his lips. Hunger gleamed in his dark eyes. "Who are you?" he hissed, taking a step toward me.

I sneered. Even possessing a Nejeret, he stood about as much chance against me—against Re's sheut—as an ant. "You are pathetic, Apep."

He stumbled, then stopped, his mouth hanging open and his eyes shining with outrage.

Laughing, I raised my hand, and just as I'd done to Ankhesenpepi, called forth vines of At. They burst up from the cavern floor and snaked around Apep's legs, restraining him. "You disgust me. If I could erase you from existence . . ." But I couldn't. And as awful as it was to admit, even if I could, I *wouldn't*.

His lips retracted, and he snarled.

I ignored his little outburst. "But you are needed in the future"—I crossed my arms over my chest—"so all I can do is take young Aset away from you and erase all of your memories of her and what you have done to her . . . and all memory of me, of course." I scanned him from head to toe, recalling something else Aset had included in her tale. "And your host body's memories as well, since he invited you to possess him in the first place." I smiled, feeling the spirit of vengeance fill me, keeping me calm, helping me focus. "And I think I shall leave you trapped in that body for a little while longer."

I willed the At vines to climb higher, capturing his arms and trapping them against his body, before stepping closer. Raising my hand, I touched my fingertips to Apep's forehead, preparing to erase both Apep and his host's memories. "It is a fitting punishment that your freedom will mean his death, but it is not enough. I think I shall add some memories of intense pain as well, though I fear that, too, will not be enough. Nothing will change what must come."

Apep started to writhe in his At bindings as I did as I'd

promised, and even through the chill that had slowly been seeping into my soul, I found pleasure in his tormented grunts and cries. Which probably should have bothered me. But in the thrall of the chill—the *oneness*—it didn't.

"Please do not hurt me," Aset whimpered, her voice small and shrill.

I shifted my focus to her, and the oneness shattered. Moving toward her slowly, I held out my hands and spoke to her, keeping my voice low, my tone calm. "I will not hurt you, Aset." I crouched in front of her, but made no move to touch her. "Your brother is waiting for you outside, just a short ways up the beach. I will take you to him, it—"

"Heru? You saw Heru?" She raised her head, meeting my eyes for the first time. Her own widened. "Oh my—your eyes are like the Great Father's."

I offered her a small smile and nodded. "Yes, they are. And I came here to rescue you because he was away and could not do it himself." I glanced over my shoulder at the shuddering form of Apep's host body. "He will not bother you again, I swear it."

Her eyes lingered on the forbidding man, still held upright by the At vines restraining him, then settled back on me. She blinked several times, tears welling in her eyes and her chin trembling, and when I reached out a hand to give her shoulder a gentle squeeze, she threw herself at me. Shuddering and sobbing, she clung to me like I was the only thing keeping her alive.

I held her tightly and rubbed her back in slow circles. She was so small, so fragile, it seemed, and it amazed me to think of the strong, graceful woman she would become.

Eventually, she quieted, and I helped her to her feet. "Do you have any clothing?"

She shook her head, her eyes flicking to the fire. "He burned my dress."

I sighed, my own eyes landing on a rough woven blanket.

Retrieving it quickly, I wrapped it around her shoulders along with my arm and guided her toward the narrow, uneven mouth of the cave. Neither of us glanced back at her abductor.

"How did you know to come?" she asked once we were out of the stifling cave and under the stars.

I laughed softly. "Now *that* is quite a story."

"I think I would very much like to hear a story right now," Aset softly. "I would like to think about anything else but what *he* did to me."

I squeezed her shoulders, my heart bleeding for her. "Very well. In about a thousand years . . ."

"*MUST* YOU GO?" ASET ASKED AS WE NEARED THE PLACE where I'd left her brother. The sand was soft and cool under our bare feet, and she'd seemed both awed and soothed by my fantastical tale of what was to come.

I nodded. "I must."

I could just make out the outline of Heru, maybe a half mile away, though I knew he wouldn't be able to see us yet, and I wanted to leave before I had a chance to complicate our relationship any further than it already was.

Stopping, I turned to face Aset and captured both of her hands. "You cannot tell Heru or any others what I have told you." I gave her hands a squeeze. "You must promise me."

She blinked in surprise, but nodded. Frowning, she said, "What about the Great Father? Surely he must already know of you and what is to come . . ."

I bit my lip, my eyebrows drawing together. "I do not think so." Talking a deep breath, I pulled the piece of papyrus Aset had given me a millennium in the future out of my satchel and unrolled it. "You must tell him this, and only this," I said, and then I relayed her own future words to her, paraphrasing only a little. "My name is Alexandra Larson, and I am the Meswett you seek. My mother is Alice, daughter of the Netjer-At Alexander and granddaughter of the Netjer-At Ivan, and my fathers are the Netjer-At Set *and* the Netjer Apep. I am Hat-hur, your wife"—I watched Aset's eyes widen—"and bond-mate to Heru."

Her mouth fell open.

I smiled, just a little. "Find me, old friend, protect me, and ma'at will be restored, for this is what has always been and will always be." I paused, studying her pretty, stunned face. "Do you need me to repeat it?"

She quirked her mouth to the side, clearly unsure.

"You will not be able to find this moment in the At to rehear it, even after you've manifested, so . . ."

Abruptly, she nodded. "Then yes, repeat it once more, and I shall remember."

I did as she requested, then once again took hold of her hands. "There is one more thing you must know—you will be with child from what that Netjer-At did to you."

She didn't look surprised, much to *my* surprise. "That was what he wanted."

"Ah . . ." I understood. "You must tell Nuin that I said that the child is not to be harmed, that he must be allowed to live—though under the guise of being Heru's firstborn rather than yours. Can you do that?"

Wide-eyed, she nodded.

"Good." I gave her hands a squeeze before releasing them. "In many years, there will be a pharaoh name Pepi Neferkare. On the day of his funeral procession, I will jump through time to arrive at a temple run by priestesses of the cult of Hat-hur in Men-nefer."

"Hat-hur . . ." Aset stared at me quizzically and shook her head. "This is *you*, correct?"

I nodded, if a bit hesitantly, though I wasn't sure why. After all, I *had* just told her to tell Nuin that *I* was Hat-hur. "But I prefer 'Lex.'"

"There is no temple cult devoted to you yet . . ."

I shivered, feeling like someone had just walked over my grave. "Then you must ensure that one exists by the time I arrive."

Aset nodded slowly. "Yes, I believe I can do this."

"And remember, when I arrive, I will not know you—not really."

"Because all that you have told me has not happened yet—for that younger version of you," Aset said, accepting it all a whole lot better and more quickly than I had.

"Aset!" Heru called.

Peering over Aset's shoulder, I could see Heru running along the beach toward us. I met Aset's eyes. "I must go before he sees enough of me that I must erase his memory."

"Very well." Unexpectedly, Aset leaned in and wrapped her arms around me. "Thank you . . . thank you so much." Her body shook as she spoke. "You cannot know how much I appreciate what you have done. My life is yours."

"But do not forget, Aset," I whispered, "it is also *yours*." Pulling back, I smiled down at her.

"Aset!" Heru was only several dozen paces away.

"Farewell," I said right before hurtling myself into the At, body, ba, and all, thinking only of the Oasis and of my own time.

Dizzily, I staggered out of the At and into Nuin's crystalline sarcophagus.

He looked just as I'd left him what felt like such a short time ago, his features glowing in a soft incandescence in a semblance of peace . . . of sleep. For a moment, as I stared at his familiar, unusually relaxed features, I thought it hadn't worked and I'd returned to the Oasis at the end of the 6th Dynasty instead of my own, native time.

"Welcome home, Lex."

I spun around, making my time-travel vertigo even worse. A trim man dressed all in black, with black hair, multiple facial piercings, and an amalgam of tattoos in various shades of gray covering his exposed arms, stood in the doorway to the right of Nuin's altar.

"Nekure," I breathed . . . right before my knees gave way, and I lost consciousness.

45

REUNITE & UNITE

Opening my eyes, I found Nekure's handsome face hovering over mine. His eyes were the palest blue, shining with a mixture of concern and excitement.

"Hey," I whispered. "Marcus?"

"On his way."

I raised my hand, touching my fingertips to his pierced eyebrow. "I like you better without all this, you know."

He grinned and briefly raised his eyebrows. "It's camouflage."

Blinking, I slid my gaze down to his tattooed forearm. "How long do they last?"

He glanced down at his arm and shrugged. "A couple years at most."

I narrowed my eyes and focused on a sliver of abdomen visible between the bottom hem of his t-shirt and the top of his black jeans, where his shirt had hiked up a bit. It was dark with ink. I raised *my* eyebrows. "And I suppose you're going to tell me *those* are for camouflage, too?"

"Not exactly." His grin became lopsided. "Come on, Lex . . .

my mom gives me enough grief about this shit. I don't think I could handle it from you, too."

I laughed, and then I groaned. "God . . . I feel like crap."

"Yeah, Re says that's normal after your first back-to-back, unaided time jumps, especially two huge-ass ones."

With another groan, I propped myself up on my elbows, and Nekure helped me the rest of the way up, settling my back against the wall. "Somehow, I doubt that he said 'huge-ass' . . ."

Chuckling, he lifted one shoulder in a quick shrug. "He also says your access to the sheut might be weak for a bit . . . which *could* be a problem, because now that it's 'complete' within you, Apep'll be able to sense it." He paused, then added, "He'll be *drawn* to it."

Squeezing my eyes shut, I took a deep breath, then squinted at Nekure. "Which means he'll be on his way, right?"

Nekure nodded.

"Can I talk to Re?"

"Yeah." He flashed me another grin, this one holding nothing but mischief. "He's been waiting for me to hand over control anyway . . . impatient fucker . . ."

"Nekure!" I said with a laugh.

Chuckling again, he leaned in and pressed a gentle kiss against my forehead. "Welcome back, Lex . . . you're in for one hell of a ride."

As he pulled away, he closed his eyes. When they opened again, they were no longer pale blue, but filled with the glimmering iridescence of opals. He smiled again, but it was entirely different from Nekure's. I knew this smile, those eyes. They belonged to Nuin—to *Re*. "Hello again, dear Alexandra," he murmured.

My chin trembled, and I swallowed, my saliva suddenly feeling too thick, my esophagus too narrow. "I wasn't sure . . . I mean, I *saw* you go into him . . ." I shook my head. "But I wasn't sure."

"Ah . . . but I would not abandon you." Re-Nekure leaned in, but instead of pressing his lips against my forehead, he brushed them across my own lips in a purely platonic kiss. His lip ring felt hard and cool compared to the soft, warm flesh.

Closing my eyes, I smiled. He was really there, inside Nekure . . . *not* dead.

"Get away from—" Dominic started to say, but his words cut short as Re-Nekure pulled away from me.

Because Re-Nekure had stretched out his arm and was holding an At blade to Dominic's neck. "Careful, *boy* . . ."

Dominic's eyes widened, but not from the razor-sharp blade nearly slicing into his flesh. He was staring at me. "Lex . . . your eyes . . ."

I looked away, feeling embarrassed for some reason I didn't understand. "Stop it," I said to Re-Nekure, reaching out to unmake the blade. But despite my best effort, the knife refused to disappear. My eyes sought out Re-Nekure's. "Why isn't it working?"

He glanced at me. "Just give it a moment to recharge."

"How long of a moment?"

"An hour, maybe two," he said. The knife evaporated into rainbow mist.

As soon as he was no longer in danger of having his neck sliced open, Dominic elbowed Re-Nekure in the side of the face. Because of his near-constant façade of courtesy and kindness, it was easy to forget that Dominic had been a highly trained, highly skilled assassin several hundred years ago and was easily one of the deadliest people alive. Pulling a knife on him was a pretty dumb move for pretty much anyone to make. But then, considering that Re-Nekure was probably one of the few people who were *even more* deadly than Dominic . . .

They were suddenly grappling on the floor, and all I could do was gape.

"Stop this at once!" Aset shouted from the top of the stairway leading down to the burial chamber. *"Now!"*

Re-Nekure and Dominic froze.

"I swear," Aset said as she started down the stairs with a huff. "*Men* . . . they're all boys, no matter their age." She shook her head and shifted her gaze to me, her honey-colored eyes warming as she smiled. "Lex."

"Aset." I clambered to my feet, using the wall because I was still a little unsteady, and threw my arms around her. "Thank you so much. You did everything perfectly. I don't know how you managed, but you did . . ." I let out a relieved laugh. "Thank you."

She placed her hands on my shoulders and, pulling back, looked up into my eyes. "I only did what I must . . ." She grinned. "But you are welcome, of course." And then she blinked several times, turned her face to the stairs, and let go of me completely.

I followed her line of sight.

Marcus.

He stood on one of the middle stairs, frozen as he stared down at me. I could see the lump that had to be the At bottle of bonding pheromones under his linen, button-down shirt. He took the remaining stairs in two strides, and in another, his arms were around me and his face was buried against my neck. And he was shaking.

His reaction paralyzed me, and I did the only thing I seemed able to do; I focused what little of the sheut I could control on the memories locked away in his mind. And released them.

Marcus stiffened, then slowly raised his head. He gazed down at me with round, wondrous eyes of molten gold and liquid onyx. Slowly, his lips spread into a broad smile. A chuckle started deep in his chest, quickly blossoming into a laugh. And then my back was against the wall and he was kissing me, pressing his whole body against mine, and I didn't care one bit that three of my closest friends were standing nearby.

Marcus's hands trailed down sides of my body before gliding behind my back, pulling me closer to him, and he did something I'd only experienced as a culmination of a sexual union between us—he slipped a tendril of his ba inside me, seeking my own, *caressing* my own. My nails dug into his lower back, pulling his hips as tight against mine as possible, and I moaned into his mouth. Pleasure rolled over me in waves.

When he broke the kiss, I took several gasping breaths and leaned my head back against the wall. I stared up into his eyes and laughed breathily. "Well . . . I think it's safe to say that you've stepped up your kissing game by *light-years*."

He leaned his forehead against mine. "And that was just the smallest amount of my ba." He grinned. "I wonder what will happen when I fill you with it completely . . ."

My entire body *and* my ba pulsed in anticipation. "I can't wait to find out . . ."

Someone cleared a throat behind Marcus.

I turned crimson. I'd forgotten about the others. Standing in the altar room. Watching us.

"Lex, I believe there are some people who would very much like to see you," Dominic said, his accent thick.

"Huh?" I forced myself to take a step away from Marcus—a *super* small one—and to face Dominic. "Who?"

His eyes scanned my face, then slid down the length of my body before focusing on Nuin's sarcophagus. His pale cheeks flushed, and he cleared his throat. "They are with Alexander and Jenny in the main palace . . . but I think you may wish to change into something a little more, uh, *substantial* before seeing them . . ."

I glanced down at my simple, belted white linen shift. "What's wrong with this?"

"Nothing," Aset said with a snort. "It is the people of this time who are the problem—they are such *prudes*." She stepped around the altar and handed me a canvas tote bag. "Clothes . . . I've had a long time to prepare for your return." She shrugged and made shooing motion. "Go. Change. We'll be out here."

Hugging the bag, I wandered down one of the hallways I'd made thousands of years ago and entered the last room I'd created. Marcus followed.

"I hope you're not intending to have your way with me," I said lightly as I pulled clothing items out of the bag—there was a pair of khaki shorts, a white tank top, a thin, ivory linen button-down shirt, a pair of tan, lace-up work boots and socks, and of course, undergarments. I stared at the bra and underwear like they were utterly foreign to me, once again assessed my current attire, and finally understood Dominic's words . . . and his blushes. The linen wasn't see-through, but it didn't come close to hiding everything, either.

Marcus's arms wrapped around me from behind, and he pressed himself against my backside. "And here I thought you would be hoping for quite the opposite . . ." His hand cupped my breast, his thumb doing very pleasant things.

"Stop that," I said, laughing as I twisted around in his hold. I peered up at him, studying the lines and angles of his face—lines and angles I knew better than my own. "I'm not about to meet a bunch of Nejerets smelling like sex."

Marcus brushed his knuckles down the side of my cheek. "And if I tell you that you always smell like sex to me—like sex and love and everything that's good in the world—does that change your mind?"

My cheeks, neck, and chest heated, again.

Marcus's easy expression melted, and worry filled his eyes.

My stomach dropped. "What?" I searched those golden depths for some hint of what he was about to reveal. "What is it?"

"The people Dom was referring to aren't Nejerets."

I raised my eyebrows. "There are *humans* here? I mean, besides J and Gen?"

Marcus said nothing for a moment, then nodded. "Susan Ivanov . . ."

My mouth fell open. "My *grandma's* here?"

He nodded again. "As are your parents."

46

WANT & NEED

Crossing my arms, I narrowed my eyes at Marcus. "Do they *know*?"

He nodded, and the blood drained from my face. My parents knew about me . . . about what I really was. They *knew* that I wasn't human. I fought the urge to panic, which wasn't easy because it was a really damn persistent urge.

"You brought them here," I said quietly.

Again, Marcus nodded.

I took a deep breath and closed my eyes for a long moment. *I will* not *panic . . . and I will* not *freak out. I will* not *. . .*

I clenched my jaw. "I can't believe you told them."

Marcus released me, letting me step back and start to change my clothes. "It was impossible not to once they were here." Not an explanation, just a statement. I took another deep breath.

I unclasped my belt and set it carefully on the floor. *Another* deep breath. "And you brought them here *because . . .* ?"

"I decided that them alive and fully aware of what you are would be a preferable situation for you to return to than Apep having slain them using your father's hands," he said matter-of-factly.

I glanced at him, unsurprised to find a hard, challenging glint in his eyes. I looked away as I tugged my dress over my head. I could practically feel Marcus's eyes raking over my bare skin.

"Thank you," I said, meeting his eyes for the briefest moment and letting him see that I meant it. "I don't know what I would've done . . ." I swallowed back unnecessary sorrow for what could have been and forced myself to meet his burning eyes, to hold that gaze. "Thank you, Marcus. Really."

His jaw clenched, and his nostrils flared. "Make a door, Little Ivanov," he said, his voice rougher than usual. He took a step toward me and started unbuckling his belt.

I took a step backward, my heartbeat already speeding up from what he intended. "But . . . my family—"

His eyes narrowed, and he took another step, unfastening the top button of his trousers. "Make a door."

I took another step backward, and my back touched the cool wall. I was breathing faster now. "But . . . but Apep—"

"Make." Step. "A." Step. "Door." He was right in front of me, only inches away. He raised one eyebrow.

I willed a door into being in the blink of an eye. "But—"

Marcus caressed me with his gaze. "You've been gone for a month, and the last time I saw you—" He squeezed his eyes shut for a brief moment. When he opened them, they burned with torment. "The last time I truly saw you, my hands were around your neck, holding you underwater, and you were about to die." His eyes searched mine. "I need to feel you . . . to know that you're really here . . . to know that you're still *mine*. I *need* you, Lex."

"But what if Apep tries to pos—"

"He cannot possess me when I am surrounded by At."

I blinked, then nodded, and not a second later, Marcus's pants were pushed down, and my legs were wrapped around his hips, and I was experiencing the full depth of his need for me . . . of *our* need for each other. It was as brief and as intense of a joining as we'd ever shared, and by the end, when my ba tangled with his, something snapped inside me. I—my ba—felt like whatever threads had been tying it to my body, whatever resistance remained, holding it back from merging with Marcus's completely, broke, and I was inside him; I was a *part* of him.

I could sense Apep's fractured sheut, threaded through Marcus's very soul. I could feel how incomplete it was, and could imagine—*knew*—how beautiful and wondrous it would be if it were whole again. And I could practically *see* the tether stretching between Marcus and Set, who was miles and miles away to the east. Suddenly, the way to return that sheut to its former glory was so obvious. So easy.

I tugged on the thin tether of sheut, a mere thread connecting the portion that was in Marcus to the portion Set's body contained. The latter resisted, and the tether groaned . . . stretched . . .

Whatever it had been anchored to on Set's end snapped, and in a rush, the remainder of Apep's sheut funneled into Marcus, combining with the splinters already embedded in his ba and swelling to a glowing, pulsating mass of power.

Gasping, I withdrew my ba from Marcus and stared into his stunned eyes—his *glowing* eyes, swirling with blues and greens and purples, just as mine did, only in every shade of red, orange, and yellow. Apep's sheut was whole, and it was *all* inside Marcus.

He was breathing hard, his features locked in a mask of shock. "Was that what I think it was?" he asked, his voice hoarse.

I nodded. "Apep's sheut . . . you have it all, now."

When my feet were once again planted on the floor and we were both working on catching our breath, Marcus's lips quirked, curving into a wicked little smile. "Then I guess the next few days will be quite busy as we do *everything* we can to restore ma'at . . ."

I pulled my head back a few inches and eyed him. "You mean, start trying to conceive?"

His little smile widened into an even more wicked grin. "I must admit that I am so looking forward to this arduous challenge . . ."

"Oh, yeah, um . . ." I swallowed roughly and looked away. It was the first time we'd actually spoken about the whole "kids" thing. Wiggling out of his hold, I headed for my modern clothes. "You know," I said, glancing back at him as he refastened his pants. He was watching me carefully. "I never told you about that—the 'we can have kids' thing—back then . . ."

"I do recall," he said. "It was an *interesting* piece of information to learn from your writings."

I pulled up my underwear. "Are you mad . . . I mean, that I didn't tell you back then?"

He hesitated, which terrified me, and then he frowned and shrugged. "I'm not mad. I don't quite understand your reasoning, but I'm not mad."

Watching his face for any hint of what he was feeling, I slipped my bra on, reaching behind me to fasten the clasp. As far as I could tell, he was being honest. "So, um . . . how do you feel about it?" I rolled my eyes at how lame the question had sounded, then snuck another peek at Marcus.

The corners of his mouth twitched and he raised his eyebrows. "How do I feel about the fact that us having children is *even possible* . . . that it's the only way to prevent eternal, divine powers from killing us . . . or that our children might become beings even greater than Nejerets and be the only way to restore balance to the universe?"

I looked down at my shorts as I zipped them up. "Um . . . the first one?"

"Honestly, Little Ivanov . . ." Marcus tugged me into his arms before I had a chance to pull the tank top on over my head. "I have never"—he kissed me—"*ever*"—kiss—"been happier." He finished with a toe-curling, breath-stealing, ba-caressing kiss that had me panting and jelly-muscled all over again.

"Well . . ." I stepped out of his hold and put on the tank top, smoothing it down unnecessarily. I sent a longing glance at my discarded shift; I was going to miss dressing so comfortably. "That's just . . . great." I cleared my throat and felt my cheeks flush as I met his eyes. "Are you planning on doing that *every* time we kiss from now on?"

A single eyebrow arched higher. "Are you getting tired of it already?"

"No, I just—" My cheeks burned hotter, and I slipped my arms into the sleeves of the thin, button-down shirt. "I would just appreciate it if you could, er, *restrain* yourself whenever other people are around. I mean, I really have no problem climaxing every five minutes, if that's your goal, but I'd rather not have it happen in front of, oh . . . I don't know, *my family* . . ."

Marcus laughed out loud, but sobered quickly. He pressed a hand to his heart. "I will try to show some restraint, but I must admit that I am quite fond of this idea of making you climax every five minutes." He grinned mischievously. "Perhaps I shall set an alarm . . ."

"I was *kidding*," I said with a laugh.

His eyes glinted with promise. "I wasn't."

I gulped.

"I believe there is one item lacking from your current attire . . ." Marcus reached behind his neck and worked the clasp of a thin silver chain that was hanging around his neck—*not*, I realized, the chain that held the bottle of bonding pheromones I'd made for him. He pulled a large pendant out from the neck of his shirt. It was an ancient lapis lazuli falcon, a symbol of the god Heru—of *him*—that he'd given me a week or so before I stepped back in time, when we were still in Florence.

I turned around for him to secure the delicate chain around

my neck and touched my fingers to the intensely blue pendant. "Thank you, Marcus."

He turned me back around and studied my face. "And what about you, Little Ivanov? How do you feel about the 'we can have kids' thing?" A tiny line appeared between his eyebrows. "I know you have said that having children is not something you had ever planned on doing, even before you learned you could not . . ."

I let out a nervous laugh. "Honestly? I'm scared shitless. I mean, they're going to be gods, like real, honest-to-God *gods*. That's insane. And horrible. And wonderful. And terrifying. And . . ." I shook my head.

Marcus smiled, and I thought it might have been to hide a frown. So I kissed him, deeply, and when I broke the kiss, I added, "But I'm also kind of ecstatic." And I meant it.

47

BEGINNING & END

The entire time that Marcus and I were walking toward Nuin's palace, Dominic, Nekure, and Aset behind us and the harsh glow of artificial light all around us, my mind was occupied by two things—worrying about my impending reunion with my very *human* family, and noticing how things under the At dome had changed and how they'd stayed the same. But mostly I just worried.

And the moment I walked through the high, arched entryway into Nuin's palace and into a huge room at the front that had been transformed into some sort of a communal dining hall, with an eclectic mixture of mismatching At tables and chairs, my eyes honed in on my mom, and I nearly lost it. Like, full-on, five-year-old-girl-who-just-skinned-her-knee lost it. It had been just over seven months since I'd seen her, a month of which had been spent in a time during which she didn't even exist, and I missed her desperately.

She was sitting at a rectangular table with my dad, Jenny, Grandma Suse, and Alexander, and she hadn't noticed me yet. It took the room falling quiet for *me* to notice that there were even any other people in there, scattered among the various tables. A quick, cursory scan told me they were all Nejerets, and many were faces I recognized. They stared, and then they stood, and then they fell to their knees in supplication.

I really hated that part of being the Meswett.

Only those who were members of my guard remained on their feet, and they rushed toward us. Marcus, Nekure, Aset, Dominic, and I were surrounded by a wall of Nejerets of every size and skin and hair color within seconds. But I couldn't focus on any of them. Not while I could hear *her* voice.

"Lex?" my mom called. "Lex? Let me through!" she demanded.

"Let her pass," I said.

Vali and Sandra, the heads of my guard, parted, and my mom rushed into the ring of deadly Nejerets. The rest of my family followed her, but she was the one who practically attacked me. Her arms were around me in an instant, and I was suddenly crying, though I didn't know *why* I was crying other than that I was happy to be in my mom's arms. Maybe that was reason enough.

Minutes passed before she pulled away with a "Well now, let me get a look at you." She scanned my face quickly, her eyes widening to saucers when they met mine. "Your eyes, Lex . . . sweetie . . ." She shook her head slowly, and there was a hint of something—fear, or maybe disgust, I wasn't sure—on her face. "I didn't really believe until now, but you really have changed . . . you really are one of *them*, aren't you?"

Tears welled anew in my eyes. My mom had just referred to me as "one of *them*," as something not the same as her . . . as something *other*.

I swiped my fingers under my eyes angrily, refusing to shed tears for what I was, especially when I was only *that* because of genes *she'd* passed onto me. Being a Nejerette was nothing to be ashamed of; it was a great gift and a great curse, and it was what I was. I wouldn't have changed it if I could.

I stood taller. "Yeah, Mom, I'm one of them . . . but I'm also still *me*."

My mom's mouth opened. Shut. She arched her eyebrows. "Like I don't know who you are? Don't be ridiculous, Alexandra Marie Larson. I am your mother, and you couldn't even bother to call me when you first became engaged with *that man*"—she waved haphazardly at Marcus—"who we'd never met, I might add."

My shoulders sagged in relief, and I couldn't help but smile. Her reaction was so *her*.

She eyed Marcus. "I hope there's some actual affection here, and it's not just physical—"

"Mom!" I grabbed her arm. "Oh my God, seriously? If you had any idea, any clue of what we've been through together—"

"But I don't, do I?" she said, her sharp tone one that only an irritated mother could achieve. "And whose fault is that, hmmm . . . ?"

And now I felt guilty. I sighed. "Mom . . ."

She leveled an even stare on me. "You could've told me, Lex. You could've told me you were a . . . I don't know, a *vampire* or something insane like that, and I would've believed you—"

"You would *not* have!"

She rolled her eyes. "Okay, no, I wouldn't have believed you, but I *would* have listened . . . and I would've loved you anyway."

"You know now," Marcus said simply, earning both my mom's and my glances. "Is that not enough?"

I held my breath. Her response mattered more than I was willing to admit, even to myself.

"Of course it is," she said in a rush. "I just wish you'd told me you were going through all this . . . that you'd fallen in love, that's all."

I rubbed my hand over my face and, of all things, started laughing. "I'm in love," I said between laughs. Again, I glanced at Marcus, sending him a questioning look. "And *engaged*."

He shrugged. I made a note to ask him about everything that had happened with my family *and* about our apparent impending "wedding." Like we could ever be wedded together any more completely than we already were . . .

My mom moved aside so the rest of my family could greet me. It was hardly dignified, and filled with a chorus of sniffles and a rainstorm of tears and loads of murmured nonsense, but Grandma Suse's reaction to my eyes was my favorite.

"Well, would you get a look at those peepers . . ." She glanced back at Alexander, who was standing just behind her, reminding me so much of Heru with Bunefer—which only made me choke back less happy tears. "Alexandra Larson, I think there's an entire sun living in your head!"

I laughed. "That's the least of my problems, Grandma . . ."

But before Grandma Suse or anyone else had a chance to interrogate me, Neffe pushed through the ring of guards, making our inner circle that much more crowded.

"So it's true," she said, her caramel eyes meeting mine. She bowed her head gracefully. "I'm so glad you have returned . . . and that you knew how to save my father. For that, I can never thank you enough."

My eyebrows rose. "Neffe . . . seriously?"

She raised her eyes to mine and grinned, and I couldn't help but return her smile.

"You are so full of it."

Her eyes sparkled.

My grin faded as I remember why I'd been so eager to see her. "Tarset . . ." I glanced at Marcus. "Did you tell her about what I did to Tarsi . . . about the poison and me freezing her in time?"

He shook his head. "We'd yet to transcribe that from your writings, and without my memory . . ." He turned an irritated look on Aset and Nekure, who were still behind me. "Someone could've apprised me of the situation, or at least let me know that Tarset is *still alive*."

Aset tsked. "Don't be ridiculous. You had enough to deal with, dear brother, and Tarsi is fine as she is for now. Once things settle, we'll move her to the Cairo palace, Lex can unfreeze her, and Neffe and I will treat her."

She was right; at the moment, we didn't have time to take care of Tarset, who would be fine in her frozen state—or to unfreeze Rus either—because Apep-Set was on his way . . . drawn to me, and now likely to Marcus as well, because of the sheuts that were finally whole within us.

I turned to Marcus. "I need to speak to everyone. Can you get their attention?" I glanced around at the guards still encircling us. "And is this really necessary? Pretty much everyone here is sworn to me . . . I doubt any of them are going to *harm* me."

Looking over my head, Marcus nodded at someone. A quick glance over my shoulder told me it was Vali, the enormous, blond, image-of-an-ideal-Viking of a man. As the guards spread out behind me and around the high-ceilinged room, Marcus helped me step onto a rather plain At chair, and then onto a small, round table.

Murmuring and whispers filled the room, quieting as soon as I held my hand up in front of me. I cleared my throat, but it did nothing for the herd of horses galloping around in my chest. "I, uh . . ." I glanced at Marcus, who smiled encouragingly and nodded as he joined me on the table. Taking a deep breath, I tried again. "This last month, I've been living over four thousand years in the past, during the time of the Great Father's death."

Stunned silence filled the room.

"I traveled into the past so I could learn to use the power Nuin bestowed upon me—and upon Marcus and Set—to resolve an issue that has been thousands and thousands of years in the making. Ma'at, universal balance, is deteriorating, and if it goes unchecked for too long, then the universe and everything in it will unravel into raw, unbridled chaos." I glanced at Nekure, whose eyes still shimmered with Re's opalescence.

He nodded.

I took a deep breath. Then another. And then I shared some of what I'd learned from Nuin about the long, complicated history of the universe—of Re and Apep and how Re had taken Apep's power and been reborn as Nuin to prevent Apep from unmaking *everything*.

I scanned the assembled crowd of Nejerets. "But this was only a bandage on the wound, and ma'at was still slowly failing, which is how we find ourselves to be in the situation we're in today." Glancing at Marcus, I reached for his hand. "Marcus and I can restore ma'at, thanks to Nuin and everything he taught me, but there's one more hurdle we have to jump over before we can begin the process." I paused, taking a deep, calming breath. "Apep is on his way here, now, by means of Set's body."

Murmurs and whispers broke out, and when Marcus's "Silence!" failed, I did the only thing I could think of; I shifted to a table in the center of the room. It was pushing the limits of what I could manage, sheut-wise, at the moment, but it was enough. When I reformed, there was absolute, complete silence, and all eyes were on me.

I stared around the cavernous room, packed with amazed Nejerets sitting and standing in nearly every available space. "When Set arrives, he *must not* be killed. We'll trap him and hold Apep prisoner in his body until the process of restoring ma'at is complete, and then we'll let ma'at deal with Apep in whatever way is necessary to retain universal balance." I paused. Waited. Let my words sink in. "But first, we have to trap him."

"Do you hear that?" someone whispered. Then another. And another. "It sounds like . . . helicopters."

They were right; I could hear it, too, now that I was paying attention—the steady *thrum-thrum-thrum* of far-off helicopter blades.

I spun around, staring wide-eyed at Marcus. "It's him, isn't it?"

Marcus nodded, his face grim, and strode across the room toward the table I was standing on.

Why I'd assumed Apep-Set would come in a cars, that it would take him hours to get to the underground Oasis, was beyond me. But I had, and now we were out of time.

A minute frown curved Marcus's lips downward, and a crease appeared between his eyebrows. "You're bleeding." He touched my shin, and his fingertips brought a tiny sting.

I glanced down to see a miniscule cut. "Huh . . . I didn't even notice." And then *I* frowned, too. "A cut that small should've healed already."

Marcus pulled his hand away, his fingertip stained with a smudge of crimson. "Unless your regeneration is being suppressed because you've already reached the bonding pheromone saturation point." He frowned. "Which would mean you're now fertile."

I nodded slowly. Nuin had claimed as much, but I'd hadn't known for sure. "I guess I thought it would be more climactic . . ."

Marcus grinned. "I can't imagine anything being *more* climactic." His expression sobered, and he brushed the backs of his fingers down the side of my leg. Concern shone in the multihued depths of his eyes. "You must be careful now, Little Ivanov. Do not injure yourself, because you *won't* regenerate."

I swallowed roughly, suddenly feeling both fragile and vulnerable.

He turned away abruptly and held his hand up to help me down from the table. "Come, Alexandra. I will take you somewhere safe, somewhere where Set will not find you while I deal with him once and for all."

I started to reach for his hand, but drew back before our fingers touched. Marcus *never* called me "Alexandra." My stomach dropped into a pool of dread. The last time his lips had uttered those syllables, he'd been possessed by Apep. *It's not possible . . .*

"Lex!" Dominic shouted.

I turned around to see him rush into the dining hall between two sleek columns, his arm outstretched and a cell phone in his hand.

"Get away from Marcus! *Now!*"

I spun around to stare at Marcus. His irises still shimmered with vibrant colors, but there was something else, something new. Mixed with the blues and violets and greens was a sickeningly familiar, inky darkness.

48

DECEPTION & CONCEPTION

No matter how impossible it seemed, no matter how much I didn't want to believe it, Apep had somehow found a way into Marcus's body.

Without warning, the world froze around us, and not by my hand. Apep had stopped time, using the sheut within Marcus.

I shook my head, denying the information my eyes showed me was truth. Apep was possessing Marcus, absolutely and completely. Apep had *full access* to his power. And the only way to get him out of Marcus's body, the only way to give the universe any kind of a chance, was to *kill* Marcus. My stomach twisted, and my heart sank.

"How . . . ?" The word was barely a whisper.

"Such a useless query, but I think I shall satisfy your curiousity anyway," Apep said, speaking with Marcus's lips and tongue, but sounding completely different from the man I loved. "When you reunited the two fractured pieces of my sheut during your little dalliance earlier, the power Set held wasn't the only thing you pulled into your lover's body." Apep-Marcus bowed his head to me. "I thank you for the rather sudden relocation." He ran his hands down the front of

Marcus's body. "I do very much enjoy the way this one fits . . . and the *power*." He closed his eyes and groaned. "To feel my sheut again, whole and throbbing with barely contained energy . . ."

I licked my lips, scanning the statue-like people all around me like one of them might hold the key to regaining access to the exhausted sheut within *me*, but all I found were faces locked in expressions of confusion and horror and shock, and the power remained unusable.

Apep-Marcus disappeared in an explosion of misty colors. Before I could suck in a breath, before I could react at all, he reappeared behind me on the table.

I spun around and stumbled backward, twisting my ankle as I slipped off the edge of the table. I landed in a heap on the floor and scrambled away from him.

Grinning, he jumped off the table and stalked after me, his shoes silent on the polished floor. "It really is a pity that tearing Re's sheut out of you will destroy your body . . . I would have enjoyed playing with it." He sighed, and I continued to flee, running into immovable chairs and table legs and people.

Vines of At burst up from the floor, wrapping around my legs and ankles, working their way up my limbs.

"But now that the process has begun and you are fertile, we can't risk—"

His eyes opened wide, and his words cut off abruptly at the exact same time as what felt like a vacuous gravitational field burst to life in my middle. It pulled at the sheut so inextricably wound throughout my ba, tearing it away and consuming the power. I felt like I'd been doused in liquid nitrogen and was being shattered, and then I was on fire, flames consuming me from the inside out. I tried to scream, but I couldn't find my breath.

At first, I thought it was Apep, ripping the sheut out of my body, killing me in the most painful way possible—eviscerating my soul. But when Apep-Marcus dropped to his knees before me, threw his head back, and roared in agony, I wasn't so sure.

Around us, time stuttered, then resumed its usual passing with a thunderous explosion of sound. People were suddenly moving all around us. But the pain continued to sear through me. Somehow, I managed to suck in a breath. And finally, I screamed.

Without warning, the agony ceased. I curled into the fetal position on the floor a few feet away from Marcus's body.

Apep-Marcus was no longer crying out. He was no longer moving. He was no longer breathing at all.

"No, no, no, no, no . . ." I crawled closer to him and shook him by the shoulder, gently at first, then using more and more force as his chest refused to rise and fall, as his heart refused to beat, as his body refused to *live*.

"Neffe!" I yelled. "Aset! Help him!"

I could hear people moving around me, heard Neffe curse at them as she pushed her way through the crowd of Nejerets, but I couldn't tear my eyes away from Marcus's face. It was absolutely devoid of any expression. Because he was gone. Dead.

Someone grasped my shoulder and started pulling me backward.

I twisted around to shove them away, and found Re-Nekure's opalescent eyes only inches from my own.

"You must get away from him, Alexandra," he said. "*Now.*"

"No!" I yanked my shoulder out of his hold and turned back to Marcus's body just as an inky darkness started oozing out of his nose and mouth and ears. It headed straight toward me.

A shimmering barrier of At appeared right in front of my face, and not a second too late. Apep slammed into it, spreading in a writhing mass like he was searching for the barrier's edge, for a way around so he could get to me.

Except there were no edges. As the last of the inky darkness left Marcus's body, Re-Nekure surrounded Apep completely with the At barrier, creating a floating, spherical prison large enough to hold several people and strong enough to contain the soul of a god. Slowly, the sphere shrunk, condensing the darkness inside. It grew deeper, denser, until an orb about the size of a baseball floated a few inches from my face, seeming to suck in the light around it.

Marcus inhaled suddenly, just as Neffe slid to her knees beside him. His eyelids opened, and eyes of molten gold—*not* shimmering with divine power—skewered me. He was alive. Apep was gone, contained in a prison of solidified At. And Apep's sheut was . . . well, I didn't know where. At that moment, I didn't care.

I threw myself on top of Marcus and sobbed against his neck. "You came back. You came back," I cried, over and over again. "You were dead, but you came back to me."

His arms encircled me, and his lips brushed feather-light kisses against my forehead and temple. He took hold of either side my face and lifted my lips to his. "Always," he murmured. "I will always come back to you. Not even death could keep me away."

My whole body was shaking. "I don't understand what just happened . . . how you—Apep—he was possessing you, then . . ." I clung to him. "There was so much pain, and then you *died*. I just don't understand."

"I do," Re-Nekure said from behind me. "Powerful new life forms within you, dear Alexandra, an irresistible host—or rather, *hosts*—for the sheuts you both carried."

Slowly, I pulled back from Marcus and looked over my shoulder at Re-Nekure. "Wha—what?"

"Congratulations to you both." He smiled, and I didn't think I'd ever seen anyone look more pleased with himself. "I'm sure you'll be wonderful parents."

49

TAKE & GIVE

Sitting at the end of one of the longer At tables near the center of the dining hall, Nekure tilted his head to the side, listening to something nobody else could hear. With a nod, he looked at me. "He says that you must've conceived when you, um"—his eyes flicked to my parents, who were seated to my right, then to me and to Marcus, who was on my left—"you know, earlier . . . underground . . . right after . . . *anyway*, and he says that the 'sucking void' you felt, followed by the burning sensation, was the two newly forming bas within you absorbing the power." He was speaking for Re, as wielding Nekure's sheut had exhausted the older being, and he could no longer maintain adequate control of Nekure's body.

Once the chaos and confusion had settled, Marcus had ordered most of the Nejerets to either tend to their regular tasks around the underground Oasis or to venture aboveground to deal with the approaching helicopter. Just a handful of my personal guards remained in the hall with us, along with my family and close Nejerets friends, who were also seated around the rectangular table.

Only Dominic was absent; as soon as Marcus had learned it had been Set who'd called to warn us of Apep's possession of Marcus, likely saving my life, he'd sent Dominic topside to await the helicopter's landing and escort Set down the tunnel into the Oasis and to Nuin's palace to join us.

"So," Nekure said, "it looks like the process that'll restore ma'at has really begun, and Apep"—Nekure tossed the crystalline orb containing Apep's inky darkness into the air a few feet, catching it easily—"is no longer a threat." He raised the orb in my direction like he was toasting with a glass. "Tiny guardians of ma'at to our rescue, just in the nick of time . . ." One pierced eyebrow arched higher. "Remind me to thank the little monsters when they're old enough."

Smiling and shaking my head, I gave Marcus's hand a squeeze under the table. It definitely hadn't sunk in yet that I was *pregnant*. With twins. Who were pretty much going to be gods. Nope, that hadn't sunk in *at all*. Because when it did, I thought I'd probably faint.

My mom shifted in her chair beside me, her attention on Nekure. "Now when you say 'monsters,' do you mean that my grandchildren will be, ahem, *in*human?"

Nekure barked a laugh. "Absolutely." Glancing at Jenny, who was seated across from me, between Alexander and Grandma Suse, he added, "Well, two of them, at least. We won't know whether Jenny's kid will manifest or not until the twins come into their power and get rid of the Nothingness and return stability to the At, and all that . . . which should happen sometime around puberty, or so Re *thinks*." He flashed my mom a grin and widened his eyes, like he was sharing some exciting news. "We're in a bit of uncharted territory here. But anyway, you could end up the proud grandma of *three* inhuman beings."

My mom blanched.

Bumping my shoulder against hers, I met her warm, brown

eyes. "They'll be human enough," I assured her, then felt some of the color drain from my own face. I didn't actually know for sure. For all I knew, they might be just as incorporeal as Re and Apep were in their natural state. Fear churned in my belly, solidifying into a heavy lump. I glanced at Nekure, and when he nodded, I forced a smile and met my mom's eyes. "Promise."

"Do not fret, Alice," Aset said. "You will find that a Nejeret child with a sheut is much like any other baby." She flashed her son an affectionate smile. "Though sometimes they prove to be a little more trouble, depending on what that sheut enables them to do."

Nekure grinned.

I sat back in my chair, the events of the past month, not to mention the past hour, *finally* starting to sink in. A relaxing combination of exhaustion and relief settled over me, overshadowing the rather hearty dose of anxiety I felt every time I thought about the divine lives taking shape within me—Marcus's and my *children*—and I sighed.

We'd done it. We'd *really* done it. The universe *wasn't* going to unravel. My family and friends—everyone—*weren't* going to die or be unmade or whatever other unpleasant mode of destruction accompanied "unraveling." We'd done it, saved the world, and now all I wanted was to sleep for about a month, safe and snug in Marcus's arms.

Marcus's desires were apparently in tune with mine, or possibly it was because our bas were so wholly entangled now, but he draped his arm over my shoulders, leaned in, and pressed his lips against my cheekbone. "Let us retire, Little Ivanov . . . little queen . . . I've always been a selfish man, and I find that I'm not in the mood for sharing you right now."

He extended the wispiest tendril of his ba and caressed the outer edges of mine, and I drew in a shuddering breath.

Heat suffused my cheeks, spread throughout my body, and

made me desperate to be alone with him. I cleared my throat. "Don't you think we should wait for Dom and Set to get down here?" I glanced at the orb of seething obsidian. "I mean, what if that's not *all* of Apep?"

Marcus pulled away, and he, too, sighed. "It is, I assure you."

"But how do you *know*?"

Laughing bitterly, Marcus shook his head. "Because Apep was so convinced of his triumph that he withheld nothing of himself, kept no part of his knowledge separate from me. So believe me, Lex, I know."

I bit my lip. "Okay," I said, pushing my chair back to rise. I glanced at the faces of the people sitting around the table, the people I loved, and opened my mouth to excuse myself for the evening.

A sharp crack boomed outside the palace, the reverberations echoing throughout the cavernous room.

I stared at Marcus. "Was that—"

"Gunfire?" He was suddenly on his feet, as were the rest of us. "Yes."

By the time we reached the main bridge crossing the canal to the tunnel side of the oasis-cavern, two figures stumbled out of the tunnel's mouth. It was Set and Dominic, father and son, looking so strikingly similar. Dominic was leaning heavily on Set, his hand pressed against the lower portion of his ribcage and his lips tinged red.

"Oh my God, Dom!" I exclaimed as I lurched across the bridge ahead of the others and ran up the slightly winding, paved pathway toward them. I glanced over my shoulder to call for Neffe, but before I could even say her name, she rushed past me, right behind her father and Aset.

I turned my attention back to Dominic; he and Set were less than a dozen paces ahead. "What happened?" I slowed as I took the final few steps. "Who—how—"

Marcus reached them first, helping to ease Dominic down onto an intricately carved At bench on the left side of the pathway. "Who did this?" he demanded, his focus intense on Set.

"I did, Heru," an impossibly familiar voice said from a ways up the pathway.

I raised my head and stared at the two shadowed forms standing several hundred yards away in the mouth of the tunnel, and when my eyes confirmed what I'd heard, my mouth fell open. "*Carson?*" My graduate school peer standing in the ancient, ancestral home of my nonhuman people was yet another impossible thing to add to those I seemed to make a habit of collecting. "What—you—what are you *doing* here?"

He flashed his familiar, boyish smile, but it appeared a little strained. "I'd love to fill you in Lex . . . some other time."

I started shaking my head ever so slowly. Was it possible that he was *Nejeret*? The implications . . . it didn't make sense.

Kat was beside him. At first I thought their arms were linked like they'd been out for a friendly stroll, but then I realized that Carson's hand was gripping Kat's arm just above the elbow. Focusing on Kat's face, I saw that tears dampened her cheeks and reddened her eyes.

"He shot Dom," she shrieked. "And my mom's—"

"*Be quiet*, Kat," Carson snapped. He lifted his other hand, and light from the LED cords lining the path glinted dully on dark metal—a handgun. He aimed it at Kat's head. "Dom, there, tells me you've managed to trap Apep," Carson said. "Give him to me, and I'll let sweet, innocent Kat here live." He tilted his head to the side and jammed the nozzle of the gun against her temple. "Don't, and, well . . . I'll start with Kat, then we'll see how many of you I can take out before you get to me." He grinned that familiar, boyish grin again, and I felt instantly ill.

"Carson . . ." I took a step toward him. Then another. Part of me felt certain that my eyes weren't seeing correctly, that my ears weren't hearing what my brain thought they were hearing. And another part of me felt like I'd been punched in the gut. Carson was one of the few people from my past, human life who I'd considered a real friend. Was that all a lie? Was he an agent of Set—of Apep—like Mike had been? I'd been lied to and betrayed by a lot of people over the past year, but that didn't make Carson's betrayal any less shocking . . . or painful. "Why are you doing this?" I asked, my voice sounding hollow as I continued my slow, stunned ascension up the pathway.

His lips spread into a weak half-smile, a mere shadow of his usual grin, and he shook his head. "You wouldn't understand."

"You swore an oath to me," Marcus said, appearing at my side.

Carson shrugged. "Some oaths supersede others." He twisted Kat's arm, making her cry out, and fixed his stare on Marcus and me. "I'd stop there, unless you want to see what the inside of a half-manifested Nejerette's brain looks like . . . and I rather like her, so I'd *appreciate it* if you didn't force my hand."

Marcus and I stopped immediately, neither of us willing to risk Kat's life in a game of chicken. "Who are you working for?" Marcus demanded.

Frowning, Carson stared up at the cavern's At ceiling like he was thinking exceptionally hard. "I suppose there's no harm in telling you now." When his eyes once again focused on Marcus, he grinned. "We call ourselves the Kin."

I was having such a hard time reconciling my memory of the young archaeologist I'd known back in Seattle with this seemingly unstable and undeniably homicidal Nejeret that his words barely registered.

"Whose kin?" Marcus asked.

Carson's grin widened. "*The* Kin. I'm sure you'll hear more about us soon."

I frowned. *The Kin?*

I could practically feel the rage crackling around Marcus. "What do they want with Apep?"

Carson shrugged. "I only know *what* my mission is, not *why* I was assigned it." His eyes flicked to some point beyond us, and I heard footsteps behind me.

I risked the briefest glance over my shoulder and saw Nekure making his way up the pathway ever so slowly. He held Apep's small, spherical prison up and gave it a little shake. "Let the girl start walking this way, and I'll throw it to you."

Eyes wide, I stared at Nekure. Was he *really* considering handing Apep over . . . after everything we'd done to trap him? But the more I considered it, the more I understood his reasoning, and the more I agreed with his decision. It didn't matter who actually had possession of the Apep orb, because only three living beings could free him—Nekure and my unborn children.

Carson shook his head. "Throw it to *her*," he said to Nekure, "and I swear I'll let her go."

"Your words are worthless," Marcus said, his voice low and cold. "You're proving that right now."

Carson shrugged. "*That* is a matter of perspective."

I met Nekure's eyes while Marcus traded barbs with Carson and, as quietly as possible, said, "Can you do anything from here?"

Nekure shook his head, which meant Carson was too far away for him to use his sheut to do anything to stop the younger Nejeret. And as far as I could tell, I no longer had access to Re's sheut *at all*, so I couldn't do anything. Which meant there was only one way out of this new tangle that didn't include anyone else getting hurt. Not that I would've minded *Carson* suffering a bit, but still . . .

"You'll let her go?" I asked Carson. "You promise?"

He nodded. "Once I have Apep, I'll keep Kat with me as collateral. When we get to the helicopter, it's her choice whether she stays with me or returns here." He paused, then added, "Either way, she'll be unharmed."

I eyed him, then Kat, who looked absolutely miserable and utterly terrified. "And why would she ever choose to go with you?"

"Because her mother is waiting for me back in the helicopter, making sure the pilot remains *obedient*."

One glance at Kat told me his words were true. And I knew, with absolute certainty, that he wouldn't hurt Kat unless he had to, not if he was working with Gen. Whatever her faults, Genevieve Dubois loved her daughter very much.

"Fine," I said with a nod. "Do it, Nekure. Give him the orb."

Marcus slipped his hand in mine and squeezed, all the while glaring at Carson. "If you go back on your word," he said, "if you harm her, we will hunt you down and make you beg for death."

"But we will *not* grant you the release of death," Set said as he took up a post between Nekure and me. "Not for years."

"And when we do," Nekure added, "your death will come in the form of a prison of At, slowly crushing you until you are no larger than this." He lobbed the orb containing Apep toward Kat, who caught it with a slight fumble.

Concern, or possibly fear, flashed across Carson's face, and he licked his lips. "Understood," he said with a nod and started backing deeper into the tunnel. "Don't follow us."

"Kat," Aset called from beside Marcus. I hadn't heard her approach, but there she stood. "I'm sure your mother must love you very much, but know that we do, too. She is not the only family you have. Remember *that* when you make your choice."

I thought Kat nodded before the darkness swallowed her completely, but it might have been a trick of the eyes.

"Poor child," Aset said. "She cared for him a great deal. I think she may even have loved him. Such a betrayal . . ."

I stared at her, stunned for about the millionth time that day. "*What?*"

Nekure grunted and crossed his arms. "It was merely an infatuation. She'll get over it."

I frowned up at the empty tunnel. "So much has changed . . ."

"Indeed, Little Ivanov," Marcus said, rubbing his thumb over the back of my hand. "Indeed."

50

NOW & ALWAYS

"I'm glad you chose to stay," I told Kat. It was the middle of the night, and we were sitting at Dominic's bedside, in his room on the second floor of the Heru palace, watching his chest rise and fall while his body healed the hole in his lung. He looked older and thinner, but he was alive, thanks to a combination of Neffe and Aset's medical skills and Dominic's own regenerative Nejeret abilities.

"It wasn't really much of a choice," Kat said. She bit her lip and shot me a sideways glance. "I mean, not really. My mom—I don't know what's going on with her. It's like she's been brainwashed or something. And then Carson . . ." She swallowed roughly and looked away, staring at Dominic's shoulder. Her chin trembled. "I *hate* him. If I ever see him again . . ." She squeezed her eyes shut and several fat tears broke free, gliding down her cheek. "I *never* want to see him again."

Shaking my head, I reached for her hand. "I'm so sorry, Kat. What he did was awful—unforgivable, I know. But your mom . . ." I shrugged. "Maybe there's still hope for her."

She glanced at me. "You think?"

"I honestly don't know, but I promise we'll do what we can to figure it out."

"That we will," Marcus said from the arched doorway.

I looked up to find him and Set walking into the room, one after the other, and felt the oddest sense of déjà vu. "It seems so strange to see you both here . . . but so normal at the same time." I laughed softly as I gave Kat's hand a squeeze and released it before standing and walking into Marcus's open, waiting arms. "If not for your clothes, I might believe I'd traveled back in time again." I smiled against his shirt. "I kind of miss the kilts . . ."

Marcus chuckled. "I must admit that I miss seeing you dressed in the attire of that time, as well."

Set cleared his throat, and my cheeks heated instantly.

I peeked at him, offering him a small smile. "I'm pooped. You'll sit with them for a bit?"

He nodded.

"I don't need a babysitter," Kat said. "I'm perfectly capable of watching Dom *do nothing* all by myself."

"I have no doubt of that," Set said. He sat in the chair I'd vacated. "But a father . . . now that is another matter entirely . . ."

I smiled up at Marcus as he guided me out of the room with an arm wrapped around my shoulders. He led me to the bedroom that had been mine during the weeks I'd spent living in this house so long ago and shut a very modern-looking At door.

I studied the door for a moment. "Nekure?" I asked Marcus.

He nodded. "He's been making his way through the palaces, fixing them up the best he can so our people can start living in them again . . . if they so choose."

Glancing around the room, taking in the ancient, familiar At furnishings and scattered, modern elements, I smiled. "You've been staying in here, haven't you?"

Again, Marcus nodded.

"But you didn't know it was my room, not really."

Moving in front of me, he ran his hands up my arms, over my shoulders, and trailed his fingertips up the sides of my neck. "No, I didn't *know*." He leaned in, brushing his lips first over one cheek, then the other. "But I *felt* you here, Little Ivanov. This was the only place besides your sanctuary where I felt closer to you. When I doubted that you'd ever find your way back to me—"

I gripped the belt loops at his sides and pulled his body flush against mine. "But I *did* find my way back to you. I'll *always* find my way back to you."

"Promise me."

My eyebrows drew together, and I tilted my head to the side, my lips curving into a faint smile. "Promise you . . . ?"

"Swear to me that you'll always come back. *Always*." His eyes, so golden and heated, held nothing but demands. So many demands.

"But I can't travel through time anymore," I said, shaking my head. "Just a plain ol' Nejerette. Why . . . ?"

"Just promise me," he demanded.

I frowned, but I also gave him what he wanted, even if I didn't understand *why* he was so desperate for such an unnecessary promise. "I swear it," I said. "I will always come back to you." And as I made the promise, some deep part of my mind wondered if maybe he knew something I didn't, if maybe I'd locked away more memories within his mind—from more time periods—than even *I* knew about. I wondered if *maybe* my stint as a time traveler wasn't actually over.

When Marcus's lips touched mine . . . when he swept me into his arms and carried me to the bed . . . when he removed my clothing piece by piece, I seared the promise I'd made him into my soul.

Whatever happens, I will *always find my way back to this man . . . always . . .*

Thanks for reading! You've reached the end of Time Anomaly (Echo Trilogy, #2), *but Lex's adventures continue in* Dissonance (Echo Trilogy, #2.5) *and* Ricochet Through Time (Echo Trilogy, #3).

GLOSSARY

- **Akhet** The first of three seasons in the ancient Egyptian year. *Akhet* is the inundation season, when the Nile floods, and is roughly correlated with fall in the northern hemisphere.
- **Ankhesenpepi** Nejerette. Nuin's eldest daughter and queen and consort to many Old Kingdom pharaohs, including Pepi I and II.
- **Apep (Apophis)** Netjer or "god." One of two Netjers responsible for maintaining balance in our universe, the other being Re. Apep was historically worshipped *against* as Re's opponent and the evil god of chaos.
- **At** Ancient Egyptian, "moment, instant, time"; The *At* is a plane of existence overlaying our own, where time and space are fluid. *At* can also be used to refer to the fabric of space and time.
- **Ankh** Ancient Egyptian, "life".
- **Ankh-At** Nuin's power. Includes (at least) the power to travel through time, to create and remove memory blocks, and to manipulate the At on this plane of existence.

- **Aset (Isis)** Nejerette. Heru's sister. Aset was worshipped as a goddess associated with motherhood, magic, and nature by the ancient Egyptians.
- **At-qed** State of stasis a Nejeret's body enters when his or her ba departs for the At.
- **Ba** Considered one of the essential parts of the soul by the ancient Egyptians. In regards to Nejerets, the ba, or the "soul," is the part of a person that can enter the At.
- **Bahur** Arabic, "of Horus" or "of Heru".
- **Blade** A ruling Nejeret's chief protector and companion.
- **Council of Seven** The body of leadership that governs the Nejerets. The Council consists of the patriarchs of the seven strongest Nejeret families: Ivan, Heru, Set, Sid, Moshe, Dedwen, and Shangdi. The Meswett, Alexandra Larson Ivanov, is also an honorary member of the Council.
- **Dedwen** A member of the Council of Seven. Dedwen was worshipped as a god associated with prosperity, wealth, and fire by the ancient Nubians.
- **Deir el-Bahri** Located on the west side of the Nile, just across the river from Luxor in Upper (southern) Egypt. Several mortuary temples and tombs are located in Deir el-Bahri, including Djeser-Djeseru, Queen Hatshepsut's mortuary temple.
- **Djeser-Djeseru** Ancient Egyptian, "Holy of Holies". Queen Hatshepsut's mortuary temple in Deir el-Bahri.
- **Hatshepsut** (ruled 1479—1457 BCE) Female Pharaoh during the Middle Kingdom of ancient Egypt. One of Heru's many wives, and mother to the Nejerette Neferure.
- **Hat-hur (Hathor)** Ancient Egyptian goddess associated with love, fertility, sexuality, music, and

dance. According to the Contendings of Heru and Set myth, Hathor is the goddess who healed Heru's eye. She is often depicted as a cow or a woman with cow ears or horns, and a sun disk is frequently cradled by the horns.

- **Heru (Horus)** Nejeret. Osiris's son, Nuin's grandson, Aset's brother, and former leader of the Council of Seven. Heru stepped down from his role as leader to function as the Council's general and assassin, when necessary. Heru was worshipped as the god of the sky, kingship, and authority by the ancient Egyptians. He is often depicted as a falcon or falcon-headed.
- **Ipwet** Human, Nejeret-carrier. Nuin's primary *human* wife at the time of his death.
- **Ivan** Nejeret. Leader of the Council of Seven. Alexander's father and Lex's great-grandfather.
- **Kemet** Ancient Egyptian, "Black Land". Kemet is one of the names ancient Egyptians called their homeland.
- **Ma'at** Ancient Egyptian concept of truth, balance, justice, and order. To the Nejeret, *ma'at* refers to universal balance.
- **Men-nefer (Memphis)** Ancient Egyptian city. *Men-nefer* was the capital city of Egypt during the Old Kingdom.
- **Meswett** Ancient Egyptian (mswtt), "girl-child". The Meswett is the prophesied savior/destroyer of the Nejerets, as supposedly foretold by Nuin upon his deathbed, though none actually remember it happening. The prophecy was later recorded by the Nejeret Senenmut.
- **Moshe (Moses)** Nejeret. Member of the Council of Seven. Central figure in most western religions.
- **Neferure (Neffe)** Nejerette. Daughter of Hatshepsut

and Heru.

- **Nejeret (male)/Nejerette (female)/Nejerets (plural)** Modern term for the Netjer-At.
- **Netjer** Ancient Egyptian, "god".
- **Netjer-At** Ancient Egyptian, "Gods of Time".
- **Netjer-At Oasis** The ancient, historic home of the Nejerets, deep in the heart of the Sahara Desert.
- **Nuin (Nun)** Netjer/Nejeret. One of two Netjers responsible for maintaining balance in our universe, the other being Apep. Also known as the "Great Father", Nuin was the original Nejeret and the father of all Nejeretkind. Nuin was worshipped as a god associated with the primordial waters and creation by the ancient Egyptians.
- **Old Kingdom** Period of Egyptian history from 2686 —2181 BCE.
- **Order of Hat-hur** An over 5,000-year-old, hereditary order of priestesses run by Aset and devoted to aiding the goddess Hat-hur (Lex) during her temporal journeys.
- **Osiris** Nejeret. Heru and Aset's father and leader of the Council of Seven until his murder a few decades after Nuin's death. Osiris was worshipped as a god associated with death, the afterlife, fertility, and agriculture by the ancient Egyptians.
- **Pepi II (Pepi Neferkare)** Pharaoh of the 6th Dynasty of ancient Egypt, 2284-2180 BCE. Final ruler of both the 6th Dynasty and of the Old Kingdom.
- **Peret** The second of three seasons in the ancient Egyptian year. *Peret* is known as the season of emergence, during which planting and growth took place.
- **Re (Ra)** Netjer. One of two Netjers responsible for maintaining balance in our universe, the other being

Apep. *Re* was historically worshipped as the ancient Egyptian solar deity.

- **Ren** Considered one of the essential parts of the soul by the ancient Egyptians, closely associated with a person's name. In regards to Nejerets, a *ren* is the soul of a Netjer, like Re or Apep, much like a *ba* is the soul of a Nejeret or human.
- **Senenmut** Nejeret. Scribe of Nuin's prophecy and architect of the underground temple housing the ankh-At at Deir el-Bahri. Senenmut was the "high steward of the king" to Queen Hatshepsut as well as Neferure's tutor. Senenmut was killed by Set after the completion of the underground temple.
- **Set (Seth)** Nejeret. Nuin's grandson, father of Dom, Genevieve, Kat, and Lex, and member of the Council of Seven. Possessed by Apep, Set went rogue when the Council of Seven chose Heru as their leader after Osiris's death around 4,000 years ago.
- **Shangdi** Nejerette. Member of the Council of Seven. Shangdi is worshipped as the supreme sky deity in the traditional Chinese religion.
- **Shemu** The third and final of three seasons in the ancient Egyptian year. *Shemu*, literally "low water," is known as the season of harvest.
- **Sheut** Considered one of the essential parts of the soul by the ancient Egyptians, closely associated with a person's shadow. In regards to Nejerets, a *sheut* is the power of a Netjer, like Re or Apep, or the less potent power of the offspring of a Nejerette and Nejeret.
- **Sid (Siddhartha Gautama)** Nejeret. More commonly known as "Buddha" to humans.
- **Wedjat (Eye of Horus)** Ancient Egyptian symbol of protection, healing, strength, and perfection.

CAN'T GET ENOUGH?

NEWSLETTER: www.lindseyfairleigh.com/join-newsletter
WEBSITE: www.lindseyfairleigh.com
FACEBOOK: Lindsey Fairleigh
INSTAGRAM: @LindseyFairleigh
PINTEREST: LindsFairleigh
PATREON: www.patreon.com/lindseyfairleigh

Reviews are always appreciated. They help indie authors like me sell books (and keep writing them!).

ALSO BY LINDSEY FAIRLEIGH

ECHO TRILOGY

Echo in Time

Resonance

Time Anomaly

Dissonance

Ricochet Through Time

KAT DUBOIS CHRONICLES

Ink Witch

Outcast

Underground

Soul Eater

Judgement

Afterlife

ATLANTIS LEGACY

Sacrifice of the Sinners

Legacy of the Lost

Fate of the Fallen

Dreams of the Damned

Song of the Soulless

THE ENDING SERIES

Beginnings: The Ending Series Origin Stories

After The Ending

Into The Fire

Out Of The Ashes

Before The Dawn

World Before

World After

FOR MORE INFORMATION ON LINDSEY FAIRLEIGH & THE ECHO TRILOGY:

www.lindseyfairleigh.com

ABOUT THE AUTHOR

Lindsey Fairleigh a bestselling Science Fiction and Fantasy author who lives her life with one foot in a book—so long as that book transports her to a magical world or bends the rules of science. Her novels, from Post-apocalyptic to Time Travel Romance, always offer up a hearty dose of unreality, along with plenty of history, mystery, adventure, and romance. When she's not working on her next novel, Lindsey spends her time walking around the foothills surrounding her home with her son, playing video games, and trying out new recipes in the kitchen. She lives in the Pacific Northwest with her family and their small pack of dogs and cats.

www.lindseyfairleigh.com

Made in the USA
Las Vegas, NV
02 October 2021

31585808R00267